Praise for Deb Caletti's

The Fortunes of Indigo Skye

★ "Caletti builds characters with so much depth. . . . [She] spins a network of relationships that feels real and enriching."

—*Publishers Weekly*, starred review

"Filled with rich characters and hilarious interactions mixed with Indigo's astute perceptions of conformity and frivolous wealth, this book encourages thought and examination of what is truly important in life."

—*School Library Journal*

"An infinitely likeable heroine and richly limned with supporting characters."

—*Booklist*

"An inspiring and memorable tale full of vivid characters."

—*Romantic Times BOOKreviews*, 4 stars

"Deb Caletti's writing was fresh and amazing. . . . It was truly unforgettable."

—*TeensReadToo.com*

"In addition to a compelling plot and realistic characters, author Deb Caletti sprinkles amazing insights throughout Indigo's story."

—*Teenreads.com*

An ALA Best Books for Young Adults
A New York Public Library Books for the Teen Age

ALSO BY DEB CALETTI

The Fortunes of Indigo Skye

by DEB CALETTI

Simon Pulse
New York London Toronto Sydney

This book is a work of fiction. Any references to historical events, real people, or real locales are used fictitiously. Other names, characters, places, and incidents are the product of the author's imagination, and any resemblance to actual events or locales or persons, living or dead, is entirely coincidental.

SIMON PULSE
An imprint of Simon & Schuster Children's Publishing Division
1230 Avenue of the Americas, New York, NY 10020
First Simon Pulse paperback edition April 2009
Copyright © 2008 by Deb Caletti
SIMON PULSE and colophon are registered trademarks of Simon & Schuster, Inc.
Also available in a Simon & Schuster Books for Young Readers hardcover edition.
For information about special discounts for bulk purchases, please contact
Simon & Schuster Special Sales at 1-866-506-1949 or business@simonandschuster.com.
The Simon & Schuster Speakers Bureau can bring authors to your live event.
For more information or to book an event contact the Simon & Schuster Speakers Bureau
at 1-866-248-3049 or visit our website at www.simonspeakers.com.
Designed by Lucy Ruth Cummins
The text of this book was set in Scala.
Manufactured in the United States of America
10 9 8 7 6 5
The Library of Congress has cataloged the hardcover edition as follows:
Caletti, Deb.
The fortunes of Indigo Skye / by Deb Caletti.
p. cm.
Summary: Eighteen-year-old Indigo is looking forward to becoming a full-time waitress
after high school graduation, but her life is turned upside down by a large check given
to her by a customer who appreciates that she cares enough to scold him about smoking.
ISBN 978-1-4169-1007-7 (hc)
[1. Waiters and waitresses—Fiction. 2. Diners (Restaurants)—Fiction. 3. Wealth—Fiction.
4. Family life—Washington (State)—Fiction. 5. Single-parent families—Fiction.] I. Title.
PZ7.C127437For 2008
[Fic]—dc22
2007008744
ISBN 978-1-4169-1008-4 (pbk)
ISBN 978-1-4391-6412-9 (eBook)

To my sister, Sue Rath.
With my love and lifelong admiration.

Acknowledgments

As always my heartfelt thanks go to Ben Camardi, my friend and agent, and Jennifer Klonsky, editor and pal. You are essential. And you are deeply appreciated. Gratitude also goes to Jaime Feldman, Michelle Fadlalla, Jodie Cohen, Kimberly Lauber, and the other fine members of my Simon & Schuster family—each of you is a treasure.

My work gives me the pleasure and privilege of being in the company of wonderful, funny, inspiring librarians. Your friendship and support have meant a great deal to me. Special thanks in particular go to Mike Denton, Dominique McCafferty, Rod Peckman, and the delightful queen of librarians, Nancy Pearl. Boundless gratitude, too, to all my sales reps, but in particular, to the tireless, book-loving gems I've come to know: Leah Hays, Victor Iannone, and Katie McGarry.

Thank you, as always, dear friends and family. You are loved and cherished a thousand fold—Mom, Dad, Jan, Mitch, Ty, Hunter, and all our extended bunch. And finally, my Sam and Nick, with whom it always begins and ends. There must be a word beyond love.

You can tell a lot about people from what they order for breakfast. Take Nick Harrison, for example. People talk about him killing his wife after she fell down a flight of stairs two years ago, but I know it's not true. Someone who killed his wife would order fried eggs, bacon, sausage—something strong and meaty. I've never served anyone who's killed his wife for sure, so I don't know this for a fact, but I can tell you they wouldn't order oatmeal with raisins like Nick Harrison does. No way. I once heard someone say you can destroy a man with a suspicious glance, and I'm sure they're right. Nick Harrison was cleared of any charges, and still he's destroyed. Oatmeal with raisins every day means you've lost hope.

And Leroy Richie. Just because he has so many tattoos, you can't think you know everything about him. Up his T-shirt sleeve snakes a dragon tail, and around his neck is a woman with her tongue that reaches out toward one of his ears. But he orders Grape-Nuts and wheat toast. He's not just about tattoos when he cares so much about fiber in his diet.

We've got two regulars at Carrera's who do the full breakfast—eggs, side meat, three dollar-size pancakes. That's Joe Awful Coffee and Funny Coyote, and it's just a coincidence that they both have strange names. Joe's name, I guess, was given to him years ago—he can't remember why, because he says his coffee was just fine. A big breakfast makes sense for him—he was a boxer about a thousand years ago, and he still feeds himself as if he's preparing to get in the ring wearing one of those silky super-hero capes (why they make tough guys wear silky Halloween costumes is another question altogether). And Funny Coyote. Can you imagine going through life with a name that sounds like you're being chased by Bugs Bunny? She's American Indian, about twenty-eight, twenty-nine, with short black spiky hair you get the urge to pat, same as a kid with a crew cut or those hedges in the shapes of animals. She eats everything on her plate, sweeps it clean of egg yolk with a swipe of pancake. Then again, she goes a thousand miles an hour when she's manic, so she probably needs the calories. She calls what she has a "chemical imbalance" because it sounds more accidental and scientific than a "mental illness." A "chemical imbalance" is no one's fault. She comes in to write poetry, pages and pages of it, not that it's ever quiet in Carrera's.

Trina, she gets pie and coffee, which fits her, because she's as rich as custard and chocolate cream and warm apples with a scoop of vanilla. She's about Funny's age, but she's all long, blond hair, lace-up boots, fur down to her knees. She leaves lipstick marks on the rim of her cup, the kind of marks that make a life seem full of secrets. She has this white and red classic Thunderbird. Nick Harrison says it's a '55, but she says it's a '53. You don't care what year it is when you see it parked by the curb. Jane, who is my boss and the owner of Carrera's, says it attracts customers, so she likes it when Trina comes in.

I know about breakfast, mostly, because breakfast was always my regular shift. Usually, I worked several mornings before school, and then the early weekend hours, meaning that my own breakfast was reckless—anything I happened to grab on the way out. A handful of Cocoa Puffs, a granola bar, my brother's beef

Deb Caletti

jerky. I'd have been at the café all day, but right then, where this story starts (where I'm *choosing* to start—most everything before was nothing in comparison), I was at the end of my senior year. I still had to clock in what was left of my school hours, and Carrera's isn't open for dinner. After I graduated, though, I wanted to work full-time there while I decided "what to do with my life." See, I loved being a waitress more than anything, but apparently, it's okay to *work* as a waitress but not to *be* a waitress. To most people, saying you want to be a waitress is like saying your dream is to be a Walgreens clerk, ringing up spearmint gum and Halloween candy and condoms, which just proves that most people miss the point about most things most of the time. Waitressing is a talent—it's about giving *nourishment*, creating *relationships*, not just about bringing the ketchup.

Anyway, before the Vespa guy, I could tell you very little about who wanted tuna salad and who wanted turkey on white and who wanted minestrone, but I could tell you about what people craved when they first woke up, what they lingered over before they got serious about making the day into something.

So, what did coffee say? Just coffee? Coffee served to you, a bill slipped under your saucer when you were finished? When anyone could whip into any Starbucks on any corner and get coffee in under five minutes, what did it mean when you decided to wait for a waitress to come to your table, to refill your cup, to ask if everything was all right?

That's what I wondered the day I first saw him. Because, here comes this guy, right? He pulls up to the curb one day on his orange Vespa. He's no one we've ever seen before, and not the type we usually get in Carrera's. He's wearing a soft, navy blue jacket, and underneath, a creamy white shirt open easily at the collar, nicely displaying his Adam's apple. And jeans. But not jeans-jeans; these are not wear-around-the-house jeans, or go-to-the-store jeans or even work-at-Microsoft jeans. There's something creative-but-wealthy about them, about him in general with his longish, tousled hair, and dark, soft leather shoes that are too elegantly simple to be inexpensive. All in all, sort of hot for an old guy in his thirties, which sounds freakishly Lolita, but still true. His face is narrow and clean-shaven. He smiles at me, lips closed, and says, "Just coffee." He smells so good—showery. A musky cologne, or maybe one of those hunky bars of soap that are supposedly made out of oatmeal but probably aren't made out of oatmeal.

Jane looks at me with raised eyebrows, and I raise one of my own, a trick I can do that neither my twin brother can, nor my little sister, ha. I'm the only one in my family, far as I know. It makes me look slightly evil, which I love. Jane's eyebrows are asking, *What's the story?* Mine are answering, *Hmm, mystery and intrigue.* We've never seen this guy before, and just so you know, when you go into a small café that mostly fills with regulars and you're not one, you'll likely get talked about after you leave. It's part of what I really like about my job. Juicy gossip and lurid conjecture. Love it. Joe Awful Coffee raises his old eyebrows too, but Nick's too busy sprinkling sugar onto his oatmeal to even notice the new arrival.

I bring the man his coffee. The glass cup clatters slightly against the saucer. "Thank you," he says. Murmurs—it's one of those soft, polite, well-dressed thank-you's that legitimately qualify as a murmur. Who murmurs anymore? And then he just looks out the window. Stirs his coffee with a spoon. *Tink, tink, tink* against the edge of the cup. Smiles up at me when I pour a refill.

Deb Caletti

Just coffee. My guess is that he has things to think about. Things that are too deep for a double-tall-foam-no-foam-lite-mocha-hazelnut-vanilla-skinny-tripleshot-decaf-iced-extra-hot-Americano-espresso type place, where every person can demand and immediately get their combination of perfect in a cardboard cup. Where everyone only pretends to think deep thoughts and discuss important subjects but it's all a piece of performance art. Maybe he needs to get past all that distraction of wants and desires and greedy-spoiled-American-hurried-up-insta-gratification and just sip coffee.

I don't know. But he stays for a while. Almost to the end of my shift. I smile, he smiles. My tip is more than the coffee itself.

"Did you see his shoes?" Jane says. "Italian." I'm pretty sure she knows nothing about this. Jane is a regular jeans and FRIENDS DON'T LET FRIENDS VOTE REPUBLICAN T-shirt wearer. Running shoes. I know she went to Italy a long time ago, and that's how she got the idea for Carrera's, but I hardly think it qualifies her as an expert on men's shoes.

"Fast track," Nick Harrison says. He'd been paying attention after all. He gets up, wipes his mouth with his napkin. Fast track—this *is* something Nick knows about. He used to be a big shot in some architectural engineering firm before his wife died and he used up all his money on lawyers. Now he works at True Value down the street, mixing paint and helping people pick out linoleum. When he reaches for change in his pants pocket, he always has one of those metal tools they give out free to pry up the paint lids. Now he wears nice-guy plaid. According-to-the-law plaid.

"Fucking beautiful Vespa," Leroy Richie says. He's sitting at a table by the window, the newspaper spread in front of him. He scratches a heart wrapped in vines, which is inked onto the underside of his wrist. "Anyone know what a 'lowboy driver' is?"

"If you don't know what it is, I'm guessing you can't do it," Jane says. She frees a stack of one-dollar bills bound together with a rubber band.

"How about a 'resolute trainer'?"

"Someone serious about training?" I take a guess.

"Hey!" Leroy says. "Pilates instructor! I could do that. I've got balls."

Leroy works for the Darigold plant in town, which is why he's up so early, but he's always looking for a second job to make more money. For retirement, Leroy says, though he's maybe only thirty. People aren't too quick to hire him because of the tattoos. *They think tattoos equal drug addict,* he says. *Like all needles are the same. Like even art has to have its designated places.* Darigold hired him years ago, when all he had was a falcon on one shoulder. Now, he told us, the only place he didn't have artwork was on his bald head, which is a picture you didn't especially want to imagine, thank you.

"He's getting on the Vespa," Nick Harrison reports. "Starting it up. There he goes."

I look out the window to watch too. I watch the back of his suit jacket disappear down the street, the flaps whipping softly against his back. It's like we've been touched by something, but I'm not sure what. Maybe it's just the twinge of thrill that comes with a stranger's story, all the possibilities that might be there until you find out he works at a bank and plays golf. Or maybe it's that down deep hope-knowledge that someone or something is bound to arrive to save you from your drab existence, that maybe this is it. We're practically *promised* that, right? That our lives will

Deb Caletti

at some point go Hollywood? That excitement will one day arrive, just like a package from the UPS driver? I don't know, but I can just feel *it*—this static, popping energy buzz. The kind that comes when there's been an epic shift in the tectonic plates of your personal universe.

After work I go to school (blah, blah, blah, nothing, something, more nothing), and after school, Trevor, my boyfriend, comes to pick me up and take me home, where he'll have dinner with us. Trevor stops me right outside in the school parking lot; he kisses me and our tongues loll around together, like seals playing in water. I'm not into public displays of affection generally, but right then I'm just so happy to see him. My hands are on his shoulders, which I like to feel because, back then, Trevor delivered refrigerators and washing machines. He's got these muscles that won't quit. He's still kissing away when he separates from me suddenly, his brain catching up to the rest of him. "You changed your hair," he says.

He looks at me, and I put my hand up to my head. My hair was still short, but I'd gone from brown with yellow highlights to a rusty orange. My friend Melanie did it for me, and she's good at it too, even though she never messes with her own color. She always says her dad would kill her, but personally, I don't think her dad would even notice.

"It looks gorgeous," Trevor says. You can see why I keep him around. I could turn it blue and he'd say the same thing. I *have* turned it blue and he's said the same thing. He grabs a hold of the beads of my necklace, pulls me to him. He rubs the beard he's trying to grow against my cheek and we kiss again. No offense to Trevor, but we all know he has reluctant facial hair. He just can't grow a beard. My legs do better. We kiss a little more, which is something he *can* do, and then we walk over to his car and he starts it up. His car has the low, hungry rumble of a muffler barely hanging in. It's an old Mustang convertible, and it's kind of a piece of shit, but Trevor always says it's a *Mustang*, which apparently means it can be a piece of shit and still be something great.

Trevor pulls up in front of my mom's house. We walk up the porch steps and past the hanging flower baskets, the flowers already turning crunchy from spring sun. Mom's gardening skills are less skills than good intentions. She'll come home all happy from Johnson's Nursery, carrying those low-sided cardboard boxes full of wet, bright flowers, and a week or so later, the plants will be as thirsty as Trevor after moving refrigerators on a hot August day. I squeak on the garden hose before we go in, tip it up into the baskets. The flowers are so dry, the water basically gushes out the hole in the bottom, but at least I like to think there's maybe a few good karma points for effort here, and I don't know about you, but I need all the good karma points I can get.

Inside, my little sister, Bex, is sitting cross-legged on the floor and watching TV. She had a little crush on Trevor then, and usually she'd have gotten carbonated at the sight of him, jumping up and jabbering away. But right then she's focused on that screen.

"What're you watching?" I ask.

"The news." She plays with the ends of her long braids, crosses them under her chin.

Sure enough, CNN. More images of small huts and tiny villages washed away by flooding waters, concerned-voiced news anchors with the kind of perfect hair that has never actually been close to tragedy. The fourth day of nonstop disaster coverage. "Bex," I say. "Look. It's beautiful out. Go outside and play. Ride your bike, or something."

Deb Caletti

"I can't," Bex says.

"She's grounded!" Mom shouts from the kitchen.

"Still?" I say.

"Too long, you think?" Mom shouts again. Trevor and I go to the kitchen, where Mom has started dinner. She's wearing jeans and a white T-shirt with hanger bumps on the shoulders. I smell onions, the bitter-sweet tang of them frying in butter. Her long hair is tied back, strands around her face frizzly from steam. "I don't know about grounding. What do I know about grounding? Bomba and Bompa never grounded Mike or me. Hi, Trevor," she says.

"Hey, Missus," he says, which is what he calls her even though she's not married. My Dad was living in Hawaii with Jennifer. Mom called Jennifer her "step wife."

"That's 'cause Uncle Mike was perfect and the only rebellious thing you did was marry Dad," I say.

"Bomba loved your Dad," Mom says. "*Loves.* So even that wasn't so rebellious." Bomba, my grandmother (who earned her name when I was a baby and couldn't pronounce "Grandma"), lives in Arizona, where she and Bompa moved a while back to make their retirement money "stretch." I like the idea of that, money stretching, the way you take a pinch of gum from your mouth and pull. Bompa died about seven years ago, when my parents were getting divorced. He said he got colon cancer from all the smoke my Dad blew up his ass, but really, he liked the joke so much, he'd use it with various people—insurance salesmen, his brother-in-law. I look at the picture of Bomba that's on our fridge, stuck there with a magnet from a pizza delivery place. She's sitting in a blow-up kiddie pool with her sunglasses on, her boobs all water-balloon saggy in her swimsuit, and she's reading a magazine. She taped on one of those cartoon bubbles, and has herself saying, "Bomba, luxuriating in the pool." I miss not seeing her. Without Bomba, we have all cookie and no chocolate chip.

"Why's Bex grounded?" Trevor asks.

"She had to go to the principal's office," I say. "This girl at school—"

"Lindsey," Mom interrupts.

"She *hates* Lindsey," Trevor says. "Suck-up. Teacher's pet." Another reason Trevor is great. He keeps up with all that stuff. He pays attention.

"Yeah, that's the one," I say. "Lindsey told Bex that Bex couldn't karate chop, so Bex proved her wrong. Knocked her on her butt."

"Oh, man," Trevor says.

"Oh, man," Chico, our parrot, says from his cage in the corner. If you have any brains, you stay away from Chico. He'll lure you to him with nice words, like *Come here, Sweetie,* or *Give me a kiss* and he'll make smooching sounds. But then when you get close, *snap!* It gets the vet every time. Trevor snitches a baby carrot from the counter, and Mom gives him a look, shoves the knife over for him to chop some instead.

"She's lucky she didn't get expelled," Mom says.

"Still, she's been grounded for a week," I say.

"I like being grounded!" Bex shouts from the other room. As you can tell, our house was pretty small. Privacy, forget it.

"That's not the idea!" Mom shouts back. "See? What do I know about grounding," she says.

Mom finishes browning beef and adds garlic, and the whole house gets rich with the blissful, hypnotic meld of butter and

Deb Caletti

garlic and onions. She's making a Joe's Special, one of her top-three favorite meals at her favorite restaurant, Thirteen Coins, somewhere we go only for a special treat, since it's pricey. Okay, actually we went there only once that I can remember, back when she and Dad were still married and she didn't have to worry in the grocery store aisle over whether she should buy shower cleaner or not. In the old days, fabric-softener sheets you tossed into the dryer and already-made juice in bottles (versus the frozen kind you mix with three cans of water) were not considered luxury items. We could get the ice cream in a round container and not in a square one.

I hear Severin, my brother, come home. Severin, Indigo, Bex—my father had this thing for individuality in names, according to Mom, which basically means, *If you don't like it, blame him.* Severin says hi to Bex, and then his bedroom door shuts. Mom adds the eggs and spinach, which may sound gross, but it's not. It's amazing. My mother is great in the kitchen, but if you really want to understand Naomi Skye, the person, you need to look at the complicated relationship she had with her old Datsun then. First of all, every smell on the road—a street being tarred, a fire, some tanker spilling exhaust—would elicit this panicky reaction along the lines of, *What's that? Do you smell that? Is that my car?* She'd roll down her window, sniff, sniff, sniff, until you said, *Mom, relax! See the flames coming out of that building? The fire trucks? The plumes of black smoke over there?* And then she'd hold a hand to her chest and breathe a sigh of relief. *Thank God,* she'd say. *I thought I was going to need a new engine or something.*

Then, second, there was that pesky little red "engine" light that flickered on the dashboard. This was a sign of certain doom, which she completely ignored. If you pointed it out, she'd say, *It's fine. It always does that. It'll go off.* And then, finally, there were the windshield wipers. We'd be driving along, and her windshield wipers would be going even though it'd stopped raining twenty minutes ago, or maybe even the day before. Still, they'd be *ke-shunk, ke-shunk*ing and she wouldn't notice until you said *Mom! Your wipers are on!* and she'd give this little surprised *Oh, right!* and shut them off. See, a triple threat existed in Mom; it's still there, really (and will probably be there always, no matter what), some anxiety-denial-distraction combo that expressed itself most clearly as soon as she was behind the wheel of that old yellow car. *That's what happens when you're a single mother and work full-time in a psychiatrist's office and are raising three kids and trying to find the time to get the laundry done,* she'd say as she sprayed Febreze on some shirt in lieu of actually using the washing machine. I don't know about that, but I do know that even if she's a bit scattered, she's great with food. She knows how to feed us.

There in the kitchen, Trevor agrees. "Mmm." He groans with smell-pleasure. His own mom runs a day care in their house, so he was lucky if he got hot dogs cut up into little pieces and Cheerios in a baggie.

"Tell your brother and sister that dinner's ready," Mom says.

"Bex! Sever-in!" I shout. "Dinner's ready!"

"Indigo, God." She sighs. "I could have done that." Which is what she always says. "*Go* and *tell* them."

"God!" Chico says.

In a few moments, we're all around the table, pouring milk, passing rolls. Mom liked us to sit and have that meal together. *We will not be one of those families that eat in the car on the way to somewhere else. Where sports practice and meetings and trips to the mall are more important than being together,* she would say. *I want us to*

Deb Caletti

share our day. Trevor was the one who really got off on this, since his mother didn't hear a word he said unless he was dripping blood and had to go to the emergency room.

"Top of the line built-in model," he says, "and they aren't even gonna *use* it. It's for the *catering kitchen.* The place the caterers go to make a mess in so guests don't see." Trevor had delivered a refrigerator earlier that day to some people on Meer Island.

"The Moores have a catering kitchen," Severin says. "And this whole room where Mrs. Moore can practice her tennis swing in virtual reality. I saw it at the Christmas party." Then, Severin worked after school for MuchMoore Industries, which I'm sure you've heard of, but if you haven't, it's this company that sells digital cameras and image transferring. They'll print your name and photo on any object from greeting cards to wallpaper. Severin's my twin, but you'd never know it. I got blessed with the part of Mom that'll reach into her purse for a pen and will pull out a tampon, and I got blessed with the part of Dad that's dissatisfied with social constraints, and that's maybe just a little dissatisfied in general. The way most people feel on Sunday nights is how I think he feels a lot of the time. This led him to get fired from his job at an advertising firm, after he submitted a proposal for a major account, Peugeot, with the slogan, "Got Peu?" After that, Dad left advertising for good, moved to Hawaii, and opened a shop that rents surfboards.

Bomba, who loves me, claims I *dance to my own drummer*, and I'm sure she's got this wrong, because it makes me sound like I'm flailing around in the focused psycho-ecstasy you see in groupies in the front row of any concert. But Severin, he doesn't dance to his own drummer. He walks in a straight line. He got the parts of our parents that remember to buy stamps and that love books and that plan for the future. Severin's one of those guys who have looks and height and brains and a sense of purpose. He worked for MuchMoore, hung out with the Skyview kids from our school, and he could fake his way through the truth that he didn't fit in with them. The fact that girls like Kristin Densley and Heather Green called our house all the time and that he got good grades didn't piss me off, though, because Severin's this really nice person. He treated Trevor like an equal even if Trevor graduated from the alternative school. Severin, my *brother*, talked to me at school, even if no one seemed to grasp the idea that we were related. He's the kind of guy that also does nice things for no reason, like once he replaced a broken string on my guitar as a surprise.

"Two kitchens to clean, is all I can think," Mom says.

"*They* don't clean them," I remind.

"No, they just hire immigrants at less than minimum wage," Mom says. She sounds like Jane, my boss.

Bex takes a swig of milk. "There are people without *homes* and *food* now, let alone refrigerators," she says.

"Detention's over, Bex," Mom says.

"No, wait. Seriously," Trevor says. His face does get serious. But serious in a way that makes you want to laugh. "What would you do if you had that kind of money?"

I know that Trevor is someone who asks a question because he's dying to give you his own answer, and I am a good girlfriend, so I say, "What would you do?"

"I know what *I'd* do," he says.

"Start your business," I say.

"What's that saying? 'Give a man a lemon, he eats lemons for a day; teach him to make lemonade and he'll always have something to drink'? I'd invest in myself," Trevor says. You can see why

Deb Caletti

I might be lacking a little faith in Trevor as a businessman.

"Nunderwear!" Bex shouts, raising a fist to the air. This is Trevor's latest brilliant plan. He'd had other ideas before, but this time he's *serious*. The last time, he was serious too, but he's forgotten that. Nunderwear is based on those days-of-the-week underwear, only with Nunderwear, they'd all read SUNDAY. Trevor's got this whole product line of gag gifts he wants to sell under the business name Lapsed Catholic Enterprises. He's sure other lapsed Catholics would find them just as hilarious as he does, and he doesn't even smoke anything (anymore). He wants to make those little packets of cheese and crackers using communion wafers, called My Body Snack Pak. Then he has the Pope's Hat Coffee Filters, which he actually sketched out on a piece of notebook paper. Shaped like the pope's hat, they'd come in a pack of fifty and fit any standard electric coffeepot, for using or wearing.

"You guys laugh, but you won't be laughing when I'm rolling in the dough."

"If I had that kind of money?" Bex says. "I'd give it away to the needy. To people whose houses have washed away, just like *that*." She snaps her fingers.

"CNN isn't good for kids," I say.

"I mean it," she says. Her blue eyes look directly at me. She's eleven years old, so I suspect her submersion into disaster coverage will fade as soon as she's in her sixth-grade class painting papier-mâché tribal masks they've made out of strips of the *Seattle Times* and Gold Medal flour and water. "I would."

"Severin?" Trevor asks.

"Easy. College."

"Like you're not going to get scholarships," I say.

"You have no idea. I get Bs! God. I'm up against these kids who've taken every SAT prep class, who've hired college counselors that have been working with them since they were zygotes, searching out scholarships and filling out applications. . . . It's nuts. And they don't even *need* the scholarships."

"What's a zygote?" Bex asks.

"I told you, we'll work out something," Mom says. But she doesn't look too sure, honestly. She stares down into her plate when she says it, picks at her salad with her fork as if the solutions are hidden somewhere under the lettuce.

"What's a zygote?" Bex asks again.

"When the egg and the sperm—"

"Oh gross, never mind," Bex says.

"Can we ditch the sperm talk at dinner, please?" I say.

"What about you, Missus?" Trevor asks. His mind is still on rich people. "What would you do if you had lots of money? Lots and lots of money."

"College. For Severin and Indigo and Bex."

"I don't want to go to college," I say.

"So you claim," Mom says. It's an ongoing argument between us, and now when the subject comes up, Mom stops it cold with some statement that indicates her irrefutable superior knowledge about my real desires. She doesn't get that I don't know what I want to study, and that it therefore seems a waste of money. I'm not going to be one of those people who spend thousands of dollars getting an art history degree and then end up working in a dentist's office.

"Okay, besides college," Trevor says. "Don't you people dream big? Swimming pools?"

"I'll take a pool," I say.

Deb Caletti

"Famous people, parties . . ." He's trying to bait me.

"Hun-ter E-den," Mom sings. Okay, so I had a little crush on Hunter Eden then. Who in their right mind didn't? My friend Melanie actually went to one of his concerts and met him, because her dad's PR firm handled Slow Change. Yeah, I'd have liked to handle Slow Change. I may not have wanted to dance to my own drummer, but I wouldn't have minded dancing to my own guitar player. Not only did I find his playing to be amazing and inspirational, but he was sexy enough to melt ice, like he did on the body of that girl in the video for "Hot."

"Okay, okay. Front row tickets, backstage pass, after-concert party. Then I'd die happy," I say.

"I could sing you 'Hot'," Trevor offers. Everyone laughs. Even Chico does his *eh, eh, eh* laugh imitation. "It wasn't *that* funny."

"You still need something for yourself, Mom," I say.

"College *is* for myself," she says. "You can take care of me in my old age."

"Diamonds!" I joke. Mom is a nonjewelry person. If she ever gets remarried (which was looking unlikely since she didn't even date) she'd probably rather strap a hefty Barnes & Noble gift card to the third finger of her left hand than a ring.

"Dahling," she says. "No, I like the blue ones. What are they? I always think topaz, but that's not right."

"Sapphires," Severin says. "How about a trip somewhere?"

"Zygote City," Bex says.

"A Jenn-Air built-in Euro-style stainless with precision temperature management system," Trevor says.

"No, I know," I say. Bex looks at me and smiles.

"I know too," she says.

"Toilet seat!" we say together.

"Eh, eh, eh," Chico says.

"Come on, guys, it is *not* that bad," Mom says. She was wrong, though—it was. It had a thin, shifty crack in it, and you had to be careful how you sat down, or it'd snip you in the ass. If you stumbled to the bathroom in the middle of the night and didn't stay alert, you'd get a zesty wake-up pinch.

"We've got the only toilet seat in all of Zygote City that bites," Bex says.

"I promise, I'll get it fixed," Mom says. "Add it to the list." Microwave oven: out of commission since Bex put a foil-wrapped Ho Ho in there. Why she wanted to warm it up is still a mystery. Vacuum: worked if you only used the hose attachment and didn't mind spending about twelve hours hunched over the carpet like you'd lost a contact lens. Iron: black on the bottom and leaking water.

"Gold toilet seat," Trevor says, as if it's decided.

"Or one of those padded ones," Severin says, and grins.

"Those give me the creeps," I say.

"Me too, but I don't exactly know why," Mom says.

Freud, our cat, saunters in from the living room, stretches his hind legs behind him. Bex dangles her fingers toward the floor and Freud nudges them with his triangle nose.

"Here, kitty, kitty," Chico says evilly. He makes smooching sounds.

That was what my life was like, before I got rich.

Deb Caletti

I might have been the only one in the world who didn't have a cell phone, but I didn't care. Or maybe I cared a little. One time Trevor and I were driving around downtown Seattle, and we saw this guy sitting on the curb with his bottle of Thunderbird in a brown bag, and a cardboard sign that read WILL WORK FOR FOOD, and he was talking on a cell phone. I'm not kidding. Unless he was on some Friends and Family plan, that's just whacked. But it did make me wonder if maybe I should spend my hard-earned money on one. I decided no, though, because I really needed a car right then, and that's what I was saving for.

Mom always said that in the real world, not everyone has cell phones and TVs in their rooms and drives their dad's BMW. She was referring to the Skyview kids that went to my school. Nine Mile Falls (the suburb just east of Seattle) has its sections, like those parfaits at Carrera's with the layers of pudding and whipped cream. There's the downtown, where we live, which sits in the valley between three mountains, Mount Solitude being the largest. The town is all small Christmas-card charm and lies along a winding river that runs with salmon in October. There's another hill, though, at the edge of town, called the Midlands, where new housing developments are continually springing up; not-there, and then there, like those toy sponges that are paper flat until you put them in water. And finally there's another part of the Midlands, the highest part of the hill, a neighborhood called Skyview. Skyview is where all the kids live whose parents make a ton of money at Microsoft. The land of SUVs, of big head-lights bearing into your back windshield with crazy-eyed caf-feinated aggression. The super rich, the only-on-television rich, MuchMoore rich, don't live in Nine Mile Falls at all, but a few miles north, on Meer Island.

And I guess there are parfaits within parfaits, layers within layers. Downtown, you've got the apartments, you've got people who rent small houses like we did from Mrs. Jesus-Freak-Homophobe Olson, and people who own their homes, like a lot of our neighbors. And then in the other places, you've got the people who have the huge house but no furniture inside, the prestigious job versus just a fat check, Meer Island waterfront or just a Meer Island address. At my school, you had the down-towners under the same roof as the Midlanders and the Skyviewers, the kid whose mom waits in the food-bank line by the library in the same PE class with the kid whose mom waits in line at Nordstrom.

Apparently, there are a lot of "real worlds."

Anyway, I didn't have a cell phone, so when Jane called my house at six a.m. to ask me to come in to work on my rare Sunday off because *Nikki has to stay home with her kid who has strep throat, and God, let's hope she didn't give it to Nikki and all of us while she was at it,* the ringing phone wakes up Mom. By the time I get dressed, she's making coffee, standing at the sink in her frizzled, high-voltage morning hair and the chenille robe she'd had forever. Its fuzz was worn down in spots, just like an old mule.

"Morning," I say.

"Here, kitty, kitty," Chico says. The cover of his cage is still on, making his tiny clown voice slightly muffled. I feel bad for him under there, just waiting to start his evil little day. I lift the fabric

Deb Caletti

so he can join us. Freud walks toward Chico in his slinky fashion, sits under his cage and just stares. We have satanic pets, and I'm not sure why. I mean, we're nice people, but our pets seem to have made a pact with the devil. Freud has some psychological issues—he's slightly sadistic and a merciless hunter. He once sat in a tree swiping at the air in the direction of a squirrel, his focus that of a hired killer, totally oblivious to the snow that was blowing around like mad and accumulating steadily on his fur like a layer of meringue. He brings you the heads of rodents and birds, lays them down in the kitchen or on your bedroom carpet. He should have been in the Mafia.

"I got water down my sleeve," Mom grouses. "I *hate* getting water down my sleeve." She dries her forearm with a kitchen towel.

"Go back to bed," I say.

"I can never get back to sleep after I've woken up. You get called to work?"

"Sorry. Yeah. Jane needs me to come in."

"I thought so." But even her *I thought so* is ragged and awake-against-your-will weary. "I'll drive you over if you bring me home a piece of Harold's pie. It'll give me something flaky and fat-laden to look forward to." Harold is Harold Zaminski, this funny old guy Jane gets our baked goods from. He likes to play practical jokes. One time he stuffed the small patch of lawn in front of the store with election signs for this baby-faced Republican running for Senate, just to give Jane a coronary. When Harold's granddaughter visits, he'll bring her in, walk behind her, hands up near her neck like he wants to strangle her. She's a bit of a monster, but you can tell he's crazy about her.

"Deal," I say. "You have plans today?" Hopeful question. I

wished Mom got out more. The last date she went on was when I still had school recess.

"Oh, I might meet Allison for coffee, or I might just have a robe day and get all the accounting done. Weed the yard with Bex, if I can bribe her."

"Mom, I love you but you need to get a life."

"I have a life," she says. "And I'm getting pie-ie, I'm getting pie-ie." She sings this and gives a little chenille-dance, neatly proving my point. One thing you can say about daughters and mothers—like it or not, they know the truth about each other.

Trina is already at Carrera's when Jane and I arrive. She's sitting in her car, head back against the seat, listening to music. It's somewhere near the end of April, I don't remember exactly, but the top of her convertible is down. She isn't wearing her fur, even though April in Seattle can still have a bite, same as our toilet seat. Trina's wearing these jeans that lace up the side and this white tank top that's zingy against her tan. It's an over-the-counter tan for the most part, kept alive with aerosol and electricity after she and her boyfriend, Roger, got back from Palm Springs a few weeks ago. She's told us this. Trina's a confessional person. She rarely has an unexpressed thought.

"My God, it's about time," she says. She follows us in before Jane even has the lights up. Luigi, our cook, is already in back, and so is Alex, this quiet boy from my school who helps with the dishes. I hear Luigi singing. He always says, *Me, I coulda been Tony Bennett. They told me I coulda made a recording, but I went into the restaurant business instead. More stable.* He sings all kinds of things—TV commercials, snippets of opera, Elton John songs, stuff he makes up. *Don't leave me outta eggs, Jane,* he'll croon. But

Deb Caletti

he likes Sinatra best. I know more Sinatra lyrics than any eighteen-year-old should, thanks to Luigi, not that I advertised that. All the white suburban kids who tried so hard to be gangsta and hip-hop but whose mothers all had cappuccino machines would have chewed my ass if they'd known I could sing "Dream" and "Fly Me to the Moon."

Trina's favorite table is Travertino Navona. At Carerra's, every table is a different kind of marble, and the name is on a round gold plate on the table itself. It must have cost Jane a bundle to have the tables made. There are something like three thousand types of marble (called "families"), and all the families have their own "faults," which give them their characteristics, just like our neighbors at home—Mrs. Denholm next door, who always snooped at us through the venetian blinds, waiting for us "teens" to commit some sort of crime; the Elberts, who let their dog bark all night; and the Navinskys, whose television was always on, and whose kids even have those miniature TVs for brief trips away from the real thing. If you saw Travertino Navona, though, you wouldn't think about it having faults. It's a creamy brown, like caramel and marshmallow fluff in a swirl.

"People are *hungry* here," Trina says.

"I've got to go home sometime," Jane says. "Just to get my mail, if nothing else." She's brought Jack, her black Lab, who gets lonely and eats things if he's left alone. He ate the golf bag that belonged to Jane's ex-husband, which she didn't mind, and the leg off of Jane's dead grandmother's rocking chair, which she did mind. Leroy said this was better than if he'd chewed the leg off the dead grandmother, but Jane didn't think that was so funny.

Jack follows us in (actually, he shoves his way past us), then flops behind the register and sighs through his nose as if the whole experience has been a terrible ordeal.

"Dear God, bring me coffee before I kill someone," Trina says.

Jane sets her bag down, disappears to talk to Luigi. I get the coffee started; leave a message for Trevor to pick me up after work. "Did you have a bad night?" I ask. Now that I really look at her, I see that the underneath part of Trina's eyes have their own coffee cup rings of no sleep.

"Bad."

"What happened?"

"Ten signs you're being dumped. Number one. Your lover leaves the country and doesn't tell you."

"No way," I say.

"Way. I waited at home for him for two nights. Almost called the police, but finally called Myrna instead."

"Myrna?"

"Roger's wife. He went to Brazil, she tells me. 'I'm sorry,' she says, 'I tried to warn you, didn't I? Once an asshole, always an asshole.'"

"Oh, man," I say. I snitch the coffeepot out of the base, interrupt the drizzle for Trina's immediate caffeine relief. I set a full cup in front of her, and she sighs. Sometimes, coffee is deliverance enough.

"Rio," Trina says. The word is an ending.

"Why Rio?"

"He's got another house there. Topless sunbathers, thong bikinis." Trina rubs her forehead. "What am I gonna do?"

"Who needs him, I say."

"I thought we had a great time in Palm Springs. The sex alone—"

Deb Caletti

"Whoa. I'm barely eighteen, here, remember? Jesus. I don't want the details."

"Your loss," she says miserably.

"I get enough details at school, thanks. Do you know there's such a thing as sex addiction? I saw it in some magazine. I'm thinking the guys at my school need a support group for sex addiction. Wait, forget the support group. Just make it sixth period."

"What kind of pie is there?" Trina asks. She sounds like she's standing at the edge of a high building. She has suicide in her voice. I know what will lure her from the edge, though.

"Chocolate cream. Apple with crumble top—"

"Stop at chocolate."

Which I also already knew. People like to have something to turn down, though. They want to be able to say no to some things, because it makes their yes more meaningful. Even if that's just scrambled instead of poached or fried, wheat and not sourdough or rye. And "no"—it's also a handy, accessible mini-capsule of power. Maybe you can't destroy your asshole boyfriend, but you can at least reject apple crumble pie.

I open the refrigerated cupboard, remove Harold's chocolate cream, cut a wide triangle of comfort. By the time I have it on the plate, Joe Awful Coffee is ambling in, and so are two women who hang around by the door, even if it's obvious that Carrera's is a seat-yourself place. I grab two plastic-covered menus and lead them anyway to Grigio Fumo, since Leroy Richie likes Verde Classico, and Nick Harrison likes Rosso Verona, and Funny likes Calacatta Fantasia, and Joe sits at the counter, which is all Carrera No. 2.

Within moments, I'm flying around, and so is Jane, and we're zipping past each other like experienced dance partners, and

Luigi is belting out something he must have heard on the radio on the way over "Why buy a mattress anywhere else!" and there's the sound of frying and plates and conversation and silverware clinking against glass plates and the smell of butter and coffee and sizzling bacon, the melded recipe of morning. Funny Coyote comes in and talks to Trina, and the two new ladies surprise me and order full stacks (when I took them for the fruit-cup type) and Joe shows Jane and me pictures he just got of his new baby grand-daughter. Nick Harrison arrives and sets a section of folded newspaper down beside him, and Leroy must be sleeping late, and a couple with a toddler wants a table and I have to fetch a booster seat.

So, who needs a gym, right? First off, I've never been the show-your-body-off-in-stretchy-fabrics type, even if I've got an okay one. (My ass is maybe a little wobbly, but big deal.) I went to one of those places once, and there were just too many guys in tight tank tops strutting around and looking at themselves in mirrors. Great big old narcissist party, minus the booze and cocktail wieners on frilly toothpicks. But man, I get plenty of exercise waitressing. It's hard work. Lifting, bending, constant motion. I give Nick his oatmeal, coo-chie-coo the toddler, take the parents' order, go back to find a pen that works, refill Joe's coffee cup. The full stacks are up and I have my back turned when I hear Nick Harrison say, too loudly, "Vespa alert. Curbside."

I'm registering what this means when in a flash, the bells on the door jangle. When I turn, there's the guy again, in tan slacks and a white shirt, a sleek leather jacket over one arm. He's everything new and clean and crispy—shopping bags, clothes with just-ironed creases, things wrapped in tissue paper. Trina's chin pops up, her head swivels, and you can practically see the circles

Deb Caletti

of her radarscope following the movement of his body. Code red. She sets her fork down. She's only one bite into her pie, since Funny came in to hear her blab about Roger in Rio. Trina's a backward pie eater. She starts at the corner, leaves the point of the pie, the tastiest bite, she says, for last. This probably says something about her, only I don't know what.

People are creatures of habit, and you learn this quickly if you work in a restaurant. Maybe we have just so much change that we can take, so much that's out of our control, that we need to keep the same what we're able to keep the same. If someone sits at a table once, there's about an 85 percent chance they'll sit there again if they can, and this man is no different. He slides into the window-side chair again at Nero Belgio, a marble that is almost pure black. It's all shiny elegance, and it's a good match for him. There's also about a 75 percent chance that a person will order the very same thing as he did before, but I'd just have to see.

"Morning," I say.

"Good morning." He smiles his closed-mouth smile.

I set a menu at the table, wait.

"Just coffee," the man says again. My inner crowd cheers. It's the gleeful rise of I-knew-it, mixed with the gladness of a continuing mystery. Eggs and sausage would have meant no more questions. A regular guy finds a new place to eat, big deal. But no, he's still here with *Just coffee.*

I pour, then set his cup down in front of him. He doesn't have a newspaper, anything. He just sits and stares out the window. Joe wipes his fingers free of bacon grease on his napkin before he puts the photos back away in their envelope. "Sad," he whispers to me, flicking his head back toward the Vespa guy.

"Maybe," I say.

Nick's taking it all in. He's filtered out the ladies talking, the toddler twisting around and dropping crusts to the floor, and he's listening to Joe and me. He nods. *Depressed*, he mouths, overemphasizing the first syllable, *Dee*, from across the room, his top row of teeth showing wide and white.

Trina suddenly needs to use the restroom, which is past the guy's table, naturally. It's a pheromone parade—they're waving and throwing their batons and eating flames and doing cartwheels as Trina saunters by the guy's table. Roger who?

But Nick's the only one watching Trina's ass in those pants. Well, me too, but I'm not watching in that way so it doesn't count. The guy doesn't even blink or break his gaze from the window. "Full and resounding failure," Jane says next to me, behind the counter.

Trina takes about two seconds in the bathroom, obviously not long enough to do anything legitimate in there. Then she's out again, swiveling those pheromones like lassoes. She stares directly at the guy, but it's Trina's eye contact zeroing in to its target, and zing! Hitting the side of the guy's head.

Funny Coyote's breakfast is up, and I set the plate in front of her. Trina slides into her adjacent booth. "Gay," Funny Coyote proclaims.

"You think?" Trina says. She sounds hopeful, but it looks like she might cry. She pushes her plate away from herself.

"You're not done." I can't believe it. Trina usually eats every bite. I've seen her put her finger to a bit of crumb and lick when she thinks no one is looking. Harold's pie—nobody pushes away Harold's pie. You eat it even if you have to unbutton the top of your pants to make room.

"I've got to go on a diet," she says.

Deb Caletti

"My God, don't be crazy," Funny Coyote says, which is pretty hilarious, because she calls herself Bipolar Babe. "Relax. He's gay, I'm telling you."

"I don't know what I'm gonna do," Trina moans.

"Trina, you're talking about a couple of *guys*. Big deal. A man is not water or shelter. Or a lottery ticket," I say.

"Maybe the kind of lottery ticket you spend a hundred bucks on, just to win five," Funny says.

"Harold's pie *is* a requirement for living," I say.

"Really," Funny says, munching on a piece of bacon. "Give it here if she doesn't want it."

"Maybe I need a boob job," Trina says.

"Oh my God," I say. "Don't even joke. I hate fake crap like that," I say. "Sure, I'll take a little cancer from silicone just to have some cleavage. Sheesh."

"No kidding," Funny says. "And what happens when you're sixty and have forever-twenty tits? Freak show."

Trina moons into her coffee. Funny pulls out her notebook and starts to write. The man stays longer this time. The two ladies leave, and so does the couple with the toddler, who went from cute to monstrous in fifty minutes as his parents did the *Now-honey-that-makes-Mommy-upset* public parenting routine that always causes Jane to turn her back and pretend to stick her finger down her throat. Thanks to little Hitler, the floor looked like its own galaxy of toast crumbs and scrambled egg bits. I consider asking the Vespa guy if he's all right, but he seems to be in that private place you shouldn't just barge in on. The only privacy some people ever get is in their thoughts. So instead, I wipe the floor clean and curse at parents who grow little dominatrix children and then set them free in the world to be the kind of adults who let everyone else pick up their messes. You get some pretty strong ideas about child rearing when you work as a waitress, let me tell you.

Finally, the guy lifts one long, elegant finger in the air, gestures for my attention. Sometimes that kind of thing can piss you off, but it all depends on how it's done. Some people have a demanding stab-the-air finger that makes you want to flip your middle one back at them. They are usually the people who ask you for this or that on the side and cooked this way or that way, and with the strawberry pointing counterclockwise and the parsley with two leaves only. Most often, this kind of thing happens with large, pompous men with large, pompous voices, and with spatula-thin women whose lack of food has turned them into restrained, yet rage-filled, maniacal bitches.

Anyway, the guy was obviously raised right, because even his finger has manners. I bring him his check, and there's the crispy bill again. He smiles, I smile, and we all watch his suit-jacket-flaps flap as he speeds off on his Vespa.

For a few minutes, it's just us. The regulars, as Jane says, which caused Leroy to dub us "the Irregulars."

"Depressed," Nick says out loud. "I ought to know."

"I vote with the gals," Joe says. "Gay. Too pretty. Manicured nails. Probably never even been to a boxing match in his life."

"But I bet he's been to Rio," Trina says.

"Italy," Jane says.

"Why buy a mattress an-y-where else," Luigi sings.

My shift is almost over when Funny lifts her head from the notebook she's been writing in. "Has anyone thought about all the places you've ever laid your head?" she asks. "All the places you've ever woken up?"

30   *Deb Caletti*

Leroy walks in then. He's so much later than usual, I had given up on him coming in at all. The bells on the door jangle, but still he's heard Funny's question. He raises up his hand, as if the teacher might call on him. Under his right forearm is a mermaid, with twisty golden hair. "Do backseats count?"

"Rough night?" Nick asks. He says it with a bit of longing. Nick is this nice, straight guy who would've had this nice, straight life had his wife not fallen down those stairs.

"Anyone got aspirin?" Leroy says.

"I do," Funny says. She lifts her purse, rattles what sounds like twenty pill bottles in there.

"Eighteen places," Jane says. She scrunches her nose around instead of itching it. Jane's got allergies. "I counted eighteen places I've woken up. No, nineteen. One airport chair in Dallas during a layover."

"Seventy, eighty?" Trina says.

Nick whistles.

"Roger and I did a lot of traveling. And then you've got . . . miscellaneous apartments."

Nick blushes. He takes a sip of water that has maybe three or four flat shards of ice left in it.

"God, Trina," I say.

"Some were just *friends*," she says.

I'm almost embarrassed to admit my answer. "Five or six," I say. Mom's, Dad's, camping trip with Dad, Bomba and Bompa's. Ramada Inn with Dad. I add another, just because five seems too pathetic. I refill Nick's water glass; the new ice sloshes in merrily.

"You're young," Leroy says. He winks at me. Leroy and I understand each other.

The Fortunes of Indigo Skye   31

"Hundreds," Joe says. "Hundreds and hundreds. But then again, I'm old."

"So old, Jesus was in your math class," I say. I crack myself up.

"You probably toured the country with your boxing, right?" Jane says. She clips Jack to his leash, getting him ready for his late-morning pee. Whenever Jack sees his leash, it's like he's looking at two plane tickets for around the world, even if he's just going to the corner and back.

"Oh yeah. For years. When I got back, my family barely knew who I was." Joe's big hand is covered with wrinkles that look like the chocolate piping on Harold's cakes. It's a hand that trembles, though, as he brings a triangle of toast to his mouth and crunches.

"Well, they know you now. Look at that picture they sent. Beautiful baby granddaughter," Jane says. Joe's got the photo propped up against a water glass.

"With her in Saint Louis, I'll be lucky to see her before I'm dead," Joe says, chewing. He has a lump of toast in one cheek.

"This is getting goddamned dark," Funny says.

"You'll see her someday," Jane says. "Don't give up hope." Jack pulls her to the door like he's a sled dog and she's the sled. Jack is an old dog, but strong, same as Joe. If you ever saw Joe arm-wrestle Leroy, you'd know what I mean.

Right then, Bill and Marty come in, these two guys that work at True Value with Nick. I pretend I don't know their names, even though I do. Actually, we all pretend we've never even seen them before. This is in keeping with the Respect Hierarchy of Names, which naturally progresses from the reverential first-name-last-name-plus-bonus-points-initial (John F. Kennedy, F. Scott

Fitzgerald, Edward R. Murrow) all the way down to the bottom of the ladder, the hazy description (That Guy from Safeway, What's-His-Name). One step below that are the folks so little deserving of respect you pretend their existence is forgettable. This is Bill and Marty.

Bill wears a camouflage baseball hat, which might tell you all you need to know. Marty has a mustache, though no one has a mustache anymore. Nick gives a little wave and smile that means *I know you, sure, but don't sit here.* But Bill and Marty don't get the finer points of social etiquette, because they head right on over to sit at Nick's table. Nick isn't dressed that differently from them—jeans and a short-sleeve chambray shirt, but it's like a couple of Coors cans have just been set on the table with a martini.

"Hey, Killer," Bill says.

Nick grimace-smiles. "It gets funnier every time you say it," Nick says. "Ha, ha, ha."

"I hope they've got corned beef hash," Marty says. He takes his napkin and wipes his mouth, as if there's some layer of slime there even he can't stand.

"Excuse me," Nick says. "I was just heading out."

Nick rises and walks to the register to pay, takes his wallet from his back pocket. He still wears his grimace-smile. "Should I spit in their coffee?" I whisper.

"Arsenic's better."

I give Nick some thin mints wrapped in green foil. Nick's face just makes you want to give him *something.* This is the kind of shit he takes from these guys day in and day out. I'd love to tell them off myself, but Jane says they're our *customers.* This means that we may secretly hate them but still have to smile and take their money.

The Fortunes of Indigo Skye

"See ya, Killer," Bill says one more time and waves.

"Ooh, boy, you got me again!" Nick says. He pushes open the door and goes through it, his back looking sadder than I've ever seen a back look.

I give the idiot bookends their menus, but luckily Zach (who works the afternoon shift) arrives, so I don't have to serve them. Instead, I untie my apron and lift it over my head and grab my backpack from the back. I cut a piece of apple pie with crumble top and wrap it up in foil for Mom, say good-bye to the Irregulars.

Trevor isn't there yet, but I see Jane and Nick talking at the curb. Jack stands politely, alert as a secret service agent, his eyes surveying the territory for any criminal cat, squirrel, or bird activity. Suddenly, though, I can't believe my eyes when I look down at Jane's hand. I feel a rising wave of anger. Now, I'm not what anyone would call conservative—people at my school probably called me anything but that. I think they thought I was weird, but I noticed that every time I changed my hair, a bunch of girls would come the very next week with an attempted version of it until I changed again. I didn't really care, which is exactly what my friend Melanie said people loved and hated about me.

But I'm straight about one thing, and that's smoking and drugs, and I'm not sure why I'm so crazy about it except that drugs fucked up Trevor's life for a while and cigarettes are just nasty. We had this police officer come to our class in the fifth grade, and she brought us glass jars filled with a healthy person's lung tissue (aside from the fact that the lung tissue was minus a body, which is not generally a healthy thing) and a smoker's lung tissue. The former was pink and spongy-looking and cheery, and the latter was this desperate, dingy shade of gray that made you

Deb Caletti

think of motel rooms where crimes had been committed. You saw this sad lung as a hopeful straight-A student who'd somehow tragically descended into a life of heroin and prostitution and had died with a needle in her arm. That's how gray and wretched it looked. I never forgot it, and it frankly just pisses me off to see people smoke, knowing what they are doing to their poor, formerly positive lungs.

So anyway, I look down, and there's this cigarette held between Jane's fingers, and it's right down by her side where Jack is just breathing all this shit. And Jane doesn't even smoke.

"What are you doing!" I shriek.

Jane looks a little shocked. She swivels her head around as if there must be some robber with a bag of loot running around somewhere nearby. There's the crime, right in her own hand, and she doesn't even realize it.

"No! You! There!" I point.

"Indigo, jeez," she says. "You scared me to death."

She thinks I'm kidding, but I'm not. "You should be scared to death, 'cause you're certainly gonna put Jack in a coffin, not to mention yourself."

She looks down at herself. I can't believe it. She still doesn't get it.

"Your cigarette," Nick offers helpfully.

She holds it up as if she has no idea how it got there. "This?"

"Ugh, God, put it out, I can smell it," I say. I wave my hand in front of my face. I hold my breath so none of the three thousand toxins and tars and chemicals can get in.

"It *is* a nasty habit," Nick says, giving me another reason why I like that guy. "I didn't even know you smoked," he says.

"I don't," Jane says.

The Fortunes of Indigo Skye

"This is just a mirage," I say.

"No, I mean, I *haven't*. For years. Wait," she says. "Why am I explaining myself to you people? I'm a grown woman. I can smoke if I want." But she tosses the burning stick of tar and chemicals to the sidewalk and smashes it with her heel.

I say the one thing I know will affect her, whether it's true or not. "Smoking is for Republicans."

"That's just mean," she says to me. "I've been under a little stress lately," she says to Nick. "In regard to what we were just discussing."

"I can imagine," he says.

"What?" I ask.

"Nothing," Jane says.

"What!" I ask again.

"If I wanted everyone to know, I'd get a billboard."

I let it go, because just then we hear knocking on the glass of Carrera's. We look that direction, and there's Bill in his yeah-right-I-almost-mistook-you-for-a-tree hat, gesturing heartily at Nick. He's waving, then pantomimes slashing his finger across his throat, drops his head down and gaggles his tongue out.

"God, I wish I could get out of this place," Nick says.

I hear the growling rumble of Trevor's Mustang before I see the car itself. Then it turns the corner, pulls up along the curb. Trevor parks, gets out, opens the door for me. For a reformed pothead, he knows how to be a gentleman.

Trevor doesn't kiss me, because he also knows how I feel about public displays of affection in front of my boss. I say goodbye to Jane and Nick, edge onto the cream-colored seats that Trevor says are "pony interior," though I don't have a clue what

Deb Caletti

that means, other than there are horses on the seat backs.

"God, I'm starving," Trevor says. "Cheeseburger. Beef attack, baby! Fries, shake. You don't mind if I stop, right?"

I guess everyone is hungry for something.

"Baby, look at this," Trevor says. He taps the odometer in front of the steering wheel, and I lean over him, my elbow on his thigh. We're in the parking lot of XXX Root Beer, which sounds like a porn theater, but is one of the last drive-ins in the history of mankind or at least in the Seattle area, and has the best hamburgers you've ever had in your life, with buns as big as salad plates. Trevor's got the top down because it has gotten warm, and there are napkins and balls of crumpled foil on the floor around us. Carnivorous massacre. The Battle of the Burger.

"Two hundred ninety-nine thousand, nine hundred sixty," I read.

"You know what that means."

I'd been with Trevor long enough to guess. We met two years ago when I was walking home from school past the Mountain Academy, which is where the druggies and pregnant girls go when they get shunned from regular society. Trevor was one of the former. Now he's formerly of the former. When we met, I was in my crunchy phase—natural, no makeup, braids, sandals, flowy gauze skirts. I'd started the guitar the year before, still couldn't play worth crap, but I wanted to be Joan Baez, who was even before Mom's time, in the days of folk music, peace, love, groovy, and love your brother. I had enough gauze for a harem by the time this got old, but I thought it was great then. Trevor started talking to me when I passed. Actually, he said, "Hey, gorgeous," which shows what a sucker for a compliment I was (am).

I liked the way his eyes danced. It was like he had an internal joy flame always lit. Other people's eyes are flat as ash, but Trevor Williams has flames. Anyway, we've been together ever since, so when he says, *You know what that means*, I know what that means.

"Three hundred thousand miles," I say. Trevor likes stuff like that. He'll call you into the kitchen to watch the microwave clock change from 1:10 to 1:11, or to 1:23, or better yet, 12:34. He'd phone me up on my birthdays, the exact minute I was born, 4:17 a.m., setting his alarm clock for four fifteen, to make sure he had time to become conscious and dial.

"This is an occasion," he says. "We should celebrate." This is another thing Trevor likes. He'll celebrate anything—the vernal equinox, Secretary's Day, not having to get X-rays at the dentist.

"What do you have in mind?" I say. I lick the inside of his ear, which usually drives him crazy, but he isn't even thinking that direction.

"Let's drive up to the falls. Let Bob turn three hundred thousand in a special place." Bob is the Mustang's name. Bob Weaver, like bob and weave, because of the time he needed a new axle, and the car curved and swerved all over the road.

"Great." I buckle up. People who drive without seat belts are asking for trouble, and I didn't want to end up as one of those sad yearbook pictures of the kid who died. On the freeway, the air whooshes at us, smelling good enough to eat, sweet and warm as ripe blackberries, and my hair whips around my face and catches in my mouth. Trevor turns some music on, that heavy metal crap that's his favorite, all electric guitar and not acoustic, but it's his celebration so I don't complain.

"I feel like we're lacking something here," I shout.

"Wha'dya say?" Trevor shouts. We head down I-90, toward the Snoqualmie Falls exit.

I turn the music down. "It's a monumental day for Bob. Let's spice things up."

"Hats?" Trevor suggests. See, before I insisted he get straight, he would've said, *A toke?* Or, *Tequila?* I didn't want some guy who was all smeary and glazey who wasn't *present.* Hey, I could've conversed with my lava lamp if I wanted that. I wanted what was *real.*

"Nah," I say. "I'll know it when I see it."

Trevor shrugs. We keep driving. We pass a storage rental facility, a couple of coffee stands, a museum set in a train car, a place where they sell garden statues. *A place where they sell garden statues!*

"Trevor. Turn around. Look." Trevor flips a U right there. Arcs into the gravel of the lot, tires crunching. He knows I love walking up and down the outdoor aisles of those places, checking out five-foot cement ladies holding cement urns spilling cement water, plaster frogs, birdbaths, and tiki heads big enough to scare God. "Let's find someone to ride in the backseat."

"Cool." He shrugs again.

We meander along the paths, to the sound of trickling fountain water and the *kershun-kershunk* of gravel under our feet. "A gnome?" I suggest, mostly because he's small and affordable and I like his red hat.

"Nah. Gnomes go on trips all the time. You know those gnomes that get abducted from some old lady's garden and then she starts getting postcards with his picture from the Eiffel Tower? Shit like that."

"Yeah, you're right." We crunch along a bit more, X-ing out huge mermaids and enormous lions for obvious reasons. Trevor's strong, but hey.

40   *Deb Caletti*

We're in the Buddha aisle. Big, bowling-ball-tummied ones that smile like they're up to something nonreligious, huge head-only's, with dangly earrings that are fashion don'ts for anyone. Then I see them on a table—medium-size Buddhas sitting cross-legged and wearing tall, bumpy hats. Their faces are long and graceful and missing the pudge of the others. Plus, they look like chick Buddhas, not guys, if that's possible. My knowledge of Buddhas is on the slim side.

"How about her?" I point.

"Is it a him or a her?"

"I can't exactly tell."

"Lift it up and look underneath," Trevor says, and chuckles. "Hey, sure, why not? She'll look good later in your mom's front yard."

There are about twelve of the same figure on the table, and we check them all out to find the best one. She's heavier than she looks when I carry her over to the sales guy.

"We better make sure she's not some fertility god or something," Trevor says, and pinches my butt. "What's her name?" he asks the chubby man who's drinking a Fresca behind the cash register.

"Ron," the guy says. Trevor and I look at each other and we try not to crack up. We both realize the guy has just misheard Trevor and told us his own name. He fishes around behind the counter, puts the statue in a Budweiser box, and hands her over. Trevor carries the box and sets it in the backseat.

"Buckle Ron in for safety," I say, and Trevor snorts a laugh. He buckles the seatbelt around the Budweiser box, and off we go. It feels more festive now that there are three of us.

Trevor heads to the falls. The music is back on, and we are in the cool, damp air of the forest, curving toward the top of the falls, where a hotel and visitor's center sit at the cliff's edge. "Two hundred ninety-nine thousand, nine hundred ninety-eight," he announces. "I want it to change right by the falls." Trevor eats up another mile finding his perfect location. He has a mile left, and drives forward and back about seven times before he uses enough mileage to fulfill his goal. Already, two cars have honked at us, and a motorcycle roars past in a pissed-off fashion.

"Here goes," Trevor says. "Three. Hundred. Thousand." He rolls neatly to the side of the road, where our view of the falls is perfect. The water is meringue white, frothy, steamy, thunderous. I can feel mist on my face.

Trevor kisses me, and his mouth is warm. After a long while, we come up for air. "How you doing back there, Ron," Trevor asks.

I'd forgotten about Ron the Buddha. I look back at her, and she seems so serious with her head sticking up over the Budweiser box that I crack up.

"We're going to have to start saving for his college," Trevor says.

"With her grades?" I say.

"His. Hers. Hermaphrodite Buddha," Trevor says. It's a compromise. We drive back to the visitor's center, stand with the tourists, and watch the falls roar and crash. I sneak my way into the background of at least four videos, so that the grandchildren and great-grandchildren of the camera owners will have yours truly saved for posterity.

We lean over the railing, let our faces get whispered with water. "Where are all the places you've laid your head?" I ask Trevor. The question has been nagging at me, hangnail-like; every time I think I've forgotten about it, it catches on a thread. Maybe I've been mentally flicking it back and forth with my finger all along without realizing it.

"That's a Funny question," Trevor says. I can tell he doesn't mean ha-ha funny, but Coyote funny. He knows she asks questions like that sometimes.

"Yeah. But I got to thinking. I haven't been *anywhere*."

"You've been to Hawaii to visit your Dad. I've never even been on a plane," he says.

"Tell me your places," I say. I put my hand into his back pocket and bring him closer to me, maybe because I feel a little superior in this regard.

"Home," Trevor says. "And all those sleepovers when you're a kid. Benjamin Cassova's basement. I slept in the woods once. Stoned. Woke up with, like, a million mosquito bites."

"Serves you right. I forgot about sleepovers."

"Did you ever put someone's pinky in a water glass while they slept 'cause it was supposed to make them pee?"

"Yeah. And Ouija boards. Oooh, ooh," I say, making ghostly noises. I tickle Trevor, who grabs my wrists.

"East, west, home is best," Trevor says.

"I think we're limited human beings," I say.

"I've got you," he says. "That's all I need. With you, there's no limit."

"How about I drive back?" I say.

"Oh, In, you know I love you. But you only made it to your eighteenth birthday because you didn't have a car."

"I'm an excellent driver," I say.

"You took out an entire line of traffic cones in a construction zone last time I let you."

The Fortunes of Indigo Skye

"Two cones. Three. Big deal."

"Forget it, gorgeous."

Trevor takes me home. Me, Bob Weaver, and Ron the Buddha. My heart is still and satisfied. Wait, not *still*—that would be a bad thing. Calm. Calm and satisfied. There's nothing else I desire right then—not a sweatshirt to be warmer or a T-shirt to be cooler or a Coke or a vacation or stereo speakers or one of those wacky sets of spoons from every state of the union. What I am is happy. And maybe that's the closest definition for the word we can get, a life equation: An absence of wanting equals happiness.

I had stuck the plate of Mom's pie in the Budweiser box, so Ron is holding it in her lap. Mrs. Denholm next door pretends to get her mail even though it is Sunday, peering my way and no doubt thrilled that she's caught me in a shocking display of teen alcohol consumption. Trevor heads home; he'd promised his mom he'd fix the wobbly day care swing before she got sued.

I don't see Bex anywhere and Severin is gone too, but I hear Mom talking on the phone in the kitchen. Actually, she stands in the back doorway, the screen door propped open with a toe. She has her eye on the backyard as she speaks. "No, I don't want to do that," she says. "Too scary. Then you got to pay it back at what, three hundred bucks a month?" Envelopes and papers are spread all over the kitchen table. Mom hears me, turns, and gives a puzzled look toward the box in my arms. I give her an *I'll-explain-later* shrug, set it on the floor, and put the pie in the fridge.

"Quick, talk to Bomba," Mom says, and hands over the phone. "That goddamned cat." I can see what she's looking at now. Freud, meowing pitifully from a high tree branch. He's a sociopath toddler who's just painted on the walls and is now try-

Deb Caletti

ing to hide his purposeful intent behind innocence.

"Goddamned cat," Chico says in his parrot mini-clown voice. "Goddamned cat. Goddamned cat."

"Hi, Bomba," I say.

"Is everything okay?" Bomba says. She and Mom both answer the phone this way, as if they're on permanent crisis-car-crash high alert. Still, it's great to hear Bomba—even her worried voice is as cushy and comfy as a beanbag chair.

"Umm . . ." I look outside. "Freud's in a tree," I say. "Oh God, Mom's standing on a lawn chair. Mom should never stand on anything."

"Maybe you better go help her." Bomba sounds nervous.

I watch. "She's waving a flip-flop at him. He's not moving. No, wait. Here we go. Freud's found reverse. He's backing up. Okay. He's down. She's . . . Whoa, hang on. O-kay. She's down too. Incident over."

Bomba sighs. "So, how are ya? How's Trevor?"

"Everyone's great," I say. "Trevor's car just turned three hundred thousand miles."

"Man, I know how that feels. My *body's* just turned three hundred thousand miles."

"Come on, you're a spring chicken," I say. "Maybe you're a summer chicken, there in Arizona."

"I'm a summer chicken bored out of my skull. Do you know how annoying endless sunshine is? How's school?"

"One and a half more months and I blow the joint for good."

"As long as you're not puffing any joints," she says.

"Bomba! God. You're not supposed to know about that stuff."

"Right. I forgot," she says. "The sixties never happened. I don't know about sex either. Your mother and uncle were conceived by immaculate conception. No, wait. Actually, immaculate misconception."

"Imagine trying to fly all that stuff by today? Sure, I'm pregnant, but it's not how it looks. God did it, when I was just minding my own business. I was sleeping, yeah. I wasn't even aware anything was happening. Ri-ight."

"Covering up some hanky-panky, yesiree," Bomba says. "Listen to us heathens. Lightning's gonna strike."

"Wait, here's Mom."

"Love you, girl," Bomba says.

"Love you, Bomba." I hand the phone back over. Mom's forehead is sweaty. Freud saunters in all cool and swingy as if maybe we've already forgotten his panicky tango up there in the tree.

"Nice try," I say to him as he strolls toward the living room.

"Here, kitty, kitty," Chico says. But it's too late. Freud is already gone.

Our house used to have a garage but didn't anymore and that's how we each had our own rooms. You walked through Bex's room to get to mine. She isn't in there, though, so I step over her clothes on the floor and her pj's and her old stuffed dog, Syphilis, who she had since she was four, and her most recent school project, a diorama of a scene from *Holes*.

I lie on my bed, on this Mexican blanket my dad sent from some trip he took a few years ago. It has this mildly icky wool smell that I love. I'm lying there for, like, a second and then pop up because I'm already bored at being still. Being a waitress, everything goes so fast; normal life seems as fast-paced as government-access television.

I pick up my guitar case, unclick the buckles, and take my

Deb Caletti

guitar out like it's a sleeping baby, which it kind of is. It's a beautiful old Gibson from the seventies—gold-toned, mahogany, and I got it cheap from Trevor's cousin's pawnshop. I wake it up slowly; try a little "Stairs to Nowhere" from Slow Change's *Yesterday* CD. That goes all right, but when I attempt to play "Just Friends," I mangle it so bad I get mad at myself. The thing is, it reminds me that I don't have the inborn talent to be a member of Slow Change or any other band, not really, not if I face facts. Here's a life truth: facing facts sucks.

Mom always says that no one should expect an eighteen-year-old to know what he or she wants in life, because, hey, most adults don't know. *Look at me*, she would say. *I work in a psychiatrist's office because I ended up working in a psychiatrist's office, blown there like a weed.* Or, when she was in a beat-up-on-Dad mood, she'd say instead, *Take your father, for example. He'll be eighty and still wondering if maybe he should get his Master's in between renting out boogie boards.*

Maybe people shouldn't expect eighteen-year-olds to know what they want, but people do expect eighteen-year-olds to know what they want. Adults, they can accept the resignation toward the accidental in other adults, they can understand one another's giving up on the Big Dream, but there's no room for the unintentional in a teen. Heck, in a child. It starts about age five, right? *What do you want to be?* And even a five-year-old realizes they cannot just answer that they want to ride their bike around the neighborhood or collect ladybugs; they know they must choose something large with importance or bravery, a cowboy or a firefighter. There must be focus and determination, an arrow aiming toward the target. *What are you going to* be? You can't say you're going to *be* a good person, be interested in people, or be a waitress, even if you love to work as a waitress. *What do you want to be, Indigo Skye?* I can just see Mrs. Ford, guidance counselor for alphabet letters *S* through *Z*, asking me. *I want to be a waitress,* I would say, because that would be the truth, and Mr. Mulgoon, guidance counselor for alphabet letters *A* through *F*, would have to give Mrs. Ford CPR on the career center floor, right under the "CAN'T" IS A FOUR-LETTER WORD poster of the guy climbing a mountain.

"Be" means something you can write on a business card. "Be" is a one-word phrase, like "lawyer" or "engineer" or "accountant," a word big enough to make college debt worthwhile and to put a sports car in the driveway. A word like "teacher"—nah, even that won't do; even they're not business-card-worthy for some whacked reason. "Teacher" would get you the clucks of sympathy disguised as admiration that people give do-gooders, the way you get a cookie after you've given blood.

And I didn't have one of those big words to use—I couldn't quite summon the largeness. I didn't know what I wanted to Be. The not-knowing of that was giving me the restless pissed-offness that questions without answers give. A sense that I had permanently botched things already, embarked on the trip without the map. And maybe it scared me too, that I might end up as a mother of three working in a psychiatrist's office, or renting surfboards in a grass shack. I guess I saw their lives as failed somehow, absent of the Big Win, two of the millions of runners-up in the Living the Good Life sweepstakes. What if fate was an inherited trait? What if luck came through the genetic line, and the ability to "succeed" at your chosen "direction" was handed down, just like the family china? Maybe I was destined to be a weed too.

Funny's question rolled around in my mind, nagging. I mean, did I really want to be stuck here forever? *Here,* meaning

Deb Caletti

in this place, living this life, with these people? Go to school here, get a job here, rot in my old age here? *Here* was not a place where TV cameras rolled, where a lifestyle was unfurled for all to envy, same as an expensive oriental rug. *Here* was anywhere. And anywhere was not *some*where. I put the guitar back into its case. I can't even look at it anymore. Instead, I want to make brownies. I want an end result there's a recipe for. I want to combine eggs and water and oil and chocolate and flour and sugar and vanilla and get something fulfilling. Besides, I can lick the bowl and feel satisfied. Thank God or Buddha or my mother for my good metabolism. And thank Trevor for not minding my slightly wobbly ass.

After dinner I ask to borrow Mom's car to go over to Melanie's. I still have this feeling, a sense of swirling water going down the bathtub drain. Mom was having a premenopausal episode at dinner—she was silent and snappish and stressed, and the vegetables turned out like someone left them on the porch during a heavy rain, and you could have strapped the beef onto the bottom of your feet and made your way across the desert. She'd devoured the pie before dinner too, another bad sign. The fork with crumbs still attached was in the sink along with a glass whitewashed from milk.

I hunt around for something slightly outrageous to wear to Melanie's, because she expects it and because it gives her parents a nervous should-we-be-worried thrill too. When landscape lighting is a priority in your life, you need a good parenting crisis to stir up some excitement. I go for a black lace tank top and my bike chain necklace. On my way out, I see Bex sitting on her floor and at first I can't believe my eyes and have to look again. She has this thick layer of coins spread out around her, some U.S. Treasury flying carpet.

"Holy shit, Bex, did you rob a bank?" I say.

"Watch your mouth, Indigo," she says. "You're supposed to be a role model." She doesn't look up. I can see only the straight line of her hair part on her head, the top of her rounded cheeks.

"Seriously, where did you get this?" I see her life flash before my eyes. Mom's premenopausal episode turning to full-fledged menopausal meltdown. I see Bex grounded until she's thirty, getting a better education than me, probably, from CNN and public television.

Bex holds up an empty coffee can, shakes it. Oops, not quite empty, a coin rattles inside, and she dumps it to the floor. The coffee can has a piece of construction paper taped around it, from the same stack of orange we got for my world studies project on Malaysia—I recognize the shade. She'd used a big fat marker to write on the side. PLEASE HELP is printed carefully in huge letters. I'm sure she's just scammed the neighbors into giving her money for an Xbox that she's wanted for years, and I consider going to Severin's room to ask for some assistance in saving Bex's life before we share this with our mother. I hear his voice coming through the wall, his talking-to-a-girl voice, which is lighter and more laughy and animated than it ever is talking to us. He won't be any help. But then I see the smaller writing on the coffee can. TSUNAMI VICTIMS. She's even spelled it right, and Bex is a lousy speller. That's what twenty-four-hour coverage'll get you.

"What, exactly, have you been doing today?"

"I rode my bike to Albertsons. They let me borrow a card table, and I sat there and collected donations."

"Wow, Bex. Wow." I can't think of what to say. I have a few

fleeting worries about her just getting money from people. Like, is it that easy? Did you need some kind of permission for that sort of thing? But I refrain from interrogating her. She looks so serious.

"Now, would you shut up?" she says. "I'm trying to count."

Mom had the kind of car that should have been embarrassed going into Melanie's neighborhood. The Datsun was that shade of yellow they don't make anymore, some color that went out of fashion and that's bound to be back twenty years from now when the car's a thin layer of metal in a garbage heap. Her windshield had acne, pockmarks from when she drove behind a dump truck and got flecked with pebbles. It had a tape deck, back from when tape decks were a big deal, and it didn't have cup holders, from the days when people went places without a perpetual liquid pacifier. It had been through a whole forest of those Christmas tree air fresheners, since Freud peed in the backseat about a thousand years ago when he was ticked off about something, who remembers what. It still smelled slightly tangy in there, but you had to know what you were smelling for.

Anyway, it's a Car o' Shame as it curves up the hillside to Skyview, where Melanie lives. I picture all the other cars of the neighborhood peeking out from their garages and getting nervous and thinking because it's yellow and is an old Datsun, it's there to commit a crime.

I pass the faux mansions with their trimmed hedges and pots of snowman-like topiary that seem to be a requirement for residence here. The yards are the gardens of Mom's crunchy-geraniumed dreams—flowers, watered. Lawns, mowed. These are the kinds of houses where the furnace filters are changed on schedule, the gutters are clean. Garages are not made into bedrooms, but are nearly empty, sometimes carpeted; tidy caverns that hold cars with rain-sensor windshields and don't-you-dare-eat-in-here leather. These are houses where whole rooms exist just for display. It's the land of living rooms no one lives in.

I push Melanie's doorbell, which rings in chimes. I listen to the mini-concert that sounds large and hollow, like church bells. It makes me want to do it again, so I do. Melanie comes running to the door. I can't see her through the leaded glass windows, but I hear the *thwap, thwap* of her feet.

"For God's sake, Indigo, quit ringing the doorbell. My dad's trying to watch the game." Allen was always trying to watch *the game*, no matter what time of the day and no matter what season. I always wondered about "the game." Was there one game? Did everyone know what "the game" was? Who knows what he was really doing. He was probably buying skin cream off the Home Shopping Network.

"If I park on the street, will one of your neighbors call the police?" I ask.

"Go to hell," she says. Typical Melanie greeting.

You wouldn't match Melanie and me up, and if we hadn't gotten stuck together as lab partners in junior high science, I doubt if we'd have matched us up either. I'm not sure why we even stuck, except that we each probably find the other to be entertaining and low maintenance the way someone very different from you can be. When one person is fast food and the other is a gourmet meal, there's no use trying to be something you're not. Might as well relax and be who you are, and this is possible as long as each really doesn't want what the other has. We didn't compete with each other, is what I'm saying, I guess, and that makes friendship easy, clear of all those weird psychodynamics that can

Deb Caletti

sometimes happen. Besides, I felt like it was a personal mission of mine to broaden Melanie's world, though I think she felt the same of me.

I have to take off my sandals at the door. There's a whole row of shoes by Melanie's door, all different styles, though she's an only child. Her mom and I must wear about the same size (Melanie has huge feet), because there are my-size leather slip-ons and a pair of white boots that remind me of Trina, and a set of heels and jogging shoes. Mini–shoe store minus the boxes and the creepy foot fetish sales guy. I put my sandals with the others, so they can play too.

We pass the kitchen (Jenn-Air appliances, espresso machine, glassed-in closet wine "cellar"), head upstairs. The library door is open, and Melanie's mom sits at the desk. All the spines of the books look the same, so I guess the books aren't for reading. Melanie's mom is at the computer, and she turns when she hears us.

"Hi, Lisa," I say. I can see her cringe, as if someone has just cranked her backbone tighter. Melanie's supposed to call everyone Mrs. This and Mr. That. I'm usually a very polite person, and I work with the public, but there's something about Melanie's parents that makes me want to act out, which is also part of why Melanie keeps me around, I know. Vicarious rebellion. Lisa Gregory is the modern equivalent of the fifties mom, which means she drives a minivan and cares about window coverings and has enough candles in her house to burn down the West Coast. The semi-hysterical order in all this just makes me want to stir my little spoon of chaos.

"Hello, Indigo," Lisa says. She turns back to her computer, where she's buying stuff off of the Web. The Internet just extends store hours for some people. Twenty-four-hour mall, minus the Orange Julius, which is the best part of a mall, if you ask me.

"We'll be in my room," Melanie says.

"Have fun," Lisa says, but she says it like a warning. *Have fu-un*, which actually translates to *I'll be able to smell any alcohol on your breath*. Lisa was sure I drank and drugged because I played around with my hair color and didn't dress in a conventional fashion, and because my parents were *divorced*. Divorced is okay, of course, if your parents have rejoined the respectable adult community and have remarried. Single parents, though—they're sure to mean C averages and sex, booze, and drugs in an empty Mom's-at-work house. Or, more accurately, "single parent" means "poor," and "poor" means C averages and sex and drugs. "Poor" supposedly means kids who are out of control because they're not babysat every minute by Mom, who's working ten-hour days. Which is all pretty ridiculous, given that at my school, it's the kids who drive their own Land Rovers and are babysat by every entertainment device possible so Mom doesn't have to that are the biggest partiers and sex addicts. Go figure.

"Let's hit the liquor cabinet," I say, too loud. Melanie socks me. In her room, Melanie hooks up her iPod, which is thinner and smaller than a chocolate bar. I'm not really up on the latest toys, but Melanie *tip, tip, tips* on her computer, and in a second, music starts playing.

"I'd know that guitar anywhere," I say.

"The CD isn't even out yet," Melanie says. It's Hunter Eden. A new release. Melanie gets this stuff because her dad's vice president of the PR firm that handles a bunch of musicians. This gives him a measure of cool factor, even if he gets manicures and his skin looks too soft and he has hair only on the sides of his

Deb Caletti

head but is snow-plowed bald straight across the top. This also gives Melanie inherited cool factor, and concert tickets, too. She's taken me to a few, which isn't a bad friendship bonus. We got to sit in this little box, separated from other people, and a waiter even came. It made me feel like I was crashing some strangers' wedding reception and eating their food.

"Turn it up," I say, and we listen for a while. Hunter Eden's playing probably two hundred thirty beats per minute, but he isn't just fast, he's good. Add sexy into that, and you just wanted to lick his leather boots. Too quickly it's over, and the little chocolate bar moves on to a new song.

"Wow," I say.

"Thought you'd appreciate that," Melanie says. She takes her shiny blond hair out of her ponytail, puts it back just the way it was. "Wanna watch a movie or something?" Melanie spins her DVD rack around, runs her fingers across the titles. Her room is a technological amusement park—TV, DVD, computer, stereo, video games. Apparently, this way you could watch anything you wanted all by yourself in your own room, nudging yourself at the funny parts and telling yourself to be quiet because you couldn't hear when you were talking.

"It makes me sick. I'll never be that good," I say.

"You can be anything you want to be," Melanie says. She got those words fed to her in her bottle. All those Army-ish recruitment lines that talk you into some state of hyped optimism that no human being regularly feels without narcotic aid are deep within her, embedded at the cellular level. *Think positive! Never say "never"! The key to success is positive self-esteem!* In my opinion? It's fine to have a reasonable amount of self-doubt. Maybe it's even necessary to avoid being an obnoxious human being. Cavemen

The Fortunes of Indigo Skye

did not do affirmations. Pilgrims fighting disease and freezing temperatures did not focus on eliminating negative self-talk. The dusty and disheveled folks trudging on the Oregon Trail made it without one-year and five-year goals tacked to the insides of their covered wagons. I don't think they even *had* self-esteem in those days.

"Are you still going to be a marine biologist?" I ask Melanie.

"I guess," she says. "How about *I Know Your Secrets*?" She shows me the DVD case. Girl running in the dark, scary house in background.

"Whatever. Why do you want to be a marine biologist?"

"God, Indigo. You've asked me this a thousand times. I like fish."

"You don't like fish," I insist.

"Yes, I do." She pops out the movie, slips it into the player.

"You hate the water." Anyone who's ever gone to a pool with Melanie knows this. First, she stands at the side of the pool for-ever, with the dread of a sacrificial virgin who must leap into the volcano. When she finally gets in, she swims like those old ladies who don't want to get their hair wet. Little cupped prissy hands. Her chin in the air. It is the kind of thing that makes me like her. She tries so hard to be a part of things that you can't help but root for her.

"So?"

"You know, maybe I'm an idiot but 'marine' and 'water' kinda go together. You might as well say you want to be a mountain climber but you hate mountains. A skydiver but you hate sky. And fish. Take fish. You don't have any. Not an aquarium, not a single guppy, not a poster of fish or a fish bedspread or books about fish."

"No one has a fish bedspread, Indigo. Can we drop this,

Deb Caletti

please?" Melanie knows what I'm getting at, that's why she's annoyed. See, I've always told her she should think for herself, but that idea freaks out Skyview people. It's as if they fear they might lose what they already have if they don't walk the tightrope of acceptability, same as people knock on wood or walk around ladders. Follow convention or the big hand of fate will reach down and grab your Mercedes and your flat-screen TV. And convention tells you what to *be*, because certain professions ease and trickle and embed themselves viruslike into the kids at school at certain times. Three years ago, everyone was going to study psychology. Then they were all going to be pediatricians, and this year it's marine biology. So many of Melanie's friends want to be marine biologists that there is practically going to be a one-to-one ratio of fish to fish-studier.

"And I thought you only made the waiting list for UC Santa Barbara. You know I love you, but shouldn't you be looking at other options?" Let's just say that when it came to taking the SATs, poor Melanie hadn't been able to bring along all of her tutors.

"Did you come over just to give me crap about my future? My parents will work out something," she says. "Now shut up and let's watch the movie."

I do and we do. I sit patiently through all the scary-movie essentials: (1) Girl gets creepy caller on telephone when her parents are away. (2) Girl hears noise—oh my God!—but, alas, it's only the family cat. (3) Girl does some incredibly stupid thing, like hunting around the front yard for creepy caller. (4) Girl finds out creepy caller is actually in her own house. (5) Girl tries to get away but her car won't start, and no one has AAA in these movies. (6) Phone lines are down by storm, so girl can't call AAA even if she had it. (7) Girl stabs creepy caller with kitchen knife. (8) Creepy caller appears dead after girl makes him into sushi, but he's not dead after all. (9) Girl summons inhuman strength and reaches the knife before he does and then administers the death blow.

"I swear, I've seen that before," I say when it's over.

"I am never, and I mean never, going to stay at home alone," Melanie says.

I gather my shoes. They're still in a line with the others, so I guess they were playing nice. I get into Mom's car, with its oil change reminder sticker on the windshield, the date listed so far past that it's when I used to watch cartoons and wear stretch pants. I'm relieved to be back in the car again, but also there's this edgy sense of what might be disappointment. I think of what Melanie said—*My parents will work out something*—and I know she's right. It's what I most like and what pisses me off about being part of Melanie's world—that there are no questions here. That money makes everything decided and possible.

Here, weeds are not allowed.

4

"Mom. God, it's not raining anymore," I say.

"Oh! Right," she says, and flicks off her windshield wipers.

Mom drops me off at Carrera's on her way to work. I was able to work before school and not just on weekends because I had all my graduation credits and could have first and second period free. So Mom and I "carpooled" the few miles downtown to the café, and from there she went on to Dr. Kaninski's office in Seattle. Right then, Mom's trying to balance a coffee cup between her knees as she shifts, which is a recipe for disaster even with a cup sporting a lid with a little slit. "Indigo, I want to apologize for snapping the other day. I feel like the worst mother in the world."

"What are you talking about?"

"Last night. At dinner. I've been up all night, thinking how terrible I acted."

"Why?" I ask. "Mom, your coffee . . ." I can see it rising from the lip of the cup. Any moment it's going to splotch onto the skirt she has on for work.

"Why! Are you kidding?" She lifts the cup, sips, downshifts into second through the stoplight by the Front Street Market. "I said I'd had enough. I told you guys you were ungrateful. I know you're not ungrateful."

"You were right. We don't help unless you ask us."

"When I got up this morning, Bex was dusting the living room." Her voice wobbles.

"So?"

"So! I was hurtful. I threw that oven mitt."

"For Christ's sake, Mom, it was an oven mitt. It's got dancing vegetables on it. It's not like you threw the knives. You know, then we'd have an issue." I swear, Mom could feel bad for days about things we never even realized happened.

"When does she ever dust? She never dusts. *I* never dust. I've had that can of lemon Pledge practically since we moved in. The bottom is all rusty. I've just been so stressed lately. God." She looks like she might cry.

"You know my friend Liz?" I say. "Art class? The cool one that moved from Oregon? Her mother's going through menopause too. You should hear her talk about it—it's hilarious. Her mother tells her, 'We never spend time together anymore! Where are you? We're growing apart!' And then when Liz makes a point to be around the house, her mom says, 'What are you doing home? You need to get a job!' Liz says she comes downstairs and sees her mom standing in front of the open refrigerator, just staring."

"Indigo, jeez. Would you quit with the menopause thing? I'm too young for menopause. You can be over forty and just be a bitch." Her guilt is disappearing, deflating, as if it has been punctured. I like her better like this.

We reach Carrera's, and I haul my backpack up and open the car door. "Have a good day," Mom says. "I'll, you know, try to keep the hot flashes down to a minimum."

"No throwing oven mitts at work," I say.

Trina's car is parked at the curb, but something horrible catches my eye. Red-block-letters-on-black-plastic-rectangle horrible. A sign in the Thunderbird's window: FOR SALE.

I shove open the café door, clattering the bells so loudly that Jack leaps to his feet and gives a woof of alarm.

Deb Caletti

"Tell me I didn't see what I thought I saw," I say.

"In the Thunderbird," Joe says.

"You saw what you thought you saw," Jane says. "Easy on the bells, huh, Indigo?"

"We all saw," Nick Harrison says.

Trina rips the top off of two sugars and pours them into her coffee. She's wearing this white cape, with white leather pants. The emerald ring from Roger that she used to wear on her left hand is gone. "For Christ's sake, you people are more attached to that car than I am."

"I'm sorry, but you cannot, I mean *cannot*, sell that car," I say.

"If it's a matter of money," Joe says, "we can help you. Not that I have any myself, but we could all pull together—"

"Hey, I'll have a bake sale," I say. "Anything—"

"It is *not* a matter of money," Trina says. I didn't think it was. Trina exhales the scent of cash. "I just want to rid myself of any reminder of Roger."

"That was two weeks ago, already," I say.

"God, Indigo, two weeks is *nothing*," Trina says.

"I'm still not over Victoria," Jane says. "That was six months ago."

"She was too controlling anyway," Funny Coyote says. "You could tell by the way she bossed you around."

"Yeah, you know, Jack never liked her. That should have told me all I needed to know right there. . . . A bad sign," Jane says, and sighs.

"I'll never be over my wife . . . ," Nick says. "Well." He clears his throat.

We are quiet for a moment, except for Luigi. "Way down among the Brazilians, coffee beans grown by the billions . . ." he sings softly. Finally Trina says, "I'm getting rid of everything that makes me think *Roger*. The car, the leopard throw rug, my diaphragm—"

"Thank you oh so much for the diaphragm status," I say. I bring Nick his orange juice and Funny her eggs and pancakes and bacon. Extra napkins, like she likes. Leroy must be sleeping late again.

"I changed the message on my answering machine. Not that I'm under any illusion that he's going to call or anything. But if he comes running back . . . I had my neighbor record it for me. He says, 'You've reached Pizza Hut. Today order a large special and get an order of cheesy bread sticks free.'"

"Roger was controlling too," Funny says.

"No, he wasn't! You never even met him!" Trina says.

"You said he told you what to wear," Funny says. "High heels. That's control."

"If Trevor ever told me to wear heels, I'd pull those little hairs on his arm," I say.

"Men should leave fashion to the ladies," Joe says.

"I didn't mind the heels," Trina says. "Roger had a great eye."

"Yeah, which he's using on chicks in thong bikinis in Rio," I remind. I can tell she needs some emotional rescue ASAP. She is in that post-breakup phase of wild swings—where the ex goes from being the saintly love of your life to the darkest wedge of evil within twenty seconds.

Trina nibbles the bit of piecrust on her fork. I can practically see her mind ditch Roger's halo and remember all the times he checked out other women when he thought she didn't notice. "I guess it's a bad sign if you like everything about someone except their personality," she says.

Deb Caletti

The bells on the door jangle and I shoot my eyes over in a flash, because it's about Vespa guy time. He'd been coming in every day, and we still hadn't gone beyond the smiles and thank-you's and the occasional *Have a nice days, Okay, you too*s. But it's not Vespa guy, it's a man and a woman who must work at the salmon hatchery, judging by their T-shirts. I'm guessing not too many people wear matching salmon life-cycle shirts for amuse-ment or glamour. I slide them a pair of plastic-covered menus, get another for the man who runs the used bookstore who comes in every now and then. It starts getting busy. Two ladies in business suits and with briefcases sit down and we're rockin' and rollin', and I'm taking the hatchery people's orders—one fruit plate, one French toast—and trying not to stare at the salmon spawning over the little pile of eggs right on the guy's left pec.

I start getting worried about the Vespa guy, but right about the time I give the bookstore man his Farm Scramble (eggs with ham and onions—I've tried to tell Jane the name of it sucks), Nick Harrison gestures my way and nods his chin out the window. Vespa, stage right. Maybe it's pathetic, but none of us has lost our fascination with him. Trina sits up straighter, though she's given up trying to get his attention. The fact that he hasn't responded to Trina the way everyone responds to Trina only adds to his mys-tery. He couldn't be moved by flesh packed into spandex, which tells you a lot about a person. Our theories so far: he is depressed, shy, a lonely newcomer, sexually confused, divorcing, evading the law, in over his head with cocaine addiction. But no one has got-ten up the nerve to just get to know him and find out. As his wait-ress, I'd had the most natural opportunity, but I just couldn't seem to get myself to do it. There was just something unap-proachable about him. He was a store you wouldn't go into, or if you did go, he was the things you didn't dare touch hanging on the rack, the glass case you wouldn't even lean against.

He sits at Nero Belgio, as usual. Caramel-colored corduroy pants and a buttery yellow shirt and a creamy suede jacket. It's not the thin, fuzz-gathering type of corduroy either, but the lush, velvety sort. We do our routine. He smiles, I smile. I hand him a menu and he says, "Just coffee, please."

"Are you sure I can't talk you into anything else? French toast? Farm Scramble?" It's the most I've ever said to him, and I'm pissed at myself that it's Farm Scramble that comes to mind. It's slightly embarrassing to say Farm Scramble to someone so well dressed.

"No, no thank you," he says.

I bring the man his coffee cup, pour in a steaming stream. He smiles his gratitude. *Tink-tinks* his spoon against the sides of the cup, stirring. He stares out the window. It's practically infuriating how little we know about him. I can feel this little burble of frustration percolating, a feeling I have to ditch because the French toast is up.

I clear Joe's plate, bring the bookstore guy a bottle of ketchup for his eggs, which is just disgusting in my opinion—an egg crime scene—but never mind. Nick asks for a second orange juice. The Vespa guy takes off his jacket and hangs it over the chair next to him, and he's right, it *is* hot in here. I have an eye on everyone and I'm pleased with myself, because it's the point in waitressing that I love—it's all going. I'm handling everything like a conductor handles an orchestra, or maybe more like a kindergarten teacher handles a room of demanding, messy five-year-olds. They're all right there in my hands and everyone's happy and has just been fed their snack. Things are running as smooth as can be. I'm God's gift to waitressing.

Deb Caletti

The Vespa guy sets his cup down, nearly empty, and I'm heading over and I'm smiling and everything's cool, the pot of coffee is in one hand, when I see something that just flips my mood. It's that fast, fast as Luigi's wrist-flick of a bubbly pancake from dough side to brown side. It's that coat hanging over the chair that gets me. This beautiful creamy suede coat with a satin lining, slits for pockets. It's what's sticking up from one slit that starts this curl of anger. A square cellophane-wrapped pack.

Cigarettes.

You see people smoking all over—kids at school, guys standing around outside the Darigold plant, women in cars with one arm out the window. I am always revolted and marginally pissed, annoyed with that low-slung irritation you feel around stupidity. But this time, I am one notch over into really mad. The Vespa guy, he's perfect. He's supposed to be perfect. And now look how he's letting us all down.

I pour his coffee, my lips pursed with disapproval. I am doing a Mom, where I'm trying to communicate with the vast vocabulary of my silence everything he's done wrong. But he's not listening, because when I tip my pot back up, he gives me only that smile, which is suspect now. I'm thinking it is perhaps insincere.

I just stand there wanting to speak, doing this yes-no, yes-no, yes-no thing in my head, and then, before I even realize the debate is over, I'm at yes and I'm talking to him.

"I wouldn't be saying this if I didn't care about your health and well-being," I say, and suddenly I'm channeling the spirit of my mother, and she's not even dead. "But do you know there are over four thousand toxic chemicals in cigarettes?" I gesture with my chin toward his jacket pocket. "Carbon monoxide, for starters.

Cyanide, formaldehyde, ammonia . . ." I count them off on my fingers. "Should I go on?"

Well, I guess I might as well have just hooked Vespa guy up to numerous electrodes and shocked him with twelve thousand volts of electricity for the way he just stares at me, blinking.

"If you care about your health and the health of others," I say.

"Well," he says. "Well."

"It's only because I'm worried about you," I remind.

"Thank you for your concern," he says. "Your concern . . . ," he repeats.

And then, oh God, something awful happens. There's this pause, and then his eyes—they get glassy, wet. He blinks. My God, I think he might be about to cry. He blinks some more. Shit. Shit! I've made the Vespa guy *cry*.

He clears his throat.

"Are you all right?" I ask.

"Yes. Yeah. It's just . . ." He coughs.

Oh, man. *Shit, Indigo,* I think. *Now you've gone and done it.* I made him feel terrible. I couldn't keep my goddamn big mouth shut. "I'm sorry," I say. "I shouldn't have . . ."

"Sorry? Don't be *sorry*. Lately . . . I don't know." He gives a laugh that isn't a laugh.

"What?"

"I don't know why I'm telling you this."

"It's okay," I say. "This is waitress-client privilege. Purely confidential." Except for all the Irregulars listening in, of course.

"I go to work and everyone's 'Yes, Mr. Howards. Of course, Mr. Howards. Can I get you anything, Mr. Howards?' And no one means a goddamn word they say. It's unreal." He runs his fingers through his hair.

Deb Caletti

"Maybe it's time for a job change," I say.

"I haven't heard a sincere expression of concern in five, six years."

"A lifestyle change, then," I say.

I'm taking too much time here, I know. The ladies have put their credit card in the plastic folder and are shifting around in their seats. The bookstore guy has pushed his plate away and I can feel his eyes tugging on me to notice. In terms of my kindergarten class, I've got one kid who's knocked over the finger paint and another who's jumping up and down with his hands in his pockets, needing to use the bathroom. It's starting to fall apart, but I don't care. This is Vespa guy we're talking about, and he needs me.

"I don't know. My situation's . . . complicated," he says. "But man, sometimes I want to just . . ." He shoves his hands away from himself as if pushing something heavy. His voice is soft.

"Whoa. You're not talking drastic measures here—"

"No, God. Suicide? No, never. *Never.* I mean, like quit my job. Give it all up. Become a basket weaver."

"Why not? My father did that. Well, he's not a basket weaver. But he up and quit one day, ditched all the high pressure and moved to Maui and now he rents surfboards."

"Wow. Sounds great."

"He loves it, I think. He's got this small house by the beach. Surfboards, and what are the things with the sails that you stand on? My mind just went blank."

"Windsurfers?"

"Yeah. Windsurfers. I went there once. It was beautiful."

"I'd love that. Maui."

"I don't even think he wears shoes anymore. Of course, you have very nice shoes," I say.

"I have very nice everything. It's exhausting."

"Look, I gotta take these people's money," I say.

"Sure, sure," he says.

I grab the ladies' credit card and give it to Jane to run. She's already cleared the bookstore guy's plate, and I give him his check and sit a Darigold worker and make change for the salmon hatchery folks. Nick's trying like crazy to catch my eye, and so is Trina and Funny, and Jane keeps nudging me every chance she gets and Joe even whispers *Well?* even though it is hardly a whisper. I ignore all of them, and it takes some doing.

The Vespa guy holds up his hand in a *Stop* motion to indicate no more coffee. When I bring him his check, he says, "Thank you, you know. Really. I have faith again that everyone doesn't give just to get."

And he seems to mean it. One little gesture, you know? The *Oh, shit* from earlier is gone, and I fill up with a fellow-man-humankind gladness. I have this sense of satisfaction. A beach-ball-just-blown-up feeling, or a full tank of gas feeling. "Hey, just promise you'll ditch the smokes," I say.

"Promise," he says.

The Vespa guy leaves the plastic padded folder on the table. On his way out, he stops me, holds out his hand. "Richard Howards," he says.

"Indigo Skye," I say.

"*S-k-y?*" he asks.

"With an *E*," I answer.

"A pleasure, Indigo Skye. And thank you again." We shake. When he leaves, I see there is something else on the table too, left in the saucer of his coffee cup. It's the package of cigarettes. It's a brand I've never seen before, a white package with a red square

Deb Caletti

in the middle, *Dunhill Special Reserve*. I hear the Vespa start up outside. I watch him ride off, and he's butterscotch, melting into the distance.

"Well?" Trina practically shrieks.

"I couldn't hear hardly anything from over here," Nick says.

"Something about quitting his job," Funny says. "Becoming a basketball player."

"Basket weaver," I say. But I feel suddenly proprietary about our talk; decide to give them crumbs and crust, not the squishy center of the bread. "He's unhappy with his work."

"He said his life was complicated," Nick Harrison says.

"I thought you said you couldn't hear," I say.

"He said he could *hardly* hear anything, is what he said." It's the bookstore guy, interjecting. We ignore him.

"A smoker?" Jane waves the package in the air, gives it a shake.

"He's quitting," I say. I hear the defensiveness in my own voice. You feel responsible to someone when they've given you something private.

"Tell me you didn't give him shit about it, Indigo. I can't afford to lose any customers."

"She's merely doing her civic duty as she sees fit," Joe says in his old, gruff voice. "Those are cancer sticks."

"Unhappy with his work. Why is he unhappy?" Trina presses, but I am saved from revealing more, because just then Leroy comes in.

He is holding up one arm, the right one, with the dragon, breathing flames that lick up the back of his hand. In that hand is the red and black sign from the window of the Thunderbird. "Trina, God. Someone put a 'For Sale' sign in your car," he says.

It's May, and on my way to school after work that day, Nine Mile Falls is all warm-weather promise. It's that perfection that comes just before something; summer, in this case. You see all that it can be before it becomes what it is. No lawns are brown yet, no one is cranky from too-high heat, there are no splinters or sunburns or bee stings. The air is just all jazzed up from school almost out, and the usual signs that the prisoners are about to be released for summer break are appearing—the telephone lines in front of the school are strung with old tennis shoes that had been flung there and are now hanging by their tied-together laces; the kids walking back home wear short sleeves and sandals and floppier, less-homework backpacks, and the ones in cars are almost required by law to shout things out windows. Prom invitations and graduation class years are written on windshields with soap. The slams of locker doors sound triumphant rather than doomed.

I was part of it all and not part of it, as always. Part of it because there were kids I liked, such as Melanie and Liz and Ali and Evan (who we call King Tut because he once wore this metallic-gold shirt), and teachers I liked—Jane Aston (art class, who never marked me late for class, even if I got there ten minutes past bell because of work), Mr. Fetterling (American Government). Not part of it because I couldn't care less about prom and rah-rah shit like that, and because there were these rituals and rules I just didn't *get*, things I was supposed to be interested in that I wasn't, like who was going out with who and like those magazines with makeup tips and who-gives-a-shit articles. "What does your favorite nut say about you? Take our quiz! If you like almonds, you're the romantic type . . ." Yeah. When you want what's *real*

Deb Caletti

and you try to find that in high school, you might as well be look-ing for a mossy rock beside a babbling brook on the corner of Sixth and Pine in downtown Seattle.

I didn't get things and people didn't get me, ever since the ninth grade. I went to this concert, and the chick at the door stamped my hand with what was supposed to be a sun. She'd probably just OD'd on coffee—her shaky hand gave me a crappy ink mark with only five solar rays in the exact shape of a marijuana leaf. I was Lady Macbeth trying to scrub that thing off. But the dyes they'd used sunk so deep they'll probably give us all cancer in thirty years. Anyway, ever since then, people decided that my unique clothing choices plus the design on my hand equaled STONER, and the closest I'd ever gotten to dried herbs was my mother's oregano. I'm sure no one would even remember that mark specifically, but it never went away in people's minds, which just goes to show how badly we have the need to sort people into groups and keep them there. It's some twisted, limited, grocery-store mentality, where people have to be dairy products or vegetables or frozen foods for us to be able to understand them and feel safe. Maybe we've just become such mega-consumers that we can't deal with anything that's slightly inconvenient (basically, any-thing that requires thought). I was the tofu amidst the Baking Products and Cleaning Supplies.

Anyway, that day I'm having what I consider to be a regular school day. My schedule is pretty light; the only truly sucky part of the semester is that I have to take PE as a senior, because I couldn't stand the idea of taking it as a freshman, or as a sopho-more, or as a junior. I'd backed myself against the take-it-or-don't-graduate wall, and now I was in there with a bunch of freshmen and Mr. Talbot, who was only a few years older than us and hadn't gotten the news flash yet that he was still the dumb jock he was back in high school. He occasionally tried to be a real teacher and gave us tests on basketball that you could take with your eyes closed. *Bouncing a ball in basketball is called (A) Dribbling. (B) Bribbling. (C) Passing.* He'd write something on the chalkboard, step back and squint at it, because the word "didn't look right," that favorite old cover of people who can't spell.

That day, we spend the period sitting on the gym floor in our PE clothes, as Mr. Talbot tries to figure out how he's going to get five volleyball teams to play on four courts in a rotation lasting two weeks. It's a bit like watching a chimp try to macramé, and beats actually getting sweaty and stinking for two periods afterward. At lunch, I think about sitting with Melanie, but she's hanging out on the front lawn with Heather Green and Amelia Swensen, and Amelia's boyfriend, Jay. Not only are they likely to give me crap about my clothes or something equally as important (they will use the word "interesting" to describe what I'm wearing, and we all know that to most people, "interesting" is not a compliment), but I don't especially want to watch Jay with his hands practically up Amy's shirt right there on the front lawn. So I decide to go with Ali and Liz, who are walking to Starbucks. I hate to spend my hard-earned money on expensive coffee when I get it free at Carrera's, but it's either that or go back and join the audience of Feel-Up Fest, and darn, I forgot my ticket.

I finish up with American Government and the Gettysburg Address, which is 2265 Alder Street, in case you want to send a postcard, ha-ha. I walk home and I pass QFC, where Bex is already there with her table and new, large sign that says PLEASE HELP THE HOMELESS and, in smaller letters, TSUNAMI VICTIMS. Underneath, she's drawn an unhappy face, two dots for eyes and

Deb Caletti

a half-circle mouth pulled down. Her bike rests against a display of bags of bark and potting soil that's out front. I put a couple of bucks into her can and ask her if Mom knows where she is, and she says yeah, and that Mom thinks it's better than her hanging out with that Lindsey, who's always getting her into trouble. This is just one of those annoying and unjust differences between you and your younger sibling, because the only place I could ever ride my bike alone was the end of the driveway. I was probably fifteen before I could go to a friend's without giving Mom an FBI dossier on the people; Bex can practically hitchhike on the freeway with a mere "Have fun, honey."

At home, Severin is there, which is pretty unusual. He's in the front yard, and he's mowing. I'm thinking Mom should get mad more often, because the chores are really starting to get done around here. The lawn mower is roaring, and I can't hear a word Severin's saying but I see his mouth moving, and I scream "Whaat?" and he tries to scream back, and we do that routine once or twice before he lets the engine cut out and it's suddenly quiet.

"Jane called," he says. "She wants you to call back as soon as you can."

"Okay," I say.

"She said it was really important."

Which probably meant she wanted me to work late tomorrow, which would mess up Trevor's and my plan to hang out at Pine Lake and swim. "What are you doing home? Did they finally come to their senses and fire you?"

"Nah. MuchMoore is having sales conferences for a few days, so they let us off early." He raises his arm, wipes the sweat from his forehead. There are big rings of sweat under his arms.

"What's with guys and sweat, for God's sake? You're, like, leaking."

"Get me a glass of water, would you?"

"What, my T-shirt says 'Personal Slave'? Forget it. You gonna give me a tip?" But I actually do go inside, and I get a glass of water and even get the tray of ice and give it a twist, chase some ice cubes around the countertop to put into his glass. He's my brother, my twin, and even though we don't do the twin-bond-till-death routine, we've been around for the same length of time so we're there for each other. From the kitchen window I can see him yank the lawn mower to life again by its string. He's wearing this grin. It's this inner-pleased that seems to be about something more than the happy that comes from the smell of cut grass.

I slam out the screen door. "Let this be the end of your macho bullshit," I say, and hand him the glass. He cuts the engine again.

"Thanks." He drinks. His Adam's apple shoots from penthouse to lobby and back again.

"What are you so happy about?" I ask.

"What? Nothing."

"Yeah. Right. I saw you smiling from the kitchen. God, see? Look, you can't help yourself."

"Quit it." He wipes his mouth with the back of his hand.

"You are. Aha, you're smiling. Look at you smiling," I sing.

"Shit," he says, and tries not to grin. "Why do you always do that?"

"Why are boys so secretive?"

"It's nothing. Get your hands off your hips. You look like Mom." He drinks more water, peeks at me over the glass. "Oh, all right. Okay, are you pleased with yourself? I asked Kayleigh Moore to our prom."

My sweaty brother is standing before me, hopeful on a hopeful day. The sun is out—birds are twittering. Okay, birds aren't actually twittering, but there's a crow on a branch of a nearby evergreen, cawing at Freud, who sits calmly on our porch step, staring with sly killer eyes. That hope, it's worrisome. It's Snow White type hope, where she's tra-la-la-ing in the forest and not realizing that (1) her stepmother is plotting her death by fruit, and (2) seven short guys who want to live with you is just sick.

"You what?" I say. "*Kayleigh Moore*–Kayleigh Moore? Or a different Kayleigh Moore?"

"No, that one. What's the problem, Indigo? Jeez. You're acting like I asked out the president's daughter."

"Well, you did, you idiot. Of your *company*."

"That's not what I meant. And you don't have to be concerned. She said yes."

Freud gets up, stretches, steps to the lawn and plops onto the grass. Closer to that evergreen tree. He's got one eye on that crow the whole time. His tail twitches.

"Oh, man."

"It's gonna be fun. It's gonna be great. Here." He hands me the water glass, but I put my hands up. Forget it, Bud.

"And she goes to what, Riverside?" The private school for gajillionaire kids. I once heard that they're required to each have their own laptop, and get lunch catered from local restaurants. "It's not like you're going to be able to give her a carnation and drive her in Mom's car. What do you see in a girl like that?" I saw her once, when I picked up Severin from work. The lasting image was her T-shirt, which read: THIS IS WHAT A PERFECT 10 LOOKS LIKE. That, and her smile. Row of teeth in a perfect line, like the white deck chairs on a cruise ship.

"She's not 'a girl like that.' First off, she's gorgeous."

"Not that you're shallow or anything." I decide I want that glass after all. I take it from him, have a long swallow of what is left of the water. It is getting hot out here. Maybe from the sudden desert drought of *real*.

"She's more down-to-earth than you think."

I almost choke on the ice cube rolling around in my cheek. A spiky, ugly feeling is starting in my chest. Some kind of green, creeping sense of them-us, of protection. This cold sense of a power game one is sure to lose. Is it jealousy I feel? I'm not sure, but if it is, I'm fucking mad at myself for feeling it for someone I already have little respect for. *Here's what a perfect ten looks like.* Maybe I want what she has without wanting to be what she is.

I watch smug Freud and the nervous crow. I hate crows, I detest crows. They are sleek and crafty and mean. They are the sinister type of sixth-grade boy who makes fun of the quiet kid, and who knows what all the dirty words mean. Crows leer. But right now, it is Freud who I want to put in his place.

"Remember when Bex was, like, four, and she cut off Freud's whiskers?" I say to Severin.

"Oh, man, that was sad," Severin says, and laughs. "She thought she would make them 'even.'"

"He kept bumping into walls," I say.

I can't explain this. But I am hoping Freud is listening.

Severin starts the lawn mower again, and I go inside to call Jane. She's not at Carrera's, so I try her cell phone number. When I reach her, her voice is almost breathless.

"Indigo! You won't believe what happened after you left!"

"Trina sold her car."

Deb Caletti

"No! It has nothing to do with Trina. It has something to do with you . . ."

"Me?"

"Yeah. You."

"Uh-oh. The guy from *America's Most Wanted* came in. They finally found me. Oh, no, wait. A Hollywood agent saw my yearbook picture. Ha! And I thought it sucked." I am just cackling away at myself when I finally realize there's that endless, cave-deep silence that means Jane's cell phone cut out. It's always so suddenly lonely when that happens.

I call her back, but her line's busy, because she's calling *me* back, and we do that annoying call me–call you dance that someone should have figured out a social rule for long ago.

"Sorry, I was going through a tunnel," she says. I can tell she's in her car. The sound is all whooshing air, some distant between-channel static. I've got to strain to hear as her voice jumps through the hoops of satellites and sonar waves and tin cans with string to get to me.

"You missed all my great jokes."

But she's too excited to bother with my award-winning humor. "The Vespa guy," she breathes. "Goddamned asshole!" she growls. For a moment I'm confused—the Vespa guy is pretty nice, actually. Then I realize I'm being treated to something that would have been inconceivable in the pre–cell phone days: the play-by-play *You Are There!* of someone's driving experience. This is a different episode from the *You Are There!* of someone's grocery store experience, and usually more exciting. *(I'm passing the yogurt. Do we need yogurt? What about eggs?)* "Jerk just cut me off," Jane says.

"The Vespa guy," I remind.

"Yeah, well, he came in. Back in. After he left. After you left. He brought you something, Indigo. An envelope. Was he supposed to bring you something?"

"No." My heart has stopped—freeze-frame photo snap, held in midair.

"It's got your name on it. How'd he know your name? I told you never to give out your name."

"What kind of an envelope?" I ask.

"Yellow. Large. The kind of envelopes that only hold important stuff."

"You didn't peek?"

"Do you want me to?"

"Yeah! Wait. I mean, no. No! Absolutely not."

"It's sitting right here on the seat beside me. Would you get the lead out? God, this woman's driving like an old lady."

"No. Just keep it for me," I say.

"Oh shit, it really *is* an old lady. She can barely see out the windshield. Maybe she didn't hear me honk. I hope she didn't hear me honk. I'm a horrible person. Do you think I'm a horrible person? I'll give it to you tomorrow, okay? Hey, by the way, could you work late? Through lunch?"

"Sure."

"That's great. Nikki's got to take her kid to baseball, or something."

"I wonder what he could have given me."

"I have no idea. But, Indigo? This is going to be interesting."

5

The whole damn house reeks of Axe deodorant, that canned male concoction of musk and helmet-bashing testosterone and a few ozone-ravishing chemicals. I cough. We should all be wearing those white face masks Mom bought in bulk after she was briefly convinced terrorists were going to come to Nine Mile Falls for, maybe, a salmon hatchery tour, or to blow up that drive-through coffee stand that's made out of an old school portable.

"Severin, man, open a window!" I shout.

"It's not *me*." His voice comes from his room.

"It's Mom," Bex says. She's sitting on the living room floor, eating a Fudgsicle and counting her money. She's wearing shorts and a T-shirt with a skateboarder on it, and he's flying high in a wild arc.

Mom's quiet, though. Guilty-quiet. I follow the scent to her room, where her work clothes are tossed onto her bed. She's just changed into a pair of khaki shorts and a tank top. "I just wanted to freshen up," she says.

"Mom! You smell like a guy!"

"I like it," she says. "It smells good."

"For guys! I've told you before! Axe isn't for women. This is what half of my school stinks like. Your supposed to be smelling like baby powder. Or flowers. Vanilla is the farthest you get to go on the masculine spectrum."

"I don't want to smell like a baby." She's reaching up to pull her hair back, giving me a galloping, fresh whiff of maleness.

"Ah. A ponytail makes you feel so much more like things are in control," she says.

"Bad day at work?"

"Probably a full moon or something. You'll never guess what the drug reps brought." Since she works in a psychiatrist's office, Mom's always getting promotional items like notepads and pens and coffee mugs with brands of drugs printed on them. The names of the drugs are either so long you quit reading after the first syllable or two (benzodiazepine, thioridazine), or are soft and airy and nasal-congested (Buspar, Zoloft). I never figured out how having benzodiazepine on your coffee mug would get you to buy more of it, but okay.

Mom's got one hand in her purse that's on the bed, and she's shifting the ingredients around in there. She gives up the hunt, removes the larger stuff so she can see better. Wallet, Kleenex pack, hairbrush, a pocket calendar thing she's never used in her life, a container of Liqui-Stitch fabric glue.

"'Sewing in a Tube'?" I read.

"My hem was coming out," she says. Then, finally, "Here. Check it out."

A small plastic rectangle, with a razor blade along the bottom. "A box cutter?"

"A razor blade box cutter. From this company that makes antidepressants."

"That's just twisted."

"Tell me about it." She tosses all the stuff back into her purse, a great big new jumbly personal object party. "Trevor coming for dinner?"

"Nah. He wants to get some more sanding done on Bob before we get together later." Bob Weaver was getting a new paint

Deb Caletti

job, and Trevor was doing most of the work to save money. Bob looked like he had a skin disease—splotches of gray primer showing through the old orange-red metallic. Bob was a Mustang leper. "Are you going out?"

Mom sighs. "I just want to wrap in a quilt and watch TV. Zone out."

"So all the people out there you could be meeting will have to come knock at our front door, huh?"

She gives me a look, takes herself and her jock-smelling armpits to the kitchen. I know that's where she ends up because I can hear Chico.

"Chico good boy," he says. In terms of self-esteem, Chico's got it to spare, which is probably why he can be so obnoxious. I eat linguine with clam sauce with Mom and Bex and Severin, and Bex gives us the statistics of how many were killed in the tsunami, how many homeless, how many children unidentified and separated from families.

She rolls her pasta on her fork. "One hundred sixty-four dollars so far," she says.

"Honey, I think maybe we should see a counselor," Mom says.

"Hey, In. Do you want to make some money waitressing at a MuchMoore party tomorrow? They really need people." Severin says from over by the blender on the counter. For the last few months, Severin has been into protein shakes—these thick, brown slurpy drinks that smell like grass and the medicinal twinge of vitamins.

"Sure," I say.

"Trevor, too?"

"Trevor with hors d'oeuvres on a tray? That's hilarious, but if he gets paid, I'm sure he'd say to count him in."

"I think maybe talking out your feelings with a professional might be helpful," Mom says. She cuts her pasta, which she never does. A careful, overly thought-out action that reeks of concern bordering on panic.

"I don't need a *counselor*," Bex says. "I just need more hours in the day. I hate wasting time playing *dodge ball*."

"Sadistic game," I agree.

"I'm not sure if my insurance would cover it, but I could check," Mom says. "This obsession . . ."

"What about your Barbies, Bex?" Severin plops some ice into the glass canister too, fits on the lid.

"She hasn't been into Barbies for two years," Mom says.

"I haven't been into Barbies for two years," Bex says. "Do you think I care about Barbies now, anyway? Do you think Barbies *matter*?"

"Honey," Mom says. But she doesn't seem to know where to go from here. The word just hangs, until Severin starts the blender and there's only the sound of crunching and grinding vitamins, the silvery core of nourishment, containing every essential thing but the nourishment itself.

Trevor's got his fingers in my hair, and I love when he's got his fingers in my hair. We're lying on the grass by Pine Lake, because Pine Lake is our place. It's not a big lake like Lake Washington or Lake Sammamish, but a summer-camp type lake, with houses tucked around it—now, in the dark, cozy and glowing from the lights inside. We have our house that we like. It's not the biggest house, but has the lawn that rolls right to the water's edge. The couple that lives there has a dog, and we see him sometimes

Deb Caletti

paddling in the water or walking on the grass with a tennis ball in his mouth. The house has a dock with two chairs on it, sometimes an inflatable inner tube on a hot day. Someone is watching television upstairs—there's the shadow-light blink of nervous, dancing images. My head is lying in Trevor's lap, and he's combing my hair with his fingers and it's baby-sleepy-soothing. We've been here awhile already; we sat quiet, just watching twilight, taking in that sweet magic that happens when the light turns golden. *Why do you feel like your heart could break when the hills turn pink and the trees turn yellow?* Trevor asked. *Why do you feel every joy and sorrow and goodness and beauty and past and present and every perfect thing?* And I kissed him then, just because he was right.

The magic light passed, and dark crept in; heartbreak time changes to the hours when you tell deep and secret things. I tell Trevor about the envelope.

"So, what do you put in an envelope?" he says. Trevor's chin is tilted up. From where I lie, even in the moonlight, I can see the narrow white place of his neck that isn't tan like the rest. He's got a shirt on over his T-shirt because it's cool at the lake. It's white cotton with pearly white snaps like cowboys wear. They make me want to pop them open with my thumb and forefinger. *He* makes me want to pop them open.

"A letter," I say up into the night. "A thank-you letter."

"That's a card. A big envelope says . . ." He thinks. "Legal."

"Business merger. I see. Wants me as his partner for my cool head and brilliant mind."

"Or he's suing you," Trevor says.

"For giving him bad advice. Like those people who sue McDonald's because their hot coffee is hot coffee."

"Maybe he's giving you his Vespa."

"Ha," I say. "Wouldn't I love that."

"You could sell it," Trevor says. "What, five, six thousand? You'd be rich."

"We could run away to Mexico and buy some big sombreros and a velvet painting," I say.

"You'd promise me that you wouldn't change, even if you had all that money," he says.

"I'd promise you," I say, and he leans down and kisses me then and his mouth is cold, but then, it's not cold for long, and I like the feel of those snaps under my fingers.

The next morning Mom's in the kitchen in her bathrobe, her old blue terry cloth that looks slouchy and depressed. She doesn't, though. Maybe she's already had too much coffee, but she's rummaging through the junk drawer with the energy and focus of someone in those Army recruitment ads. "You're up early," I say.

"Couldn't sleep," she says. "Do you have any batteries?"

"On me?" I pat my pockets humorously (*I* think), but she just scowls. "Nope. None here."

"Wait," she says. "Aha." Victory—she holds up the thin cylinder of a double A. By the time I've got the milk carton out of the fridge, she's pulling a kitchen chair over to the counter and is climbing up. She shoves aside all of Severin's cans of liquid protein and mystery powders that are lined up there.

"Good God," I say, and I set down my cereal bowl and move to spot her. This is what you do as a daughter to Naomi Skye— you steady wobbly ladders as she puts up Christmas lights, you grip chairs when she screws in lightbulbs. You stand close to her jean-clad legs, or robe-clad ones, you hold on. It's not that she's ever actually had an accident, or fallen or broken anything, ever.

Deb Caletti

Just that Mom seems perpetually at the edge of the precarious-almost. "What are you doing?" I ask.

"I am just so sick of it being ten twenty, I cannot tell you," she says. She reaches up, plucks the kitchen clock off the wall. She flicks the battery out with her fingernail, puts the new one in, spins the hands, and sets the clock on the nail again. It's true that it's been ten twenty for a long time. Weeks, maybe even months. After a while, I guess, you just stop noticing.

The clock is ticking away with a newfound sense of purpose. Mom climbs down from the chair. "When you get that envelope today, just make sure Jane or someone's there when you open it. You don't know this guy. Maybe he's some kind of sicko."

"Sicko," Chico agrees.

"He's not a sicko," I say. I told Mom about the envelope last night at dinner, but I didn't think she even really heard. She was so wrapped up in Bex's tsunami obsession that she brushed it off with an *Oh really?* that was an *I didn't actually hear that* in disguise. I look for a clean spoon for my cereal, but no one's turned on the dishwasher, so there are only those spiky-tipped ones for eating grapefruit and Bex's short baby spoon with Ariel the mermaid on it. I go for Ariel.

"You don't know that," she says. "He might seem normal, but look at Ted Bundy."

"So, what, there's going to be a bloody knife in the envelope?"

"Don't even joke," she says.

"No, that white powder terrorists use. I'll give you a call before I go meet him alone in a dark alley," I say.

"Sicko, sicko," Chico says.

I decide to walk to work. First of all, Mom's get-it-done has been ignited—she's cleaned the junk drawer of old keys and dried-up pens and a manual for a VCR that died a choking death long ago after a video got stuck inside, and she's moved on to the pantry, stacking up nearly-empty-but-never-thrown-out cracker boxes, stale cereal we all hated, a plastic bear of honey that's crystallized, and a Fruit Roll-Up that survived World War II.

Asking her to take me now would be like asking a tornado to kindly stop for a sec. I can only hope she'll run out of energy in the kitchen, because I can see me coming home to a bedroom empty of everything except a stripped mattress.

Anyway, it's spring delicious out, and I don't mind walking. We had nearly two weeks of sun so far in May, which in the Seattle area means that any day now, Mother Nature will make you PAY. Better enjoy while you can. The air smells like juniper and roses and warm cement, and Mrs. Denholm next door has her sprinkler on already, one of those old-fashioned sorts that look like a miniature fountain and only cover a three by three area, and Buddy, the Yeslers' golden retriever, follows me only as far as the mailboxes, like a good child who stays in the yard like he's told.

Visions of envelopes are dancing in my head, or maybe not dancing, but walking really fast. I've thought so much about the envelope that the idea of it is close to being worn and tired, as if it had stayed up too late having more than its share of a good time. Caution is creeping in, not bloody-knife caution, but the guardians of disappointment. The excitement of not knowing has been so fulfilling that the knowing can't possibly compare.

Trina isn't at Carerra's yet, no Thunderbird at the curb. Jack the dog rises from his tired haunches and greets me with a nose to my palm as I go in.

I do a double take when I see Trina already at her booth. "Where's your . . . Oh, shit," I say.

"I don't want to hear a word. Not one word," Trina says.

"It's gone," I say.

"Good riddance," Trina says. But something's wrong with her face. Her cheeks seem bigger and her eyes smaller, and then I realize her face is puffy from crying.

I get this hollow-horrible feeling, that cavern of loss. Along with it comes an awareness—the kind that comes when you realize a situation is a few layers deeper than what it seemed. Getting rid of the Thunderbird is not a way to exorcise Roger. Trina needs the *money*. Suddenly that fact is a secret we're all keeping—Trina from us, us from Trina. I don't know what to do. "Pie," I say. I put my stuff down quick, put on my apron and wash my hands, and understand why people feed grief with macaroni casseroles.

Joe ambles, shakes his head sadly, and then Nick, too.

"Who bought it?" Nick says. "Tell me it at least went to a good home."

"Tell us you got a fair price," Joe says. He lifts himself up onto the counter stool, opens a menu and peruses, as if it's the first time he's seen it.

"My cousin," Trina says. "He's always . . ." She clears her throat, straightens the wobble in her voice. "Admired it."

The kitchen door swings open. Jane's got a new haircut, and it's short and swoopy-banged, youthful around her strong face. "Come on, people, it's a *car*." Her voice has the buoyancy of the well-intentioned lie. "Indigo! God. The envelope! Let me go get it."

She bustles to the back and Funny Coyote comes in, her backpack over one shoulder, and so does the same couple with the toddler from the weekend before. Just my luck, they liked the place. I fetch the high chair and the menus and then Jane is back.

"Cute new hair," I say.

She combs the ends with her fingers, the ones that are not holding the large yellow envelope. "You think?"

"Absolutely," I say.

She hands the envelope to me. "Well? Here it is. Do you think he'll be in today?"

"I don't know," I say. But I do know. Because as I hold that envelope and see my name on it, written in the lovely, polite loops of the Vespa guy's handwriting in black ink pen, I understand it holds something decisive.

"What are you waiting for?" Nick Harrison says.

I turn the envelope over, run my finger against the licked-down edge. And then: "No," I say. I don't want to open it like this, as if its contents are a party trick for the amusement of all involved. It's my name that's there, it's to me, and it's between me and Vespa guy. I feel like this requires special surroundings, the right time. Me alone, sitting at the edge of my bed, unhurried.

"You've got to be kidding me," Funny Coyote says. "You're not gonna open it? Somebody hand me a knife."

Trina hands Funny her butter knife over the back of the booth, and Funny brandishes it menacingly for a moment before setting it down on her napkin. I'm saved, though, because the people with the toddler catch my attention and ask for a banana for Junior, *To help keep him busy*, because Junior is scootching and squirreling way down in the high chair seat, so that his chin is nearly on the tray and his body is dangling beneath.

I fetch the banana and Junior is righted again with screaming protests and then a couple comes in and sits at Leroy's table, which is going to piss him off. Leroy comes in and glares at the

Deb Caletti

couple who will eye him nervously through the rest of their meal, though Leroy joins Joe at the counter and does something he never does: orders Joe's same full breakfast. Bill, the creep that works at True Value, comes in and sits with Nick when he's just been served his oatmeal, and the toddler is tossing pancakes to the floor and watching them drop, and Joe and Leroy begin to arm-wrestle and knock over a ketchup bottle.

Finally, Nick leaves; his bowl sports two leftover raisins looking at me like slightly crazed google-eyes, and I wipe the cold glue of banana off the floor and legs of the high chair. Someone comes in with the name of Ronald Reagan; he's young and tall and has dreadlocked ringlets, and tries to disguise his name by signing his credit card slip "Ronny." I add his name to the list of "famous" customers that we keep behind the counter. You wouldn't believe how many regular people are saddled with the names of the rich and famous—we've had James Bond and Daniel Boone and Jenny Craig and Martha Stewart and even a guy named Tom Cruise, who, if I remember right, was about eighty years old. I'm working late, late enough to see Trina leave next, and she walks down the street with the saddest pair of knee-high boots you've ever seen, scissor flicks of despondent white disappearing around the corner. After Trina, Joe and Leroy leave together and Funny takes out her tablet and starts to write. No Vespa guy, I am right, and I work the lunch crowd of corned beef and turkey and mounds of potato salad and pickle spears until it's time to go. I do a last favor for Jane and take Jack out for a pee, and it makes him so happy and satisfied that it makes me happy and satisfied.

Jane seems to have forgotten all about the envelope, because she is fully submerged in new haircut love/insecurity. I've caught her peeking at her reflection in the glass of the dessert case with the intermittent smiles/scowls of acceptance/rejection we give our new selves. There are few things that can make as us vulnerable as new hair.

"God, Jane," I say. "You just look like a whole new person."

"Really?" she says. She scrunches her nose. Either it's self-doubt or her allergies are bothering her again.

"It's great," I say.

I pat Jack's black satin head and leave with my envelope in my hands. *Indigo Skye*, it still says. When I get home, I place it under my pillow, and smooth out the cotton of the pillowcase with my palm. If I open it now, what's coming will be instead what has come. This time, right now—it's the instrumental before the vocals, the love before love's been admitted, the Christmas eve before the Christmas. Some things need a delicious *before*, and this envelope is one of them.

We're almost late to the MuchMoore party because I worked the lunch shift and Severin says we need to be there by four and then he tells me I need to wear nylons, which makes me want to shoot him because I hate nylons, and then I have to go hunt through Mom's underwear drawer for a pair, and the only ones she has make my legs look Ace-bandage-y and granny pale. Nylons are in my top three worst feelings, along with tight jeans and clothes still wet from the dryer, so my legs are already cranky. Then Trevor comes, and Severin says he needs to wear a tie, and now Trevor's gaze is murderous because he hates ties, and required strangulation clothing was not part of this deal. Severin looks around for an extra tie, and plucks out this hideous clip-on that he has from when he was maybe ten, and it's not only too short, but it's got penguins on it. Already, I'm getting a bad feeling about all the *need to's* that apparently must

Deb Caletti

be met to be acceptable in the presence of the wealthy.

We pile into Trevor's Mustang; Bob Weaver looks hideously splotchy with the flat, steely gray of primer. A few days ago, the car developed a death rattle, which has now turned to some serious and hugely loud, thunderously pained cry for help. I clap my hands over my ears.

"The muffler," Trevor shouts in his too-short penguin tie.

"Oh, great," Severin says. He's already shifting around in pre-embarrassment and it's only us. He's all spiffed up himself, looking sharp in the shirt and tie he wore to homecoming last year, and his face is smooth from just being shaved.

"You don't have to ride with us, you know. You could walk," I say.

"I'm fine," he says, or rather, it's what his moving lips mouth, since you can't hear a word anyone's saying. It's the kind of fine that's obviously not fine.

We drive across town, and I imagine people ducking in fear at what they think is a descending jet; I picture dogs with sensitive hearing whimpering and hiding under beds. We cross over Lake Washington, and Trevor's driving only about thirty-five, because every time he accelerates, you can feel your kidneys rattle from the vibration. The Moores live on Meer Island, this dollop of land in an inlet of Lake Washington, which is full of waterfront houses set down at the end of secluded, gated drives.

Severin is shouting directions that he reads from a piece of paper. There's a right here and then a left and you can feel yourself curving closer to the water. Severin has been here before, but he's getting nervous and snappish and we make a wrong turn and have to turn around in someone's driveway, meaning Trevor's Mustang has just shattered all the crystal in their cabinets.

Severin's head is still bent over that piece of paper, but there's no need to look anymore, because it's suddenly obvious we're here. There's a spotlight, one of those huge, rotating, blinding columns of light outside a high pair of open iron gates, flanked by a couple of guys in black pants and vests. The guys are talking into walkie-talkies.

Trevor lets out a low whistle.

"Are they expecting the president, or something?" I ask.

"That's just Mike," Severin says. "He works with me in shipping. I don't know the other one. Roll down your window."

Mike steps over to the car. "This is a private party," Mike says. His vest has got some man's face on it, with HAPPY 55, CHIEF! printed underneath.

"Mike, it's me," Severin says from the back. "Severin?"

Mike peers inside with narrow eyes. "Oh, cool," he says. "The waitstaff is supposed to meet in the catering kitchen. Man, you realize you got something wrong with your muffler?"

"No, hey, thanks for letting me know," Trevor says. We roll up the window. "Maybe he should be a car mechanic," Trevor says. "He's obviously got some kind of intuition." He rolls his eyes at me, and I roll mine back at him. Mike is talking on his walkie-talkie, which seems pretty ridiculous, because he's talking to another kid with that same old guy on his vest, who's just standing on the other end of the driveway, and who's now gesturing wildly for us to stop.

"I'm supposed to park the car," the guy says. "Valet." We pile out, and Trevor hands the kid his key. "You better bring me back a Mercedes or something," Trevor says. "Little key mix-up, heh, heh, heh."

Trevor's swingy and relaxed, but I'm getting this dark, rolling feeling in my stomach, black clouds moving across gray sky—maybe not dread, but the self-protective distancing that dread brings.

The house itself is sprawled and layered, three that I can count, and there are wide steps that lead to the doorway, and each step is lit with toddler-size hurricane candles and decorated with vases of tall stalks of lilies. Musicians in black suits and long black skirts set up chairs and music stands on a balcony overlooking the entry, and they are all wearing the vest with Chief's face. The door has a big basket of umbrellas (in case of a sudden storm, I guess), and his image is on those, too. It's getting a little bad-dream creepy, this old guy's face everywhere. A little man with a bald head and one of those cowboy string ties runs around rabbit-like, talking into the sort of microphone head pieces that you see on movie directors or air traffic controllers. We descend the stairs and my ace-bandage nylons feel scratchy with shame. Trevor senses my nerves and takes my hand, but I let it go—displays of support seem weak and middle-class. In the entryway of the house itself, on the wide marble floor, are cutouts of Chief; his head is on various bodies—Elvis, Han Solo, Einstein (he's wearing a wild white wig and small glasses, carrying a book that's labeled *Theory of Relativity*). Chief is a bodybuilder, with perfect six-pack muscles. Chief is God, with a white robe and a halo of light behind his head. A photographer with a long lens is already snapping photos, and another black-vested man stands on a ladder and adjusts the lights that shine down on every Chief cutout.

I see a woman who can only be Mrs. Moore, wearing a stiff-skirted outfit with a jewelly sweater. "Anna! Anna!" she calls, and a barrel-shaped blond woman comes hurrying over with spot

cleaner and a cloth to dab at the hem of Mrs. Moore's sweater. We
follow Severin past a stairwell with a rope across it, past huge windows overlooking the lake, past more vases now even taller than
any of us. It's a stage show, I see, because there's the lighting
man, and the soundman, the costume woman, and the set director. The only problem is, not only have I forgotten my lines, but
the only play I've ever been to was *Death of a Salesman* with my
freshman class, and even though Chief's apparently being
memorialized, he's not dead yet, as he's there in the kitchen, eye-
ing the cake, which has this huge photo of him and his wife on it,
on the deck of some ship. Nope, this is not another cardboard
cutout of Chief, it's the real, living, breathing him, because his
finger is moving toward the frosting.

"Hello, Mr. Moore," Severin says, and the man turns. It's the
face that we've already seen in replicated miniature.

"Welcome," he says. He holds his hand out and shakes
Severin's, and it's obvious he hasn't a clue who Severin is.

"Severin Skye," Severin says. "This is my sister Indigo, and
her friend Trevor."

Mr. Moore is a little disappointing, really. You expect someone
who is that rich to have dashing jet-black hair or melting charisma.
But Mr. Moore is plain; he's got an average, amiable smile and
folding wrinkles in his forehead, the kind a tiny dune buggy
would have a blast on. He is still looking at Severin with that half-
quizzical smile you give the oddly familiar—he's seen him somewhere, but where? Trimming a hedge? Detailing his car? Dating
his daughter?

Right then, with that thought, Kayleigh Moore enters, stage
left. Her hair has a snowboard gloss and she's wearing a shorter
version of her mother's stiff skirt and sweater. It's beginning to

Deb Caletti

feel like those movies where the poor boy dates some girl named Buffy, who calls her father *Daddy*.

But not quite. "You're not eating that frosting, are you, Chief?" she says. "Hi, Severin."

"Oh, you know each other," Mr. Moore says, mystery cleared. His voice sounds familiar. Who does he sound like? Kermit? No, that's not right. A cartoon character. A cartoon character puppet?

"I'll show you where you're supposed to be," Kayleigh says.

"This is Indigo and Trev—," Severin says, but Kayleigh interrupts.

"The Chief shouldn't eat so much sugar—he's got a touch of diabetes," she says. We follow her to a separate kitchen; this is obviously the infamous catering kitchen, because here there are actually plates and food and chopping blocks and crumbs hidden from view, unlike the other kitchen, a "kitchen" in quotation marks, like those living rooms people have that no one lives in, only a kitchen no one cooks in. Where the other room had silvery wall-size appliances that look like art in a museum, and metallic pillars topped with huge blown-glass bowls, this one has people moving around and placing things on trays, and the black vests worn by all flash Chief's miniature face. It darts and dashes and lands and dashes again, like a room of Chief flies. And speaking of vests, here are ours, placed in our hands by the caterer, a white woman in some kind of African caftan, wearing an African turban.

"Boy, do we get to take these home?" Trevor jokes. "It'd look really good with my 'Happy 80th, Grandma' bowling shirt."

"Actually, we'll want you to leave those behind," the woman in the caftan says.

"Sure, next year you can cross out fifty-five and write in fifty-six," I say.

Severin looks at me with a homicidal stare.

"The Chief likes to donate these to the needy," Kayleigh says. "Well, I'll let you people do what you need to do," she says. She gives Severin's hand a squeeze, and as she makes her way across the room, she lifts her skirt, already short, as she steps over some pieces of cut carrot that have fallen to the ground.

The faux African woman, who is attempting to abduct the African culture and take it as her own for borrowed depth, tells us her name is Denise. Her catering business has a reputation for being "the best," or so she tells us. The food is some bizarre collection of cultures—there's a sushi chef in the corner, bent over his knife and his platter of edible art, and Denise has us fill trays of Moroccan beef-tipped skewers (beef on sticks), fresh mahimahi on whole grain flat breads (tuna on crackers), and free-range chicken with sesame teriyaki and rice wine glaze (chicken on sticks). The director with the cowboy tie rushes in after a while and stirs everyone up like a wooden spoon in a soup pot, shouts that there are only five minutes to go, then four minutes, and so on, and I'm hoping we'll have a chance to duck before the rocket ship takes off. We all (the three of us and about six other helpers) are supposed to burst into the room at once with trays of food.

The director gives us the cue and we're off. The lights have been dimmed and the guests mingle in with glasses of champagne, handed to them as they enter. Everything's aglitter, and the orchestra is playing—violins, cellos—"Hail to the Chief." I'm having this overwhelming sense of the odd and laughable, only no one seems to be laughing. The women all have the same hair and are wearing clothes that probably cost what a month in college would. A booming, God-like voice comes over an intercom (kudos to the sound man), and suddenly there's this film being

Deb Caletti

played on the white walls of the second- and third-floor balconies, and it's apparently a documentary of The Chief, and God is saying, "The Chief is a man who likes the finest things in life," and the crowd laughs, and there's the Chief in the film, smoking a cigar, a cap over his wrinkled forehead. "The Chief is a man who's earned his reputation . . ."

It's a group ass-kissing orgy, but I don't have much time to think about that, because my tray is empty, and off I go to refill it, and it's almost hard to see with all the people and the lightbulbs going constantly off. I head back to the kitchen, put Baked Egg and Red Pepper in Mediterranean Pastry (little previously frozen quiches) onto my tray. I pass Trevor, who says, "The Chief is a man who likes to bonk girls half his age," in a God-like whisper. He nods his chin toward Mr. Moore, who is chatting with a young woman with a spilling cleavage, a grin splashed across his face, rolling forehead wrinkles in an upward arc.

The champagne glasses are refilled, and there is food also on long tables across the living room. The paintings in here are bigger than the walls of my house. I offer my tray to three women standing in a group. *I hear they really give little to charity,* one says. She's too tan and has short, curly black hair and a beaky nose. *I hear they had a poor relation who had leukemia who asked them for money. They turned her down,* says another, in a sexy, glittery gold top whose skirt is way too short for her age. *The girl died,* she says, and plucks a second quiche to set onto her napkin.

I smile my polite servant-girl smile, but it doesn't matter, because no one sees me. I have no money, so I am a shadow. I am so far beneath, that I am not on the plane of existence. I move to another group, a woman in long silver crepe and wearing a diamond that's so big, it looks like the kind I had in the dress-up box when I was a kid. She's talking to another woman with the same short curly brown hair, who's looking resplendent (I always wanted to use the word "resplendent" and never had a chance before) in some swaying, beaded skirt. *It's obvious that he's on the B list if he got the invitation so late. I don't know if I even want to go with him.*

Trevor cruises past again. "The Chief is a man who's gonna get sloshed if he drinks any more champagne," Trevor-God says. I sneak a pinch to his butt, which is the most fun I've had all night.

More food, more circles round the room. There's an open bar, and the bartender has a vest on too. "Groovy vest," I say to him.

"Hey, you too," he says, and grins. "I saw it in *GQ*."

A group of two men and their wives. *How's it going, Bob, since I saw you last? Sweetheart, can you move? They want to take our picture.* I step aside, refrain from doing a Bex chop to the guy's family jewels for calling me sweetheart. The couples stand in a group. Smiles all around, dropped after the flash goes off. One woman shakes her head at the tray; the other plucks a Fresh-Garlic-and-Lemon-Squeezed Hummus on Traditional Naan (bean dip on bread). *Since you saw me last?* The other man says. *You mean last weekend?*

I've lost track of Severin, but I see his girlfriend everywhere. She's there, the real her, talking with three frat boys in suits and half-spiky haircuts. But there's lots of fake hers, too (these people love photographs). She's in various poses in several electronic frames of rotating photos. She's skiing. Fade out to her in a bikini. Fade out to her and her brother on horses. Fade out to her and The Chief and Mrs. Chief on a green lawn. Appearing and disappearing images of the perfect life.

My calves are starting to burn, and the bottoms of my feet,

Deb Caletti

too. I haven't sat down in hours. My biggest wish at the moment is to take off these horrible nylons and fling them, slingshot-style, into one of the two swimming pools. There's something about being here that's making me feel like there's a slow gas leak somewhere. My head hurts. Nothing feels quite real. There's an absence of honesty, and it's actually squeezing the blood vessels in my brain. Even the hors d'oeuvres lie.

But we're not done yet, because plates need to be gathered, and someone claps their hands to make a speech. It's Mrs. Moore, with her stiff face and stiff skirt; she's giving a jingly but firm laugh that means she wants everyone's attention. People start that *tink-tink*ing of knives on drink glasses.

She thanks everyone for coming, then reads some poem she wrote, choking up midway at the power and beauty of her own words, which rhyme "happiest years" with "shedding of tears." Mr. Moore takes the microphone, says a few words, thank you blah, blah, blah. It's driving me nuts, trying to think who he sounds like. Someone on *The Simpsons* maybe? *On this special day* blah, blah, blah, he says, and then it hits me—Grover. Mr. Moore, CEO of MuchMoore Industries, is a dead-on ringer for your furry pal. Then Mrs. Moore takes the microphone back, tells everyone that there's something very special about to happen, which turns out to be a hip-hop group singing and dancing some Chief rap, just in case you thought the Moores were out of touch with contemporary black culture. Mr. Moore watches and snaps his fingers, and Mrs. Moore sort of sways from side to side until she notices some crumbs on her skirt, which she brushes off and looks concerned with, but apparently not concerned enough to interrupt her show of finger-on-the-pulse fun (and support of inner-city blacks, to boot).

Finally, the cake is sliced up into smeary images of the now cut-up Moores. People dig in to Moore noses and elbows and shoes with the edges of their forks, eating bits of their host in a twisted version of a religious ritual. We weave around serving coffee, and then guests start to amble out, and are handed cups of hot cocoa on their way through the door. We are free to turn in our vests and go; the cleaning staff takes over from here. I've lost Severin, who I want to nag about going home. Trevor and I aim out into the big room, where some guests still linger, unwilling to part from the magic and memories. I'm afraid I'm going to have George Orwell dreams about the Chief.

I spot Severin, who is aiming straight toward Jim Riley, who's on this television show called *Seattle Tonight*. Now, I would never go right up to the guy and introduce myself, but Severin would and is. In my opinion, there are two kinds of people in the world—the ones who actually ask salespeople for help, and the ones whose most often-used shopping phrase is *Oh God, here she comes again*. Severin is in the camp of the former.

Jim Riley looks just like he does on TV. Blond, with a perfect smile, and a clean, putty-smooth face. Severin holds out his hand.

"Hello, Mr. Riley," he says. "My name's Severin Skye and I work for Mr. Moore. I just wanted to tell you how much I enjoy your show, and that it's an honor to meet you."

I can hear Severin's words just as I am walking up to him, catch the tilt of Jim Riley's blond head, the rising of one corner of his mouth. He looks at Severin. "They sure packed you into that shirt," he says.

Severin gives a little laugh, that uncertain kind you give when you're faced with cloudy intentions. I look at his shirt, and I guess it's true. Severin has grown since last year's homecoming—the cloth pulls across his shoulders and there's a gape at the buttons; the cuffs hit the bones of his wrists. My insides gnarl, a winding sense of shame. "Come on, Severin, let's get out of here," I say.

Jim Riley has already turned away. The people who should be most ashamed of themselves generally aren't. Kayleigh Moore appears at Severin's side to say good-bye, squeezes his hand. "Wasn't it a great party?" She doesn't speak as much as *exude*. "All the most important people in the city were here for the Chief."

The arrow on my internal Had Enough scale suddenly shoots to the outer reaches. Hey, you know, I deal with the most important people too. I deal with James Bond, and Martha Stewart, and Daniel Boone. And they happen to be very nice people.

Trevor has retrieved the car—alas, still the Mustang. He's got a bunch of Polaroids on the front seat—him in his penguin tie standing next to the Einstein Chief and the Bodybuilding Chief and the God Chief. I dance a Polaroid around. "Hey look, everyone, I think I'm God," I say in a Grover voice, only I can't do Grover, and Trevor looks at me like I've truly lost it this time.

"Did you inhale helium?" he asks.

Kayleigh Moore stands outside the door of the house with her frat boyfriends. Trevor's got the car running, and I'm not sure how it's possible, but the sound has gotten worse. Kayleigh claps her hands over her ears.

"Can we *please* get out of here," I say.

"Later, Chief," Trevor says. He hits the gas and the car rolls maybe two feet before there's this horrible clanging metal crash, and then the catastrophic sound of iron scraping against cement. "Uh-oh," Trevor says. He stops the car.

"Shit! What happened?" I say. "Did you run over someone's wheelchair?"

"Oh my God," Severin says. "They're all watching."

"Please excuse me for a moment," Trevor says. He opens his car door and steps out.

"What's going on?" I ask.

"Oh my God," Severin says again. "The muffler fell out. It's lying on the drive. Behind the car."

He's right, I see. There's a huge metal object sitting behind Bob Weaver. Kayleigh and her friends are laughing, but Trevor just lifts up that muffler and carries it to the car. He places it in the backseat. Trevor does this as if mufflers falling from cars are a mere nuisance, a trifle, something that happens all the time in front of the houses of gajillionaires, no big deal. He does this with a great deal of dignity. It is one more reason to love Trevor Williams. And then he starts the car, and we rumble off, leaving the sound of a thousand fighter jets in our wake.

The night gives me the sense that I want to shake something off of me, some film of unkindness. I am sure I wear its secret odor, detectable by people with good hearts, same as the way dogs can smell when you've been with other, unknown dogs.

The amount of money spent tonight on flowers alone could have fed a small African village, I'm guessing; it was no doubt more than what Mom makes in several months. Something about this knowledge makes me feel slightly sick. This is not about jealousy. This is severe sadness about things unjust. A queasy shame that the rightful owners of it don't feel. A sense that something is seriously wrong with us. I wash my hands, strip off those hideous stockings, and get into my flannel pajamas. Even though the night is warm, flannel is your most understanding clothing.

Deb Caletti

I sit at the edge of my bed, aware that the time has come to open the Vespa guy's envelope. I lift my pillow and remove it. The house is quiet; the night is quiet, except for the faraway sound of some neighborhood dogs barking. I hold the envelope on my lap and run my fingertip across the ink. I carefully lift the flap, edge my finger along the opening. It is a letter, with a few other papers attached. *Dear Indigo Skye,* it reads. *Consider this thanks for your kindness. I decided to do as you suggested and make my life my own . . .*

I stop reading. A paperclip attaches all the pages, and I slip it off. At that moment, a piece of rectangular paper flutters to the floor, lands upside down. It is a check, I can see that. I crouch to my knees, turn the paper over. His name is there, Richard Howards, a signature at the bottom. I am on my knees, almost in a position of prayer, when I see the numbers.

Two and a half million dollars, it reads. *Two and a half million dollars.*

When I see those numbers, they are not real. It could just as well read *two and a half million antelope,* or *two and a half million red apples* or *two and a half million sailing ships.* It is not a number I understand. And for a long time, I cannot even rise from where I kneel.

6

"No one just gives away two and a half million dollars," Mom says. It's one a.m. but her eyes are bright. I am sitting on her bed and so are Severin and Bex; everyone awakened when I screamed. Even Trevor is there, sort of—the phone is lying on the bed too, and the speakerphone is on.

"You still smell like Axe," I say to Mom.

"That might be me," Severin says.

"It's definitely not me," Bex says, but she smells her underarms anyway. "I don't even wear deodorant." She picks at the fuzz of her moon and stars pajamas.

"You people can't smell me." Trevor states the obvious, his voice coming from down by the bedspread.

"Maybe it's not real," Mom says. She looks at the check for the millionth time. The two and a half millionth time.

"It's the biggest tip I've ever heard of," Severin says.

"It's a fucking big tip," Trevor says, as if it was his own idea.

"We should all go back to bed. We'll have to figure out what to do in the morning," Mom says.

"Figure out what to do? Figure out how we're going to spend it," Severin says.

"A nice fat donation to tsunami relief, for starters," Bex suggests. "An Xbox."

"We can get a new muffler," Trevor says.

"We? Hey, people. This is my check here," I say.

"Who can sleep anyway," Bex says.

"I'm starved," Severin says.

"It's because you drink that protein shake shit instead of really eating," I say.

"I have the sudden urge to make pancakes," Mom says. "No, French toast." She leaps up from the bed.

"Man, I can't believe I'm not there," comes the little voice from the bedspread.

"Powdered sugar on it," Bex says. She bounces on her knees around the mattress and Freud bolts out the door like there's a fire.

Mom hunts under the bed for her slippers. She can find only one, gives up and puts on a pair of socks. I say good night to Trevor, and in a few moments, there's the smell of melting butter and the ziss of egg-and-butter-soaked bread in a hot pan.

"It's like some movie," Mom says, waving around the spatula. "Like one of those movies where a waitress wins the lottery, or something."

"Holl-ee-wood," Bex says.

Mom just stands there shaking her head and holding the spatula, and you know that the bread needs turning over.

"Mom," Severin reminds.

"Mom," Chico says, under the cover of his cage. He's supposed to be sleeping. "Mom! Mo-om!"

"Oh! Right," she says, and saves the bread just before it burns. In a short while we're sitting around the table, now flecked with snowy white that's drifted from our plates.

"I don't know if any of this is really happening," I say.

Bex pinches me on the arm, then Mom does, then Severin leans over the table to do it too. "Ouch," I say.

"It's happening," Bex says.

When I wake up the next morning, reality takes a slow train back to my brain. In my bed, I've convinced myself it's some weird dream, brought on by a bizarre night of wealth and emotional poverty. But, no, there's the envelope on my floor. *Richard Howards.*

"I called your father," Mom says. She's standing outside the bathroom door. She pounds on it with her fist. "Did you fall asleep in there, Severin? Come on, you'll use all the hot water."

"You what?" I ask. We all seriously need some coffee.

"Your father? Well, first I called Bomba, and after I got tired of hearing her screaming 'Oh my God, oh my God, oh my God,' I called him."

Mom calling Dad has happened only twice in the last few years since my father remarried—as far as I know, anyway. The first time, Mom phoned Dad when Bex was taken to the emergency room with a high fever and possible meningitis. The second time, Severin was three hours late coming home because the car battery died, and Mom was sure he'd been kidnapped or murdered. So this was right up there with illness and death and homicide.

"What'd he say?"

"Well, he agreed with me. We have to find some way of giving it back."

I feel nettle prickles of irritation. "Wait a sec," I say. "I'm eighteen, here. This isn't something everyone else decides." I might have agreed with them. In fact, I *did* agree with them. It was annoying, though, when parents got so, well, *parental.* For God's sake, give me my bottle and a graham cracker, you know?

Deb Caletti

And the money—I was excited about the money, sure, but not in any real way. It reminded me of when Severin and I were seven and my parents were still married and my dad told us he was taking us to Disneyland. Severin and I shrieked and ran around the house and hit each other and my Mom smiled and told us to calm down and they kissed. Dad even had slick pamphlets that Severin and I spread out on the kitchen table and read aloud. We fought over which ride we would go on first. But even then I knew in my deep inner pieces that we were never going. Dad, my father of restlessness and poetry and soul-searching, who kept Thoreau and Emerson on his bedside table like people keep Bibles—he couldn't be on the teacup ride, and I understood that, even at seven, even as I hit my brother in giddy thrill and snatched the pamphlets from his hands. He couldn't be on the teacup ride, and I couldn't be the sudden owner of a shiny new two and a half million dollars.

"For God's sake, Severin." Mom pounds. "Now! I'm going to be late for work!"

"Jeez, chill, Mom," he says.

"Estrogen surge," I say.

The doorknob turns and we back away and Severin escapes with a towel around his waist and his hair wet. A whoosh of steam dashes from the bathroom, a ghost running out. The mirror is a moist haze that Mom will have to wipe away with a towel or her robe sleeve.

"Do you smell what I smell?" I say.

"Yeah, Severin. Lay off my Axe," Mom says.

"You used half a can, apparently," I say to him, but Severin's in his room already, slams the door on us.

"God, I love that smell," Mom says.

"No one just gives away two and a half million dollars," Melanie says. We are in her room. She has a new poster on her wall, in a frame. The posters in my room—a close-up of hands on guitar strings and the back of Hunter Eden onstage (yeah, we all know his ass could keep Levi's in business for all eternity)—those posters were hung up using bits of masking tape looped into circles of stickiness. But this has glass and a mat, the whole works. It has six rows of fish, with their scientific names in italics underneath. I'm surprised it doesn't have one of those little let's-pretend-we're-in-a-museum lights over it.

"Nice poster, Mel," I say.

"Shut up," she says. "My father gave it to me."

"You should ask him for the bedspread."

She ignores me. "This is mind-blowing. I just can't believe it." She shakes her head. "Who would do that? No one would do that. He wants something. Maybe he wants *you*."

"No, he doesn't. He's not some Internet perv, trust me."

"Pervs don't wear T-shirts saying they're pervs," Melanie says.

"Don't tell anyone about this, okay?" I say. I don't want this to be some running conversation at school, like when Lauren Liu got chosen for a Coke commercial or when Zen Markson's mother committed suicide. I am not other people's entertainment.

"I won't," she says. And then, "Oh my God," Melanie shrieks. It's the kind of girly sound that makes me hate her and love her at the same time. Being friends with Melanie makes me feel like I'm in junior high and have just been asked to walk to the bathroom with a cheerleader when I know she's perfectly capable of going on her own. Melanie is fascinating and baffling, exciting

Deb Caletti

and annoying as hell. "I just realized something."

I shriek too, just to try it out. I sound a little like Freud, the time Mom had to give him a bath after he'd knocked over a bottle of motor oil Trevor was using in our driveway.

"I'm going to Malibu this summer," she says.

"Malibu, like where Barbie is from?" I say.

"Indigo, you could come with me."

I laugh.

"No, I mean it. I wanted to ask you before, but Dad says you'd have to pay for your own plane fare, and . . ."

"You knew it would be an issue."

"You could buy your own plane now," she says.

"That's ridiculous. Plane fare will still be an issue." But Melanie has popped up from her folded-leg position on the bed and has gotten her cell phone, which is the kind that has the calendar and the camera and does everything for you but clean your room and balance the national debt.

"Okay, look." She taps the screen with a little metal stick, shows me the screen. "The end of June. You can come down for a few weeks. We can rent a convertible. Hell, you can buy a convertible."

"I don't know, Mel, that's a lot of time to take off work." I imagine Mel and me in a pink Barbie Camero, wearing little plastic Barbie shoes and Barbie wedding dresses, our veils flying out, some giant hand driving us around on the kitchen floor.

"You've got to be kidding me. You're still going to *work*?"

"I told you, I'm going to give it back."

Melanie pretends to punch numbers into her phone. "Hello? Yeah, I want to report that I've got an idiot in my house? Uh-huh. A certified f-ing lunatic. Please come and take her away before I kill her myself."

"Hey, let's play Name the Fish. I'll hold my hand over the labels and you can tell me what they are."

"You are a millionaire!" she shrieks. She is hugging me. I picture a cartoon scene where my tongue is gaggling out from the force of her embrace.

"Air, air," I Freud-shriek back.

"Girls," Melanie's mother says, her head suddenly in Melanie's room. "I told you, I'd like you to keep the door open when you're visiting."

Melanie's mom is gone again, but I can feel her presence still lingering in the hall. "Quick, hide the pot," I say loudly.

Do you ever have those moments when your dream life and your real life intersect like spirits from the dead who appear in the here and now to knock over vases and picture frames? When you wake from a dream of a long kiss or an angry moment and you take that feeling into the new day? The sense floats, looks for something to latch on to, feels both right and not right, too present for something imaginary. This is where I am now, when I walk into Carrera's, my work shoes on and laced, the news I have to share trailing ahead of me and behind me, wispy but insistent as perfume samples in a magazine. The news is the real and not real of a dream. The here and now but not now.

"Well?" Jane says from behind the register. She is wearing dangly bead earrings, jeans, and a T-shirt, a white one, which has the smeary gray haze of once having been washed with a blue towel. Clothes that may not understand two and a half million dollars. Even Jack lifts up his head. His red cloth collar with the bone hanging from it with his address and name etched on—I'm suddenly sure that even he won't understand two and a half million dollars.

Deb Caletti

"You were right," I say. "It was big."

"Oh God," she sighs. She shares this with Mom—the equation of "big" with "disaster." It makes me wonder, right then, if the Moores, or even Melanie's mother and father, would ever feel this equation, and I don't think so. Wealth gives you the expectation of more wealth, and struggle gives you the expectation of more struggle. The willingness to embrace the idea of "a surprise" is dependent on our past surprises being good ones. Maybe this is obvious, but I don't think so. Pessimism and caution and cynicism and the inability to be spontaneous are character flaws to those who've had good fortune, and common sense to those who haven't.

I put on my apron, tie it behind my back. I shout a hello to Luigi, who greets me with a "Ciao" that comes through the open rectangle window that leads to the kitchen. Poor Luigi—he's like those other isolated workers stuck behind small openings—bank tellers and limo drivers and movie theater ticket sellers. The most we see of him is his dark, hairy arm sliding plates through to the other side, though he doesn't seem to mind.

"For Christ's sake, Indigo. How much longer are you going to make us wait?" Trina says.

I peek under the foil of Harold's pie dishes. "Lemon or berry?" I ask her.

"No chocolate?" she says. She looks slightly panicked. "Berry. Chocolate ice cream." It sounds disgusting, but it's not my job to argue with the customers. I notice something shocking about Trina. There. Under the table. No boots. No knee-high boots or calf-high ones or even ankle-high. No I'm-no-virgin white ones, no you-can't-handle-what's-in-these red ones, no tie-me-up black ones. She's wearing Reeboks, oh God. She had to walk here, I realize. I realize, little bits of Trina are disappearing.

"Until everyone else gets here. I don't want to tell this a thousand times," I say.

Nick is next, and he looks like hell. He's got a sweatshirt on from some resort, and this looks rudely prosperous and overconfident next to his jeans that have seen too many wearings without being washed—you can tell because they're loose and low-slung without meaning to be. He's unshaven—whiskers sprouting up sure as the lawn our neighbors, the Elberts, just reseeded. He doesn't even greet us. Just slides and slumps into his table.

"Look who the cat dragged in," Trina says. She's as direct as she likes her coffee. Black, no sugar or cream.

"Yeah, well," Nick says.

Jane goes to him, sets her strong hands on his shoulders. "Today's the anniversary?" she asks.

He nods. He pushes his palms to his eyes.

"You said it was coming," Jane says.

"Year two," he says.

"It's so hard," Jane says. "When my mother died . . ."

"I thought this was supposed to get easier," he says. He takes his palms from his eyes, which are red and baggy; they have the new wrinkles of apricots left too long in the fridge.

"They don't tell you that the second anniversary is harder," Jane says. "You think you're supposed to be better. Hits you worse."

"You're telling me."

"Grief is harder when it simmers than when it boils," she says.

"I wish I still smoked," Trina says.

I don't even bother getting on Trina's case for this. I put in

Deb Caletti

Nick's order without asking him, add an order of toast that I'll take from my tips, or rather, tip, if necessary. I want him to have something to crunch, rather than just swallow down. You are not completely helpless if you can crunch. I also ask for a hot chocolate with whipped cream, because whipped cream can remind you why it's good to be alive.

I am wondering how I will be able to share my news, lay this gold egg on a battleground. Some kind of feeling is working around my insides; this finger, looping and curving on steamed-up glass. My conscience. Guilt, maybe. But I don't have time to think about it; a mismatched couple comes in—a very large woman and a tiny man, one of those couples that bring to mind Bomba's expression, "There's a lid to every pot." And then Funny arrives and she's bouncing and smiling, her dark eyes gleamy, the corners of her mouth turned up like an elf's. Her smile relieves some of my guilt.

"People, people, people," Funny says. Funny is small. Tiny, really, but you forget she's tiny because of her intense dark hair and sharp, focused eyes. But I see it now, with her thin wrists and small fingers clutching a magazine. It's not a regular magazine, all shiny and bold and shouting, but a quiet, whispering one with thick paper and thoughtful fonts.

"What's that?" I ask.

"People, people, people," she says again. "I'd like everyone's attention." Even the large woman and tiny man raise their heads. They have the look of restaurant dread you get in those places where you're supposed to interrupt your dinner to join in to some rousing group-singing of "Happy Birthday," belted out by over-enthusiastic waiters and waitresses as a sparkling candle melts into an oversize sundae.

"Funny Louise Coyote is officially a published poet," she says.

"What?" Jane clasps her hands together. Her eyes are wide. "You sold a poem?"

"Well, 'sell' is a relative word. I get ten copies of the magazine. You know, the landlord won't take those instead of rent—"

"My God, Funny, that's wonderful," Jane says.

Even Nick smiles. "Well done, Funny," he says. That's the kind of good man he is. A man who looks outside himself, a non-murdering man, a man who never leaves a messy table and wipes up sugar he's spilled.

"It's in there? Let us see," I say.

"It's not in this one," Funny says. "This is just the magazine. It won't come out for two more years." She holds it close to her chest.

"Wow," I say.

"If the magazine stays in business that long. I mean, I know no one really reads it, but that's beside the point," Funny says. Funny sets the magazine carefully on the seat beside her. She places the napkin onto her lap daintily. She lines up her silverware. She makes the bottoms of her knife and fork and spoon all even.

"It's not something you do for fame and fortune," Jane says. "It's a heart thing."

"Right," Funny says. "Pancakes," she tells me. "Eggs, bacon." I write it down.

"Beware of heart things," Trina says. "That's all I can say."

Big lady and small man have gone back to their uneven conversation, and the bookstore guy comes in and so does Joe. Joe eases up onto his counter stool and sighs. He reminds me of Eeyore. His bald head is shiny but has a terrain of its own; bumpy,

Deb Caletti

a barren planet. His thumbs grasp the edge of the plastic menu that he could recite by heart. His jacket smells like smoky outside morning. I pour Joe's coffee.

"Come on, Indigo," Jane says after I take the bookstore guy's order. An omelette, which means he's okay with things mixed together. He's not fussy about clarity. The rest of him shows this too. His shirt is untucked and the orange T-shirt peeking from underneath is a color that doesn't match. He's got an earring, but earrings don't necessarily mean cool anymore, just trying to be. He's edging through his thirties reluctantly, the earring says. He's a walking omelet of contradictions. "Leroy's always late, if he even comes. I'd say we're all here."

"He's coming," Trina says. "I see him." She leans forward to look out the window, showing us the small of her back from her shirt that's eeked up. "He's parking that piece of crap car. Okay, he's locking the door, not that there's anything to steal. Keys in his shirt pocket. Whistling. He's whistling. Almost at the door, and . . ."

"Give me your best hangover cure," Leroy says.

"You want to stay in shape, you gotta lay off that, what did I tell you?" Joe says. He shakes his dark, bumpy head.

"Lack of *sleep* hangover," Leroy says. "No booze involved. I worked all day, then all night. I got this job watching this old lady because they're worrying about her falling and I'm supposed to stay up all night because she walks around. She isn't gonna fall. She's steadier than me. I put on some music, and she danced. I wasn't supposed to let her dance. Why bother being alive if you can't dance?" He snaps a vine-covered finger.

"I can see this job's going to last," Trina says.

"I shimmied her around the room." He chuckles. "Man, she loved that."

"Come on, Indigo," Jane says. "Everyone's here. Spill it."

"Oh man, that's right," Leroy says. "What was in the envelope? He suing you or something?"

I think about making this big. For a moment, I see it cinematic. Indigo lifts her pant legs, steps up onto a counter stool, onto the counter itself. She holds her hands out, makes her grand statement, and they swarm her, lift her, carry her around, turn circles with her in their arms. It's a joy moment, the arms of friends, their goodwill.

But instead, I see their faces, and I can't speak. There's Nick, and he is wiping the edges of his mouth with a napkin, and Jane, hands on her hips. Trina in her Reeboks and Joe, looking like a visual sigh. Leroy, grinning. Both inked hands clasped in expectation. Leafy fingers intertwined, the forearm mermaid, upside down in waiting. And Funny, leaning back, smiling, whose good news no longer feels like relief to my strange guilt. It is an ace to my four aces. News I will trump.

"He gave me two and a half million dollars," I say quietly.

"Holy fuck," Leroy breathes.

"What?" the bookstore guy says. "I didn't hear."

"Nobody gives away two and a half million dollars," Jane says.

"I knew he was loaded," Trina says sadly. "Damn it."

"Can you repeat that?" Nick says. "I think I didn't hear right."

"You heard right." I grab a towel, start wiping the counter. I wipe the same spot over and again. I make circles. I make circles because circles are starts and middles and ends and starts again.

"My, my, my," Joe says. He whistles long and low. It's a ten-syllable whistle. "Now you've got yourself some trouble."

"What are you talking about?" Leroy says. "Joe, you don't know jack." Jack raises his head from where he lies on the floor.

Joe hears the friendly punch, boxes the air in Leroy's direction. "This is an *opportunity*. An opportunity? No, wait. This is a new universe. He handed you a universe."

"Who would do that? No one does that," Jane says. "Unless he wants something."

"Some psycho," the bookstore guy says.

"No," I say. "He doesn't want anything."

"My God," Trina says. Her hand is to her heart.

"And I thought I was having a good day," Funny says.

"I'm giving it back," I say. They stare at me. And I have a weird sense of me here and them over there. Like there is the breeze of sudden space between us. I have my first two-and-a-half-million-dollar realization: Having money requires the ability to ignore the selfishness of having money.

"Are you okay?" Jane asks. She's at my elbow. Takes the towel from me. "You look really pale. Sit down, Indigo."

"I'm a little . . . in shock." I know it sounds crazy. I know it does. But I feel like I might cry. I suddenly see where I'm standing, and that's at the edge of change—really, really big change. Not the small, daily movements of regular change. Not the regular breaths of life-movements. It's tectonic-plate change. A shift so monumental that the landscape will be forever altered, and my toes are at the edge of it, and it's jolting, and then all at once the ground really does seem to move. The actual ground is really slipping under my feet, and . . .

"Someone get a cold washrag," Jane says. She's peering down at me, and I don't know what's going on, because I have a sudden, strange view of the ceiling. What I realize is there's some crap up there, stuck, above Rosso Verona, probably flung there by that Hitler toddler. Someone's going to have to get a chair and get it off.

"There's pancake on the ceiling," I say.

"Indigo, are you all right? You fainted," Jane says. "Give her some space, everyone."

Leroy's looking down at me, and so is Nick, and the bookstore guy, who is being elbowed out of the way. Even Jack is looking down—I see the underside of his furry chin. Funny appears with some hard brown paper towels from the bathroom, soaked in water. Nick's holding napkins that he dunked in his ice-water glass. Joe's got the towel I used, but there's crap on that, too. Restaurant work is messy.

I sit up on my elbows. "Whoa, I've never fainted before," I say. "That was weird. Like human consciousness melting. Kind of cool."

"Yeah, it's cool how you scared the shit out of us," Leroy says. "That was cool." He acts pissed at me.

Joe leans over, pulls down the skin under my eyes, stares inside. His brown eyes are staring right into mine. His eyes look huge. "Hey, quit that," I say. "You're creeping me out."

"She's fine," he says.

"Should we call 911?" Jane asks.

"She's ready for another round," Joe says.

"I bet you didn't eat a good breakfast," Funny says. "In all your excitement." I sit up.

"You're right." She is right, I realize. I didn't eat anything since French toast at two a.m. I had completely forgotten about food in all the talk about money. I look around at my new world. I realize the tiny man and the big woman are gone.

"Dine and dash," I say, and point.

"They left bills on the table," Nick says.

"Fifty dollars." Jane counts. "For two breakfasts."

Deb Caletti

"They left rather in a hurry," Nick says. "When you hit the ground." Now that I'm standing again, he wipes his own face with the napkins.

"Sit down, for God's sake," Trina says to me.

"Hey, fifty bucks. Another big tip," I say.

Jane hands me a piece of Harold's pie on a plate. "Ha, not on your life," she says. "Eat. Indigo, my God. I don't know how to process this."

"Me either," I say.

"Finish all of that," Trina says. "If you faint again, I'm going to faint. I can't handle anything medical."

"Those emergency room shows . . . ," Nick says.

"The worst," Trina says.

"She's fine," Joe says. He seems pleased at being the expert. He even hitches his belt up. He crosses his arms and gives a small nod.

"Two and a half million dollars? It's a dream come true," Trina says. "God, I wish I'd waited on him."

For the rest of my shift, Jane insists I either go home or take it easy. Everyone is treating me as if I'm fragile and new. Nick asks when I'll be quitting Carrera's. Trina asks if my family will be moving. Funny says I won't have to work for the rest of my life. Leroy tells them to back off, for God's sake.

I know I'm not saying good-bye when I leave that day. But it feels like a kind of good-bye. I feel that empty place of something left behind.

Leroy calls my name as I head toward Trevor's Mustang.

"Indigo!" he shouts.

"Leroy!" I shout back.

"This is a good thing," he says. "Got it? A *universe*."

It takes me a minute to realize what's different. It's Sunday afternoon, and I'm sitting on the seat with pony interior and Trevor has kissed me and he gently pushes the lever into drive and we're passing Chuck's BBQ and the bookstore and the Front Street Market and I watch some man crossing the street carrying his dog, and I'm wondering about that when it hits me.

"The car's quiet," I say. "No, it's *purring*."

Trevor cracks up, slaps the steering wheel with his palm. "Finally. I was wondering when you were going to say something."

"When did you fix it? I thought you worked today."

"Baby, did you see that guy carrying his dog? What's up with a guy carrying his dog on a walk?"

But I don't care about that anymore. "Focus," I say. "The car?"

"I had it fixed. Doesn't Bob sound happy? I never heard Bob sound so happy." Trevor peers at me from under his shaggy bangs.

"What do you mean you had it fixed?" Trevor always fixes Bob himself.

We stop at the red light by the library. I see Erik Dobbs from my school coming out of the 76 station, holding a bottle of Coke and, what is that? A yellow bag of Funyuns? Who eats Funyuns, for God's sake? But Trevor's right. The Mustang is purring, and when the light turns green, it pulls out with a confidence Bob's never shown before. I'm not sure I like Bob like this.

"Trevor!" I say.

He's apparently engrossed in the sound too, because he tosses his head as if shaking himself into reality. "He just sounds sooo good." He grins. "I'm loving this! I bring it to the Mustang place, right? Downtown Seattle. Let them replace the muffler, a few other things . . ."

"Trevor, God, how much did that cost?" I feel a little panic-flutter. Butterfly wings of anxiety. I have a feeling I know where this is going.

"I took it out of my savings. Baby, you should see your face," Trevor says, and chuckles. "Relax. Have you forgotten that we're rich?"

He stops at the next light just turning yellow, by the True Value where Nick works. There's a stuffed collie outside. He used to belong to the owner, Terry, and I guess, technically, he still does. The dog wears a True Value baseball cap, and he gets dragged out every morning and dragged back in at night. The light turns red, and Trevor grabs my shoulders, kisses me long and hard. He's forgotten I'm not into public displays of affection; still, his tongue lulls and makes a right turn, then left, and it's the kind of kiss that would make me usually forget what century I lived in or what planet I was on. The light must have turned green, because the car behind us honks and Trevor separates from me, my lips cool with the sudden air.

"We're rich!" he says again.

Usually that kiss would have acted like some tingling, hypnotic spell, but this time, I feel something else. A small, internal stepping back. A slight shove to his chest with my palm that I see only in my mind. Just, this little echo of *away*.

Mom sits at the desk that's against one wall in the living room, tapping on our computer. It's heavy and prehistoric, bulky and as large as old televisions, and it is the yellow-tan color of a corn tortilla. Occasionally you'll hear it groan and creak and grind when it's just sitting there, like it's trying to remember something painful from the past. You kind of feel bad for it, like it should be on an IV and allowed to just rest. It's a terminal terminal, ha-ha.

Mom's got a pencil behind one ear. She's looking all over for something, lifting papers and scanning the floor, and my bet is, it's that pencil she's missing. Trevor's out front showing Severin under the hood of the car, and I hear Bex in the kitchen. By the warm, thick smell in our house, I'm guessing she's making brownies.

I snitch the pencil from Mom's ear. "Looking for this?" I ask.

"Aah. I knew it was here somewhere."

"What are you doing?" I ask. Actually, I snoop at the computer screen, which usually pisses her off. This time, though, she leans to one side to show me. It's an Alaska Airlines website, a grid of travel dates and times and prices.

"Well, you said you thought he went to Maui, right? That was your guess?"

"Yeah," I say.

"Well, Dad did some asking around. Okay, really? He did more than ask around. He says he called everyone he knew and they called everyone *they* knew and it was practically an all-out man hunt."

"Oh my God, you're kidding," I say. I can't believe this. I picture poor Richard Howards, gone to Maui to escape his life, to get

Deb Caletti

a little rest and relaxation, descended on by helicopter tour guys and parasailers and surfers. I feel horrible.

"No, no," Mom says. "It's okay. It's good. No one talked to him. But they did find him, Indigo. You were right. He went to Maui."

"That was easy," I say. I feel a swoop of disappointment. "I think we should be grateful he apparently lacks imagination. Or just wanted to get the hell out, fast."

"He's been there five days. The first few nights he stayed at the Four Seasons, but then he rented a house."

"What, does Dad have a spy ring?"

"You know your dad. People love him. He probably knows everyone on the island."

I sigh. I'm getting a headache. Mom's eyes have those coffee-ring moons underneath, and her hair is in the same ponytail from this morning.

"So, you're going to fly out there?" I ask.

"No, I thought you'd fly out there." She taps the screen with her pencil. "Next week? Thursday? Stay the weekend with your dad?"

"And what do I do when I get there? 'Hey, hi, remember me? Am I blocking your sun? I'm the waitress you gave two and a half million dollars to. Where'd you get that piña colada, it looks delicious'?"

"I don't know," Mom says. "Your dad will help you."

My mother is under the permanent delusion that my dad can fix things she can't. Anytime something breaks, she sighs and makes some comment along the lines of *If your father hadn't run off to Hawaii* . . . She'll stand and look at the dripping sink or the broken shower head or the leaking dishwasher and imagine my father as this home repair hero, when the truth is, he sucked at home repair. He would stand there scratching his head and knocking on pipes with his knuckles like they might knock back an answer in secret code. I watched him hang a picture once, and it took him five tries and he hammered the nail in with the bottom of a nearby vase. You could see the Holes of Failure surrounding the upper edge of the picture frame. He's really not great at any other crisis either. He supposedly got lost on the way to the emergency room when Mom was having Bex, and they kept turning around in the parking lot of a 7-Eleven until the cashier stood at the door with folded arms, probably thinking they were casing the joint for a robbery. I could just picture Mom giving birth right there in a parking space littered with a Slurpee lid and cigarette butts and one of those white, ruffly paper trays they put hot dogs in. You could be having a heart attack and Dad would be looking for his car keys under the couch cushions. Yet somehow in Mom's mind, if Dad were still with us, we'd never have car problems or a brown lawn or printer jams. To her, he had some ability to make things right and keep things running in a way she'd never be able to.

"Severin can come with me," I say.

"Indigo, no. Sweetie. Even you—this is going on my credit card. I don't have the money for this ticket. I didn't want to say, but Mrs. Olson was over a week or so ago . . ." She rubs one eye with her palm.

I know what this means. Mrs. Olson is our landlady. Mrs. Olson looks sweet as a box of See's candy. She wears thin sweaters and has brown spots on the back of her hands and a little gold cross necklace around her woggly chicken neck. If you got to talking to her, though, she would tell you about her ring, with a stone

Deb Caletti

to represent each child, that Mr. Olson gave her on their thirtieth wedding anniversary, and then she'd tell you how the liberals are messing up the country, giving money away like it grows on trees, and how the last great Democrat was Franklin Delano Roosevelt, but those days are long gone, and even he would never allow men to marry other men when that was just against nature. Just *against* nature, and those people ought to be hung. She actually said "hung," which made you realize that in another life she'd be the sort to bring her knitting to the public executions. According to my mother, Mrs. Olson is one of those people who have a fat checkbook but a thin heart. After Mrs. Olson would come over to raise our rent, my mother would go into her room and shut the door for a long time, and the bottle of aspirin would be on the bathroom counter, the fluff of cotton left out and the lid off. Mrs. Olson never had any *funds* (as she called them) to fix anything. Instead, she'd dock a couple of dollars from the rent for a month and then turn around and raise it permanently, which, according to my mom, was the same thing insurance companies do whenever you use the insurance you paid for.

"Can't we subtract airline tickets from the money?" I say. "It seems only fair."

"That'd be nice, but is this someone who's working with a full deck, here?" She sighs. "If it's not one thing, it's another. Who would have thought too much money would be a problem. I'm agreeing to this flight, okay?" She lifts her eyebrows, poises her finger dramatically over the enter key. I nod. "Done," she says. "Done. I did it. You're going." Mom scrolls down the screen and back up again, presses a button and then stares at the printer, which just sits there politely.

"Wait—I'm going to have to be alone with Dad," I say. "I've

hardly ever been alone with Dad for an extended period of time." I feel a wash of nerves, that edgy discomfort you get when you're in an elevator with strangers. "What if we don't have anything to talk about?"

"It's not like you don't ever talk to him," Mom says. But she's not really listening. She's opening up the lid of the printer and peering inside, the same way she does when the car starts making weird noises. She pokes her finger around in there.

"Talking to him for five minutes on the phone every few weeks is different from finding things to say for a few *days*." *How is school?* will take up all of about a minute and a half. *How is your brother and Bex,* another three minutes. What if we complete our conversational repertoire before we even get out of the airport parking lot?

"You used to *live* with him, remember," Mom says. Barely remember. It doesn't even seem real anymore, our time as a family altogether. Dad left when I was eleven, when he decided his life was becoming a frightening suburban cliché. Mom told us this one night when she'd had a second beer and let both her tongue and the image of him loosen. I like my dad, don't get me wrong—the five-minute bits of conversation every now and then and the few times we've all visited him have been great. He's a likeable guy. But we haven't really gotten to know each other, him and me. Time and place have been barriers to that, but so has the intermittent sense that I have something to forgive him for—the fact that he left people who loved him for something better than that, I guess—and that delicate sense is the architectural frame our relationship is built on.

"You'll have Jennifer," Mom says. "Jennifer never stops talking." Mom slams the printer door shut, same as she would the hood of the car when there's nothing wrong, far as she can tell. Jennifer is my mom's stepwife, but we don't call her our step-mother. She's ten years older than I am, so "mother" is just not the word that comes to mind. Mom's right, though. All I'd have to do is bring a stack of quarters and keep pumping them in and Jennifer would keep on going.

"God," I say.

"He's *your* father," Mom says, as if somehow this is my fault. As if I was the one who chose him, not her. She tries the printer button again, and the machine cranks to life. "Ha!" she says. When it's done, she snitches the page from the tray, turns off the computer without shutting it down properly. It exhales in exhaustion.

We hear Bex making the "ooh eee ooh ahh" noises of someone taking something hot from the oven. Mom yells at her to use a pot holder, for God's sake (knowing Bex, she used the hem of her shirt). *"For God's sake!"* I hear Chico screech. This is just another example of sibling unfairness. I didn't get to use the oven until I was, maybe, fifteen, and even then Mom hovered over me like I was holding a torch and a can of gasoline. Under normal circumstances, I would have complained about this injustice (shouldn't we all have to suffer equally?), but this involves food, chocolate food. In a few minutes Bex appears with a plate of brownies.

"This is an obvious display of butt-kissing now that you're rich," she says. At least she's honest about it. "All I ask in exchange is that you remember the people without homes in Malaysia."

"She has to give it back, Bex," Mom says.

"But we want brownies anyway," I say.

"Do we ever," Mom says.

"Fine," Bex says. She holds out the plate and some napkins. The brownies were cut when they were too warm, so they fall apart a little when you lift them. Two bites and I'm feeling better already. There's something about consumption—chocolate-to-mouth, receipt-in-bottom-of-shopping-bag—that fills empty places. We need our empty places filled, and what are the speedy, available options? Material things, God, love, nachos with everything. Consuming something, anything, smoothes out the gnawing of need and stitches the gaping of angst, and if only a brownie is available, a brownie will do.

There are places where time seems to slow down in some alien-planet way, where everything is on football-game time, a minute equaling fifteen minutes. Any math class is one of those places, as is the Department of Motor Vehicles, and the waiting rooms of doctor's offices. And airports. Time oozes in airports, some primordial flow from before there were clocks, when thousands of years was a relatively short period of time measured against eons. That's airport time. I've been waiting to board for twenty minutes, which in regular-life time feels like four or five days have passed. My good-byes to everyone and Trevor's farewell kiss are already hazy and long-ago soft.

I go to the bathroom just for something to do. I've already gone to the gift shop full of overpriced candy bars and trashy novels and Seattle key chains and playing cards and those scenic spoons that you thought had disappeared long ago. Things almost impossible to imagine that people desire. I find the bathroom sign with the chick in the triangle skirt, and the rolling suitcase Mom made me bring follows behind me like Bex used to when she was younger. I want to make it go to its room, but we're stuck as traveling partners. Ha, it'll probably have a more interesting conversation with Dad than I will.

I do the nervous push-open-the-door-quick maneuver you do in bathrooms to be on guard against unpleasant surprises. I've got a real knack for out-in-public bad luck. If some cash register is going to run out of tape, that's the line I'll be in; if there's some stalker salesperson in the store, I'm the one she'll follow. And if there's a stall without toilet paper, I'm in it.

I've been on an airplane twice in my life, both times to see Dad. He came to visit us, but it was awkward—he stayed at the Ramada Inn near the airport and we stayed with him, Bex and me in one bed and he and Severin in the other, the sound of airplanes taking off and landing and the tiny bottles of shampoo reminding us all that it was temporary. The only lively part was Bex jumping around in her bathing suit and asking if it was time to swim yet, and Severin eating crackers out of the minibar before he realized you had to pay for them, at five dollars for maybe six Wheat Thins. The last time I was in the airport was a few years ago, and since then the airport has acquired these creepy, revolving plastic seats on the toilets. Me and my little following rolling friend cannot believe our eyes. There's this thin skin of plastic on the seat that eeks around after you flush. I try it a few times just to watch it work, and let me tell you, whoever sat in some boardroom with this great idea was really a sicko, or at the very least, the overachieving son of the president of the company. I have the sudden fear that this is actually the same piece of plastic going around the same circle, and wish I had a Post-it note or a piece of gum or something to stick on and see if I am right. I get out of there fast. I stand at the sink and before my suitcase has even rolled up behind me, the faucet shoots on.

"Hey, I'm not ready," I say to it, because no one else is in there. The faucet goes off. I position my hands nicely underneath and . . . nothing. I wave them around. Still, nothing. I turn my back to try another sink and wham, the old one shoots on. God, I hate presumptuous, overachieving appliances. Toilets that flush before you're ready; automatic, attacking seatbelts; refrigerators that beep when the door is open too long. Melanie has one of those. For God's sake, it makes me feel like my inability to decide is a criminal act. To all the pushy appliances out there, back off.

I had previously been trying out wearing the air of an owner of two and a half million dollars, something casual and leaning and not nervous and wary, some sort of new cool, but the bathroom experience has reminded me that I am just one of the masses that must deal with creepy, revolving plastic on toilets. My inability to control an automatic faucet has zapped my confidence, and so I sit back down in a hard plastic chair formed to the supposed contours of my body and look around for possible terrorists instead. Some kid sits on his dad's lap and pats the man's head, which the dad puts up with amiably. An old guy in a World War II Veterans cap and a snazzy pair of red Keds high-tops asks me to take a picture of him and his wife, who's sporting a crocheted cap and a pair of velvety leopard pants. I try to find the *big button there* she is gesturing toward, as she leans back against the man and smiles.

"Cool shoes," I say to the man. More than the shoes themselves, I like the fact that he's wearing them. He has a cane and some huge elastic band around his waist as if trying to keep his internal organs in. "You two are stylin'."

The woman beams. "We're from New Jersey," she says.

I hand back the camera, wait for another eon. I watch a creature

Deb Caletti

emerge from the sea, grow legs, begin to walk upright, and then it's time to board. The flight attendants flash their credit card smiles and I haul my bag up and take my seat by the window, which is good, because I can keep an eye on the wing this way and make sure it stays on. I watch the line of people sludge past, waiting for the human lottery of who will sit next to me if I happen to die a fiery death today. This turns out to be an older man with a neatly trimmed gray beard and a laptop, which he stows under his seat. Then he lays his head back and closes his eyes, and I'm alone again. The seat between us is empty, lucky me. I read the plastic card and follow along about the yellow evacuation slide and the seat as a flotation device, which we all know is a lie, but okay. Apparently the life jacket has a whistle attached, so that if you crash into the water from thousands upon thousands of feet and still manage to bob along in the sea, you can tweet for attention. People are reading magazines and eating snacks and sleeping while the rest of us are looking around for exit rows and thinking about death.

After we've nosed up and we're not wavering around and the blond lady starts bending over and fussing with the drink cart, I figure I can stop listening for noises of disaster and smelling for burning plane parts. No one would hunt for ginger ale if we were about to plunge. I turn my inner alert switch to standby, flip through the catalogue of expensive watches and dog carriers and minibars for the office. I read the in-flight magazine and look at pictures of Portugal and try to see if we're getting a movie.

I get a Diet Coke and a package of four peanuts and decide not to pay five bucks for headphones. I've got a hundred dollars Mom gave me for the whole trip, and I don't want to waste it. She took it from the envelope of money she keeps in her underwear drawer for emergencies, and I know there isn't much in there. So instead, I watch the movie with no sound—cars chasing each other and things blowing up and people's lips moving, and I don't feel I've missed much at all. Finally, we're about to land and I hunt under my seat for my shoes and accidentally grab the toe of the sneaker of the guy behind me and yank, which cracks me up. I even peek between the seats to see whose shoe I've just pulled, and it's some Asian guy with big glasses, who now has both feet tucked protectively to the side, which cracks me up further. My shoulders are going up and down, up and down in that laugh that tries not to be a laugh. You can see why I am never going to be the type to have two and a half million dollars.

I can tell the moment I'm off the plane that yanking on some stranger's foot will be the highlight of my trip. I walk down the airplane steps onto the tarmac, and even though it's evening, the air is balmy and breezy. The warmth, the strangeness of the climate, is a surprise. It's always a surprise, a sudden climate change, even when you know what to expect when you arrive. Maybe our mind can grasp the going from one part of the world to another in a few hours, but our body still works on some pretechnology basis that feels the wrongness of this. I almost don't recognize Dad—he has his hair cut very short on the sides and he's a lot more gray than the last time. But Jennifer is easy to spot. Her hair is piled on top of her head and she's wearing a sundress of manic oranges and yellows, and her sunglasses are still on even though it's dusk. She dangles a lei over one wrist, an oversize flower bracelet.

"There she is!" Jennifer says. She drops the lei around my head and there's the sudden bright smell of gardenias. "Aloha!"

"Sorry," Dad says. He looks dressed in an outfit not in his con-

Deb Caletti

trol—tan shorts with lots of adventuresome pockets, a T-shirt advertising some band called Dead Center with the picture of a bull's-eye (Dad's musical interest, far as I know, gravitates to, say, Elton John). He has a sweatshirt tied jauntily around his shoulders.

"What do you mean, 'Sorry'?" Jennifer says to my dad. "It's *tradition*." Jennifer is actually from Portland, Oregon. She met Dad when she came to the islands on a cruise ship with two girlfriends. Now she's embraced Hawaii as if her ancestors had paddled over from Polynesia in boats made from the husks of a banana tree.

"Good flight?" Dad says. Dad is funny with words. He can have an economy with language, like his conversation is on a diet. Then it can come spilling out in some dialogue binge.

We do the bad airport bumbling dance, where unfamiliar bodies and bags struggle for rhythm. Their car is parked in the airport lot. It's a small convertible, and my suitcase won't fit into the trunk in spite of a great deal of struggling on my father's part—various geometric shoves. So it sits beside me, just when I thought we were finally going to have time apart. Jennifer flips down the visor to make sure her face hasn't changed since the last time she looked. She hunts around in her bag and finds a circle container of lip gloss, smears one finger in a circle and applies it. She makes a gummy smack with now-shiny lips and the car has the limp odor of something fruity.

"Well," Dad says.

"I know," I say. "Pretty weird, huh?"

Jennifer takes a breath. "I just think, if this is what he wants to do, then why not just let him? I mean, the guy has obviously thought this over before he did it. I don't understand why you can't just say, 'Hey, thanks,' you know, send him a note and tell him you understand what he's doing, what he's wanting . . ." She's shouting a bit, sitting sideways in her seat so both Dad and I can hear. We're out on the main road now, and the wind is loosening the strands of hair around her face, making a few stick to her shiny lips.

"Jen," Dad says. It is only one word; no, not even a whole word, and to me it could mean anything. *Jen, can I change lanes or are we about to be hit by a papaya truck? Jen, are you sitting on my sunglasses? Jen, you have hair stuck on your lips.* But apparently Jen understands Dad's shorthand language. She's got the internal lemon juice that's rubbed on his words to make the secret message appear underneath.

"Oh, come on," she says to him. "Don't even give me that."

This time he merely gives his head a tiny shake. I see it in the rearview mirror. "I don't believe you, I really don't," she says to this. "You honestly find that immoral in some way? Sheesh."

Perhaps I am learning the trick to conversing with this man who is my father. It's like talking to one of the palm trees lining the road where we are driving. You say whatever you want, and when they swish and shush a bit in the breeze, you respond how you please.

I sit quietly in the backseat, feeling suddenly prim and awkward. I sneak a look over to my traveling companion, who just sits in solid black stodginess. Their arguing, if you can call it that, has brought on a bout of good behavior on my part, the nervous silence of an unwanted guest. I wonder what's going on at home. Three hours' time difference, and Mom would be back from work. I picture her hunting under the bed for her second slipper and see Severin clicking open a three-ring binder to put in his AP Government homework, thoughts of Kayleigh Moore dancing in

Deb Caletti

his head. Trevor would be finishing his last delivery, slamming the rolling metal door on the back of the delivery truck down for the last time of the day, locking it up and saying *See ya* to Larry Jakes or Vic Xavier, who is half Trevor's size, but who can lift an Amana Radar Range off the truck by himself, according to Trevor.

We pull up to Dad and Jennifer's house, a bungalow just a few steps from the beach, with tile floors and pictures of orchids and birds of paradise that Jennifer has painted in watercolors, and furniture that's all bamboo and tropical-flower cushions. The doors and windows have been left open and Dad drops his sweatshirt immediately onto a kitchen chair when we come in. Jennifer says she's tired and goes off into their room, and Dad pours some pineapple juice into a cup in the shape of a tiki man and hands it to me. He makes me a tuna sandwich, puts potato chips inside. It's just the way I like a tuna sandwich, without even telling him, and I wonder how he knows this. Keiko, Jennifer's golden retriever, has devotedly followed me around since I arrived and is now sleeping in a half circle at my feet.

"How's everyone?" Dad says. "How's your mom?" He looks toward the bedroom door as he says this, as if the word will seep through the crack under the door for Jennifer to hear.

"Fine, yeah," I say. "Good."

"How's Bex? Your brother?"

"Great. Bex is in this new phase. She's collecting money for tsunami victims."

"No way. No kidding?" He smiles, chuckles. "A school project? That reminds me of you, selling those magazines in the first grade. Remember that? They gave you some prize you wanted, an AM/FM pen radio or something, and we went all around the neighborhood, knocking on doors? I bought, like, four magazines myself. It would have been cheaper to buy you a stereo. I got a yachting magazine, or something, golf . . ."

"Better than *Cosmo*," I say. I chuckle with him. I crunch into my sandwich. His face looks happy for the first time that night, so I don't want to tell the truth, that I don't remember this at all. Actually, I'd forgotten that he knew things about me, things I didn't know. But a good chunk of our relationship is based on things that happened in the past, and if I decide not to acknowledge his memories, we might be left standing on an empty ballroom floor, not knowing how to dance.

"We had so many damn magazines coming," he says, laughing. "But you got your radio."

"That made me so happy," I say, but I'm only guessing.

"Happy," he says. He rubs his jawline. "Have you thought about it, In? What it might mean, having that money? The effect of it? Who you might be, with it or without it?"

"I'd be myself, richer, I guess."

"I don't know, In. I don't know. Maybe you'd be less of yourself. I worry. A person can rely on what they have, rather than what they are. . . . Isn't that what the chorus of voices even tells us? To look away from ourselves and toward *things*?"

"I don't know," I say.

"Buy it, have it, get this and you'll be that? I think this is the world's opinion, In. And I distrust the world's opinion."

"You rebel," I say. I ball up my napkin, toss it at him.

"I'll take that as a compliment, thank you. It's easy to go along. But all the great men have been nonconformists."

"Get some dreadlocks, Philosopher Dad," I say.

"Ha, can you see that? Jennifer would shoot me. Just, In? Listen to yourself. It's harder than it sounds."

Deb Caletti

"Myself says that potato chips are awesome in tuna," I say. "Myself says that the thought of you in dreadlocks is hilarious." He tosses my napkin back at me. We stay up a little while more, talking about Bex and Severin. We make a plan to see the Vespa guy in the morning. It's not as bad talking to him as I imagined, not at all. We're clicking along really nicely, as a matter of fact. It's him and me, which I thought would be bad, but it's him and me, and that's what's actually kind of nice. I'd forgotten that part about Dad, the misplaced dreamer-academic, the human equivalent of a soul walking an empty beach. I'd forgotten that I like those kind of people. And besides, he has lines around his eyes that crinkle when he smiles.

"Want more juice?" he says. I accept another glass, to bring to my room.

"I'm sick to death of pineapple juice, you want to know the truth," he says as he pours. "But Jennifer likes to have it around. Vitamin C, all that. Healthy diet food."

We say good night. He gives me a sort-of hug, an arm around my shoulders. "You're getting so big," he says.

"Maybe I'd better start on the pineapple juice diet," I say.

"You know what I mean," he says. "Grown up. A young woman. Well, let me know if you need anything."

I pat Keiko's head, close my door with the abandoned dog on the other side. I can feel her there, her eyes on the door, watching over me. My room is a small rectangle with twin beds that have palm tree bedspreads. There's a large photo of a sunset on one wall, and a painted sign that says, KO KAUA PALEKAIKO! with OUR PARADISE! underneath. Jennifer's paint supplies are stacked in one corner and Dad's books creep along one wall. I set my tiki man on a shiny teak bedside table. I feel like I'm inside a suntan lotion commercial or one of those old Elvis movies where he surfs. The pillowcase smells like no one's been in the room in a while. Keiko is whining on the other side of the door. I have a pang of sympathy for my dad then. It's regret on his behalf, something he may or may not feel for himself. It had to be hard, being the kind of person who always thinks. The sad part was, he left one cliché for another—suburban cliché to a Hawaiian-themed one. I wonder then if it's easier to forgive when the life of the person you're forgiving seems to not have gone the way they intended. Maybe it's easier to be generous in that case. But I feel a small piece of something else inside too—I'm a little pissed. If he left us who loved him, he should have at least made sure it was worth it.

I guess forgiveness, like happiness, isn't a final destination. You don't one day end up there and get to stay. It's there, it's not there. It's in and out, like the surf I could hear outside my window as I lay in that bed. Sometimes forgiveness is so far away you can barely imagine its possibility, and other times, surprising times, like when a tiki man is looking at you from a bedside table, it is a sudden, unexpected visitor who stays briefly before moving on.

Deb Caletti

8

The next morning Jennifer emerges from the bedroom with a wide smile; she's wearing a tiny sarong skirt and a tight white tank top spilling boobs. It's cloudy out, but they're the kind of clouds that lack any real ambition other than to temporarily annoy. They'll blow off soon; you can tell because the air is warm, minus any true marine-cool bite. Dad has already opened the windows again, and you can hear the *tick-tick-tick* of palm leaves swishing. He's reading the paper while we drink coffee, and I don't mind that. There's no angsty-hollow in our silence, just sleepy morning comfort, which may be in part because I barely slept last night. I had that other-place alertness, where you hear the air conditioner whoosh and the refrigerator buzz; where it's dark and still dark and still still dark, where the dark hours go on forever, and you think about everything that can't be solved as you lie in bed until you finally get sleepy when the windows begin to edge with light.

Even if I'd gotten the best rest of my life, I think I still might be sleepy here, because everything's sleepy—the breeze, and the sound of the surf, and the warmth. It's like living in a nap. We're supposed to pack the car in another fifteen minutes or so to head over to Richard Howard's house. I'd be nervous, but it's hard to be nervous where people are usually barefoot.

"Aloha!" Jennifer says. Her voice is pink and cheery as the inside of a grapefruit.

"Morning," I say.

"You've made a friend," she says to me, and Dad looks up from his paper, his glasses at the end of his nose. "Keiko slept outside your door all night."

Dad tilts his head back to view her better from the bottom half of his glasses.

"What?" she says. She knits her eyebrows together. Her voice has slid to a ledge and stopped.

"Nothing," he says.

"My outfit," she says.

"It's fine," he says. But even I can tell it's not completely fine to him. Maybe it's the spilling boobs that bug him, I don't know. He can be conservative in ways that aren't Republican.

"What's sa-rong with it," I say. "Ha-ha."

"You look great," he tries again, and this time, I'm convinced too. Whatever bothered him is gone now, and he goes back to his paper, his toes hooked behind him on the rung of the counter stool.

"I feel bad, just surprising the guy like this. I wish we could call," I say. I pour another cup of coffee. I'm hoping it'll work some reality magic on me. My eyes are hot with fatigue and I'm having one of those out-of-body moments when I see where I am but can't quite grasp it. I'm in my father's kitchen. I am holding a glazed brown sloped mug decorated with Polynesian flowers, which has a chip in it. We are discussing the return of more money than I might see in my lifetime. There should be music playing behind us, or a laugh track. I should be eating popcorn, watching me, wondering what will happen next.

"His phone's not hooked up yet," Dad says to his paper. "Not much else we can do."

"Hopefully he'll be there."

Deb Caletti

"Five minutes away," Dad says. "We'll go back later if not."

He turns the page. Sleepy ease is being shoved and bullied from the room by Jennifer's ice-cave silence. She walks to the kitchen, her feet making soft slaps on the tile. She looks in the refrigerator and brings out the pineapple juice, clanks the can on the counter. You can feel the pissed-off chords playing in the room, so hey, I'm outta here.

"You guys ready in ten, fifteen?" I say. I'm hoping to have this done with, quick. I'll give back a check that could change my life, maybe go to the beach and swim. Maybe I can't fund my dream to stalk Hunter Eden from concert to concert, but I can make Melanie jealous by bringing back a good tan.

"Meet you at the car," Dad says.

I brush away my coffee breath, change out of my sweatshirt to my T-shirt from the guitar exhibit at the Experience Music Project. It's getting hot already. I find my flip-flops in my backpack. Dad and Jennifer are back in their room with the door shut, so I head out front and wait by the car.

Dad's house is in a clump of other, various-size homes near the beach. His is the closest (and the smallest)—you can actually walk right out onto the sand through a small gate from his backyard. I lean against his car and the metal is warm; it zaps straight through the fabric of my shorts and T-shirt. It smells so good out here—salty and sweet-flowers both, a pinch of that ocean odor of cold, seaweedy vines washed up. Trevor would love it here. I wonder if Mom would—I picture her here in this house instead of Jennifer, but my parents have been divorced long enough that the thought of them together seems odd and even makes me feel slightly panicked. Mom would fuss with sun lotion and worry about jellyfish and warn Bex to come in from the surf, and Dad's dreamy semi-there-ness would drive her nuts. It would be too hot to cook, too hot for quilts or tea that Mom likes. Then again, maybe she would like to drag a stick behind her to make a line in the wet sand. Maybe she'd like to wear a ponytail all the time and eat food that doesn't require constant supervision.

I watch a muscle-y neighbor strap his surfboard to his car (you'd have watched too), and then when that fun's done, I realize I've been standing out here for too long. Keiko sits under a palm tree in the shade, eyes glued to me. It's funny about dogs, how they have these jobs they take so seriously—the guarding, the watching, the following. We just go about our business and don't even notice the singular, focused intent of their world and of their life's work. They should all get raises.

Keiko's tongue is lolling out, so I check her water bowl and refill it with the garden hose and take a drink myself and spill water down my front and then start to get the restless pissed-offness of waiting in the heat. Especially now that I realize I am completely wrong about nerves and the islands. My stomach is starting to tap-dance at the thought of seeing the Vespa guy. *Richard Howards*, I remind myself. I see his name in my mind, signed on that line of the check. "Dad!" I yell childishly.

No answer and I wait a few more minutes until *can't-wait* surges with sudden urgency. I'm fine one minute, but now I'm not fine, and filled with Now. I lean through the open window of the car and beep the horn. I'm done being the polite guest because I'm just me after all, and that's my annoying father.

Dad emerges, running his hand over his hair. His Hawaiian shirt is flapping as he trots to the car. "Longer than ten minutes," he admits.

"I'm getting gray as you," I say. "How long will Jennifer be?"

Deb Caletti

"She's staying."

"Oh," I say.

"Keiko can come," he says.

I clap my hands and she runs over in full-out dog joy. Keiko climbs into the car, her beard dripping water from her bowl, and I climb in the front. The seat is hot on my legs and I lift them up, set my feet on the dashboard with intention to ride like that. "Trade one bitch for another," I say, and it's out of my mouth before I realize it. I don't even mean it how it sounds. It's just one of those jokes that slip past the guards of rightness. Look, I don't see the guy very often and I want things to go well, and insulting his wife is not exactly the way to make that happen. I don't even really think she's a bitch. Just slightly grating the way fluorescent lights are grating. Maybe slightly greedy, too; the kind of people whose self-focus seems a small and daily thing.

I sit upright and look over at Dad in marginal horror, grasping around for apology, when he opens his mouth wide and lets out this huge laugh. My God, it's just this big *Ha!* and I relax and smile and apologize anyway.

"I didn't mean that how it sounded," I say.

"It's okay," he says, and I see that it is. Maybe more than okay. I think he likes having someone on his side. He seems to be a man who's been on a deserted island, and I'm the one who appears with sympathy for his situation and some food and a phone made out of a coconut.

We drive, and Keiko's lips are blown open in a windy dog smile. We are curving our way along the ocean, and bits of clouds are peeking open and showing blue, and when this happens the ocean gets sparkly and the waves tipped with white. It's funny, but Hawaii looks just like Hawaii. Like it should, from the pictures.

"So pretty," I shout, and Dad just nods. He turns on the radio and there's some seventies song and he lurches his head to the beat, which is something I'd advise him against, as he looks a bit like those dashboard figures with the bobbing heads. The song is from the time when guys called their woman "Pretty Mama" and people were doing it in Chevy vans. It's okay, though, as he looks really happy. It's like I'm just getting to watch him be himself when no one's around. And then I look down, at the yellow envelope at my feet. When I see it, the lightness I feel is shoved aside and a gnarl of nerves wind in my stomach.

"How far?" I say.

"Five miles?" Dad shrugs. "Dan Shugman's old place," he says, though this means nothing to me.

"Weird. So close to you. Do you think if I'd have mentioned Costa Rica he would have gone to Costa Rica?"

"When I was in college? I once took a trip to Jamaica because I overheard some guy talking about it on the bus," Dad says. "Then again, Hawaii's sort of all-purpose, user-friendly for disappearing, right? You can drink the water."

We drive past an outdoor shopping mall, with dresses and shirts in Hawaiian fabrics hung in doorways of stores to attract tourists. There's a grocery store, the clang of shopping carts, and then we are back by the ocean again, driving against the backdrop of a lush mountain painted in a hundred shades of green. We pass a string of big hotels and then a busy stretch of road, with cars parked along both sides. Here, the ocean is dotted with reds and yellows and greens, colors of surfboards, people riding waves and crashing; long, smooth rides, and short, ditched ones, ending in arcs of white splashes.

"Wow, look," I say, though of course he's seen this a million

Deb Caletti

times. Dad only nods, flips his turn signal on. We curve our way up a hillside; climb a small cliff until the ocean is below us, looking suddenly both smaller and larger. The houses here are newer, not the small shaky haphazard ones of Dad's neighborhood. Some are huge, with walls of glass and peeks of swimming pools. Dad turns into a driveway of a creamy house that's notched into the cliff side. There's a small patch of lawn and two palm trees, and while the house is smaller than its neighbors, it's new and clean and the view is wide and stretches along the coast.

"We're here," Dad says. He cuts the engine, and Keiko is already trying to shove to get out.

"Dan Shugman's old place? I was expecting something with a grass roof and a Folger's can to pee in," I say.

"Dan Shugman's a classy guy. He moved out to the golf course," Dad says. "How about I'll check and see if Mr. Howards is here." Dad pops out of the car, but hey, forget it. I pop out after him. It's bad enough that *I'm* surprising the Vespa guy, let alone my dad. I close the door on Keiko, who looks shocked and affronted. I trot to the front door. Dad rings the doorbell. I hear its hollow sound echo in the house.

We wait for the sound of footsteps. Nothing. Dad cups his hands around his eyes, leans up against the glass next to the front door. "Lots of boxes," he says.

"Move over," I say. I cup my hands too, and look inside. Boxes, all right. Stretches of wood floor empty of furniture. Wadded-up paper, a couple of glasses unwrapped and set on the countertop bar that separates living room from kitchen. A large, ugly black and brown clay vase is lying on its side on some bubble wrap. Glass doors lead to a pool hanging over the cliff. Not a bad way to run away from home.

"He's not here," Dad announces.

"Brilliant deduction, Sherlock," I say.

"Let's go and come back."

It's disappointing, because now I'm ready. Ready is like that. Ready is the reluctant guy on the dance floor. You ask him and he says no; you ask again, drag him by his wrists, and when he's finally there, after a few steps, the music fills him and he's cutting loose like there's no tomorrow.

"Lunch?" Dad says.

"Didn't we just eat?"

"What's that got to do with anything?" he says, pretty sensibly, if you ask me. "Onion rings? Let's go by and see Neal first. We've got two new guys and your old Pop can't stay away from work one day, right? If you tell Jennifer we stopped, she'll say she was right."

"It's our secret," I say. We're pals now, and this and the idea of onion rings fills me with a singular gladness. I feel a lift of hope, new things coming. Dad taps his thumbs on the steering wheel to the music that's not playing anymore. Keiko sticks her head between the seats so she can be part of things up front.

"I'm going to whack you with my elbow when I shift," Dad tells her, gives her head a soft push back. Keiko has a flexible personality, though. She changes her plan enthusiastically, shifts around in a needless circle and watches for other dogs out my side of the car. I hear her breathing just behind my ear.

We're back down the hill again, out where the hotels are, huge places with filled parking lots and open-air lobbies and layered, identical balconies. There are older hotels too, across the street, with names like Sea View written in blue script on their white-cement sides, little kids in partial bathing suits running up

Deb Caletti

and down outside corridors, pissing off their neighbors, though what can you expect at this price, honey? It's a place where wives wear their hair up in huge butterfly hair clips, and husbands look for the water wings in the suitcases and wish they'd stayed single. The buildings look past tense, the pools a bit murky, though maybe it's only by comparison that they suffer. Comparison is like that—we'd all be more satisfied without it, because across the road are bellboys in Hawaiian shirts and crisp tan shorts, greeting airport shuttle vans with luggage carts made from leggy curved brass.

Dad parks at a public beach entrance. The asphalt of the lot is covered with a coat of sand and my footsteps are gritty. Keiko knows this place, starts ahead without us. I take my shoes off when we reach the beach, and the sand is warm, but cool when I dig down my toes. The sky is only patchy clouds now, wisps on their way elsewhere, though a poofy train of looming white is on the horizon.

The beach is already filling. People from the hotels sit under grass-roofed umbrellas and shade tents; they lean against chairs with adjustable backs and foam cushions and fluffy, white hotel towels. Everyone else (including the poor suckers from across the street) lugs armfuls of stuff, bringing as many of the comforts of home as possible—red-and-white coolers of food and striped canvas bags of sun lotion and beach toys and magazines and sunglasses and cameras to record it all. I hear a radio—*You make a grown man cryyy-iiii*—owned by someone who either assumes we all share his love for Mick Jagger or else doesn't care if we do or not.

"Any of this look familiar?" Dad says. We're trekking across the sand and toward a block of beach layered with windsurf boards and sails and even a paddleboat or two. A little building behind us houses surfboards and boogie boards and life jackets and scuba gear. Two guys are out by the equipment, and one shouts, "Hey, Keiko! Hey, girl," and slaps his hands on his knees, and Keiko's rear starts swiveling like mad and then she's off, running toward her glorious, thrilled, dog-human reunion. Dad waves, and Neal takes one hand from the thick fur around Keiko's collar and waves back.

"You missed me, huh, boss? Can't stay away for two days. Or else you think I boarded up the place and ran off with the till? Right? Like that'd maybe get me to the other side of the island, if that," Neal says. "Maybe buy me a Coke. No, no, don't tell me. This can't be little Indigo. No way. No friggin' way. You picked up some hot chick at the Sunset Grill. You finally came to your senses and are gonna dump Miss High Maintenance. You're all grown up." He holds out his hand to me.

"Neal, you look exactly the same. Probably the same shirt, even," I say.

"I only got the one," he says, and gives up the handshake and puts one big paw around my shoulders in a hug. Neal was Dad's first employee, and we had lunch with him when we visited before. You can tell he and Dad are close, but in the teasing, punching-arm way a lot of grown men are close. Verbal jabs mean love, and that plus many years means they'll be there for each other's hospital visits and family funerals. Neal is a native Hawaiian, and I mean it when I say he hasn't changed. He's got the age-defying genes of Polynesian men, and he's brown and bulky-muscled in his tank top, wide-smiled, kindly-eyed. He could be twenty-five as easily as forty-five. I think he's got something like five kids, which makes me wonder if Mrs. Neal shows her age for both of them.

Deb Caletti

One of the guys from the shack calls out to Neal "Windsurfer!" And a paunchy tourist in his midforties with dark hair dyed blond and a mean-looking goatee approaches Neal while tucking his wallet into his back pocket.

"What's your name?" Neal says.

"Dean," the guy says.

"Okay, Dean, you done this before? Big guy like you knows what he's doing before he takes this baby out, right?"

"Of course," the guy says. His *of course* is an insulted one, a shove to the front of some competition. I can tell which one is his wife on the beach. She's sitting on a towel and looking nervously our way. "I know what I'm doing."

"We got a lesson today," Neal says. He checks his watch. "Thirty minutes."

"I don't need lessons," Dean says. "I'm a soccer player."

Neal shrugs. He hauls the Windsurfer to the edge of the water. He's so strong, he looks like he's carrying an envelope. He trots back to us, leaves Dean to struggle with the Windsurfer as if he's suddenly been handed a squirming sumo wrestler. I can see his arm muscles quivering from the beach. He gets the sail upright at just the moment a wind gust comes, and he shoots out to sea. His wife has her hand up to her eyes, shading out the sun, watching Dean get smaller in the distance.

"Chump," Neal says. "He'll need the rescue boat, I guarantee it. Friggin' mainland athletes. Friggin' *jocks*."

Dad chuckles. We follow Neal to the shack. Keiko's already there, getting a drink from her work bowl.

"That guy signed all the waivers, right?" Neal says.

"Yesiree," one of the guys behind the counter says. He taps the clipboard with his knuckles. "Hey, boss."

"Zach," Dad says. He uses the guy's name instead of a hello. "This is my daughter Indigo. And Eric, over there."

"Hey," Eric says. He's drinking from a bottle of Koala, a mixed-continent metaphor, and is peeling the label with his fingernails. New guy.

"Hi," I say.

"Great name," Zach says. "Indigo, not Eric." He chuckles at himself.

"Credit her brilliant father," Dad says. "Thoreau. 'The night is a different season. . . . Sweet-fern and indigo weed in overgrown wood-paths. . . .'"

"Etcetera, etcetera," Neal says.

"I was named after a weed? That explains a lot," I say.

"A beautiful weed," Dad says. "I never told you?"

I shake my head. "I just thought you had a thing for different names. Maybe you liked blue."

He throws his hands up in a *What're-you-going-to-do-with-a-father-like-me* gesture. "Now you know it was Thoreau's fault. So, we're going to go eat. Onion rings."

"Yesss!" Zach pumps one arm, giving us a fluffy view of a swath of armpit hair.

"Looks like everything's under control here," Dad says.

"The minute he's gone, bring the dancing girls back out," Neal says.

Keiko's a bit confused at the short workday. Dad has to call her three times, and Neal has to urge her on before she heads out with us. Keiko's obviously very responsible on the job. We head down the beach. Dean's just a dot on the horizon now.

"What's going to happen to Dean with the mean goatee?" I ask.

Deb Caletti

"Lost at sea, eaten by sharks. But he sure could play soccer," Dad says. "Nah, his wife there is going to have to pay sixty-five bucks for the barge to go and fetch him. We make more profit on guys like that."

We trudge over to Crabby Bill's, a beach bar with outdoor seating. We sit at the counter, on high stools with woven seats. They obviously know Dad; the bartender puts in his order between pushing blender buttons. "Two," Dad says. The bartender nods. He's quick—he's facing us and then there are the apron strings tied behind his back and then he's with us again. "Wade here," Dad says, "is a real talented singer. If you were staying longer, I'd take you out to the Kingfisher, where he performs. This is my daughter, visiting from the mainland," Dad says.

"Aloha," he says. "I'm a better singer than a bartender, that's for damn sure." But I wonder. He's off again, zipped to the other side of the counter. Wade is fun to watch. He's shooting colorful liquid into cups and flipping down soda handles and pouring icy deliciousness from blenders and chatting with the customers and joking and making people smile. It's just before noon, so the place is starting to fill, but Wade's got it handled. I know what this feels like. He's swinging in the rhythm of his work and loving it, and it makes me miss Leroy and Jane and everyone back at Carrera's.

Wade sets down two tall icy glasses of piña colada. "No booze. Sorry, kiddo, it's the way he likes it, what can I say. We're not all sane, rational people, are we?" He smiles and then he's off again, wipes down the counter and sets two coasters down in front of a new couple at the bar. "Hot enough for you folks," he says. "What can I getcha?"

We're actually having piña coladas in Hawaii, which seems

pretty hysterical, but as I sip through my straw, I find it cool and frothy, a coconutty heaven. And, well now, the onion rings arrive, and they're beautiful oniony art. Large and piled high, the Leaning Tower of Pisa in fried brown crisp. They're so hot, I can barely touch them, but Dad plucks one right off and bites. Keiko sits up straight, hoping Dad'll notice her best behavior and fine posture and reward her with a dropped nibble.

"I like Wade," I tell Dad. "All your friends." And I do. I'm feeling bighearted. I like the entire world right then. I like every single soul, with those onion rings in front of me. I even have a pang of fond goodwill for poor windsurfer Dean, who is probably about now coming face-to-face with his own mortality.

"It's a fine life, it really is," Dad says, though he too is under the spell of grease and salt. "But I miss you kids. Sometimes I wonder—"

"Oh, shit!" I say. You may think I just spilled ranch dipping sauce right down my front just then, but that's not what happened. No, not at all. "Oh my God." I grab Dad's elbow.

"Indigo, what?"

"It's him."

"Who?" Dad's lips are shiny. He wipes them with a napkin.

"Vespa guy. Shit! Right there! Stage right."

He's sitting at a table in the covered outdoor section of the restaurant in front of us, a grass-roofed place with ceiling fans and fishing nets and glass balls decorating the walls. He's wearing blue swim trunks and his shirt is a bright, thirst-quenching green. The waitress moves away from his table after placing down a hefty plate of a hamburger and fries in front of him. He's progressed beyond just coffee, I see.

I slap my hand to my heart. "Oh, man. This is so weird. It's

Deb Caletti

him. He was there, in Nine Mile Falls. Now he's here in Hawaii and I'm in Hawaii."

Dad knows what I mean. "That guy gave you two and a half million dollars," he says.

Seeing him, the real him, makes this suddenly more unbelievable. I can almost wrap my mind around the fact when it's just me and the fact, alone in my own mind. You can talk yourself into making sense of almost anything. We still have wars and capital punishment and guns in people's houses and we all go, uh-huh, yeah. Women talk themselves into writing to convicted murderers. So, you know, the mind is fairly flexible. Still, I can't grasp the idea that the man there—who is now lifting the bun from his hamburger and placing the lettuce and pickle inside, leaving behind the onion, reaching for the ketchup bottle—has given me a fortune as a tip for a cup of coffee.

"That's him?" Dad says. "I pictured him different."

"Like how? Dashing jet-black hair?" I think of the disappointing Mr. Moore.

"Top hat and tails? Uberhuman?" Dad says. The Vespa guy is thwopping the bottom of the ketchup bottle. "Look at that shirt, though. That's not Jack's Shirt Shack."

"Elegance followed him here," I say.

"Want me to go and talk to him?"

My eyes don't leave Vespa guy. He's leaning over a hamburger, his blond head tilted slightly to the side for the bite.

"No. I've got an idea. Hang here a sec."

I scooch back my stool; take an on-the-way sip of my drink. Dad calls Keiko to stay. My heart is whumping away, but it's not a dread whump, more an excited one. Funny thing is, I'm really glad to see him. I feel like I would if I turned a corner on this island of Maui and there was Leroy crossing the street, or Funny, emerging from a store with a shopping bag under one arm. I came to see this man, but the actual him is a happy surprise.

My grand entrance sucks, because I can't figure out how to get to that part of the restaurant, and on first try, I end up near the restrooms. Chick in triangle skirt, boy in boxy suit. Back up and try again, and I see Dad gesturing like a madman from his seat, arm flinging and pointing the other direction, thanks Dad. There's a little gate to walk through and then I'm in the restaurant, passing tables, and I swear Vespa guy looks up and right at me, but he doesn't know it's me-me. He probably thinks I'm familiar but can't think of from where.

I approach his table. "Can I get you some extra napkins," I say. "Or a refill? They're free." I don't know if they're free or not.

"No, thanks," he says. He looks down. I don't move. He looks up again. "No. Wait. Wait a minute." And then he breaks into a big toothpaste-ad smile. "My God, wait a minute. Indigo Skye? My God. What are you doing here? I didn't even recognize you."

"Mr. Howards. I'm here to see you."

"You're kidding. How did you find me? How did you know where I was?"

"You said . . . I said—I told you about my dad. Maui. It was the first place we checked. You could have been anywhere . . ."

"Note to self: Work on predictability."

I laugh. "It's a good thing your imagination wasn't more wild."

"In my defense, I also considered Bali. All right? Give me a few points for that. But, passports . . . What are you *doing* here?" He seems genuinely baffled. "Because of the *money*?"

"It's not exactly what people . . . People don't just do that."

Deb Caletti

"Well, I highly recommend it. It feels great. I wanted you to have it. That's why I gave it to you."

"It was . . . a lot." I laugh, maybe a little hysterically. "Okay, this was beyond a lot. Fifty bucks is a lot."

"Look, I didn't give you my last dime or anything. I just spread it around. Got rid of it—gave it to people it made me happy to give it to. This is the best decision I've ever made. You've got to understand that. *I wanted to.* Trust me, I've never felt better. Here. You want to sit?" He pushes out the chair across from him with his foot.

"My dad's over there." My dad, apparently a skilled lip-reader, raises his arm and waves.

"Your dad. You mentioned him." Richard Howards arcs his arm, gestures my father over. Dad winds his way to us, balancing the dish of onion rings and our glasses. Keiko follows, even though I doubt she's supposed to be in this part of the restaurant. No one seems to mind.

Dad holds out his hand. "William Skye. Will. I'm the dad."

"Richard Howards. I guess you played a part in my being here. Maui—I heard the word, and it was . . . *yeah.*"

"Well, at least the hamburgers are good," Dad says.

"Oh man, the best. Hey, pup," he says to Keiko, who sits down politely. "I'm sorry you went to the trouble of flying out here, though," he says to me. "If you're trying to give me my money back, I don't want it."

"It was very generous . . . ," Dad says.

"You say "generous," but you think "crazy," right? Or that I want something? I don't, okay? That's exactly it—I don't want anything. I don't want anything anymore. Just this." He gestures to the air in front of him, the right-now air. "Here, it's enough. A cheeseburger is enough." He lifts the second half of his hamburger, shakes it a little in Dad's direction. "If you moved out here, you understand why I am too."

"I didn't give away two and a half million dollars when I came. Of course, I didn't have two and a half million dollars," Dad says.

The waitress comes, offers Richard Howards a refill, which I guess they really do have. I smile at her—I'm always especially nice to other restaurant workers. When she leaves, Richard Howards leans forward on his elbows. "So, you may know this. But I started this little computer company," he says. "Zeus?"

Dad's eyes widen, and I have one of those shock-moments, when you actually stop breathing. Even Dad, who thinks a "hard drive" is something that happens only when there's bad traffic, knows that Zeus is one of the biggest search engine companies around.

"So, you've heard of it," he says.

"I thought your name sounded familiar," Dad says.

"Listen, it was great at first. But a lot of things that you think will widen your world can eventually imprison you. Right? Am I right? A marriage, some relationship, a job, a *concept*—success, religion? Can start to swallow you whole, if you let it. You don't watch out for your spirit, and before you know it, *bam*. You're in service to this *it*. I don't know if I'm making sense."

"To me you are," Dad says.

"You end up feeling like you've been put in a box. And then a smaller box yet. You can't even breathe."

"Yeah, I remember I lost sight of my ability to just go for a *walk*. To watch the sky and be a human being," Dad says.

Richard Howards nods. "I know. You can't even remember

Deb Caletti

who you once were. I wanted out so bad but I didn't know how. I couldn't see beyond the walls. I don't know why. I'm a smart guy. But I couldn't get loose from the way I was seeing and the way I was living. The top flaps of the box were open all along for me to escape, but it seemed . . . impossible."

"Well, you lose the energy for escape. Until the balance tips somehow and it's finally harder to stay where you are—," Dad says.

"Exactly."

"Than to make that change."

"Exactly right."

"What happens is, you become a slave to another person's need, to other people's idea of what you should be. And hey, I wasn't anywhere near where you were. But, you listen to all the outside noise, and your own voice just doesn't have a chance," Dad says. "A lesson for you, In." He waggles his finger at me.

"It feels like a hundred years ago already. Lifetimes. I feel giddy with freedom," Richard Howards says. He looks it too. Younger, maybe? He is swirling a fry in a splotch of ketchup, pops it into his mouth. He's a different guy from the one who sat so very still at Carrera's, sipping that black coffee, staring outside.

"I'm glad you two understand each other," I say. There's a small scritch of irk lying somewhere near my surface, though. Dad's leaving meant leaving Mom, Severin, Bex, and me. Dad's box was a house with us in it.

Dad and Richard Howards look at each other for a moment, a man's moment, not too long to be intimate, long enough to convey the fact that they're not alone. "I don't want that money," Richard Howards says. "I'm not going to let another person or a group of people box me into who I'm supposed to be. Getting rid of this money—it's the emotional equivalent of dropping it from a skyscraper and letting it rain down. I'm having the time of my life giving it away."

"It was a bit of a shock," Dad says. "For Indigo."

"Was it too much? I was thinking, the taxes alone . . . Does it feel like a burden?"

I think of Mom, and Mrs. Olson with her liver spots and her cross necklace. I think of all those little envelopes on our kitchen table, with their narrow tissue-paper windows. Those envelopes, so heavy, and sometimes so feared that Mom would leave them unopened. I noticed that. The way she'd open the ones from school, or from magazine subscriptions she'd never order, or from Bomba. But she'd take those ones with the tissue-paper windows and set them aside, like they might burn her fingers if she touched them too long. Menopause was not her real problem, I knew. The money is not a burden. It is the end of all burdens. "It didn't seem right to take," I say.

"I'm giving freely. If you gave it back, it would hurt my feelings."

"I don't know how we could ever repay you," Dad says.

"Listen. Indigo? Just promise me one thing. Let it make you bigger, not smaller. Okay? Right? That's repayment enough."

I just look at him, and he's smiling at me, and I suddenly feel this largeness, this solemn swell of the momentous. This is real. And I'm not in shock anymore, I'm just . . . overcome. I blink. I could burst into tears right here, I think, into the now salty napkins. But the moment is too important even for that, held still in the tiny space of time between now and then, before and after. We're quiet, but Jimmy Buffett is singing about wasting away in Margaritaville and there's a burst of laughter from a table of six,

Deb Caletti

and a guy shouts, "And she wasn't even dressed yet!" and there's more laughter. But in my world, this world, there's the Vespa guy and Dad and Keiko and me, and my heart, which is trying its best to hold the fullness of unimaginable gratitude.

"Why me?" I say. Dad takes my hand and gives it a squeeze. My eyes prick with tears.

"That's exactly why, Indigo Skye," the Vespa guy says. "You ask 'Why me?' instead of 'Why not me?'"

9

Richard Howards invites us back to his house after he finishes his lunch. He has rented a motor scooter, not quite his orange Vespa back in Washington State, but he is obviously right at home on it. His shirt flaps as he drives. When we get back to Dan Shugman's place, there's a golf cart parked in the driveway, and some old guy who turns out to be Dan Shugman himself.

"Just seeing that you've got everything you need," he says. "And dropping off those extra keys I promised. Hey, William."

Dan Shugman's wearing crispy white old-guy shorts and a plaid shirt. He's got bright blue eyes and silver, straight Republican hair. But his twinkle is nonpartisan. You can tell he thinks the world is a fine place to play within. I like Dan Shugman right off.

"Come on in." Richard Howards is happy. "Dogs, too. My humble abode." He steps aside.

"Not too humble," Dan Shugman says. We step in, and the room is wide and bright. The windows look over a pool, and beyond, the sea. It feels good in here. I could sit and look out this window forever. "Looks so odd without the furniture," Dan Shugman says. "We had a piano over there." He points to the large windows. You can see the round indents from the piano legs still in the carpet.

"It's a beautiful place," I say.

"Now you won't worry that I gave away my last dime and am sleeping in a dim room on a thin mattress."

"I hereby stop worrying," I say. Keiko sits by my heels.

"You play the piano?" Dad asks Dan Shugman.

"Hell, no. No one played. Stupidest thing in the world, having pianos you don't play and dining room tables you don't sit at and china you look at."

"Big jewelry you never wear, or maybe worse, do wear," Richard Howards says.

"You've got an ex-wife," Dan Shugman says.

"And ex-jewelry," Richard Howards laughs. He's standing in front of the refrigerator. There's not much in there, I can see. Bottles of Henry Weinhard's Private Reserve, some cans of 7UP, several Styrofoam containers of leftovers. He hands Dad and Dan a beer, me a 7UP. I crack open the top, take a cool sip.

"I got some ex-diamonds," Dan Shugman says. "The wife would pick 'em out and I'd write the check." Dan Shugman's thumb and forefinger make pen squiggles in the air.

"Ex–exercise equipment," Richard Howards says.

"Amazing the shit you accumulate," Dad says. He's happy here too. "We have a teak hook to hang bananas on. At what moment in your life do you think you gotta have a teak hook to hang bananas on?" He takes a swog of beer.

"Right about the time you buy the 'I Heart My Pekinese' golf sweater," Dan Shugman says. "Sorry, all, but I've got to run."

Out the front windows I can see Dan Shugman drive away in his golf cart. We sit in Richard Howards's empty living room and talk until Dad finishes his beer and we come to that winding-down place, that feeling of a battery run down, when you know it's time to go. Dad and Richard Howards are pals now. Dad's promised to show him the place with the best Scotch in town. Richard Howards shakes Dad's hand and gives him a clap on the back.

The Fortunes of Indigo Skye   161

"See, Indigo Skye?" Richard Howards says. "You give it up and it all comes your way."

I guess it's true, because the Vespa guy is as light as a soda bubble. You can feel the good air in and around him. He is a wide sky, the same wide sky he can look at every morning and every night now. I nod. He takes my hand and we shake, and then I give up on that and give him a hug. You never know, you see, when or where you will stumble on a sudden connection, a lifelong bond with another human being. A hundred people can sit down in a booth and it will be eggs and toast. And another one, just one, will sit down and will change your life, be monumental with just coffee.

"Thank you," I say. The words are so small.

"Thank *you*," he says. "If it weren't for you, I might still be ingesting four thousand toxic chemicals."

"Stay away from those nasty things," I say.

"Never again," says the Vespa guy.

The next day, my plane doesn't leave until late afternoon. There's one more thing Dad wants to do with me, he says. So we put on our swimsuits that morning, leave Jennifer behind with her magazine and her Special K. Keiko's got to stay behind, because we'll be in the water. Dad's got the gear in his trunk already.

The beach where Dad finally parks is spotted with Dr. Seuss–ish beings with masks and snorkels and flippers, bodies of various shapes—large, bloated stomachs and tiny flat ones, muscled brown chests and bright pomegranate shoulders, noses smeared with streaks of white lotion. It's an I-don't-care beach, a beach of equals, a beach with a higher purpose than showing one perfect body to another perfect body. In the water the backs of people

Deb Caletti

float along the surface, the underside of flippers making an occa-sional showy flap, the curve of snorkels pointing skyward.

I'm a little afraid of snorkeling, I admit. There's a very rational (I think) fear of trying to breathe underwater, and then the strange-ness of oversize feet, and the occasional bursts of salt water in the mouth, and the coordination of all of the above. I did it once before when Severin and Bex and I visited, and even Bex, who's not the best swimmer, was paddling around fine while I was busy repeating the *don't panic, don't panic* mantra. I could stay under there only awhile before I'd flail around with the sudden splashy realization that I was doing something unnatural.

"So I'm going to give your mom the name of a financial advis-er I know over there. He's a great guy, you can trust him, even if he's . . . boring, okay? So don't give him trouble for being boring, Indigo. We need boring people in the world too, or else no one would be there to do our taxes."

"Okay," I say, because I don't know shit about financial advis-ers or accountants or banking. Mom set up a savings account for me years ago, and before last year when I started working at Carrera's, I had all of about twenty-six bucks in there. I've got maybe five hundred now, enough to pay for maybe a few college textbooks if I change my mind about going, not enough for col-lege itself. Certainly not enough to interest a boring accountant.

We sit on a rocky beach and Dad puts on his flippers, sliding his thumb under his heel with a thwap of rubber against skin. The mask is stuck on his forehead, so he looks like he's some kind of a large insect. "And I don't have any great advice for you, In. I wish I did. I want to say . . . stay true to yourself, but I know you'll laugh."

"Only because you look like a fly," I say. "I'm not worrying about staying true to myself. I know myself pretty well."

"Money changes things, In."

"What's all the ooh-ahh about money and change? It's like it's some voodoo curse. I plan on being me with more money."

"Okay, In."

"I don't see why that's not possible."

"I never had a lot of it, okay? But even when I had maybe more than average? It makes you see things differently. Like yourself. What you expect from other people." He's tucking his keys and our sun lotion and shoes under three layers of towels, protection against marauding thieves.

"I will stand true against the forces of e-vil," I say in a super-hero voice.

"I don't know how to explain it," he says. He's still tucking and hiding. "Not to say there's some kind of glory to being poor, because there isn't. There's nothing glorious about fear." Dad stands, brushes the sand off the butt of his swimsuit. "Just that for some reason, money can make you expect certain things, owed certain things. And some people think they're owed them just by virtue of having, not by virtue of earning. I guess that's the easiest way to put it. Are you ever going to put your flippers on?"

"Flippers are the most ridiculous thing one could put on their body," I say.

"Rainbow wig," Dad suggests.

"Bowling shoes," I say. I snap the flippers on, and Dad holds out his hand to help me stand. We flap, flap down to the water's edge, balancing with arms out like tightrope walkers, as everyone around does a version of the same act.

Dad gets there before I do. His feet are in the water, and he turns to wait for me. It's just another blue-sky day in Hawaii, and

Deb Caletti

the black lava cove we're in bends around us. "Here's my great advice," he says. He reaches out his hand, and I take it, hobbling the last few steps. "When it seems like too much, remember, *this* is the real world. Nature. Under here, no one cares about money, or about what race you are, or what car you drive. It's just another day of everyone swimming different directions, looking for food, staying well, being beautiful."

"One, two, three," I say, and we dive. It's the only way to do it, because no matter how warm the water is, diving in is always oh-shit cold.

At first, it's just murky green, small bits of floating algae, Dad's legs, the color of someone else's swimsuit going past. I keep focused on Dad (*don't panic, don't panic*), push my fins against the push back of the water. I follow, and then suddenly, right there below us, is a school of fish, bright yellow, and a few orange striped ones (clown fish, I think), and I remember all this, the unreal National Geographic thrill, the am-I-really-here astonishment, the creepy unease that a fish might swim against your bare legs, mixed with complete, goose-bumpy wonder. Dad's hair is serpent-wild, and he's gesturing to the fish below as if I could miss them. I nod, not that he can see me. I hear my own Darth Vader breathing, try to forget that I do, and then, with a few pushes of my legs, there's another color—blue like you've never seen blue, narrow fish with the vibrancy and shine of a first-place ribbon. And then a sad, scary guy, a spiky ugly brown puffer fish, headed right my way. I thrash around in sudden panic, flail my legs around, pop my head from the water. It seems so deep, but it's really shallow where we are. I can stand. The beach is right there—not a thousand worlds away like it seemed it would be. There's our rolled-up towels, that kid throwing rocks while his mom lies back on her towel with one eye peeking halfway open.

Dad stands beside me. I raise my mask. "That was amazing!"

He takes the rubber piece from his mouth. "Isn't it? It is amazing, each and every time."

"That puffer fish was coming right at me."

"He's more afraid of you than—"

"Don't even try that line on me. Let's go under again," I say.

We duck down again, and I follow Dad where he leads. It is up and down again, up and down, through my moments of panicky standing. We go one more time down, and Dad is pointing to sea anemones hiding in the rocks, when I see something round and large, heading past with purpose, wide feet paddling peacefully. I cannot believe my eyes; no, I cannot, because it is a sea turtle. A real, alive sea turtle swimming past in his own ocean home. I want to shout, do my flailing routine, but Dad takes my hand and for a moment we swim behind the turtle, giving him polite distance, paddle in his bubbly wake. And then he makes a right turn and he is gone, faster than us, the speed he's learned from being ancient.

I paddle back quickly to where I can stand, fling off my mask. "Oh my God, oh my God, oh my God, oh my God."

Dad's mask is on his forehead. His eyes are bright. "The real world, In," he says.

Jennifer stands with Dad at the airport, by his side. She hugs me good-bye, and I know I'll be taking her perfume home with me as a parting gift. Dad hugs me too. He holds my arms, looks at me hard. This is the first time I've been with him by myself, without Severin or Bex. It wasn't us kids and Dad this time, just me and him, two people. His eyes are wet. I think he might cry. I kiss his cheek.

Deb Caletti

"I love you," I say. It's true, I realize.

"I love you," he says. And that is true too, I know.

"I'll call you tomorrow," he says.

They stand there together when I leave, and when I look back over my shoulder to wave, they are still standing there. Jennifer is fishing for something in her purse, already moving beyond my visit, back to her own life, but Dad just stands there watching me, one hand tucked under his arm, the other cupping the side of his face. He sees me turn, puts his fingers to his lips, sends a kiss my way.

My eyes are hot with tears. That's my dad there. See? I am leaving him to go back to his life, of pineapple juice and Jennifer's paintbrushes and Neal and surfboards and windsurfers and Wade the bartender and the devoted Keiko. This time, I am leaving him behind. And I make a little vow then, to myself. To not let the backs and forths of forgiveness interrupt the steadiness of love. Dogs go on doing their job and we don't stop to notice, but sometimes, so do people. Maybe I didn't notice it before, but Dad was there, he was, his eyes never leaving my door. It was time, I guess, to let him in.

10

If I had a quarter for every time I heard the word "money" in the next few weeks at home, I'd be a millionaire if I weren't already a millionaire. Melanie was averaging four calls a day to either ask how I was going to spend it or recommending ways to, and Severin and Bex kept looking at me with the wide eyes of those starving African kids in the ads. Jane was acting weird, as if me and the me who had money were two separate people—she seemed irritated, as if I'd gone off and done something she disapproved of, and even pulled me aside to ask if she needed to find a replacement since I was probably leaving. Trina invited me to go shopping, and Funny suggested she write up a story about me for the paper. Not only did I tell her no, I vowed everyone else to silence, didn't breathe a word of it at school (not even to Liz or Ali or Evan). Still, KMTT, a local radio station, phoned and asked to speak to the waitress who got a really big tip, and KING 5 News knocked on the door. Severin told both that someone was playing a joke, but Severin's a crappy liar.

And Trevor—a few days after I get back home, he tells me he has a surprise for me. Surprise—you think flowers. Balloons. A life-size cutout of Hunter Eden he might have gotten at Tower Records. No way am I expecting what I do see when he pulls into our driveway. I hear him honking, and I run outside barefoot ready to be happily grateful. I stop on the walkway.

"Wow," I say.

There is an odd weight in my chest suddenly at the sight—

Bob Weaver, gleaming in brand-new orange-red metallic glory, and Trevor, leaning out the window, his smile as bright as the glints of sun on the Mustang's freshly painted hood.

"Doesn't he look like a fucking king? Some king of cars?"

"Wow," I say again. "You had him painted."

"I didn't think you'd mind. It would have taken me, what, five, six more months to save up the rest of the money? But now, why not just get it done? I couldn't wait to see your face."

Trevor springs from the car. The car door is still flung open, and he takes my face in his hands and kisses me hard.

He pulls back. "Baby, what's wrong?"

I wipe my wet mouth with the back of my hand. It is hard to say the words, because he looks so happy. They feel heavy, like I am pulling something hard but necessary. "Don't you think you should have *asked*?"

"You're kidding, right?" he says. He shakes his head, as if he didn't hear right.

"I think you should have asked," I say. My voice sounds thin, even to me. It stretches far and long, across some great expanse of distance that seems suddenly possible between us, some vast space I've never seen before.

"God, In," he says. "This is what, *crumbs*? A drop in the bucket? I thought you'd be *happy*. This doesn't even sound like you. We share everything."

Twisty tree roots of guilt wind up my insides. I shake my own head, to exile those thoughts. He is right. Crumbs. And yet, the small voice inside says, "everything" isn't the same everything it was before. "I'm sorry," I say. And I *am* sorry. "It's beautiful. I'd want you to have it done. Of course I do."

He pulls me close again. Kisses my hair. I close my eyes,

against the sight of new differences. "It's for us, In. Let's put the top down. I want you to see it with the top down too."

And let's not forget Mom. Mom, who is on her third talk with me. Now she calls me to the kitchen. She's got her yellow legal pad and pen and sits at the table with me across from her, same as the other two times. A yellow legal pad and a pen means a PLAN. She even has *PLAN* written across the top of the paper, same as she did during the last two talks that went nowhere.

"Indigo, we've got to make some decisions here," she says.

"I want to buy a house," I say. "For you."

"No, Indigo. I told you. No."

"No," Chico says. "No, no, no."

We might as well play a tape recorder. It's the same conversation we've had twice before. "Why are you being like this, Mom? I want to help. I want to make things easier for you."

"Pride, okay? Just let me have it." *College,* she writes. "We need to talk about college."

"As I said before. Of course we'll use the money for Severin's college. And Bex."

"And you."

"Mom."

She slaps the pen down on the paper.

"Cars," I say. "For everyone. You, me, Severin—"

"Too much. Too much at once," she says. "I don't want this to change us all suddenly."

"Then I'll buy my own."

"Fine," she says. But her voice has edges. She doesn't write down the word "car." Instead she doodles a dark spiral on the page, circle within a circle within a circle.

We are at some sort of standstill, and the argument is so new

Deb Caletti

and strange, we might as well be attempting to argue in a foreign language. "Look," I say. "I've had the money all of, what, a few weeks now? It's sitting nice and cozy in the bank. We don't have to make any decisions about it right this minute, do we? Can't I have a little time to get used to this?"

Mom sighs. She tilts her head back, looks up at the ceiling and shakes her head. "Money, money, money," she says. And right there, three more quarters earned.

"You know what the problem is?" Trevor says. "The problem is, you're treating this like a problem." We're talking on the phone. I'm sitting on my bed, legs folded. I stare at my guitar case across the room. For some reason, since I got the money, I can't open it. I haven't felt like playing. I don't know why, except that I don't know if I'm the girl who plays that guitar or not. I've got old-me and new-me pieces, and I'm not sure where they belong.

"You don't understand," I say. "Maybe it's just new. But everyone's different and it's bugging me. I don't know. Maybe I'm just adjusting to it." *"It"*—the word has its own definition. *"It"* means the money.

"In, you're not having any fun with this. This should be fun. This is, like, every person's *dream.*"

"It's hard to have fun when everyone is acting so weird. They're not relating to me. Just me with money. Already. My family, the Irregulars . . ." I don't mention Trevor himself. That'd put us on opposite sides, and I need him now on mine. "You should hear Jane. Her voice is all distant-cool. I don't get it."

"It's all new, In. And maybe, are you maybe reading too much into things?"

"I don't know." I trace the squares of my quilt with my finger.

"In, God! This is great! You're forgetting it's great. Okay, I know what we're going to do. We're going to go shopping."

"Shopping." Maybe he's right. I *have* forgotten the fun parts, haven't I? I've been sucked up suddenly into the weighty and spinning frenzy of Important Decisions.

"What's the point of having money if you don't spend it? What's the fucking *point*, In? Come on."

And right then, I'm sure he *is* right. I'm sure, because this small spoon starts stirring a little pot of glee inside. The glee of the traitor, the swapping over from *you shouldn't* to *why not?* Fun—permission internally granted.

"I don't understand why you don't just go for the big stuff right away," Trevor says. We're in Bob Weaver, who is gleaming so hard it's nearly a gloat, heading out for our planned outing of disposable income amusement. We just got fueled up with a double espresso and a brownie, and I am officially and legally high. "If it were me, I'd be getting a stainless steel beauty, freezer on the bottom, an ice maker, cubed or crushed."

A refrigerator. Hmm. With caffeine jazzing through me, everything seems like an exceptional idea. I have to force myself to stop and think. "Maybe tomorrow," I say. I see a folded sheet of notebook paper sticking out from underneath Trevor. He's sitting on it. I give a little tug and he moves a leg to free it. I unfold it and read.

"What?" I say. Happiness jets over to irritation. "What's this?"

"It's nothing," he says. "Just a few ideas." *Refrigerator*, it actually reads. *Car stereo. Floor mats.* The words run down the paper and extend to the other side.

"A list," I say. "But *your* list." And there it is again, suddenly,

Deb Caletti

some heavy feeling in my chest. Something that feels like anger but that might be disappointment. I'm hoping for anger. Anger is brief and vacates the premises quickly; disappointment is the uninvited guest that never leaves. I try for anger. "What, am I Santa and you've been a good boy?"

"*Ideas*, In. Come on, lighten up."

Nothing makes you feel less like lightening up than someone telling you to lighten up. But this is supposed to be a fun day. We have planned for fun, and when you plan for fun, you don't want a fight. Fights on days you've planned for fun are especially upsetting. I don't want to argue, not today. So I forcibly shove aside my prickles of pissed-off, which is easier than it sounds when millions of little sequined caffeine dancers are doing their big Broadway number on your internal stage.

We go to the mall. For the record, I hate the mall. I hate the mall music and the mall lights and the mall chicks with their mall chick outfits, and the mall foam boat that the screaming kids play on. I hate the mall women spraying you with mall perfume and the mall escalators (I always find the down when I need the up) and the mall parking lot. The only thing worse than the mall is the mall at Christmas.

But let me tell you something about the mall. The mall is a very different experience when you have money as opposed to when you don't. It's the difference between standing outside of somewhere and going in.

You can tell that Trevor and I are mall virgins, because we make strategic error number one right off the bat. Trevor doesn't want the Mustang scratched, so he parks on the top level of the garage, in the farthest-away spot, a spot that has its own zip code and isn't close to anything except the JCPenney photographer and the catalogue purchase return counter. I should have brought my hiking boots and compass and trail mix.

The main part of the mall . . . well, it's like being on the inside of a pinball machine. We bounce from flashing lights to flippers to bells. My mood improves by the second. This is way better even than the caffeine rush. By the time I get out of Radio Shack, Trevor has to make a trip to the car. I buy tiny televisions and travel alarm clocks and five cell phones (family plan), and a DVD player and a big-screen TV that will be delivered the next day. Headphones. Xbox for Bex. Games for aforementioned Xbox. Digital camera. Ipods, docking stations (whatever those are—Trevor says we need them), a laptop, a remote control robot.

Trevor wants to go into Victoria's Secret, but I say fuck off. It's my money, and I go into Sharper Image instead and I buy a travel pillow and massagers and something that measures your golf swing (Trevor likes this) and a weather forecaster and a machine to make our air pure and this thing to clean our jewelry, even though we don't have jewelry yet.

Trevor makes two more trips to the car, and I go clothes shopping. I start to get the hang of this, see, because I'm feeling this mall-with-money difference, this *I'd-own-the-world-if-I-wanted-to* buzz. Something is happening to me in here. I feel swingy and powerful, like Freud after he brings you a mouse head. The more I get into it, the more I get into it, if that makes sense. The noise, the lights, the credit card slide across the table; it's some Las Vegas high minus the Elvis impersonators. I buy shirts and jackets and a robe for Mom and shoes for Severin and a coat for him too, and outfits for Bex, skirts and sweaters, and this Harley shirt that comes with a matching key ring that Trevor likes.

I'm pretending I'm a millionaire and can buy anything I want

Deb Caletti

and I'm starting to believe me. We're walking through Nordstrom when Trevor starts to get whiny.

"Can we eat yet," he says. "C'mon, In. I'm tiii-red."

But there in the center of the store on the first floor is a place I've never gone. A non-Indigo place. A small perfumey universe of swively white chairs and women with high cheekbones and powdery faces and lab coats, which are supposed to make us think that eyeliner is a science that requires an expert. A place that says that real beauty can be bought only there; that the plastic packages of the drugstore mascaras and lipsticks are merely clownish frauds. Even looking over there gives me some scritch of insecurity, something I suddenly feel I need to overcome now that I could belong there. When you have money, you have Ziploc bags and not fold-over baggies. You drink Diet Coke and 7UP, not the "Diet Cola" and "Lemon Lime Drink" of the store brand. You fill up the whole gas tank, instead of buying the few dollars' worth you have in your wallet. You go to a salon, rather than cut your own hair or get a ten-dollar chop job at a place where everyone rushes out looking the same. And you come to this place, where a skilled professional with a cool demeanor guides you toward the power of beauty. It's a test. The big test. A fitting-in right of passage. A metaphorical journey from the two-dollar Wet n Wild lipstick of the masses to the seventeen-dollar lipstick that comes in its own glossy bag with a braided rope handle.

I step forward and try out a wealthy confidence. I sit down in one of the swively chairs. I am a millionaire. Once the lab coat is off, once they remove the jacket of superiority, these makeup counter women just go home and make a salad and get up the next day and put the lab coat on again.

"I'd like a whole new look," I say. The woman standing over

me has blond hair swooped up crescent-roll style, a poofy, decisive makeup brush already poised in her hand.

"The colors you're wearing are too harsh," she says. La-ti-dah, big deal.

"Your colors are fiii-iine, In. I want to go-oooo," Trevor whines.

The woman is wiping my face with a cotton ball dunked in something cool and stingy. "You have good lines," she says. "Let's make the most of them." It's a compliment and an insult both. She starts dabbing and dobbing, her face close to mine, warm breath smelling like what she had for lunch, making me shut my eyes and hold my own breath. I pop my eyes open, and yikes, hers are right there, large and staring at my mouth, and I slam my eyes shut again. Lip liner, eyes, brows—my skin pulls different directions, and then finally, "There. I'd recommend the number seventeen moisturizer, and the skin care line. You have large pores."

I look in the round mirror on the counter in front of me. I look airbrushed. Finished in a way I've never looked finished before. I'm afraid to blink, lest I crack myself.

"You look great," the woman says.

"Right," Trevor says. "Except for the hair, she looks like you. Fuck, they all look like you," Trevor grouses, swooping his hand in a wide motion to include all the women in all the swively chairs.

"Don't mind him," I say, moving my lips like a ventriloquist. "He just needs lunch. I'll take it all," I say.

I have to ride home sitting on the Motorized Bumper Boat, with the Turbo Hair Groomer and the shower radio wedged under my

Deb Caletti

elbows and the espresso machine and alcohol breath-screening device under my feet. Trevor perked up after I bought him a hot dog and fries and an Orange Julius, extra large. We pull into the driveway and he honks the horn like mad, scaring Freud, who leaps from the open window of Mom's car, where he was sleeping but knows he shouldn't have been sleeping. He jets across the lawn and hides under the front hedge. Bex runs out the front door.

"Christmas and every birthday anyone's ever had," she shrieks. "Now we're talking!"

"Xbox," I say.

"No," she breathes.

"Yes."

"OH MY GOD!" she jumps up and down the way she used to when she was younger and had to go to the bathroom badly. I carry in an armload of boxes, passing Ron the Buddha on the way in, who eyes us serenely from over by the rhododendron bush. I flop onto the sofa when I get in, take my shoes off. Mom's wearing a pot holder on one hand, with a lethal amount of happy toasters on it. "Well, look at you," she says.

I put my hand to my face, forgetting the layers pasted there. I look at my fingertips, splotched with dots of brown. I haven't figured out yet that you're not supposed to do this. "I had a makeover."

"So I see," she says.

Severin pushes open the front door with his hip. "Clear the living room, we're coming in!" His arms are full of boxes. "Make room!" He shoves Mom's rocker with his foot, and it sits against the wall pointed the wrong direction. It looks somehow offended.

Trevor sets some boxes down with a thump.

"Hey, easy with the merchandise," Bex says. The room is filling. "Check it out!" Bex holds up a musical soap dispenser for Mom to see. Mom nods. She looks overwhelmed. Picks at a piece of packing tape with her finger.

"Let me get a knife," Severin says. He trots to the kitchen and comes back, starts slitting the lids of boxes.

"Maybe we should do this in some sort of . . . order," Mom says.

"Nah," Bex says.

Trevor returns. He passes out the boxes of cell phones. "For you, Missus," he says to Mom. "And you, and you, and *you*," to me, kissing me. "And me."

"A CELL PHONE!" Bex shrieks.

I remove mine. I decide I want to take a picture of all this.

"Wait, we've got to charge them first," Severin says.

Trevor takes control of this, lines them up on the floor by the TV. In a few minutes, the room is filled with blocks of Styrofoam and plastic wrappings and instruction manuals. I hear Bex's voice, locate the top of her head as she sits cross-legged on the floor in a bare spot surrounded by cardboard towers.

"Cool," she says. She's wearing a pair of the headphones, and she's got the alcohol-level breath analyzer, Alcohawk, held in her palm.

"Indigo," Mom says. "You don't even drink."

I shrug. I hand her the barbecue fork that's also a thermometer.

"We don't have a barbecue, either," she says.

"I think that's coming with the TV," Trevor says.

"I'm sober!" Bex says.

Deb Caletti

At dinner Mom opens a bottle of wine, but not before Trevor hunts around in the paper and packing bubbles and locates the new one-touch bottle opener. Mom doesn't drink—I think someone from work gave her the wine last Christmas. But now she sips it gratefully, sighs as if she's just descended into a hot bath after a long day.

"Oh. My. God," she says.

"This is the best day of my life," Bex says. She's wearing all three shirts I got her, and this cool hat with a feather in it that looks a little like Robin Hood's.

"I thought your best day was when you collected a hundred and sixty-three dollars at QFC for tsunami victims," Mom says.

"Oh, that," Bex says.

Severin is wearing this abdomen exerciser we bought him that increases muscle size without any actual physical activity. He forks in a few bites of meatloaf, then undoes the Velcro strap with a *shh-shwick*. "I don't think I can eat with this on," he says.

"You look buffer already. More buff," I say.

"Yeah, In, a buffer is something you shine a car with," Trevor says, and I stick my tongue out at him. "Wait. Can we get a buffer? For Bob Weaver?"

"Honey, I don't know if I can take another day like this," Mom says. "Undoing all that packing tape and twisty ties alone has given me a migraine." She's not even eating. She's just drinking wine and nibbling at bread crusts. "And the makeup . . . Honey, you're a natural beauty. All that foundation—I think of bodies in caskets."

I decide to ignore her. I decide she just needs time to get used to the new me. "Wait. Something's missing," I say.

"How could you even tell," she says.

"Something I got for you. It's probably with my clothes."

I go into the living room, kick my way through paper and plastic. Freud is sleeping on an open instruction booklet Severin was reading. I find the shopping bags with my new clothes still inside. I reach my hand around the crispy new fabric, feel for a small bag.

"Aha!" I shout.

"Oh, God," Mom groans.

"Oh, God," Chico says.

Back in the kitchen, I hold the bag out to her. Trevor chuckles. "I know what it i-is," he sings.

Mom takes out a small box, decorated with color tiles. She opens the lid. "It's a pillbox," she says. She knits her eyebrows together, baffled.

"For your hormone replacement therapy," I say.

"I am not in menopause!" she says.

"Yet," Bex says.

"Wow. What can I say," she says. "That was very thoughtful."

"It's got the little squares so you can remember to take them every day," I say.

"Just what I needed," she says. Sips her wine again.

Just then, one of the cell phones rings in the other room.

"Hello?" Chico says.

"Cell phone!" Bex shrieks, and runs there. "It's mine!" she announces. Hers is pink. She's standing in the kitchen doorway, pushes the talk button, then holds it up to her ear. "This is Bex," she says. "Huh?" She covers the mouthpiece with one hand. "They want to order a pizza."

"Ask them what kind," Severin says.

"What kind?" Bex says into the phone. She listens a moment,

Deb Caletti

covers the mouthpiece again. "Large Canadian bacon and sausage."

"Where are they calling from?" Severin says.

"Take their credit card number!" Trevor says. We're all laughing now.

"Where are you calling from?" Bex says. "Astoria?"

"Tell them we'll be there in about five hours," Severin says.

"Bex, tell them they have the wrong number," Mom says, but she's laughing too.

"We'll be there in five hours," Bex says. She listens. "They hung up," she tells us. "My first call. Cool." She punches in a few numbers and in a moment our home phone rings.

"Hello?" Chico says.

"I wonder who it is," Mom says.

In the middle of the night I am awakened by a sound. I sit up abruptly in bed. I hear it again. It's music. Wait, it sounds like the ice cream man, in our house. Is this some kind of twisted nightmare? The fucking ice cream man, breaking in to chop us all up in our beds, to the tune of "Zippity Do Dah"?

I listen. It's coming from the bathroom. My heart slows. I remember. There is no psycho ice cream man here. It is just our new musical soap dispenser/alarm clock, singing at midnight.

Leroy is looking at the want ads again.

"What happened, Leroy?" I ask.

"The old lady I was watching? She wanted to get out of the house. I took her out to see the salmon hatchery. She wanted a smoke, so we were just sitting there on a bench, having—"

"You deserve whatever you got, then, Leroy." I tie my apron behind my back. "You let an old lady smoke? You let yourself smoke?"

"Hey, now, I haven't for years. Things have been a little stressful in my life lately, you know. . . . And anyway—"

"She died on you. Right there on the bench," Trina guesses.

"No—," Leroy says.

"She fell in the water," Nick guesses. "Slipped and fell in."

"And then got chewed on by a giant salmon," Funny says. She cackles evilly.

"Broken hip," Joe says.

"I vote with Joe," Jane says. "Broken hip."

"God, you people." Leroy gives up. He takes a crunch of his wheat toast, goes back to his paper.

"What, Leroy, what?" I plead. "Come on."

He chews as if we are all invisible. There's only the *tink* sound of Funny's fork against her plate, and Luigi whistling in the back.

"Oh, well," Trina says. "We'll never know. Big deal. I'll have the chocolate pie," she says to me.

"Yeah, really," I say. "Who cares."

"All right, all right," Leroy says. His cheek still has a round ball of toast in it. "We were sitting there having a smoke, and who should walk up, of all people, but her grandson. Her grandson! He works at the Ale House across the street, but Grandma didn't tell me that. I think she wanted to get in trouble. Just to liven things up, only now she's gonna get some nurse and the high-light of her day is gonna be when she gets her pulse taken."

My cell phone rings from my backpack behind the counter. I ignore it since I'm in the middle of my shift, but it goes off again. Bex set up my ring tones, and now every time anyone calls it sounds like a fucking circus. "Just a sec," I say to Trina. I trot over. Flip it open. Melanie.

"You told me you'd call me right back," she says.

"I'm at work," I say. I feel the little twingy unease of wrong-doing, can see Jane's back straightening slightly at my voice on this phone, now, during work hours. She's told me she doesn't want my phone ringing every two seconds, that I should turn it off. Since no one hardly ever calls me, I just keep it on low, in case of emergencies. Once you have a cell phone, you can't imagine how you ever lived without it.

"I need to know if you want to go or not."

"I told you, I've got to think about it. I'd have to get time off of work, and I'd miss Trevor . . ."

"Oh my God, Indigo. That's ridiculous. This is a lifetime opportunity. There are going to be *parties*. The kind that Hunter Eden goes to, do you hear me? Hunter *Eden*. And you are worry-ing about missing *Trevor*?"

Let's just say Melanie doesn't understand Trevor. To her, Trevor doesn't have a future. And having a future apparently means hav-ing the means to make money. If she didn't understand Trevor before, she really doesn't understand him now. "Melanie," I say. I'm ready to fight her on this, but just then two ladies with laptops walk in the door, and Jane catches my eye.

"I've got to go."

"I need to know by the end of the week," Melanie says. "Hey, did you get a dress? For prom?"

"What are you talking about? You know I'm not going to prom. You know it'd take armed men to forcibly drag me to prom."

"I just thought that now—"

"Right. I have money, so I'd want to go. That not wanting to go was some sort of fake principle disguising the fact that I couldn't afford a limo."

"Okay, okay, I'm sorry."

Jane gives me a real look this time. She grabs the menus and seats the couple herself.

"I'm saying good-bye now." But for a moment, just a moment, I picture myself back at the mall. I get the revved thrill imagining buying dresses and earrings and shoes and beaded purses and shawls and stockings; the image is shattered, though, when I picture Trevor and me in front of a fake sunset.

I hang up, tuck my phone into my backpack. Jane shoots me her displeasure through eye contact, but doesn't say anything. I take the order of the laptop ladies (coffee for both, fruit, one poached egg). I seat the bookstore guy, then an elderly man and wife.

"Shit. Look who's coming," Nick says. Bill and Marty, the True Value guys. Bill is wearing his camouflage hat again, and a T-shirt that reads GET HAMMERED, with a picture of a big hammer on it. Marty's in a flannel shirt, even though it's seventy-five degrees

Deb Caletti

and beautiful out. In the Seattle area, in case you don't know, when it's above sixty, convertible tops go down and people start wearing shorts. Hey, our season in the sun is so brief, why let goose bumps stop you? What's the big deal about hypothermia? But seventy-five and flannel? This means his skin probably hasn't seen the light of day since chicks drooled over Peter Frampton.

"Hey, Killer," Bill says.

"You polish the old pistol today?" Marty says, chuckling. They sit down beside Nick.

"Marty, you idiot, it wasn't a pistol. He shoved her down stairs."

Marty looks up. His mustached mouth hangs open. There really are those people whose mouths hang open upon shock or attempt at deep thought. It's hard for them to think and operate parts of their body at the same time. "No, it was a pistol."

"Stairs, you dumb shit," Bill says.

"No, Nick, tell him. Pistol."

Nick sighs. "She fell down stairs. Carrying laundry."

A sick feeling, a solid regret, sits in my stomach. And I wonder then, you know, why he puts up with this. Why not tell them to shove off, to sit somewhere else? Why not take it up with his boss, or get up and leave? It's true that there are two of them, and that they are both larger than Nick, which may be part of it. It's always wise to be careful who you say *Fuck off* to. But there is something else at work here, I understand now. Nick has reached the point when a person stops fighting for themselves. When a sense of powerlessness seems larger than any ability you have to fight back. He has gotten to the place where the words "destiny" and "fate" are not used as expressions of possibility, but as the words for forces that always win. It is the way early settlers saw fate (a storm, famine, disease, a harsh winter that would take half the family), or maybe the way sailors did (too much wind, no wind, a raging sea, a drowned ship). Maybe just anyone who's up against things too large. He has lost the ability to wrestle and rail against; he's given up his will to make things better for himself. It makes me sad for him. But more than that, it makes me pissed off.

I bring the plastic menus to the table. And here's what I do. I slap one down so hard onto the marble surface that all three men jump. I point my finger at them, make it a weapon in the air.

"I want you to listen to me, and listen to me good," I say, channeling some sheriff in a western my mother must have watched while I was in the womb. "If you ever—and I mean *ever*—give Nick any more crap about his wife again, God help me I will take you both down." I realize I have raised my voice, not in a yell, but loud enough to still all silverware and cups and dishes and even Luigi. The kitchen is quiet. Jack's ears are perked up into two alert triangles.

"Indigo . . . ," Nick says.

Bill smirks. "Are you smirking?" I say. "You think I can't do it? Well, sweetie, you may want to wipe that look right off your face, because I have a black belt. Got it? These hands are lethal, understand? And if you still don't believe me, I'll be happy to write down the name of the man I put in the hospital when he laid a hand on me in an ungentlemanly fashion."

Bill gets serious. But the corners of Marty's mouth are still turned up, ever so slightly. "Give me a napkin," I say. "Hand over that napkin right now." I click my pen into working position, think quickly. *Peter Frampton*, I write. Okay, so thinking quickly is not always my strong suit.

"Wasn't he a singer?" Marty says. "Kinky-haired guy?"

Deb Caletti

"Not that Peter Frampton, you asshole," I say. I ball up the napkin in anger. "You better remember this. It's the last warning you're gonna get."

I turn my back. I hold my breath.

"This place sucks," Bill says.

"Let's go to Starbucks," Marty says.

They ease out of the seat. The bells of the door jangle hard behind them. When the two men pass by the window, Leroy starts to applaud. Then Trina joins in, and then Joe, and even the bookstore guy. It's just a smattering of applause, not the full-fledged all-out type you'd get if this were a movie, but still. The old couple, who I'm guessing are visiting from out of town, look up like gaping fish, eyes big and scared behind their glasses.

"I've always wanted to do that to those guys," Leroy says.

"Me too," Joe says.

"Do you really have a black belt?" Funny asks.

"Sure," I say. "I also have a brown one, and a fake snakeskin one that I don't wear because it looks like an endangered species."

"Why didn't we ever DO that?" Leroy says. "We just sat there and let it happen, and no one said a word to those assholes."

"Why didn't I ever do that, is more like it," Nick says.

"Those guys were shaking. Did you see that?" Trina holds up a hand, makes it tremble.

"Indigo?" Jane says. "I need to talk with you. When your shift is over." Her voice is stretched tight, like the snappy skin of a polish sausage.

"Dum da dum dum." Trina hums uh-oh music.

"She's not in trouble for that. Tell me she's not in trouble for that," Leroy says. Jane ignores him. She gives the old couple their check and smiles nicely at them.

"If I were younger, I would have *pow*, popped those guys in the kisser," Joe says.

I know Jane isn't exactly pleased with me, but I figure it'll wear off by the time the morning's over. She'd been pissed at me before—for taking too long at tables (it's not my fault if people want to tell me their life stories), for flipping off nasty customers behind their back. But I just act remorseful and everything is fine. Even with her weird new attitude toward me, I figure that's how it'll go. So I work my shift and the Irregulars start heading out, and I hang up my apron and say good-bye to Luigi, and expect Jane to give me a few serious words using her eyebrows of concern, the end.

"Indigo," she says. We are by the coatrack in the back room. It is past coat-wearing season, but the rack is filled. There's a blue puffy parka, and a navy nylon jacket and a zip-up gray sweatshirt. Who knows who the coats belong to—they've been here for as long as I've worked here, gaining new members periodically (a red jacket with ski tags on the zipper, an orange slicker like crossing guards wear). It's like the shelter for homeless coats. Coats with no places to go and be a coat.

I sigh.

"Look, I'm not kidding around here," she says.

"I didn't say anything," I say.

"Not *yet*," she says, and her tone surprises me. The "yet" is a word with edges, the sharp angles of hostility.

"Jeez, Jane," I say. Here's where I am supposed to apologize. She's supposed to accept. I make a joke and all is well again. But her tone jabs in a way she's never jabbed before. And I'm not so sure I like being jabbed. "Ever since I got the money, you've been like this," I say.

Deb Caletti

"And *you've* been like *this*," she says. "You leave me in the lurch when you go off to Hawaii. Your cell phone's making me freaking nuts and I told you I wanted it off. You tell off my *customers*—"

"I had to go, you *knew* that. And your customers are hurting your other customer," I say.

"I can't exactly afford to lose people here, Indigo." She folds her arms. Her face is actually flushed red. "They're probably not going to come back."

"You shouldn't even let guys like that in," I say. I start to cross my own arms, then let them hang at my sides. It feels like a face-off, and this is Jane and I love her, but the edge is in my own voice now. "They treat Nick that way—"

"It's up to Nick to take care of himself. I've got my own things to take care of here. I've got people who count on me. What you did might have been amusing to everyone else—"

"Amusing isn't the point, Jane," I breathe. "Caring about *people* more than a twenty-dollar check is the point."

"That's all fine when you have the luxury of being able to have principles."

I do fold my arms then. We are arguing. We're actually arguing. And then comes what I know is coming. What I knew all along was coming.

"You may have the money to say and do whatever you want, Indigo, but I don't," she says. "I've got *responsibilities*. I have bills to pay. No one gave me two and a half million dollars." Her forehead is shiny with sweat. She wipes it with her palm.

"I didn't ask him to give me that money. It just happened," I say.

Jane takes a deep breath, blows out slowly. She looks at me, and for a minute I see just Jane, the old Jane. "I know you didn't," she says. "I apologize for being bitchy. I'm under a lot of stress here lately. And the whole money thing—I'm sorry. I confess to feeling very human about it. Ungenerous. Jealous in a way I'm not proud of. And then there's your own behavior recently . . ."

"Okay," I say.

But I don't say I'm sorry. She's being unfair. It's not my fault I'm suddenly rich. The apology is noticeably absent. I stare at the coats. Jane stares at the coats. I hear the siss of Luigi cooking something in oil. Jane looks at me briefly, then shakes her head and walks back out to the dining area. "I want the phone off," she says over one shoulder. I watch her silver earrings flash their disappointment, then the round curve of her shoulders heading away.

I don't think of those shoulders hunched over the spreadsheet on a computer screen, or at the counter of her bank, or even up late at night in bed, the light on when lights should be off, joining all of the other lights lit in midnight worry. Instead, I think about Leroy's question, of why no one stopped the True Value guys, even Nick himself. It was hopelessness, I decide, and the word, just that word, makes me feel ticked off and even slightly disgusted. Hope is not something that fate bestows, like Willy Wonka and the golden ticket, I think then. Hope is a decision. And sure, maybe money allows you to make that decision more easily, but still.

I let the bells slam against the glass, and if Jane doesn't like that, either, it's just too bad.

Severin bounds out of the house when Trevor and I drive up. The front door bangs against the wall with a bash—it lost its springy

Deb Caletti

little doorstop long ago. Mrs. Denholm is watering her plants—i.e., spying on us. The stream of water that's supposed to be hitting a rosebush is actually hitting a cement garden frog, and she is squinting in the effort to get a good look at us. She keeps studying other things intently—the mailboxes, her own porch—in an effort, I guess, not to stare. She's no doubt convinced that Trevor and Severin are part of some robbery or heist or credit card scam due to the amount of boxes that have been entering our house in the last week, and she's probably working hard at remembering everything to tell the police. Mrs. Denholm used to make those offers that were really demands—*Would you like to borrow my clippers so that you can trim that hedge? If your lawn mower's not working, you can certainly use mine . . .*—but she has changed tactics lately and has taken to making statements that are really quests for information. *There's certainly been a lot of commotion at your house lately.* Or, *A delivery truck was here, but you weren't home.*

This is what she says now. "A delivery truck was here, but you weren't home," she shouts, cupping one hand around her mouth, megaphone-style. That cement frog is getting the watering of his life.

"Thanks," I shout back, and give a little wave. I love the fact that this gives her no additional detail. I love the fact that this will make her stew in her own juices of curiosity, and that it will send her into a frenzy of peeking through her venetian blinds.

"We missed FedEx, but I was here for UPS," Severin says. He's getting tan already, and I'm surprised right then how much he looks like Dad. "Trev, I need your help. What'd you guys do, buy the biggest TV in the store?"

"Flat screen," Trevor says. "It can hang right on the wall."

"If we had a wall that size. Come on, I can't even get it out of the box by myself. The UPS man had to use a cart."

"UPS men don't lift refrigerators," Trevor says. This reminds me to admire his muscles, which reminds me to pinch his cute little ass. I love that little ass. It isn't Hunter Eden cute, not cute enough for screaming masses, but it's cute enough for one Indigo Skye.

Mom isn't home from work yet, which is probably a good thing. Severin was right about the TV—he and Trevor are hauling it around and trying it in different places, and it looks a little like a drive-in movie screen suddenly in our living room.

"We'll get used to it," Trevor says, and in spite of his refrigerator comment, his arm muscles are bulgy with effort, and a thin stream of sweat is cruising down his temple.

"I can't wait to see it on," Severin says. "Where were you today at school, In?" he says. "Mr. Fetterling asked where you were. He said he heard some rumor that you came into a fortune and were going to drop out three weeks before graduation. I told him you had strep throat."

"I got in a fight with Jane and didn't feel like going," I say.

"She came with me on my rounds. You should have seen her lift this microwave oven by herself," Trevor says. He shakes his head and his hair swivels with crazy blond pride.

"Small but mighty," I say, and flex my arm for him.

"Strong and beautiful," Trevor says. "And rich."

I wish he wouldn't say that and I'm about to tell him so, when Severin says, "Well, you better get Mom to call. Okay, I think this wall is as good as we're going to get."

It's the wall where Mom's rocker is, and Trevor lifts the rocker in one hand and plops it onto the middle of the carpet. The TV sticks out into the hall a little, but it's either that or hanging it in the hall itself.

Deb Caletti

"Screwdriver," Severin says.

I search around on the floor. "Check." I hand it over.

"Metal hanger," Severin says.

"Check." That too.

Severin fusses with bolts and hangers while Trevor hunts in the fridge for something cool to boost his strength before we have to lift the thing up again.

"Hey, didn't you guys buy a drill?" Severin says.

"Yeah, it makes holes to the tune of the 'Star-Spangled Banner,'" Trevor shouts from the kitchen, and chuckles. The soap dispenser had been keeping everyone up at night. Mom hid it under some towels in the bathroom cabinet, and it is still there now.

"Just a sec, I'll get it," I say.

Severin *zzzzz*'s with the drill and Trevor leans in the doorway and swigs a Fresca.

"Speaking of rich, In? I've got to ask you something," Severin says. "I wouldn't bring it up, but it's sort of an emergency and I figured you wouldn't mind. . . . Does that look straight?" He stands back, appraises the hooks now firmly in the wall.

"I'm not buying you steroids. The protein shakes are bad enough."

"Ha. And, no jokes, okay? Just because you're not going? It's important to me. The prom. I don't want Kayleigh to think I'm some poor kid . . ."

"You are some poor kid," Trevor reminds. "At least, no one puts your head on God's body."

"You know, a few hundred dollars? I have the tux money, but I know she'd expect a limo. And a nice dinner. A really nice dinner. A dozen roses, maybe."

"A corsage, not roses," I say. "She can't wear a dozen roses pinned to her dress."

"Well, she could, it'd just make dancing painful." Trevor tilts the Fresca can and takes another swig.

"I just thought, both, you know? A special night? Why not?"

Why not? Because I don't like Kayleigh Moore? Because I think she's like some child who would only look down her nose at the other children grappling on the floor for the candy that fell from the piñata? Because I worry she's going with Severin to do a good deed for the kid who works in the warehouse? Because in her case, Moore is less?

"I don't get why a prom is like a mini-wedding these days and a wedding is like royal nuptials. No one should spend that kind of money for a high school dance."

"You sound like Mom," Severin says.

"He's right," Trevor says. "You never say 'nuptials.' No one says 'nuptials.'"

"Fine," I say. "Anything you want, Severin."

"Hey, you don't have to . . . ," Severin says. "Okay, we're ready to lift."

Trevor sets down his Fresca. Lifts one corner of the TV as Severin lifts the other.

"No," I say. "Knock yourself out."

"Okay, I think it's hanging. Yeah, it's on the hooks," Severin says. "In? Hey, thanks. I don't want to look stupid with her, you know?"

"Yeah," I say.

Trevor screws in the cable, and I push the power button. The image is huge. Two kids at a table, eating breakfast. Their father enters, snitches a handful of cereal from the box. His figure fills the screen.

Deb Caletti

"Holy shit," Mom screams. She is in the doorway, suddenly. Her hand is to her chest. Bex stands beside her.

"We thought a man was in the house," Bex says.

"That's a television?" my mother says.

"It's hanging over into the hall," Bex says.

"What's wrong with your voice?" I ask her. She's talking funny, like she can't manage her own tongue.

"I went to the dentist," she says. "I can't feel my lips."

The image on the television changes. Now some woman is walking in a field of flowers, blowing her nose and looking miserable.

"Huge nose," Bex says.

"Guys, this is ridiculous," Mom says. She tosses her purse onto the seat of the poor rocker, which is adrift in the middle of the room. "No one even watches TV around here."

"Because our TV is about four inches across and you have to bang on it to get the color to come back," Severin says. He leans back on his heels, crosses his arms, and stares at the woman blowing her nose as if he's never seen anything quite so fascinating. Trevor aims the remote at the television and shoots, and the image changes to some bald man heavy with middle age, yabbing on about city government.

"Talking head. Get rid of him," Bex says. *Thalking head. Ge rih a him.*

She moves Mom's purse and sits in the rocker, scoots it in the direction of the TV.

"This doesn't fit the room. This doesn't fit *us*," Mom says.

Trevor clicks and the government guy disappears.

"Spanish channel," Bex says. Click. "Religion. Whoa, big hair religion."

"Let's call the number," Trevor says, but he's already moved on.

"Home shopping!" Bex yells. "Look! In? You want that necklace?" My mind flashes on Dan Shugman and Richard Howards and their ex-jewelry.

"Nah," I say. "Ugly."

"Guys. No one is listening!" Mom is raising her voice.

"Warning! It's the hormone hour. Do you need a pot holder to throw?" I say.

"Cooking channel. What IS that? Eyuw, gross," Bex says.

"Fancy shit," Trevor says.

"Hmm, I don't know," I say. "It looks kind of good."

"History . . . Sharks . . . Cartoons! Keep it there," Bex says.

Trevor has the power, though, and he's loving it. Click, click, go the enormous images, and Severin hasn't moved. It's understandable—I haven't either. It's all so large that it's hypnotizing. You could fall in there and never get out.

"People!" Mom shouts. She snaps her fingers, like trying to break a spell.

Erectile dysfunction ad (thanks for sharing), shower cleaner. Guys in a bar drinking beer. And then Trevor stops. There's a guy walking on a beach. A chick in a bikini walks up to him and sniffs the air around him. "You smell sooo good," she hums.

"Missus!" Trevor says. He looks over his shoulder at Mom. "Check it out!"

"Mom, your favorite!" Bex says.

"Axe!" Severin says.

"Whoo-hoo," I laugh. "Look, Ma, giant Axe ad."

Mom sighs. "I give up," she says.

Deb Caletti

"I don't get how people think God and science don't go together," I say as I look up at the starry night. My head is in Trevor's lap, and we are on the dock at Pine Lake Park, our park, our place. We arrived at twilight; Trevor pushed me on the playground swings and we watched the trees turn yellow as I flew toward the sky. Then it got dark and the light lost its magic, and the trees became secretive. "Just look at those stars and tell me, how can you not believe in God? Yet, all these wacky people think if you talk science you're some kind of atheist."

"We could buy a house here, you know, In," Trevor says. He is wrapping my hair around one finger.

"And why can't evolution and God go together, anyway? Sure, that's not what the book says, but what are they gonna do, try to explain the whole process to people who still thought the world was flat? I mean, come on. God created, presto chango, that everyone could understand. But why can't God have created evolution? I don't get it."

"We could probably even buy our house. You think? We could knock on their door and offer them some fucking-tastic amount they couldn't say no to."

"You're not even listening." I sit up. I circle my knees with my arms.

"We've got some decisions to make here, In. I mean, I think it's time we talk seriously about Nunderwear."

An ugly wave rises up inside of me. "And *I* think it's time we talk seriously about you talking about my money every fucking second."

The swell of anger—it's not the worst thing. What's worst is that Trevor looks at me then, gauging whether I'm kidding or not. He thinks I am. It is not the kind of mistake Trevor-Indigo of the past could have made. We always saw each other. But he doesn't see me. He doesn't see *me*. He actually laughs. Like I'm just a great big kidder.

"Anyway, I think if we get it started? It's a way, you know, to have money make more money. It's a great idea, In. People are going to love Nunderwear. People will love the Jesus lip balm. 'Lookin' smooth for the Lord.' You gotta love it."

"I can't believe it," I say. But it's the *I can't believe it* that means you *can* believe it. Maybe that you even expected it. The water is black and twinkly. A mosquito annoys my bare legs and I swat him away. "Take me home." I stand up.

"What's the matter? In? What's going on?" He stands up too. He holds my arms. I look at his blue eyes, under his shaggy bangs. He is someone I know and don't know. Or maybe that's actually me.

"If you keep talking about we and us and my money, I'll start thinking we're a threesome," I say. I twist my head to the side so I don't have to look at him.

He ducks and dodges so that he can meet my eyes. "It's always been we and us," he says. "Is it wrong to want to make some plans?"

I feel the pressure of his fingertips against my skin. "You're holding me too hard," I say, even if this isn't exactly true.

He lets go. "I don't get you, In. I don't get what's going on here."

"I told you, I want to go home," I say.

We walk to the parking lot. My arms are folded. It was foolish to think nothing would change. I get in Bob Weaver and slam the door.

Deb Caletti

"Easy, In. Jesus," Trevor says.

For some reason, this pisses me off more. That there's this object he cares about more than my feelings at the moment. When we get home, my house is dark, except for the porch light glowing. A few mosquitoes buzz there, too, like the last holdovers at a party. Trevor kisses me good night and I kiss back, but it's a weird, absent kiss, performed by my body double. And when he says he loves me and I tell him I love him in return, that, too, is faraway, distant and echoey, like words spoken in a too-large and empty room.

12

Over the next three weeks Severin went to the prom, and we both finished classes and had our graduation ceremony. Trevor and Bex and Mom held up cards when Severin and I paraded in. Bex held WE, and Mom held LOVE, and Trevor held YOU. They screamed their heads off when they saw us, and Mom tried to take pictures with our new digital camera, but most of them were a sea of purple gowns or the curly brown head of the woman seated in front of her. She's not so good on the technical end. There were a lot of prom pictures, though; Severin bought the super-deluxe pack, and he had wallets of him and Kayleigh and refrigerator magnets and this huge eight-by-ten that sat in a frame on the desk in his room. Kayleigh, in white satin and carrying a dozen roses with roses at her wrist, looked like a prom queen who'd been hit by a floral delivery truck, and Severin was tall and handsome beside her, his arm around her waist.

Dad's graduation present to me was a book of Emerson's essays. The note inside said *The source of my fatherly wisdom. Remember who you are. Love, Dad.* I cracked it open, but was assaulted with what seemed like a million tiny words; a *Hark!* leapt from the page, and I shut the book again. Dad had planned on coming to graduation, but Jennifer had slipped in a splotch of water sloshed from Keiko's bowl and had broken her ankle and Dad needed to be there to take care of her. He sounded sad and disappointed and he sent flowers and cards and called us twice that day, once beforehand to wish us luck and once after to see how it went. He pressed me on my future plans, urged college now that money wasn't an issue. I had missed all application deadlines so I had time to think, I told him.

Mom bugged me daily until I finally visited Dad's financial adviser, who discussed investments with me and who gave me a spending budget and set me up with a debit card. I hadn't made any Big Decisions about the money yet. I bought a car—a VW Rabbit. I tried again to talk Mom into getting one for herself, tried to talk her into moving, but she just got that hard-as-marble face. *Save it for your future,* she said. I gave her rent money one month, but found it later propped up on my pillow with a note: *We're fine, In. But thank you. XXXOOO Mom.* So, here I was with people asking me for money I wasn't sure I wanted to give and people not taking money I *was* sure I wanted to give. Melanie gave up on me coming with her to Malibu. She was leaving the next day for the summer, moving on to UC Santa Barbara. Just like she said, her parents "worked something out."

"I cannot believe you are giving up this chance," she says when she calls me that morning from the gym. Melanie's one of those baffling people who get up at insane hours to work out when all other sensible people are repeatedly hitting their snooze button. Right then, I'm driving Severin over to Kayleigh Moore's before heading to work, and I'm balancing my phone between ear and shoulder as I drive. "With all the people my Dad knows? You could bring your guitar. You could play for some big-name producer, who knows?"

"Who Knows is a big-name record producer? Never heard of him," I say. Besides, my guitar and I are taking a break from our relationship.

"Left up here," Severin says. He's all hyped up because it's the first time he's seen Kayleigh Moore since prom, and the first time he's been invited to her house since we worked there the night of Chief's birthday. They're having some kind of swimming party, and Severin is wearing his swimming suit. He has a rolled-up towel beside him, and he smells like coconutty sun lotion. It seems a little early for a swimming party, but hey, maybe seven a.m. swimming is some new fad among the superwealthy.

"Don't you care about doing something other than staying here with your family and working and being with Trevor? Don't you find all this a little *small*? Someone has opened the door to your cage, and you're just sitting there. How many places have you even been? And you think Trevor's going to widen your world?" I hear someone shouting on her end, "Hey, Wiley, stellar abs, man!" and then laughter.

The question scritches at my nerves. I think of Funny, *How many places have you laid your head?* It occurs to me that there are two and a half million ways not to measure up. "Isn't your Amazing Abs class about to start?" I say.

"Aerobics and then weight training," she says. "*I'll* be ready when I go to put on a bikini."

"Pump it, work it," I say. "With buns of steel, you can sit anywhere. You are my exercise role model. Ha, now that I have a role model, can I skip doing it myself?"

"Left! Back there!" Severin says.

I glare at him. "Mel? I gotta go. I can't do this driving-and-talking thing."

"I'm sorry you won't be coming, Indigo. I'd love to have you. And I think you're missing out."

"Send me a postcard," I say.

I have to make a U-turn into a neighborhood with a SLOW

Deb Caletti

CHILDREN AT PLAY sign. This would be the time for Severin to make our same lame joke about fast children, and the fact that they must be playing somewhere else. But he misses the sign entirely. One hand is clinging to the door handle, and the other is clenching a clump of fabric from his swim shorts.

"Would you relax?" I say.

"God, In, the way you drive makes that slightly impossible," he says. "You almost took out that lady with the stroller, and then you slid through that stop sign and now we're having the grand tour of this neighborhood, with that cocker spaniel practically riding on our front fender."

"No children or animals were hurt in the making of this film," I say. "Backseat drivers must get out at the next stop."

"That poor dog. I saw the terror in his eyes," he says. Maybe I have made Severin a little nervous with my defensive driving. I've got the air conditioner on, but he's got a mustache of perspiration.

"You want your own car? Work on Mom for me. Until then, it better be 'Thank you, Indigo, my beautiful, wonderful sister, for going out of your way for me this morning so that I can visit my spoiled girlfriend, Buffy.'"

"Now take a right. Right, here! Shit, man. Okay, that next left, by that willow tree." He points, but thanks, I can see it two feet in front of me. "God, I'd love a car. Why's Mom freaking out like this? She doesn't want it to change us in some drastic way, but she's the one going to extremes, if you ask me."

"Hormones!" I sing.

We reach Kayleigh Moore's house, if you can call that place a house. I had wondered if it would look different to me now. I couldn't buy it, or anything close to it, even if I spent everything

I had. But I have seventeen-dollar lipstick on now, from my binge at the makeup counter. I view the house with new, expensive lips and realize it looks the same to me as before. It feels cold and unreal, like a movie set. It is not a place where your Mom would go into the kitchen in her robe in the morning and make hot chocolate. It is not a place where you could find the bag of marsh-mallows for that hot chocolate, fastened closed with a rubber band.

I leave Meer Island and hit the gas so I won't be late to work. I breathe better once I am out of that place. There's something about it that makes me feel like I've got a plastic bag tied around my head. At the next stop light, I drag race a King County Library bookmobile and a minivan with the bumper sticker PROUD PARENT OF AN HONOR ROLL STUDENT. I beat them both soundly, then take the on-ramp to the freeway. I get off at the Nine Mile Falls exit, curve around the Texaco station and Old Country Buffet, one of those all-you-can-eat places that no one who lives here actually goes to, one of those places with gravy that makes you have sec-ond thoughts. My eye is caught by something at the roadside.

It's a man, and he's wearing some huge, spongy yellow upright rectangle costume, with some orange glob coming from the top. He is dancing around and holding a sign that says, SPEND THE MORNING AT OLD COUNTRY BUFFET. Usually, I wouldn't pay much attention, but my eyes travel from the mysterious costume down, and I see the legs that stick from under it. Tattooed legs. Legs with zodiac signs—rams and bulls and water bearers and intertwined fish—that edge down into the top of his sneakers.

Maybe I forget my turn signal, because someone honks, and maybe I swerve just a little, because the spongy yellow upright

Deb Caletti

rectangle hightails it into the restaurant bushes. I yank the parking brake, get out. The yellow rectangle has had the orange goop scared out of him, and he's taken a tumble—he's horizontal in the junipers and it appears that he's unable to right himself again.

"Leroy?" I call.

"Who is it?" His arms and legs are flailing like a tortoise stuck on his back.

"Me. Indigo."

"Oh, thank God! Did you see that car try to run me over?"

"Leroy, jeez, I'm sorry. That was me! I was just pulling over. I saw this yellow rectangle with your legs . . ."

"I'm a breakfast burrito. Help me up."

I pick my way across the junipers, hold out my hand and foist him upright. "You have shit all on the back of you," I say. I swat off the back of him, freeing bits of prickly green and dirt and leaves.

"That was you? What were you doing? I thought you were going to kill me."

"I was pulling over!" I say. "That's all! That guy didn't need to honk and shake his fist! I couldn't believe this was you! What are you doing?"

"It's a job, Indigo." A car with a bunch of teenagers passes by and they beep their horn and wave. "I needed a job, you know, after I got canned from the old lady."

"But, Leroy . . . ," I say. "This?" It's a humiliating job. It makes me sad to see him here, those Leroy eyes under that orange . . . "What's that orange stuff on your head?"

"Cheese. Melted cheese," he says.

Under that melted cheese. Leroy's eyes. This makes him

smaller than he deserves to be. Face it—adults plus costumes equals humiliation. No adult should ever have to wear one for money. Wearing a Dopey-the-dwarf costume or a mattress sale sandwich board and dancing around so some big shot can make a profit, well, it's almost unconstitutional. Cruel and inhuman.

"Beggars can't be choosers, okay? Not too many people want to hire me with my tattoos. These people don't care. I'm all covered up."

"Except for your legs." I point.

"I was supposed to have yellow socks, but I forgot them," he says.

"God, Leroy. A breakfast burrito."

"At night I get to be a kidney bean. It's their house soup special."

A large old-people car pulls up and a lady with blue-white hair rolls down her window. "Can you tell us how to get back on the freeway?"

"Back straight that way." Leroy points with a yellow arm. I missed a clunk of juniper that dangles from his elbow. "Stay to your right." The car drives on. "What do they think I am, the visitor's bureau? I've given directions to triple X drive-in, Lake Sammamish, and the post office, and I've only been here an hour."

"Why do you need to do this at all, Leroy? You have a job at Darigold."

"It's complicated, okay? Indigo, I don't mean to be unfriendly here, but I've got some arm waving and jumping around to do."

I leave Leroy, and make my way over to Carrera's. I'm a little late, I admit.

Deb Caletti

"You're late," Jane says.

"Jane cut me a chintzy piece of pie," Trina says. "You better be on time tomorrow." I hurry to the back room, drop my bag, wave a hello to Luigi, and put on my apron.

"Leroy won't be coming in," I announce to the Irregulars. "He's dressed as a breakfast burrito outside of Old Country Buffet."

"And I thought I was the crazy one," Funny says. Her head is bent over her notebook.

"Anyone says one word against Leroy, I'm gonna, pow, pop him in the kisser," Joe says. Since my encounter with Nick's coworkers, everyone's been a little . . . aggressive.

"We all do what we've got to do," Trina says. "Since Roger left, I'm answering the psychic hotline." She licks the back of her fork.

"What!" I scream.

"God, Indigo. Not so loud," Jane says. "You scared Jack." Which is true. Jack has leapt to his feet.

"I'm sorry, but . . . Trina, come on. What, you tell people that tomorrow will bring a new day?" I bring Nick his oatmeal. He rips open two packages of sugar and pours them on top.

"'A day without sunshine is like night,'" Nick says.

"Yesterday, she told some woman that she was going to meet a man named Roger who would run off to Rio," Funny says.

"So?" Trina says. "The way Roger gets around, it's probably true."

"Wait, guys," Nick says. He suddenly scoots himself out from the table, knocking his spoon from balance on the side of his bowl. "Is that—Look. Look! Outside!"

I almost expect to see the Vespa. The Vespa, with the Vespa guy back on it. Richard Howards, looking for me, asking for his money back. I picture it all disappearing—me returning the TV, the digital cameras, the raft, the soap dispenser, damaged from when Mom threw it against the bathtub tiles. The cell phones. God, no, we love those.

But it isn't the Vespa. I see a flash of red and white. It's Trina's Thunderbird. Parked down the block in front of True Value hardware.

"It's my cousin, that idiot," Trina says. "Do you know he hasn't washed that car since he got it? There's an empty McDonald's cup in the backseat. One of those insulting 'Sorry you're not a winner' scratch tickets. There's a catalogue thrown on the floor too. The kind that sells sausages and cheese logs?" She puts a knee on the seat, cranes her neck to get a better look. She looks like a mother who's given up her child, now sure she's caught a glimpse of him.

"It's the Thunderbird, all right," Nick says. I stand beside him at the window. Jane is there too, and Joe, who has risen from his stool to join us. Funny leans across Trina's booth to get a look.

"She's still a beauty," Joe says. "Mmm, mmm, mmm."

We watch the cousin, a tall man in tight jeans and a black T-shirt. His head cocks at an angle that says *These sunglasses make me look hot*. He tucks the keys into the back pocket of his jeans, slams the car door so hard we can hear it.

"Ouch," Nick says. I can feel Jane flinch beside me.

The cousin peers in the window of the True Value door, then bangs on the glass.

"It's not open yet, asshole," Nick growls. Another happy graduate of Indigo's School of Assertiveness Training.

The cousin bangs the door a few more times, then kicks at the sidewalk with the toe of his boot. He gets back into the car, slams

Deb Caletti

the door shut again, and then revs the engine. He sits there for a minute, trying to decide what to do. He apparently has forgotten this prior sequence of events, because he turns the key again, when the engine is already on. The car screams in mechanical outrage. Trina gasps, releases a whimper-cry.

"It makes me sick," Funny says. "God, I need a Xanax."

We watch him drive off. Jack feels the heaviness in the room and wants out. He noses Jane's palm to plead for a walk. We're all quiet. I bring Trina a second piece of pie. Nick clears his throat. I feel weighted with other people's misery. There is a part of me that understands Jack. I just want out of here too.

The bookstore guy arrives; and then there's one of the Nine Mile Falls librarians, who comes in with Joe Davis, the minister/handyman who fixed our plumbing once. I'm starting to swing into full gear again, when I hear the circus come to town—meaning, my phone is ringing. Shit, I forgot to turn it off. I can sense Jane snap to attention as she waits for my response, but I just ignore the phone. The ringing stops, then starts up again. Stops and starts again, in that insistent way that means emergency. I can feel the choice in front me—phone emergency versus Jane's anger, but what really wins out is curiosity. It's probably one of those urgent wrong numbers you get that immediately insert you into stranger's lives—*Uh, Beth? I'm running late, because Dan's wife Sue had this thing with her pancreas . . .*—but I can't stand not knowing. On the fourth call, I drop my menus onto the counter and dash.

I fish madly for my phone. Severin, the screen says. *Severin?*

"Man, this better be good, because I probably just lost my job," I say.

"Indigo," he says.

"I cannot be-lieve you are calling me at work."

"I started walking, but, fuck, it's a long way. Can you come and get me? Indigo, please."

"Where are you? I'm in the middle of my shift."

"I wouldn't ask, you know it. But I started walking from Meer Island, and I'm on the freeway, and it's a lot farther than it seems when you're driving." His voice is ragged. It sounds thin, thin as those really, really old Levi's of his, the ones that had been washed so much they got a new hole every time he kneeled down.

"What happened?"

"The swimming party? I get to the door, and she asks me why I'm dressed like that. Why I'm not wearing pants and a tie."

"Who swims in a tie?" I'm not getting this.

"She wasn't asking me to the party. She was asking me to be a *waiter* at the party."

"Oh my God," I say. "Goddamn it."

"I know, Indigo, okay? I know. Don't start. Just come and get me. Please?"

"I'm coming," I say.

"What do you mean, you're leaving? You can't leave."

I untie my apron. The bookstore guy's Farm Scramble is up. Joe needs a coffee refill. "It's my brother. An emergency."

"What kind of emergency, Indigo? It better be good, okay? He'd better be in the hospital or something."

It's one of those times when you can tell the truth won't do. "He's . . ." I think quickly. "He *is* in the hospital. With a . . . With a . . ." Shit. "His pancreas burst."

"Pancreases don't burst!" Jane says.

"Burst pancreas." Joe chuckles. "Heh, heh, heh."

Deb Caletti

"I gotta go," I say.

"We both know you're lying, Indigo. The least you could do is respect me enough to tell the truth," Jane says. She looks calm. She sounds calm, even. Severin's desperate voice, though, has filled me with urgent, hurry-up. I speak fast.

"Severin, okay? He needs me to come get him. His girlfriend invited him to this swimming party that wasn't a swimming party, and now he's . . ."

I realize how lame it sounds. I should have stuck with the burst pancreas. Jane folds her arms. She shakes her head, and I see that her face is getting the red flush again. "Honestly," she says. "He can't wait? You're willing to pick up and ditch me like this because your brother's girlfriend did a shitty thing?"

"He's really upset. *Really* upset." The words hang. They sound silly and frivolous, tinsel words.

Jane unfolds her arms, twists her watchband around in circles. "Listen, Indigo . . . Honestly," she says again.

"Jane, I'll make up my shift, I promise."

"You know, this all just doesn't seem . . . I'm not sure this is working."

"Wait a minute," I say.

"If you leave me in the lurch like this . . . I'm just thinking. Maybe you should take some time off. Until you get your head straight about this money and all. . . ."

I'm standing behind the counter and she's in front of it, and something seems backward in this, so I go out front too. "You're firing me," I say.

"Oh, no," Nick says.

"Indigo—"

"You are." I'll tell you one little thing about me, and that is that I'm not too keen on being bossed around. If, say, my Mom tells me to empty the dishwasher, I like to wait a little bit, you know, not hop up and do it right away, because then it feels more like my own idea. That's a little problematic when you have an actual boss. But Jane, she's more like a friend than a boss, and we understand each other. Friends don't fire you, though. Bosses do. And the fact that my boss is suddenly all bosslike is making this awful feeling rise up, like when you shake a can of Coke before opening it. This firing? If there's going to be a firing it's going to be my own idea.

"Indigo. I can't keep making concessions for you. Your priorities seem—"

"I quit."

"Wait. Let's sort this through, okay? I'm just saying you might need a little time . . ."

"Quit. *Finit*. Finished. The end. *Sayonara*."

Trina waves her fork in my direction. "Just a second here. You can't quit."

"Everyone needs to go to their corners," Joe says. "Time out."

Funny just sits there with her pen raised above her notebook, and Nick looks struck. The bookstore guy's Farm Scramble is getting cold. "I think those are my eggs," he says.

But there is no way to back out now. I've said the words. And there are some words you can't take back. It's like trying to get popcorn back into the kernel. *It's over. I'm leaving. We're through.* You can try, but there's no forgetting that someone wanted out.

I toss my apron right there onto the floor where I stand. I swing my backpack over my shoulder. I let the bells bang on the door behind me. And I try to ignore this feeling in my chest. This heaviness, a searing rip. The sense that my heart is

Deb Caletti

breaking. I ignore it, get into my car, and step on the gas.

A Hostess delivery truck driver lays down on his horn. "Watch it, you lunatic!" he shouts out his rolled-down window.

"Shut it, Twinkie," I shout back.

13

I bring Severin home. He doesn't say anything on the drive, and once we're back, he goes to his room and shuts the door. I sit down in the rocker, which has found a new place by the shoved-aside coffee table. I quit my job. I can't believe it. I quit my job.

"Do you think God's a baseball fan?" Bex asks. Since school let out and since we bought the new TV and Xbox, Bex has given up on tsunami victims, given up on her friends Max and An Ling, who she used to play with after school sometimes. Bex just wants to lie on the floor in front of the TV, be swallowed up and devoured by the huge screen and whatever is on—*Wheel of Fortune*, Animal Planet, the Travel Channel, the Daytona 500 racing game. Now a field of green fills our living room, as do men in white uniforms, cool and pure as vanilla ice cream.

"I don't know, Bex, why?"

"They always pray before a game," she says.

"Do you want to go swimming or something? I'll take you to Pine Lake."

"No." Her chin rests in her open palms. Her legs are crossed at the ankle. She has a Band-Aid on one shin, but I have no idea how she could have gotten scratched, since she hasn't moved from the TV in days. Freud is curled up in a spot of sun by the front window.

"I don't really want to either," I say. "How about CNN?"

"Nah. There are so many more choices now that you got Premium Cable."

We watch baseball. We watch a men's diving championship, which is more interesting, due to the embarrassing bathing suits. Bex does a lot of snickering and pointing. We share a bag of Cheetos and then we watch some woman trying out Paris restaurants. Bex puts in a video game and her cartoon car makes cartoon loops around a cartoon track.

Mom comes home just after six. "God, what a shitty day," she says. "Bex, I *told* you no TV today." She heads straight for the kitchen, and I get up and follow. I'm actually stiff and creaky from sitting in that chair so long.

Mom drops her purse onto the kitchen chair, and her mail onto the table. "Indigo, please. Don't let her sit and be a zombie like that."

"You don't mind if I'm a zombie," I say.

"Zombie," Chico says. "Zombie. Zombie. Zombie."

"Would you feed Chico, please? I don't worry about you being a zombie because you never were exposed to endless entertainment on a life-size television when you were her age. *You* didn't go from compassionate Samaritan to hypnotized TV child. The other day, she was watching *bass fishing*." Mom rubs her temples with the tips of her fingers. "Of course, you were never as prone to extremes as Bex either. I'm worried she'll join a cult someday, or get involved with some guy she'll never leave even if he's jobless and wears a Budweiser cap. . . ."

"Maybe we should sign her up for some summer camp thing. Horseback riding or crafts, or—"

"They're just so expen— No! Jeez. I didn't mean to say that. Forget I said that. We're not having this conversation. Ack!" She pounds her head twice with her fist.

"Mom, this is stupid! What good is this money if I can't share it with you? You, who needs it? This is ridiculous."

"So, it's ridiculous. I don't like the idea of crazy spending. It worries me. If there was a thoughtful plan, it'd be another matter. Some sense of applying the brakes. But it feels like all, buy this, buy that, buy whatever." She does what we do when we don't know what to do. She opens the refrigerator and stares inside. She lets the door slap shut again. "Indigo—you know, I just haven't processed how to handle all this money stuff yet."

"I know," I say. I lift the door to Chico's cage. Chico eats these bird pellets, but he also needs regular, healthy human food too. I give him some broccoli from the fridge, a bit of wheat bread, a little pinch of leftover chicken. "Chico good boy," he says. Sure.

"And I can't process it right at this moment. This has been one shitty day." She drops into a kitchen chair. She shoves aside the stack of mail. She rubs her temples with her fingertips. "There's a full moon, or something, because Dr. Kaninski's schedule was just *packed*. So we're seeing twice the amount of people, and no one's got their insurance cards, and then there's an emergency call from this father who says his son's locked himself in his room and he's got a *gun*, and Dr. Kaninski's at *lunch* and then it turns out the son doesn't have a gun, after I interrupt the doctor's pad thai, and then this woman calls for the second time in a month to get more meds when she has a three-month supply, and then the day is finally over and I go to my car and I've got a *flat*."

"Oh, man," I say. "You should have called me."

"For you to do what? Change my tire? Offer me moral support while I panic?"

"I can change a tire!" I say. "Okay, maybe I can't change a tire."

Deb Caletti

"Dr. Kaninski changed it for me." She chuckles. "A psychiatrist changing a tire. His golf ball tie was flipped over one shoulder. I feel stupid not knowing how to change it myself. I doubt I could have jacked the thing up, though . . ."

"I think that means you have penis envy," I say.

"Male arm muscle envy, and no other body parts, thank you." Mom takes off her shoes. There's the clunk of her heels under the table. "Hot, tired, and sick of humanity. This calls for fast food," she says.

"Agreed," I say. "It's been a shitty day for everyone."

"What happened?"

"Trust me."

"Do me a favor? Take a poll and figure out what everyone wants to eat. I'll meet you at the car."

"I'll drive" I say.

"Forget it," she says. "I value my life."

Taco Time, we decide. I'm counting on insta-fat and salt served in cardboard food boxes to lift my mood, which has gone gray and senseless as ash. I'm not the sort to get depressed. Usually, the times I can count on it hitting are when we've had two weeks of straight, gloomy rain, and when I hear those ads for some depression medicine or clinical study on the radio. *Are you feeling helpless or hopeless? Does your life seem meaningless and empty? Are you full of the awareness that we just put up with a bunch of endless crap, punctuated by brief moments of brightness, and then we die?* Depression ads are so depressing. If you don't have it before one of those things, you have it after. Those usually are the only real times a fuzz of gloom descends on me. But now I feel this tug and pull at my inner joy, a gradual darkening, the way they used to get the room ready for a movie in elementary school. The screen is yanked down. The heavy curtains dragged shut, first one, then the other. Finally, *Justin, get the lights.* I've just graduated from the inane prison that's high school and I'm the relatively new owner of two and a half million dollars and I'm feeling *depressed?* Melanie (and most of my peers and a few teachers and Severin and sometimes Mom) may have been right after all—I *am* crazy.

We get into Mom's car, which now has three regular wheels and one tiny, undersize spare that looks both forlorn and wrongly hopeful. Then Mom forgets her keys and has to go back in again. It's practically a law in our house that you can't leave the house without forgetting something. You say good-bye to a member of my family, and it's just a rehearsal, because a second later they'll come dashing back in. Finally, we're buckled up, and the minute Mom starts up the car, my phone rings.

"In, listen. I've just had a brilliant idea."

Uh-oh. The last brilliant idea Trevor had was when he thought he'd surprise his mom and give her the afternoon off from day-care work. He carted off six little kids and put them into her minivan while they were playing outside. When Mrs. Williams came out to the backyard and found it empty, she screamed with the full-power open-throttle fear and outrage of a bear whose cubs have been snatched. It was so loud, the guy on parole across the street took off running even though he didn't do anything wrong, and old Mrs. Jaynes, the neighbor lady next door, who'd been on a ladder picking apples from her tree, flew from it in airborne surprise, breaking a hip and flinging apples in all directions. An apple was even later found in one of Trevor's mom's flowerpots, and another, weirdly, in a baseball mitt one of the toddlers had brought over. Poor Mrs. Jaynes has used a walker

Deb Caletti

ever since; she shouldn't have been on a ladder at her age, but still. The police stopped Trevor and the minivan as they were pulling out of Burger King; they were all wearing golden crowns and singing a sloppy rendition of "Wheels on the Bus."

"I've had a lousy day, Trevor," I warn. Mom backs out of the driveway, looking both ways. Ever since I got my own car, everyone else's driving has been driving me crazy. I never realized how slow she goes. We're moving at maybe five miles an hour. I wouldn't even have known we'd left, except the trees and houses are stepping backward oh so slightly out my window. At this rate, we'll be at the mailboxes by Tuesday.

What happened? Mom doesn't say, but mouths instead.

I'm expecting Trevor to ask the same thing. He's always been a good boyfriend that way, and is alert to comfort and misery clues. Offering his sweatshirt, remembering that girls actually need to use the bathroom, stuff like that. But this time, I'm not sure he even hears me.

"I was just driving home from work, and it hit me," Trevor says.

"A Hostess truck?" I say. I still hear that jerk's horn.

"What? No, this idea. I've been thinking about how to expand my product line, you know. I mean, I've got a good line of Catholic products, I think. But what about other religions? Am I limiting my sales base? So, I'm just running through the list in my head, okay? Methodists. Well, the fact of the matter is, Methodists aren't funny. Protestants, Methodists, Lutherans— none of them are funny. They're pot roast, green beans, potatoes. What's funny there? Then I realize. Mormons. You've got the whole bigamy thing. Bigamy's hilarious."

"That's kind of going low, Trevor. Kind of cliché. They don't even really practice bigamy." Irritation rushes in. I know where this is heading. Another way to spend my money. I hate the way he sees me lately. Like I'm a human ATM machine.

Mom scrunches her eyebrows. *Bigamy?* she mouths.

"What's the matter with you, In? Jesus, you're sounding uptight."

"I told you, I had a bad day."

"Well, then I guess you're not going to like my 'I Heart My Wives' T-shirts."

He's still being a Teflon listener. Everything I'm saying is sliding right off of him.

"Why don't we talk about this another time," I say. "Right now? I'm tired of the whole topic."

There's silence on the other end, the kind of silence that's very noisy. Unsaids say so much more than saids. I feel the sharp corners and dangerous ledges in the quiet.

"I know what you're thinking," he says. Trevor's voice has a snap. And Trevor's voice never has a snap—Trevor has the perpetual cheer of a Hawaiian shirt. My throat closes. There are so many words there that want to come out, that nothing can come out. I watch as Mom eeks through the neighborhood. We finally make the left turn heading toward town; we inch in the direction of the small bridge that hooks over Nine Mile Falls Creek, where the salmon run. "You're thinking I'm after your money. It's what you're always thinking lately." I look at fir trees, every fir tree, and wish for more space between Trevor's words and what might come after them.

"I'm not your ticket someplace," I say.

It comes out before I realize it. Mom shoots an alarmed look my way. There is silence. I just sit there, holding the phone. I

Deb Caletti

don't even hear him breathe. I've shocked him, and I've shocked myself. The words are horrible, I realize. I want to snatch them back, but there's too much truth in them to do that.

"Wow," Trevor says finally. "Wow. I guess after two—more than two—years of being together, I thought we could handle anything. Even this, In. But you haven't even given us a chance to handle it. You put yourself in one place and you put me over here."

"I *am* in a different place," I say.

"Funny, I thought we were heading somewhere together. I thought this—the money. I thought it was something that happened to *us*. But apparently I was wrong."

I don't say anything. His words are too close, and so I shove them far.

"And maybe you ought to know something else," he says. "Just now? I didn't call you to talk about your money. Maybe you might remember that I had this idea long before that. I don't need your money."

And suddenly I feel something I've never felt with Trevor before. A corner I could turn, down a street away from him. I can see that corner so clearly that I feel a choice in front of me. To walk ahead and make the turn or to run back the way I came. The space ahead seems so large, so frighteningly unknown; the space behind is known. It's where a sense of home is, even if home doesn't fit anymore. And so I rush back. I run back to safety like a little kid who thought for a moment he was lost.

"Trevor, I'm sorry, okay? I'm sitting in the car with Mom. I love you, all right? Just, let's do this later."

Silence again. "Fine."

We hang up our cell phones I bought us. The thing about

running back to safety—its relief abandons you fast. The things-are-still-okay comfort is fleeting, like touching base in a tag game before you know you have to run off again. Change is the most relentless nag. For about thirty seconds, I'm so glad I didn't do something crazy and end things with Trevor right there. And then, the scritch of annoyance starts. He thought the money was something that happened to us? Wasn't he making an awful lot of assumptions here, without checking with me first? And, really? My money wasn't going to be brought up? When it has come up in practically every conversation we've had in the last six weeks?

"Are you all right?" Mom sneaks a look at me.

"Yeah," I sigh, but shake my head. My body isn't so sure. Along with my resumed annoyance is something else. Supreme inner disappointment, the big daddy of guilt, aka shame. I said *I love you* and didn't mean love. I meant *Please don't leave me*. I meant *Please don't inflict change on me*. I meant *Let's just ignore this. I'm not ready for this right now*. I'm embarrassed at my own self for using Love and Cling interchangeably.

"Do you want to talk about it?" Mom asks. She has finally crept over the other side of the bridge. One of us, anyway, is capable of forward motion, even at the pace of a marble on a barely tilted surface.

I shake my head, which is starting to hurt. I realize this about the inner voice—it whispers, then it shouts, and then it back-hands you one with a headache for not listening. You can fool the mind, but you can't fool the body. The body is more honest. "Can we just get there?" I ask.

"I'll take the freeway, instead of going through town," she says.

I roll down my window, lean one elbow out. I sniff the green,

Deb Caletti

hopeful air of summer. Mom sits at the freeway entrance, her turn signal making an endless *click, clock, click clock*. Finally, she hits the accelerator and we are off, and then there is a horrible, screeching cry in the backseat, and a sudden moment of confusion and fur and the long searing scrape of a claw down my forearm.

"Oh my God, oh my God. Freud!" Mom screams.

"Shit, what's he doing in here?"

Freud is wondering the same thing. The car as a stationary sleeping palace is one thing, but as a speeding, scenery flying, wind-sucking metallic force of nature—Freud is having none of it. Freud is in full get-me-outta-here panic, and Mom is trying to merge and a corvette with its radio blaring screams past, the driver flipping her off, and her turn signal is still on, and now she's flicked on her windshield wipers by mistake and sent a fountain of wiper fluid shooting across the windshield and Freud has leapt to the backseat and now the front again and is clinging halfway up Mom's shoulder. I try to pull him off so she can drive and we won't be killed as Mom yells, "Ow! Ow! Ow!"

"Move him! Ow, damnit! I can't see!"

"Pull over, pull over!" I say, and finally Mom eases over to the side of the freeway. She turns off the engine. A semi rattles and whooshes past, and the car shakes with apparent fear. Freud still clings to her shoulder, his eyes wild.

"How did we not see him?" she says.

"I don't know. I didn't even look. He was probably on the floor."

"When we started going fast . . ."

I remove Freud's claws from Mom, and he lunges to my lap, sinks his little needles into my bare shorts-clad legs. I let out a scream, clench shut my eyes, and feel his squirming mass rise from my grasp. Shit, he bounds from me, and all I see when I open my eyes is his furry narrow ass and his hideous, villainous tail escape through my open window.

"Freud!" Mom yells. "Oh, God!"

I have a vision of a flattened Freud; Freud as a thin roadkill animal crepe. Trodden by Sears radials, guts insta-compressed into a new layer of asphalt, his soul hightailing it from the premises (heading for you know where), leaving glassy eyes behind. I don't want to see that happen to Freud, even if Mom and I look like we've just made a joint jaunt through a paper shredder. Freud's one of those relatives that you aren't especially fond of but who is still part of the family, damn it.

But Freud's plan does not involve a leap into speeding traffic. He's running as fast as his hairy hide can take him, into the woods adjoining the freeway. I barely notice the SUV pulling over ahead of us, its monstrous emergency lights blinking on-off. A woman with short brown hair pops her head from the driver's side window. Her mouth is a gash of open anger.

"You sicko!" she screams. "I saw what you did!"

Nothing is making sense. Mom is flinging open her door, her eyes glued to Freud's little gray body heading for the evergreens, but this woman is shouting from her massive, environment-smashing car.

"You animal killer! I'm going to call the police! Sicko!" she screams again. And then her huge tires are in motion and the tanklike back of her SUV rolls back into traffic to suck more life from our planet.

"She thinks we threw him out the window. She thinks we brought him here to ditch him," I say.

Deb Caletti

But Mom isn't paying attention to any of this. She's hiking one leg over the highway barrier, her arms flailing around for something to hold on to. Oh, God, this is Mom putting up Christmas lights and changing smoke detector batteries all over again.

"Wait for me," I say. I unclasp my seat belt and go out after her. She's stumbling toward the forest and shouting Freud's name. His evil little behind disappears into some ferns and then appears again out the other side. He looks over one shoulder at us.

"It's okay, Freud," Mom croons. "Stay there. I'll come get you. It's okay." Mom is using her talk-the-suicide-from-the-ledge voice, which she perfected at work. Well, maybe not perfected, because Freud takes off again. We scramble after him, branches breaking under our feet, and holly and blackberries scraping our legs, already in shambles. Freud eyes a tree trunk. He isn't quite crouched to leap, but his shoulders are in that considering-it pose.

"No," Mom pleads. She's gone from rational and calm to desperate. "Freud, no."

But cats love a yes when you need a no. He slings his body back then forward, slingshot-style, and up the tree he goes.

We watch him clutch and climb and settle onto a branch just out of reach. He makes himself comfy.

"Oh, Freud," Mom says.

"This isn't funny, Freud, goddamnit," I say.

Mom hides her face in her hands. I look around for something, anything that might help us. The freeway hums behind us. There's nothing here but huckleberry bushes and . . . I don't know, green bushes, I'm not some kind of horticulture expert. We're in a forest, that's the point.

"This is ridiculous," I say.

"I don't know what to do. I just don't know."

"We ought to leave you here, Freud. You can be eaten by coyotes and mountain lions. You could be a tasty little morsel," I sneer.

Mom clasps her hands and looks skyward. Man, we are in trouble if Mom's praying. Mom says she doesn't generally like to bother God unless there's a crisis, same as she does with Dad.

"Mom!" I say. I'm trying to snap her back to the here and now. At the moment, we need a higher power that will actually return our phone calls.

Mom looks back at Freud. "Please," she says. "Come on, Freud. Here, kitty. Come here."

But Freud's twisted little sadistic self is just beginning to enjoy this. If cats love a yes when you need a no, they love a no when you need a yes even more.

"Fine. Let's leave him," I say.

"Indigo, no. We can't do that."

"Why not? This is a power trip. Look at him."

"He looks scared," she says.

"Scared, my ass. He looks smug."

Mom looks at Freud, considers this. "Well, still. We need something to climb up. Maybe we can call someone. Someone with a big ladder."

Right as she says that, we hear the *crack-snap* of footsteps in a forest. A big square-shouldered figure approaches. A big square-shouldered figure in a uniform. My God, a cop.

"Is everything all right here?" he says. "What seems to be the trouble?" He must have watched plenty of cop shows, because he has the lines down.

Deb Caletti

"Officer! Oh my gosh," Mom gushes. She's suddenly turned all Catholic girl in the presence of authority. Mom never says "gosh." "My cat . . ."

"You need to understand that we take animal cruelty cases very seriously," he says.

I don't doubt him. He looks like he takes everything very seriously. He has a square jaw, too, and his eyes are hidden behind sunglasses. His hips are bulked up by radios and other cop stuff that hangs off of him. If he actually had to run, it'd be as awkward as having a toddler strapped around your waist. "No, there's been a misunderstanding," Mom says.

"Mmmm-hmmm," Officer Friendly says. "We got a call about someone throwing a cat onto the freeway."

"I wasn't throwing a cat. . . . This is my pet. We'd never hurt him."

"Ha," I say.

Mom shoots me a look. "He was in the backseat."

"The caller witnessed a cat being thrown," the officer says.

"We didn't throw him! He jumped up . . . My daughter had her window open . . . He panicked when we got on the freeway, and now . . . I don't know how to get him down . . ." Mom's voice cracks. Mom's voice cracks and Mom cracks. She lets out a small sob. She puts her palms to her eyes.

"Ma'am?" the officer says.

"I would never hurt my cat. Never. Any living being . . ." She's crying now. "He's part of my family. His shots are all up to date. . . ."

"Ma'am? It's okay, all right?" The officer removes a radio from his hip. Clicks it on, holds it up to his mouth. He spits a few words into it, hooks it back to his hip again.

"He gets this special medicine for his eye. . . ."

"Mom, it's okay," I say. She has branches in her hair.

"The fire department will be here in a minute to get him down," the police officer says.

"I'm sorry," she says. "It's just been one of those days. . . . One thing after another. You know?"

He lifts his glasses off his head. Maybe his eyes aren't so bad underneath. Maybe they're slightly kind. "You look really familiar to me," he says. "You didn't happen to go to Lake Washington High, did you? In Kirkland? Mr. Cassady, history?"

"Yes . . . ," Mom says. "I did."

"Brian Murphy?" he says.

She squints her eyes, like he's a tiny, fuzzy place on a map that she can't see without her glasses. "Brian? Oh my God, I'd have never recognized you."

"Naomi Connors? You look great!"

She doesn't correct her last name. I can hear the heaving sound of a truck pulling up, and see the spin of red lights through the trees. The fire truck is here.

"The fire truck's here," I say.

But they ignore me. Mom is flashing this smile as bright as an amusement park at night, and Officer Brian Murphy is grinning like a goofy kid who just won a ribbon for his volcano at the science fair.

"So, how've you been?" he asks. "God, you haven't changed a bit."

"I'm not sure if that's a good thing." She laughs.

"Oh it is, it is," he says.

Two firemen are picking their way through the forest, hauling a mega ladder between them. Freud must see it too, because

Deb Caletti

he stands lazily, and begins inching his way back along the branch.

"Mom! Freud . . . ," I say. But Mom has forgotten the reason we are standing out in the middle of a forest. Mom has forgotten we are out in a forest at all. She may as well be at a cocktail party, swirling her ice cubes in a glass and contemplating the basket of tortilla chips.

"You live here in town, then?" Officer Brian Murphy asks. He folds his arms and leans his weight on one foot, turning his shape from intimidating square to friendly triangle.

"I do. After my divorce . . ."

Blah, blah, blah. I leave the exciting plot right there and wait under the tree, scooping up Freud when he touches down. The firemen barely make it halfway, when I head toward them with Freud in my death grip.

"He's a hideous beast who came down the minute he saw you. I'm sorry," I say.

"Cats," the fireman says to his partner, and shakes his head.

I roll up the car window, place Freud in the backseat. I sit up front, waiting for Mom and Officer Brian. When she finally gets into the car, she's all cheerful. "Okay, Freudy Boy," she says. "We had quite a little adventure, didn't we?"

"Did he give you happy drugs from some bust?"

"He asked for my number. Isn't that funny?" she says. "Now, I don't want you to ever, ever do that naughty thing again," Mom addresses Freud. "Indigo, hold his collar from here so he stays in the back."

"You sure are cheery," I say. "For just getting mauled by the cat and almost arrested."

She laughs. "Brian would never have arrested me." She flips

The Fortunes of Indigo Skye

down her visor, smiles at herself and makes sure there's nothing in her teeth. Satisfied, she pulls out into traffic. Her windshield wipers are on. *Flick-flick. Flick-flick.*

"Mom, your wipers, for God's sake," I say.

"Oh!" she says.

She swipes at the wiper handle. But she doesn't turn them all the way off. They're set at that annoying channel where they seem off, but give a single, sudden burst of on after fifteen seconds. Mom doesn't seem to notice. The wipers are silent, then fifteen seconds later, on again.

I consider letting out a single, bloodcurdling scream. Then I consider pulling a Freud and leaping out of the window myself. It all suddenly seems too much. Firing myself from my job; Leroy's and Trina's and Severin's humiliation; a near breakup with Trevor; Mom in all her Mom-ness. I feel the sudden Had Enough that is quiet but powerful in its certainty. I want out of here. Away from all of them. I want into a different "real world." Everyone wants a Big Decision? Fine, my Big Decision is going to be to make my world bigger. I will take my two and a half million dollars and head to the only place I have an invitation—with Melanie to Malibu. Indigo Skye, phase two.

Deb Caletti

14

What I did next was shitty. Only I didn't feel like it was shitty at the time. I felt it was my right, and "my right" is the guilt-avoiding umbrella under which most shitty things are done. It was my right to call Melanie as soon as we got home, the very second after the Taco Time papers had been balled up and thrown away, the splotches of hot sauce wiped from the table. It was my right to not tell anyone where I was going, until I left the next morning. It was my right to tell only Bex, who was still hypnotized in front of the television.

"I'm going to California for a while with Melanie," I say. "Tell everyone."

"Okay." Bex watches an enormous wooden spoon stir an even bigger pot of a rice concoction the yellowish tones of risotto.

"Tell Trevor I'm gone," I say.

"Mmmm-hmmm," Bex says.

Every conflict, I've decided, is about power. Every one. Wars are about power, sure, and immigration, and crime, and poverty, but so is who gets the parking space and if you go to the movies or out to dinner and if he thinks you look fat in those jeans and if she'll let you change shifts and whose turn it is to let the dog out and if he loves her more than you and if she snubbed you at that party. Power—who has it and who doesn't, and who has what the other person doesn't have. Who's up and who's down. Sandbox stuff. He took my tractor. We both want that shovel.

Power.

And what's the shortcut to power? The winner, the king, the

insta-got-it? Money, naturally. Take it from me, someone who didn't have it and then did, you feel different when you've got it. You've got rights. You've got a voice. You've got power-over. And maybe, just maybe, you feel a little smug about that. Maybe you feel a little entitled. You, after all, sit in the part of the plane where they use china and linen, or better yet, a different plane entirely from those poor slobs whose knees are scrunched to their chins all the way to their destination.

Maybe, too, my father was right. And maybe I didn't care that he was.

Money, see, it gives you the ability to say *Fuck you*. And that ability feels good. It feels swingy and wide and soaring. It feels large and strong and without borders. Borders? YOU make the borders, if you want them. And when you've got the ability to say *Fuck you*, you want to use it. Money is power, all right, but that in no way should indicate that those who have it will do the right thing by it. You feel different when you have money, set apart, and for most people, I'd guess that "set apart" is not even a half step from "better than." You can meet everyone's eyes, unlike the kids at school, the poor ones, who often look at their shoes when they speak. You're in the mental box seat, and they're in the last, upper rows. "Set apart" means *you* and *them*. It can get away from you. It can spin out of control and make you ugly. But hey, you've got a right to be ugly.

That's my explanation for my shitty behavior, anyway. Why I ignore my phone ringing and ringing until I finally shut it off. How I manage to enjoy the literal first class on the plane, and disregard the spinning elf of guilt in my gut. How I've justified my no-plan plan. Maybe I'll stay a week. Maybe I'll stay forever. Maybe I'll do whatever I damn well please.

Deb Caletti

"Put that thing away, Indigo, it's giving me the creeps," Melanie says. She flicks the laminated corner of the safety card. I didn't realize I was still holding it. The cartoon people seem to be enjoying going down the poofy yellow slide. It makes me think of a birthday party Melanie had, where her parents rented one of those inflatable tents you jump in and the same sort of slide, minus the life jackets. "Remember that party your parents had for you with the slide?" I ask.

"Oh my God, don't remind me. Given the fact that I was fourteen at the time . . ." Melanie's chair is reclined all the way. The man behind her could almost clean her teeth, if he had one of those spiky tools and a paper bib. Melanie raises one finger to get the flight attendant's attention. The woman has blond hair combed up in a tight twist. She seems familiar but I don't know from where, and it's driving me crazy. Then I realize she looks like the woman at the makeup counter. Same hair, same creamy tan powdery face, same outlined lips. "I'd like a sparkling water with no ice and a lime," Melanie says. "Indigo, do you want anything?"

"No, thanks," I say, and smile at the flight attendant/makeup counter woman. She smiles back at me, but it's only a tight exercise of facial muscles merely posing as actual pleasantry. Maybe I know that because I've given that same smile myself sometimes.

The flight attendant returns a moment later with Melanie's glass. In first class, you get real glasses, and real knives, too—apparently, the terrorists sit with the general public.

Melanie doesn't acknowledge the flight attendant; she only takes the glass and sets it onto her tray and flips another page in one of the catalogues she's brought along.

"Thank you," I remind. People with no manners suck.

"No problem," Melanie says. She focuses on the rectangular photos of leggy women in shorts, T-shirts, this skirt, that skirt. Melanie reads the catalogue like it has an engrossing plot. After a while, her chin pops up suddenly. "Feel that? We're descending."

It's true—we're not so much descending, which implies easing gradually downward, as seeming to drop down a staircase with very large steps. It makes me remember that we are in a hunk of metal in the sky, which is downright crazy when you think about it. It's best not to think about it. My body knows the truth, though, and is protesting this situation to the best of its ability, with a fluttery panic in my chest, and ears that are balloons suddenly filling. I fight the urge to grab Melanie's arm and sink my nails in, but she just sits there, folding down the top corner of a page of some pair of pants she likes.

This is the second flight I've been on in just a few short months, but I already have the necessary information to compare the skill and expertise of pilots. The wheels hit the ground with enough of a bump that my ass rises briefly into the air, and the wheels make this grinding metal-on-metal screech that reminds me of this semi truck I recently encountered, which tried to stop suddenly just because I changed lanes. I clutch my arm rests against the g-force, dig my heels against the floor to aid in the braking, same as Fred Flintstone in his foot-powered car.

"I like this sweater, but I'm not so hot on V-necks," Melanie says.

"Jesus, I think this plane should have had a 'Student Driver' sign on the back," I say.

Melanie gives me her usual Melanie look of scrunched, quizzical eyebrows. These are usually released a moment later with a barely discernable shoulder shrug, a physical demonstration of *Whatever*.

Deb Caletti

"My dad will meet us at baggage claim," she says. "But tomorrow let's just rent our own car." She's told me this plan about a thousand times now, which means she's excited enough about it that she's anxious it won't actually happen. It must be the second part of this she's worried about, though, because, sure enough, her dad's right there by the silver carousel, his arms folded across his chest. He looks like a completely different guy from the one who's always in the media room in the perfect house in Nine Mile Falls. He's already tan, and has his sunglasses on his head. His black hair is slicked back, as if he's permanently just gotten out of the pool.

"I see you two made it okay," he says, and I swear to God, Allen has been replaced by his twin brother. I can't quite figure out what's different. At home, he's quiet and sort of slinks around before he disappears again. But here, even though he hasn't said anything yet, he's louder. He's larger. And as if to prove my very thinking, his cell phone rings and he's suddenly smiling hugely and performing into it.

"HEY!" he says in capital letters. "It's ALLEN! Yeah, back in town!" His words backslap and shmooze.

"God, watch my bag not make it," Melanie says, although right now the carousel just sits still and looks tired.

I take my cell phone out of my bag; turn it on. I've gone from three messages to fourteen in a two-and-a-half-hour plane ride.

Indigo, it's Mom. What have you done? Why are you doing this? I called Jane and . . . I erase the message. *Indigo. I'm very worried about you. Call me, please. The least you could do is tell . . .* Erase. *Goddamnit, Indigo. Call and tell us what's going on. I've tried to reach Melanie's parents, and no one . . .* Erase. *In? What the fuck is going on? I'm assuming this is your way of saying we're through, but Christ, your mom is a wreck . . . Erase. Indigo, Trevor's been here and he's just heartbroken. Heartbroken. If you want a little adventure, fine, but to treat us . . . Erase. In? Trevor. Fuck. Never mind. Click. Erase. Indigo, shit. Severin. Would you please call Mom? She's a mess. Erase.* Then Bex's voice. *A role model doesn't just take off.* And then, finally: *Indigo? It's Dad. Your mom phoned me. I'm just . . . here if you need me.*

I don't want to hear their voices. I don't want to think about them. So, away they go. *No new messages,* the voice mail chick reports.

"We'll get together for a drink!" Allen says.

The carousel groans and lurches into motion. Melanie stands at its edge, but I just wait there with my bag between my feet. Some kid sits on the edge of her Winnie-the-Pooh suitcase and looks weary, and a man in a golf shirt and slacks and silver hair waits beside her while Grandma, I'm guessing, with her gold-white hair, jiggles a little boy with chubby legs and saltwater sandals and a face rosy from sleep. The various pieces of luggage start to bamp down the ramp, spin to place and ride slowly around. A black bag falls. Another black bag. Another black bag. Golf clubs. Another black bag. Luggage makers must be either extraordinarily lacking in creativity or extraordinarily depressed. Down slides a car seat, which Grandpa snatches up. A mystery box all taped up, more golf clubs. Another black bag, to which Melanie says, "There it is," although I have no idea how she can tell.

Allen is still exclaiming away on his cell phone, and we follow behind him. Melanie has put her sunglasses on, even though we're inside.

"Is that so you won't be recognized?" I joke, but then notice that all kinds of people have their sunglasses on. We follow Allen

Deb Caletti

outside. There are two black limos waiting at the curb, and a Hummer limo, which looks like a military command center on wheels. I think my brother had one of those when he was a kid. It came with little guys with guns that my mom told him he couldn't play with, so he was forced to make the happy Fisher-Price people, with their molded plastic brown and yellow hair, ride in there instead.

Allen points a key fob at a slick black Mercedes, and the car makes a series of chirps that sound like Chico when his claw gets stuck in his cage. The trunk pops open, and we put our bags in. It's early evening but it's hot. Allen sits in the driver's seat while we put our stuff in, and then Melanie sits in front with him. The car is arctic freezing inside—Allen has the air conditioner blasting, I guess, but it's so quiet, you don't hear a sound now that he's hung up his phone. We wind our way out of the airport, and join the long stretch of traffic.

"You should have a convertible, Dad," Melanie says.

"And suck exhaust every time I get on the road? No thanks," Allen says. He keeps taking peeks in the rearview mirror, and at first I think he's making sure I'm not putting gum in his ashtrays. But then I realize he's not looking at me at all. He leans back a bit so that he can see his own reflection in the side mirror too. *Hey there, Hot Stuff,* I can hear him say to himself. *Hey, Good Lookin'.* I wonder what Lisa would say if she could see this routine. I wonder if he's available later that night for a date with himself.

"Doesn't your mom like to come on these trips?" I ask.

"She doesn't like to fly," Allen says. I get a flash of an image— Allen opening the newspaper every morning to some plane crash article, placing it right next to Lisa's cereal bowl.

Driving in this car is like driving in some padded, soundproof chamber, protected from every discomfort, glitch, or minor annoyance. The windows are tinted to soften every visual harshness of life (even the strip mall we pass, with its teriyaki place, Laundromat, and Spanish video store, looks muted and calm), and you can control the climate from every seat. But the car is creepy, somehow—airtight and squishy like some Travel Casket made by Sharper Image.

We edge forward in bursts, then brake. Eventually the landscape changes and there are hills of large homes and the dots of palm trees. It was not long ago that I was in a sunny, unfamiliar place with palm trees and a dad driving a car, and yet this is a completely different experience. I'm apart here, not a part.

I feel some twisty sadness, something that's edging toward regret. *Shit, Indigo,* I tell myself. *You only just got here. You wanted a bigger world. Enjoy the experience! This is an adventure! Maybe this is a NEW LIFE.*

I give myself a talking to. Nothing new is comfortable at first. If I am intent on expanding out of my narrow existence, I need to give it time. Six months. A month. Me and myself compromise. The summer, at least. I try to change my attitude. I play Count the BMWs, which gets unchallenging quickly. The sun is beginning to set, though, and the sky through the tinted windows looks pink-and-blue beautiful. I want to see the real thing for a moment, and I crack my window, breaking the suction of the car and causing Allen to whip his head around and exclaim "Hey!" in protest.

I roll it back up. Maybe he was right about the exhaust. When the window is down, I see that the colors are not pink and blue, but a hazy, muddy gray-brown. "I just wanted to see the sunset," I say.

Deb Caletti

"It's just smog," he says.

"A smogset," Melanie says. This cracks them both up.

"Just look at it with the window up. It looks better that way," Allen says.

It takes us a long time to get to the house Allen rents in Malibu. It's on the beach, with lots of angles and large glass windows and an entryway with a marble floor the color of Travertino Navona, Trina's table. Trina would love this place. There's a white carpet in a living room no one goes in (the carpets still look springy and the vacuum tracks are linear and undisturbed) and shiny wood floors in the kitchen. The furniture is sleek—trim leather sofas and geometric pillows. It smells like new paint and new leather, and there are books about art and architecture posing at angles on the end tables, and dimmed lights and some ooh-ah New Agey chime-and-water type music that's playing in every room. "I guess I'm not going to be drinking tomato juice in there," I say, and nod toward the living room.

"He's got a housekeeper, so don't worry if you make a mess," Melanie says. She drops her bags where she stands. "Let me show you your room."

My room is white too, with black accents—a black headboard and black end tables. There's a painting of something splotchy and orange over the bed. The music has followed us in here.

"It's great, Mel," I say. "But the music's freaking me out a little. I feel like I should meditate at the altar of Citibank, or something."

"He says it relaxes him," Melanie says. "If you like this, wait'll you see the pool."

"Your dad is a different guy here," I say.

"Thank God," Melanie says. "I think he's his more natural

self. A place can bring out your more natural self, don't you think? I feel more like the real me here. This is just . . . my place."

I keep my mouth shut, which should earn me some karma points. I'm hoping Melanie is just showing off a little for me here, in this new place, like people do when they present their territory— lifting their metaphorical leg on the this's and that's that they've got and want to flaunt, demonstrating the superiority of possessions that are theirs, not yours. Bex does it whenever she has a friend over—she'll show the little kid Chico's cage and say, "Chico can learn words faster than you." And then, "But he doesn't like new people." This latter part, of course, is an outright lie—Chico doesn't like anyone, except maybe Mom.

Melanie opens the French doors to the deck, where the pool is. It's like Vespa guy's, but with little blue-and-white tiles inside in a design, and padded deck chairs. The house is smack on the beach itself, which stretches left and right for miles; the other houses in rows on either side are layered like expensive desserts, making this huge house seem small and shivering. It's getting dark now, and the only light comes from the windows of the houses. The ocean itself, *shh-shuuu*-ing its whispered rhythms, is dark, dark. The sand is white fading into black where it meets the sea edge. We stand at the deck rail and listen and look at blackness, and my hair feels stringy and damp from sticky ocean air. I am here when I once was there. I am so different, I'm not sure who stands here.

"Maybe I should call home. Let them know I'm okay," I say.

"You're braver than I'd be," Melanie says. "O-kay. You know where your room is."

"Hey, Mel? Thanks. This is really amazing."

"Isn't it?" she says. "I *told* you."

Deb Caletti

Mom picks up on the first ring. "My God, Indigo, how could you do this? How could you just go take off without telling me? I can't believe you'd treat your own mother like this, let alone the rest of us. Trevor? He's a wreck. I've never seen him without the most perfect and happy disposition, and he had tears in his eyes, Indigo. He had tears in his eyes after the way you treated him. Bex has been crying—she feels like she did something wrong. . . . Indigo? Are you there?"

"Yes."

"Just . . ." Mom's voice breaks now. "Why?"

"I needed to," I say, and realize that at least this much is true. "I had to get away. I felt all this pressure . . ." I hear her voice and I remember it all again, the *all* that seems a hundred years ago already. Jane and Trina and Leroy and the gang; Trevor and Severin and Mom and the bills and Bex in front of that damn television.

"When are you coming back?"

The two-and-a-half-million-dollar question. "I don't know," I say.

She's quiet. Her voice is a whisper and I force myself to not let it twist my heart. "And that's how you leave home? No plan, no good-bye?"

"It's fine, Mom. Everything's fine. Nothing has really changed, except that I'm not there."

"Everything has changed, Indigo. You can do that, you know, with one action. You should know that. "

Silence. My stomach drops. "I'm sorry," I say. I'm not sure how much I mean it. The words seem far away again. They just feel sort of available and convenient—the way you pluck your blue T-shirt from the floor because it's on top of the pile and it's clean.

"We deserve better," Mom says.

"I've got to go."

I'm expecting a rush of protest, pleading, maybe even tears. But Mom is silent. I feel the sadness in the silence. It is so large and heavy it feels as solid and permanent as marble.

"Bye," I say.

"Good-bye, Indigo," Mom says.

And then she hangs up. There is just emptiness on the other end of the phone, and I sit at the edge of that deck chair and listen to the endless *shh-shuuu* of the waves, the in-out rasp of them, water on sand, water off sand. The trees make a shimmery-paper sound. The house is so bright the bright is almost noisy behind me, but in front there is only the stretch of blackness.

I rub the canvas fabric of the deck chair cushion with my palm. Finally I go inside, to my own room, that's all white and smells unopened. I prepare to sleep in the sixth place I have laid my head, and I feel lonelier than I ever have in my life.

15

"I told him, we are *not* waiting around all day for rides from him. I'm just not. So he's having the car place send over a car. We can just give them your credit card number when they get here."

"MY credit card number?"

"Well, Indigo, come on. There's no way he's paying for us to have a car here, and you know, we do get to stay here on the company account."

"Fine. You're right."

"You've got plenty of money. Don't be cheap." This should bother me maybe, but it doesn't. It feels like my share. There is this house she's invited me to. A glimmering pool outside. Melanie socks my arm playfully. We're hunting for breakfast in the fridge.

"I still can't believe you got a one-way ticket," she says.

"Why? Maybe I'll want to stay. Maybe this is my place too."

"Well, then the car lease is a good idea. I told him to get it for the summer, is that okay? Since that's how long we'll have the house? I thought maybe you could drive me down to school. If you decide you want to stay, you can go from there."

"Perfect," I say. And it feels closer to perfect today. The house is bright, and you can feel the ocean urging possibilities. I'd just forbid myself to think about Trevor and home. I'd use some mental flyswatter, smack away any slightly buzzing thought.

"There's nothing to eat around here," Melanie says. And she's right. Well, there's food, but there's nothing to *eat*. This is food for decoration. There's a package of pine nuts that cost more than a good breakfast at Carrera's, and a wedge of cheese that was more expensive than three packages of the pine nuts. There's a cellophane bag of dried figs in a designer bow, and a glass container of anchovies. It's impressive, but lacks the general requirements of actual food—nourishment, say. "We can stop somewhere on the way to the beach," Melanie says.

A few moments later, the doorbell chimes and two car lease guys poke their heads in our front door. Sitting outside is a red Porsche with the top down. I laugh. "You're kidding, right?" I say.

Melanie gives me a big smile. "They're going to need your card and your license. Dad's taken care of the rest."

I fill out forms in triplicate, no doubt giving the Porsche company my firstborn child if I scratch the car. Melanie is dangling the keys on the end of her finger. "No way," I say. "If I just paid to use this thing, you're Skipper and I'm Barbie."

The car is brand new. This all feels pretend. Melanie gets in and so do I, and I try to figure out how to get the parking brake off. I hunt around down by my legs and feel up the dashboard, like a seventh-grade boy on his second date. "I just felt up the dashboard," I say to Melanie, and we break up into the nervous, hysterical giggles of people doing something they sense they shouldn't. I finally spring something loose, and the car starts to roll backward.

"Indigo!" Melanie shrieks.

"Would you relax, for God's sake."

"The landscaping!"

"It's fine! These desert plants are sturdy! This is the land of the sturdy plants." I give the accelerator a little tap and it roars, a big *VROOM!* like a cartoon car. It always cracks me up when

Deb Caletti

sounds actually sound like the word used to describe them. A cat, for example, never says "meow." But occasionally a dog will really say "arf" or "woof" and this car actually says "vroom." Things are looking up. Maybe last night was mere homesickness, over now. Trevor would love this car, but I'm not thinking about Trevor.

I hear the click of Melanie's seat belt. We sort of lurch forward and back, and then forward again as I figure out the gears. There's a bit of a *reeech!* and we leave behind a skid of black and we are off.

"Oh my God," Melanie says. "Oh my God." Melanie's hands grip her seat.

"You are so overdramatic sometimes. Tell me how to get out of here."

Melanie just gapes, her mouth a black open half circle, like some hole on a miniature golf course. She points. I'm starting to like this a little. It's way better, let me tell you, than driving one of these things around the living room floor with Barbie and G.I. Joe. You can feel this car's power right under your hands, and in the way the seat curves around your butt. It's *there*, ready to do your command. This thrum of energy . . . You can feel the possibility of speed. I bet it can go *fast*.

"Holy fuck, Indigo, SLOW DOWN!"

"Take a laxative, Mel. God. I was just *seeing*."

"There's a speed trap here. Lots of people have lost their lives here. What's that guy with the movie-star hair? Jimmy Dean."

"That's a sausage."

"Jim. James, okay? And what's that other one. The guy, the rock guy. Jim Morrison. Right here."

"You only have to worry if your name is Jim," I say.

"All kinds of Hollywood people, Indigo. My point is, the

road's dangerous. You always see those wreaths and things here."

I know she's lying. Melanie's mouth always gets obvious sewn-up stitches in the corners when she lies. Her mouth looks like any hem my mom tries to sew without using the Sewing in a Tube. "Liar," I say. I point at her.

"I am not. Keep your hands on the wheel!"

"Mel, we're going to the beach, right? And the beach is supposed to be fun and relaxing. Anyway, where is 'the beach'? There's beach all over the place."

"Yeah, but nobody goes *here*. Just keep going, and you'll see it off to the left."

Melanie is right. There it is, and my stomach gives some kind of lurch of dread. No, more like a LURCH OF DREAD. I don't know what I was picturing—maybe Dad's beach, where we could rent some snorkeling gear, and swim in the waves and make fun of old guys in Speedos. This is a whole different game; I can tell before I even make my twentieth circle of the parking lot to find a place for my car. My car, by the way, isn't so special here. I see several of them, in various colors, most of them red, though, just like mine. A red Porsche here is like a black suitcase at the airport. Music blares from a couple of canopy tents on the beach. Perfect bodies play volleyball, reach for that serve. Only a few people are actually in the water—most are propped on half chairs or stretched on mats or towels. There are no little kids, no old people. Only perfect bodies and more perfect bodies holding plastic cups and laughing and jostling each other so boobs jiggle and liquid spills from cups.

Melanie is twisting and adjusting various triangles of her bikini, which is suddenly revealed, her shorts and top having been whipped off with record speed and shoved down onto the

Deb Caletti

floor of the car. I realize that my tank suit is Quaker and nunlike for this place. My insides creep, attempting to make a retreat that I'm unable to make. I'm not a prude, but this is NOT my place— everyone here is posed and styled and has put a great deal of thought into what they're wearing. Here, my slightly wobbly ass is weird and out of place. It wants to go home, where it's normal and even appreciated.

I start wondering when we can leave before I'm even out of the car. I want to protect the self-esteem of my imperfect body, and so I keep my shorts on. Melanie is striding over to a group of people, oblivious to the fact that the sand, sinking over the edges of my flip-flops, is searing hot.

"Desiree? Is that you?" she squeals.

"Melanie?" A girl with waist-length brown hair hugs Melanie, and looks at my shorts. "Aren't you hot?" she asks.

"I have an unsightly rash," I say.

Melanie gives me the *God, Indigo!* eyes. "This is Indigo," Melanie says. "And Desiree. We knew each other from last summer."

"And Glenn," Desiree says. No one is named Glenn anymore, but Glenn doesn't know that. He comes alive at the sound of his own name, same as Freud when he hears the can opener. He lifts his head and strides our way, ditching the guy he's talking to in order to join us.

"Your dad has the record company," he says to Melanie. He has brown, shaggy hair, a tattoo of a jet on one arm.

"Yeah," Melanie says, even though it isn't true. Her mouth doesn't have the little lines, though.

"Why are you wearing your shorts?" Glenn asks me. Obviously people here are entitled to rudeness.

"Why do you have an airplane on your shoulder?" I ask.

Glenn pats his own arm. "Oooh, that's my baby. I can't bear to be away from her for one minute. So I put her picture here."

"That's your plane?"

"Fuck yeah, it is. My Learjet 60."

"It's your dad's, Glenn," Desiree says.

"You don't know what you're talking about," he says. "It's mine. Is your car yours?"

"It *is* mine," Desiree says.

"Well, it's *mine*," Glenn says.

Mine, mine, mine. I'm getting a headache already.

"Great to meet you, but we've got to head out," I say.

"Real funny, Indigo," Melanie says. "Let's get something to drink."

"We've got beer over there," Glenn says. He points to one of the tents, where there are coolers and tables of food. "Cold beer makes me hot," he says. He sticks his tongue in Desiree's ear, and she swats him.

"We'll be right back," Melanie says. We head for the tent. I feel like she's George in *Of Mice and Men*, while I'm the retarded Lennie, following along. "That Desiree is such a bitch," she says. "But, God, did you see Glenn? I've had a crush on him for three summers."

"Glenn?" I look at him. I try to see what the big deal is. Trevor appears in my mind. I try to force the thought away, but it insists. My heart squeezes, lurches with ache. No way does Glenn have Trevor's sweet eyes or smile or arm muscles that could lift you right up and spin you around. I flash on a Trevor memory, the time we were at Pine Lake, looking at the trees; when the light made you sense that promises could be held in your hands. *Why*

Deb Caletti

do you feel like your heart could break when the hills turn pink and the trees turn yellow? Trevor asked. *Why do you feel every joy and sorrow and goodness and beauty and past and present and every perfect thing?* I banish the thought. I don't want to think of Trevor right now, at least the good parts of Trevor. I can't move into a new, bigger life, dragging my old furniture.

"Why do you say 'Glenn' like there's a question?" Melanie asks.

"He's got a plane tattoo on his arm." Leroy's tattoos are ART. This is advertising copy.

"He's got a *plane*."

"So you've got a crush on his plane."

"His father is a big shot at Universal."

"Do you think his father's hot too? I don't get your point."

Melanie blows exasperated air out her nose. She rummages around on the table of food for something to eat, but this looks like her dad's fridge, part two. Tortilla chips that are different colors. Olives, goat cheese. Various bottles of sauce but nothing to put it on. Melanie sticks her hand in a bag of chips and crunches, and then I do my Lennie routine and follow her to the volleyball game in progress. She seems to know these people too, and Glenn is playing, so she joins in and jumps around and squeals and holds her hands in that clasped-together way that means she's ready for the ball to come to her. Anytime it does, Glenn shoves his way in front of her and attacks it, like a pig after a corn-cob.

It is my general policy not to play sports in public, as it is against Section Five, Paragraph Three, in the humiliation clause of my personal contract. I once played a game of softball at a school picnic, and I can still hear the laughter. And hey, any nonathlete is doing a public service, because an athlete craves an audience like a guy with new sunglasses craves a mirror.

So I watch the volleyball game until I can't stand it anymore. Okay, I saw the perfect bodies, let's move on to something more interesting. Great spike, whoopee. A spike like that could change the world. My life was forever changed by witnessing it.

"Mel!" I shout. "We're gonna be late!" Okay, true, we have no plans, but this seems better than shouting that I am officially bored out of my skull. Melanie either doesn't hear me or pretends not to. I cup my hand around my mouth and try again, and she gives me the look a Doberman behind a chain-link fence gives the mailman. She obviously is having a great old time with Glenn, who acts like one of those asshole guys who has big-titted women reclining on the mud flaps of their trucks. You wonder how another woman could raise a man like that. His mother should be ashamed.

I survey my options. Well, I have the car key in my pocket. I could just leave. If I'm going to try to like this new place, I'd better get to know it better, find a beach that isn't your worst mall nightmare, only with everyone basically naked. Not everyone around here is like this, I'm sure. So I could just sneak away while Mel's vision is blocked by the bulk of Glenn's body in front of her. She could get a ride home from Glenn himself, something she might even thank me for. Or I could sit here and wait until . . . nah.

Then again, driving off without her might make Mel slightly pissed, and given the fact that Mel is currently my only friend here and that she is providing the roof over my head, making Mel pissed is probably not in my best interests.

I can feel my skin ripple with heat and sunburn and skin cancer. I'm going to go through a lot of sun protection factor

Deb Caletti

forty-five while I'm here, I realize. Maybe it's because I'm starving, but I'm getting that edgy feeling that is just this side of enraged, and I want out of here. I look around for ideas, and as I whip my head back toward the volleyball game, I feel a tiny little spin, brought on only by sudden movement and lack of food, but it makes me remember fainting in Carrera's, and, yes, what a brilliant idea.

Faking a faint is a little trickier than I thought. Should I keel over like a fence post, or crumple like a delicate woman in an old movie? I stand in a very obvious location, right at the sidelines of the volleyball "court," at the point where the net post is stuck into the sand. I make what I hope is a fainting sound, some sort of combo of Ah! and Oh! and give my best crumple.

At first it seems no one notices. Shit. Should I stand up and do it again? Glenn yells, "Our serve!" and there is the splat sound of a ball landing against waiting palms. I consider peeking or giving some sort of groan, but it turns out to be unnecessary.

"Oh, God!" some girl screams. "She passed out!"

"Too much fucking beer," some guy says.

"Indigo? Indigo! Are you all right?" Melanie.

"Maybe we better call 911," a girl says.

This, I do not want. I pop open my eyes at the very moment someone pours their water bottle over my head. Peachy.

"Heat stroke." A guy with brown hair streaked blond crouches beside me. His breath smells like corn chips. He holds an empty water bottle. "I was a lifeguard. Saw it all the time. Are you all right?"

"I don't know what happened," I say.

"Too much fucking beer," the other guy says again.

"Maybe you'd better get out of the sun for a while," the former lifeguard says.

"We'll do that," Melanie says. Now things are rolling. I sit up. My hair is drenched, and my bathing suit and shorts, too. I could have done without the bottle of water dumped over my head, but oh well. Now that the shock is over, it's really quite refreshing.

"God, that freaked me out," a girl in a white bikini says. "I need a beer."

"Just remember it was our serve," Glenn says.

"Are you sure you're okay to drive?" Melanie says.

"I'm feeling much better now," I say. "A hundred percent."

"Let's get something to eat," Melanie says. "If you're positive you don't need a doctor or something. We could call Dad . . ."

"A cheeseburger would help more than any doctor. And a shake. Low blood sugar . . ."

Melanie and I finally eat real food, and when she sees I'm not dying, she suggests we go shopping. At least stores are air-conditioned, she says.

I feel like it's my secret duty to make it up to her, so I park the car and we walk to a street of stores. These, too, are different from home. There is no True Value here, with the owner's stuffed dog out front. These are all small, expensive shops, you can tell, with names written on awnings. The first place is quiet, and the racks along the walls have maybe eight or ten things hanging on them. The two tables in front have maybe four or five items of clothing laid out.

"Are they going out of business?" I joke. "There's nothing here." I think I'm pretty funny, but Melanie's jaw clenches.

"Indigo, can we just look around nicely?" she says.

Deb Caletti

The woman behind the counter—now this is getting weird. She has blond hair in an upsweep, obvious cheekbones, and an air-conditioned demeanor. I swear to God, she looks just like the woman at the makeup counter, and just like the flight attendant in first class. I squinch at her in a *Hey, do we know each other* look, but she only lowers her eyebrows disapprovingly.

Melanie scrapes the hangers of the three skirts and two blouses and one shirt against the rack. "This is cute," she says. She holds up the T-shirt. I conduct the first order of business required after the uttering of the words "This is cute." I flip over the price tag. I've learned this from Mom, or perhaps it's an action that came down the genetic line, same as that tongue curling trick that we can all do but Trevor can't.

"Seventy-five dollars!" I say.

"Indigo, shhh, for God's sake." Melanie sneak-peeks at the blond woman.

"No, you're kidding me, right? That's seventy-five dollars for a T-shirt. It looks like any T-shirt. It looks like any and all T-shirts."

"It's not any and all. It's a really nice T-shirt. A very good quality T-shirt," Melanie says.

I rub the fabric between my fingers, prompting the blond woman to say too loudly, "Is there something I can help you with?"

"We're just looking," Melanie says.

Now, the blond chick and I and Melanie all know that "We're just looking" means Melanie's supposed to put the hanger back on the rack and that I am supposed to remove my pinching, soiled fingers from the fine fabric. The sense that I'd better do this is edging through my nervous system, but reaches some stop sign in my brain that makes me remember that I've got two and a half million dollars and can buy every item of clothing in this sparse, icy, over-air-conditioned store from this over-air-conditioned woman.

If I want to. And I don't want to. I want to argue with Melanie about a T-shirt being seventy-five dollars.

"Mel, this is ridiculous. This is not some fine fabric. One hundred percent cotton, okay? The same one hundred percent cotton that's in every other T-shirt."

"I can tell you're not a shopper. They are not the same."

"If I put on that T-shirt and one that cost ten bucks, you would not know the difference."

"You might not, but other people would," Melanie says.

"You know what? That's just insulting. No one could tell the difference. And the reason they can charge that is because you're insecure enough to worry that people *can* tell the difference. The T-shirt isn't just about being a T-shirt. It's about being a seventy-five-dollar T-shirt. It's about giving you a false sense of superiority. Remember, Mel, you cut the price tag *off*—no one's gonna see it."

"That's ridiculous," Melanie says, but she puts it back on the rack. "You have to pay more, Indigo, for better-quality things. It's the way they're *made*."

"Aspirin is aspirin and laundry soap is laundry soap and one hundred percent cotton is one hundred percent cotton."

"What about Egyptian cotton?" Melanie says.

"Does this say Egyptian cotton?" I flip the tags around and point. " 'Made in Sri Lanka.' I can't honestly believe I'm standing here arguing about cotton."

"Let's just go," Melanie says.

"Have a good afternoon, ladies," the saleswoman says. Her breath shoots a blast of arctic air at our backs.

Deb Caletti

Back at home by the pool, Mel moves her bathing suit straps up, down, over, untied, tied, down again to avoid tan lines.

"I cannot believe you don't like shopping, Indigo," she says. "What is wrong with you? You're the wrong person to give two million dollars to." She leans over to pick up her glass of lemonade from the table, holding her top with one hand. She takes a drink, then has to rearrange all the straps again.

I'm on the diving board. "Not all shopping. Just not that shopping today. God, those stores. That beach . . . ," I say, then leap. I like the *thwacka-thwacka-thwacka* noise it makes when I jump off. It sounds like I've done some fantastic dive, even though I can't dive worth shit. I feel the delicious, sudden swoosh of descent into a watery world. An impressive, bubbly display of bubbles bubble around me. This is the most fun I've had all day. It's vacation fun. I can't quite get it to feel like real-life fun.

I pop my head up, paddle to the pool edge, hold on to the curve of concrete with my fingertips.

"Indigo, this isn't like home here. You're just going to have to relax and go with it."

"Go with the flow. Hang loose. When in Rome, roam," I say.

"You want to experience all the things your money can buy? Here it is."

"Here it is. Huh," I say.

"Indigo, come on. You're going to get out of it what you put into it. You didn't even try to meet anyone at the beach. I know you just broke up with Trevor after a really long time, but it was *Trevor*."

"What's that supposed to mean?"

"You know what I mean. Just look at all your less-limited options here."

I feel pissed-offness hovering, but then again, what's so wrong with what she said? Isn't that what I felt too? Isn't that part of why I left Trevor, and everyone else?

Melanie's head is back against the lounge chair. Her eyes are closed. She's lying still to keep the pieces of clothing in place. "You know, you could have stayed home, but you didn't want to be home."

"I *don't* want to be home." I say this and the words sound brave, but inside they feel like a large ornate door that hides an empty room. I want to be beyond missing home, beyond my family and Trevor. I want to be big as two and a half million dollars, but I can't help wonder about all the things—all the people, all the places—that make me *me*.

I duck down under again, pop up so that my hair is sleeked back on my head. "God, those people at the beach, though," I say. "I thought the kids at our school were bad."

"They're rich; they're not *bad*. Just because they have money, they're not bad."

"I know that." I did know that. "Richard Howards had money, and look at him. You have money."

"Not like this. Not nearly like this. Not like you even have," Melanie says.

"Maybe it's just *the way* they have money."

"The way they have money."

"Maybe that it makes them smaller, when it should make them bigger," I say. "I don't know. I'm still figuring it out."

"Well, stop thinking so much," Melanie says. She twists, releases the lounge chair so that it lies flat, and rolls onto her stomach. "This all, right here—this is what everyone's after."

Deb Caletti

16

The next day I call Mom when she's at work. I leave a message, and don't answer when she calls back, doing that oops-we-missed-each-other lie that cell phones are so handy for. If I talk to her, I'm afraid I'll feel too much. Too guilty, too sad, too lonely, all the pulls of *old* that can keep you from *new*. My two-and-a-half-million-dollar self expects more from me. There are no more messages from Trevor. I check again. Still no messages. I want there to be messages and I don't want there to be messages. I feel these small shots of hollowness that I refuse to label as missing him. They're just the leftover echoes of routine, old habits; they're just my own fear, looking for a safe place to hide.

Melanie and I go back to the beach, and I take off my shorts and talk to the streaky blond-haired guy whose name is Jason Lindstrom. Jason surfs. No, he actually *surfs*, like in the movies. He has this thing on his car to attach his board to and everything. He shows me the lines on his ankle from where the umbilical cord that attaches him to his board cut into his skin. It looks like a suicide attempt by a very ignorant person.

We take a walk down the beach and Jason tells me about his grandmother who has Alzheimer's and how every time they see her she thinks it's his birthday and she gives him money. He tells me his favorite cereal is Cheerios, because he likes how the sugar falls between all the little holes and gathers in a sloopy splotch of syrup in the bottom of the bowl. I like this. I'm glad to find someone here I like besides Melanie.

That night, Allen comes home, the first time we've seen him since the airport. We are in the "media room" (it's actually called that, which seemed obnoxiously self-congratulatory) when he pops his head in the doorway. My liquor knowledge is spotty, so I don't know exactly what he smells like, only that he smells fumey, like little wavy alcohol lines are coming off of him. It's the odor of one of the brown alcohols, poured into short glasses over ice. He would give the glass a spin in his hand before sipping, I imagine, so the ice didn't collide with his nose. He smells like cocktail napkins filled with hors d'oeuvres, like the cling of cigarette smoke on jackets and gazes both too intent and glazey from false interest.

"So there's a thing this weekend. Saturday night? You can come—bring a friend," Allen says. "Just one, though. Tickets required." He pats his jacket pocket.

"What kind of thing?" Melanie asks. She'd been trying to figure out the DVD player, but ditches the whole effort when he says this, as if she was unwrapping a stick of gum and has just been handed an ice cream cone instead.

"Little party for friends of Two Heads Records. Sunset boat cruise."

"Oh my God," Melanie says. She looks at me and I look back because Slow Change, Hunter Eden's band, is part of the Two Heads label.

"Can't promise who'll be there," he says, then takes his bleary self down the hall to his room.

"Did I tell you?" Melanie says. She grabs my arms. Her eyes are as shiny as grocery store paperbacks.

"Two Heads Records," I say. My heart gives a little flop of anxious-excited. "You don't think he'll actually be there, do you?"

"I told you, I saw him at one of these things before."

Deb Caletti

"You said you saw his *ass.*"

"Like anyone would not know that ass?"

"Oh my God, it was probably some guy that works with your father's ass," I say. But my voice is high and jazzed, speeding like a Porsche with my own foot on the accelerator. High, jazzed, and a wind-in-your-hair thrill, even though we're inside, just clutching each other's arms and jumping up and down.

The day of the party we skip the beach, but Melanie calls Glenn and Jason and asks them to come to the party that night. Mom calls, but doesn't leave a message. A strange number appears on my call log, and I hear the uncertain voice of Bomba. . . . *miss you and hope you'll . . . Wait, shit, there was a beep. Indigo? Did I press the right number? Can you hear this? I hate these blasted cell phones. That's supposed to make your life easier? It's Bomba, if you hear any of this. I miss you. Call me.* I picture the photo we have of Bomba on our fridge at home, with her saggy boobs in her funny bathing suit, sitting in a wading pool. I wonder what she would think of where I am right now, in this house on the beach, with the house-keeper that makes every dirty dish vanish as if nothing unseemly like eating has ever really taken place here. I wonder what she would think if she knew that I am going tonight on a yacht to cruise the coastline with the rich and famous. I feel a pang of disloyalty. I'm an economic traitor.

We spend the day getting ready. Or rather, Melanie spends the day getting ready and I splash in the pool and clear the fridge of pine nuts and cheese and some flat bread crackers that are made with spirolina, which sounds like it has the capacity to kill me. It is one of those days when the day is just something to get through until night comes. One big giant endless bowl of soup before the main course. I let Melanie take the Porsche to go shopping, and when she gets home, she tries her hair in various styles and shaves her legs twice. She wants us to get pedicures, but I'm sorry, people buffing and painting your toes is just twisted.

Jason and Glenn are picking us up in Glenn's Jaguar. I thought only old ladies with tanned purse-leather necks and golf handicaps and aging husband CEOs had Jaguars, but apparently I was mistaken. I sit on the leather couch to wait for them. Melanie hasn't appeared yet.

"Melanie! Come on! I want to see what you finally decided to wear!" Me, I'm just in my orange skirt and orange tank top. Orange always makes me happy. An orange is a fine thing, itself, and there isn't anything much nicer than having someone peel one for you. "They're going to be here any minute!"

I'm in a fine mood, thinking about oranges and wearing orange and being here starting a new life and getting to go on a yacht and maybe seeing Hunter Eden. All the angst about leaving home is missing right now. I'm having a is-this-really-my-life moment, but in a good way. Usually you have those when you have the flu, or when you step in something the cat hecked up, or when you leave your wallet somewhere when you are starving. But this—if I'd thought it up, imagined it, if I'd wished on birthday candles on a cake, it wouldn't be this moment. It was a moment I wouldn't even think to dream.

And then Melanie walks in.

"What are you wearing?" I ask. I think I might be seeing things, because I can't believe it. I really just can't believe it.

"Indigo, don't give me any shit about it."

I stand up. I walk over to her, because I think maybe it's just the same color. Maybe it's just a different green T-shirt. I take a

Deb Caletti

pinch between my fingers. "It's that same T-shirt," I say.

"Indigo, quit it. You're going to get it all wrinkled."

"I cannot *believe* you would do something so stupid," I say. I'm not mad. I'm still sort of in my happy-orange mood. I'm not mad, I just think she's an idiot. You know, fine. Go spend seventy-five dollars on a saltine cracker. Go spend it on a rubber band. Go for it. "What a waste of good money," I say.

"Well, I didn't actually *spend* it," she says. You can tell she knows she has made a mistake the second the words are out her mouth. She actually looks over her shoulder, back down to her room where she came from, as if she could reverse all this and try again.

"What?" It can't be that. She didn't mean *that*. "What do you mean?" But I'm afraid I know. Suddenly, I'm sure I know.

"Never mind. In? Never mind."

"Fuck never mind. You didn't actually spend it. That's what you said. What do you mean? You didn't shoplift that, did you?"

"No!" she says.

But she has those little lines around her mouth. The sewn-up lines. And the thing about a conscience is, we're not the full, single owners of it. We may think we hold it, like an orange, ours, in our hands; we may think we can toss that orange away into a patch of blackberry brambles. But we forget it is made of sections; sections that belong to the people who love us and look out for us. Your mother has a section of that conscience, your father, your family, and I have a section of Melanie's. Maybe she could lie to Glenn, but she could not lie to me. Maybe because we most successfully lie to the people who we don't care (never cared, no longer care) if we disappoint.

"Melanie. You did. My God. You did! How could you do such

a thing? WHY did you do such a thing? You have money to pay for that if you wanted it so bad." I look at Melanie, with her silly green T-shirt and her jeans, her manicure, her hair straight and long, and her wide eyes, still showing shock at the way her mouth has betrayed her, and she looks so small to me. At home, she was large; in her circle of friends she was loud and in command and so large. But here she is small. If this is her place, it is a place that makes her small and faded and wrong.

"I just . . . I wanted it."

"You wanted it? So you just took it?"

"I wanted it, Indigo, okay? There's no great big psychological issue here. I just wanted it."

The doorbell rings then. And then too, a *bang, bang, bang*, as Glenn and/or Jason knocks on the door. I can hear Jason say something that makes Glenn laugh. I realize Melanie is right about what she said, and the realization makes me slightly sick. It disgusts me. There is no great big psychological issue here. There is no contemporary-society pseudo-psycho-sham explanation of *lack of self-esteem* or childhood wounds or other such shit. The truth is much more simple. We think a lot about not having. When we don't have and we think about not having, it's called dreaming. When we do have and think about not having, it's called greed.

I sit with Jason in the backseat of Glenn's Jaguar, and Melanie sits in the front. The back of her head looks guilty to me. I feel the cringing tangle of electricity between Melanie and me, disappointed energy that might as well be solid and real and not just air and feelings. I could almost touch it, but it might burn my fingers. Neither Glenn nor Jason seems to notice the fifth entity in the car.

"Do you think Twisted Minds will be there?" Glenn asks.

Deb Caletti

"I don't know, you know, there are no guarantees," Melanie says. "I don't want everyone getting disappointed if not."

"How about Raw?" Glenn asks.

"As long as Hunter Eden's there, that's all I care about," Melanie says.

"Oh man, he's so gay," Jason says.

"That's what all guys say when another guy is really hot," Melanie says. She may be right, but I'm in no mood to agree with her.

Jason goes on to tell us about some gay surfer he knew who dropped out of school, and then Glenn tells some story about his sister dropping out of school and his parents going nuts, and then Melanie tells some story about the time her mother freaked out and threatened to put her brother in the hospital for depression if his grades didn't improve, and then we are at the marina. There is a young Latino valet and Glenn hands over the keys and says, *If you scratch it, you'll never say 'green card' again* to us as we walk off, cracking up Jason and Melanie, and causing me to step on the heel of his shoe on "accident."

"Hey!" he says.

"Oh, I'm sorry," I say. Asshole.

It's a beautiful night, that's true. The water sparkles glittery white, and the marina boats are strung with lights, their windows glowy and gold. The air shimmers with sound—laughter, and the slam of car doors, and voices lifted with anticipation. There is a warm breeze that makes the palm fronds sway and sing their *tick-tick-tick* song. Melanie hands over our tickets. Her dad is supposed to be there already. We walk up the ramp of the yacht. We, I, *walk up the ramp of a yacht*. Do you understand? A yacht that looks like a yacht, long and sleek-nosed and demanding a compliment.

Jason holds my arm. "You okay?" he asks.

"Oh, yeah," I say. "Fine."

It looks like a house inside here—a house with paintings and furniture, jammed with people holding glasses of tinkling ice cubes and . . . Wait a sec, someone I recognize. The blond woman in the upswept hair. There she is, over by the stairwell, a portly man's hand around her waist, and there she is again, in a black dress, getting something from the bar, and there she is, pressed up against a guy wearing a Hawaiian shirt, his stomach bloated and his gray beard full and bragging.

"Let's find the food," Jason says.

"Let's find the booze," Glenn says.

We are in a little clump, like ducklings who've lost their mother. Even Jason and Glenn seem uncomfortable here. The boat begins to move, the scene changing, sliding past, in the windows beyond. We follow Glenn in a line, weaving in between men and women balancing cocktail napkins and drinks, until Glenn reaches the bar. A band starts up, no songs I recognize, but suddenly the sound is thick and the volume on the boat rises so that you have to shout to be heard.

I smile at the bartender, a young guy who has a goatee-in-training. This is his job, which means he is viewing it all from the outside in, same as me. I'm a waitress, see? "Pretty crazy, huh?" I shout to him.

"Indeed," he shouts.

I roll my eyes, indicating that we're on the same team. Somehow, for some reason, it's important to me to have him know that. To know that this is not my place. That his home, somewhere, an apartment maybe, with a wife and new baby and old Bob Dylan albums and leftover lasagna in the fridge is more my place, likely. But he is wary of me. I can feel it in his cautious smile.

Deb Caletti

"You're not drinking," Jason says. He has a glass of clear liquid with a lime in it, and Glenn and Melanie both hold martini glasses with olives skewered by miniature swords. Obviously, no one is carded on this trip.

"The brain is a terrible thing to taste—I mean, waste," I joke. But I don't know if he hears me. Jason just shrugs. We follow Glenn to the food table, which is lined with various items served by waiters in white. Glenn maneuvers us toward a living room table where we can set our glasses down.

"I've heard this band," Glenn says. "Flying Something . . ."

Melanie nods. She looks nervous and uncomfortable, like the hostess of an unsuccessful party. She bites the edge of her nail, then remembers her manicure and stops. Three people sit on the couch next to us. The man in the Hawaiian shirt is there, along with another barrel-chested guy wearing tiny glasses, and a fifty-ish woman who is still aiming for the bimbo look. Allen appears at Melanie's elbow.

"Having fun?" he shouts.

"Oh yeah, this is great," Melanie says.

Wavy lines are coming off of him already. "Isn't this the most amazing food? Let me introduce you," he says. He turns and snags the first available audience, the three people on the couch. The woman is the wife of producer-somebody; Mr. Aloha is somebody-somebody; and the barrel-chested man with the tiny glasses is a photographer. I hear that part.

"His photos are amazing." Aging Bimbo touches the barrel-chested man's hand.

"Well," he says.

"Really. That tomato," she says.

"Tomato?" I shout to Jason.

"He photographs *food*. They just said—"

"Have any of you seen his work?" Bimbo says. "This tomato was unforgettable. Sitting on a white plate . . ."

"That red tomato?" I shout. "Is that the one?"

"You've seen it," Bimbo says.

I feel a pinch on the fleshy part of my arm. Melanie. How dare she pinch me. She shoplifted a T-shirt. I don't even want her hands on my arm until she goes back to that store and does the right thing.

"You just really captured its essence," Bimbo says.

"Well, I try. It's a matter of what Michelangelo says—about finding the character in the marble," he says.

"You're an artist," Bimbo shouts.

"I saw the most amazing photographic display while I was in New York," Aloha man says. "The most incredible you've ever seen. Nudes with pomegranates. I *know* about photography. I've seen the best exhibitions around the world, but this . . ."

"So much of it is having the right eye," Vegetable Michelangelo says.

"And you do. You have such an eye," Bimbo says.

"Well . . ."

"And blah, blah, blah, bullshit, bullshit, bullshit", Bimbo says.

Glenn is looking into the bottom of his martini glass. Allen has ditched us, veering off to refill his glass. I am beginning to see how it works. It is just like the Moore party. Everything and everyone is amazing. The best. And all you have to do is pat yourself and one another on the back, in some great big old narcissist backslapping orgy. These people—they are walking PR firms for themselves. Breathing human advertising. But this time I am here. I am inside, not outside. And I feel something about that. Something moldy and wrong.

Deb Caletti

"What about his cucumber?" I say to Bimbo. "It was *amazing*. So . . . green."

"Nice to meet you all," Melanie says. "We're supposed to go say hi to some people."

But they aren't paying attention, anyway. Any words that aren't self-reflected glory disappear into the din, mere lips moving.

"Green!" Glenn is busting up. "Fucking cucumbers."

"Indigo, don't," Melanie says.

"The true art is seeing the inner tomato," I say. "Of course, I always *loved* Michelangelo's fruits and vegetables. He always did an *amazing* grapefruit."

"I saw the exhibit the other guy was talking about. In New York. It wasn't so hot," Jason says. "Fucking naked people with pomegranates."

"I thought you said Raw was going to be here," Glenn says. Little wavy alcohol lines are starting to come off him, too.

"We're going to go outside for a while, okay guys?" Jason says. "We'll catch up to you."

"We are?" I say. But Jason already has my arm and is steering me through the crowd. Another band starts up. We step outside two glass doors that lead onto the ship's deck. It's a little quieter out here. And this seems to be where all the performers are. You can tell—instead of aging-rich-people clothes and young-wives-of-aging-rich-men clothes, there are who-cares performer clothes. We-are-supposed-to-be-subversive-and-or-avant-garde clothes. And okay, sure, these are just other costumes, but I feel better out here, among the leather pants and pierced noses and vintage shirts that appear casually chosen but that were probably in and out of the reject/possibility pile same as Melanie's.

"See anyone you recognize?" Jason says.

"Hey, aren't you the drummer from Raw?" I say to him.

The ship has two floors, and we are on the upper deck. God, it's beautiful out here. The black sea shines with moonlight; the sky has unfurled the stars. The city lights twitter and gleam in red and yellow and white along the shore. The air is just-right warm. Two and a half million dollars, though, could not buy the beauty of that sea, and the intoxicating temperature of that ever-slight wind.

Jason leans over the railing, and I do too.

"Light is *amazing*," I say.

Jason laughs.

"No, really. It is. Look, it's like light-magic out there. Light makes things magic. Think about it. Christmas trees. Fireworks. Glow in the dark stars. Fireflies. Phosphorous. Jet planes in a night sky."

"I can sit in a dark room and just watch the lights of my stereo," Jason says.

"Exactly," I say. "And what about that dusky time of night when the hills turn pink and the trees turn yellow?"

"Well, they don't really *turn yellow*," Jason says.

"You know what I mean," I say. But I'm not so sure he does.

"I guess," Jason says.

We are standing very close together. Our arms are touching. Maybe it's the way the breeze is blowing, I don't know, but I notice something then that I didn't notice even sitting next to him in the backseat of the car or standing beside him inside. It's a smell—a familiar smell. Maybe I was too angry to smell or hear or see properly in the car, and maybe there were too many distractions inside, but here—yes, there it is. I know that smell. Jason—

Deb Caletti

he smells like Axe. He smells like Axe, and it might have been funny, but suddenly it feels anything but that. It isn't funny at all, because all at once it's unbearably, overwhelmingly sad. I am here, and those people who I love, my family, my own Trevor, are somewhere else, under this moon too, but not here.

"Axe," I say. I whisper. And my God, suddenly I just miss them so much. I can't fool myself about it—the feeling is too large and whole, and the wall I have built against it just breaks down and I am alone with it, this missing. This monumental missing of the people who make me *me*. Absence is so much louder than presence. Axe. I swallow. Suddenly my eyes get hot with tears.

"Are you okay?" Jason asks.

I nod. But I'm not okay. I just . . . I want to be *home*. The loneliness you feel with another person, the wrong person, is the loneliest of all.

He turns to me and kisses me then. Jason, with these unfamiliar lips and this odd mouth that feels thin and wrong and moves in ways I don't know. I remember again how the body is more honest than the mind most of the time, because this kiss tells me one thing, and that one thing is that I don't want to be kissing Jason Lindstrom from Malibu. I want to be kissing Trevor Williams from Nine Mile Falls, who understands the way I feel about twilight-yellow trees. You need someone in your life who sees trees the same way you do.

The kiss ends. Jason looks happy. "Wow, that was great," he says. "I can't wait to have more of where that came from. You thirsty? I'll go get us something. Stay here."

I stay. I watch the water beneath me, rushing past. I lean far enough down to feel the force of wind at my face. I need the waking up. I stand straight, take a deep breath, and SHIT! Inhale twelve thousand toxins from some asshole's secondhand smoke! I turn around, and that's when I see him. There he is, standing not three feet away from me, in the center of the deck.

Hunter Eden.

Hunter Eden, standing and talking to my friend, the blond woman with the upswept hair and red nails. Hunter Eden, with a cigarette pinched between his index and middle finger, sending black tar my way through its glowing orange tip.

I have to look several times to be sure it's him. The top of his head comes up just under the woman's nose. He's short, that's the point. He doesn't look at all like he did in the videos. He's thin; scrawny as the type of dog you see tied up to a streetlight outside a tavern. Even his ass looks different. Diminished. Small and human. It is NOT the ass I know from the cover of "Hot"— no way is that the same ass. No way. The woman says something that makes him throw back his head and laugh, and I can see his teeth, yellowed from nicotine. Maybe I just imagine them yellowed from nicotine. But I don't imagine the woman's voice.

"Your last album was *amazing*," she says.

"Well . . . ," he says. "I was so stoned I could barely play. Thank the sound techs. Thank some kid they brought in to fill in where I fucked up." He laughs. She laughs. He takes a drag from his cigarette, and two streams of smoke jets exhale from his nose. He coughs a phlegmy, gray-lunged cough. Spits a hunk of something over the rail, into the ocean. The woman doesn't seem to mind. He's famous, he's rich, and so who he is doesn't much matter.

I can't believe what I'm seeing. I can't. If I close my eyes and open them again, maybe I'll see the real Hunter Eden. Because

Deb Caletti

this isn't Hunter Eden. This isn't him *at all*. This is some guy you'd see in a 7-Eleven, buying a box of rubbers and a six pack. How could they do this to us, whoever *they* are? How could they give us something so false to want? He doesn't even play all his own songs? I'd been had. I'd worshipped something that wasn't even real. I'd wasted my time and my belief on a *lie*.

The Hunter Eden I knew? He was product marketing with a stand-in ass.

I want out of here. It's too much. I've got to get out of here, away from Melanie and Jason, away from Hunter Eden, away from these people at this party. I ran from the wrong things, to the wrong things, and the realization makes me sick with shame. I've hurt good people. I need to make it right.

There's one small problem, though, with this pressing, now urgent, need. I am on a ship. Cruising around the coastline. I am stuck here, at the mercy of these people at this stupid party, until they decide when and where I get to leave.

I go back inside. Decide to find a bathroom. A bathroom is a great place to hide. There is no good excuse for anyone to bother you there. On the way, I see Melanie, fixated on a bleary-eyed Glenn, who has one hand up the back of her stolen T-shirt. I head down a quiet hall, find a bathroom with a sink and a basket of little rolled-up towels. I sit for a while. I consider my options. I can stay in here, play Let's Use All the Towels until I get bored. I could be in here for a good long while. Option two: go back out. Put myself in my own Indigo bubble so that nothing these people say or do can affect me until we get back.

Neither of these ideas is satisfactory. What I want, what I NEED, is to get off this boat. But I can't exactly tell them I want off, right? These are important people, partying on a fancy yacht, cruising in the ocean, and I am only Indigo Skye, sitting on a fancy toilet, hiding in a bathroom.

A woman pounds on the door. "Is anyone in there? Can you hurry it up?" she says. And right then, for some reason, I think of Nick. Nick and his oatmeal with raisins. The True Value guys. I think of Leroy, and of Mom, and of Jane, whose circumstances make them feel smaller than they need to feel.

"Watch the flusher," I say to the woman waiting outside. "It gets stuck. Took me forever to get it working." And then I find one of the stewards, in his white uniform.

"Do these things ever stop? The boat. I mean, does it make a stop? Like if someone needed to get off?"

"Can you wait ten minutes?" he says. "We're letting off a passenger in Santa Barbara. She's not feeling well."

Ten minutes. I can wait ten minutes, all right.

"Sure," I say. "Thanks."

The party carries on, as the boat slips into harbor. I feel two seconds' worth of bad about ditching Jason. I don't feel bad enough, though, because when the boat stops, I am waiting at the bridge with the ill woman and her husband, who holds her elbow.

"I never could do boats," she says to me. She waves her hand in the air as if to dismiss the whole sordid experience. She has a diamond on her finger the size of a cannonball.

"Go on ahead," the husband says to me when the bridge comes down. "We're going to take it slow."

And so I do. I go on ahead, because I, Indigo Skye, have the power to stop yachts. Well, maybe not quite stop yachts, but I have the ability to end things I don't like and to say something isn't okay when it isn't okay. I have the power to insist on good and real things for myself. Most of all, I have the right to change my mind.

17

"Dad?" Dad is the one I call. Dad is who you call in a crisis.

"Indigo? Are you all right? My God, what time is it?"

"I'm sorry to be calling so late."

"No, Indigo! Please. What's going on? Are you okay?"

"I just . . . Dad?" I start crying. I am crying right here.

"Sweetheart, it's okay. Okay? I'm here."

"I broke my promise to Richard Howards," I cry. "I'm becoming smaller, not bigger."

"Where are you, In?"

"I don't even know. Santa Barbara? I'm sitting at this boat dock. I'm looking at cars in the parking lot. Jaguar, Jaguar, Porsche, Lexus, Lexus, BMW. I'm sorry. I've been so stupid."

"Honey. What's going on?"

"I was on this yacht." I sniff. I take a breath. I feel like I'm in pieces and parts. I feel like a Picasso. "At a party. I hated it. Like everything that was supposed to be beautiful was ugly. So I just got off. I just got off because I couldn't stand it anymore. And now, here I am. I'm sorry I woke you guys. But I don't have a car, and I'm not sure where I am and it's late. I broke my promise. It was *so easy* to break, Dad."

"I know, In."

"I just got sucked right up."

"I'm just going to call you a taxi, okay?"

"I haven't even been gone a week," I say.

"Long enough to find out what you needed to know," Dad says.

"Tell Jennifer I'm sorry to wake her. She'll probably be pissed."

"In, don't worry about it. She's not even here. Let's just worry about you."

"What do you mean, she isn't there?"

"This isn't the time to talk about it, okay? Let's try to figure out where you are."

"Oh my God. She left. She left, didn't she? Are you all right?" My heart is still. It holds its breath.

"Absolutely. It's necessary. But now what's really necessary is calling you a taxi."

"It's kind of a long way for a taxi," I say.

"It doesn't matter. What do you see where you are?"

"This big-ass camper. It's got this license plate that says 'Captain Ed.' A bumper sticker—'Home of the Big Redwoods.' Hey—it's a Washington State plate."

"Honey, okay. Do you see a sign of any kind?"

"Bel Harbor Marina," I say.

"Perfect. In? I'm going to find out who to call and have them come, okay?"

"Okay. And then I want to come home," I say.

"I'll call you right back."

I close my cell phone. I really do love this little phone. It is so helpful, like a tiny silver friend.

It is late when I get back to Allen's house, but Melanie and Allen aren't home yet. I know I should stay the night and go to the airport the next morning but I don't want to wait. I don't want to lay my head there one more night. Dad and I make a plan. I write a note to Mel.

Deb Caletti

Thanks for everything, but this is not my place.

I look in the fridge for some snacks to bring, but there is nothing but bottled water. A huge beefsteak tomato sits on a shelf, though, and at the last moment, I go back for it, place the tomato on my note to hold it down. Michelangelo would have approved.

The Porsche vrooms to life. I let my hair whip around my face. I let the giddiness of relief, of speaking my own truth, fill me. It's the orange soda happy feeling you get when things are going right, or when you're finally going to make them right again.

All I have to do is get on I-5 and go north. Straight north, until I get there. If Captain Ed could do it, so could I. I take Dad's advice and when fatigue strikes, I get off at the first city I find. I turn in to the Holiday Inn off the interstate, in Redding, California. Nothing goes wrong at Holiday Inns. This is no creepy motel of sandy-feeling sheets and clingy, molesting shower curtains; this is a Holiday Inn where kids could swim in a pool and where there is always a place right next door that serves breakfast twenty-four hours.

It is very late, but I can't sleep. I think about Dad and Jennifer. About Mom and Severin and Bex and Jane and the Irregulars and Trevor. All my people. I don't want to call home this late, and so I put the TV on for company. Once I eliminate home shopping channels and crime shows, I'm stuck watching bird migration. Someone has stolen the phone book and Bible (so much for nothing going wrong at Holiday Inns), and the hotel service pamphlet takes me only two seconds to flip through. Finally, I hunt around in my bag for Dad's Emerson book that I brought along. I open to the page he folded down, the essay "Self-Reliance." It seems at first a sure cure for my insomnia. A long-dead guy talking long-dead-guy talk, fleur-de-lis language, words as curved and ancient and small as old-lady embroidery.

But then I start to listen to him. This once alive, real man talking. His rhythms are soothing and draw me in; he is almost religious without all the God part. And if I cut out all the curlicue words, ignore the thou's and thee's, I see that the man had stuff to say. About how we should trust ourselves. About how nature and the good and right stuff inside is our real fortune. We are swayed too much, he said, by the wrong things, by what each other has, not what each other is. We must be nonconformists, he wrote. We must think for ourselves, because the only sacred thing is the integrity of our own minds. *Insist on yourself,* he said.

"Insist on yourself," I say.

"You read it," Dad says.

"Yeah."

"I can't believe you read it."

"Honestly? Me either. I actually liked it."

"I knew you could never be a conformist for long, In. You promised you'd call if you needed anything last night, so I'm assuming all went well," Dad says.

"I just went north, like you said. Are *you* all right?"

"I'm fine. I don't want you to worry. It's what I need. The truth isn't the problem, In, just what you have to do to face it. Where are you?"

"I'm here in a Josie's Pancake House, pouring blueberry syrup over the biggest stack of pancakes you've ever seen in your life." I hold the phone in the crick of my shoulder, cut a triangle of pancakes.

Deb Caletti

"Yum," Dad says.

"Bacon, too," I say.

"What next?" Dad says.

"I-5 north. Stay straight until I get home."

"Grandpa Sam?" Dad says. That was Dad's own father. He died before I was born. "He told me to see the world. 'Home is not the center of the world,' he said. It wasn't bad advice, not entirely. I mean, how do you get a sense of something without its comparison? But we forget—anyplace can be the center, depending on how you turn the globe. Who's there, who's not there, that's what makes a place worth staying in. That's what makes it ours."

I chew away. Swallow. "So, there's no place like home, click my heels three times?" I say.

"Not necessarily. But sometimes, yes. Often."

I think about this. I swirl the tines of my fork in the thickness of the syrup. "I've got some making up to do to the people there," I say. "To all the people I love."

"Indigo?"

"Yeah?"

"So do I," Dad says.

I drive, and drive and drive. I have a lot of time to think. About what I really want, about the things that mean something to me. That sounds so simple, and yet it isn't simple. Sometimes, stopping to think is hard work. The sun is out the whole way. It is the kind of day where dogs' heads stick out from car windows. All types of heads—Doberman heads and cocker spaniel heads and mixed-up-dog-family heads. But they are all out, ears flapping, noses up, filled with the joy of the journey.

The Fortunes of Indigo Skye

I have two milk shakes and one cheeseburger on the way, eating with one hand and driving with the other, because I'm in too much of a hurry to stop. I speed through southern Oregon, its farmland middle, then arrive in Portland. My heart lifts when I make it over the state line into Washington. *Stay straight on I-5 into Seattle,* my Dad said, and that's what I do, ignoring my numb ass and legs that feel permanently crunched into their new *L* shape.

I am starving again when I arrive in Seattle; I want to go straight home, but my stomach aches with hunger and so I stop for something before I cross the floating bridge to go back home to Nine Mile Falls. I stop at the Frankfurter right on Pier 54 on the waterfront, and have a huge hot dog with sauerkraut, just the way I like it. Then I get back into the Porsche and head through Pioneer Square.

It stuns me to think how easily I could have missed it. My eyes are humming with fatigue, and the city traffic and one-way streets are distracting, as is the effort required in trying to find the signs for the freeway entrance. But I don't miss it. I don't miss *him.* I am sitting at a red light and look over and there he is. I swear to God, this is what I see—a homeless man, sitting on one of the benches under the glass pergola of Pioneer Square. His head is down, his hair a dirty tangle. This is not an uncommon sight, not at all, because a lot of homeless people hang out here on these benches, under this awning of glass squares. But what is unusual, what shocks me, what stops me so thoroughly that the car behind me honks when the light turns green, is what he is wearing. A T-shirt, but over that, a vest. A vest with Mr. Moore's face on it, a vest from the party, HAPPY 55, CHIEF! written underneath his image.

I think I am perhaps hallucinating. I think the sun and wind and endless miles are messing with my head. I drive around the block again, to be sure. My heart is beating very fast, with the urgency of importance. They had said, hadn't they, that they give the vests to the needy? I drive past slowly, and if I am hallucinating, I am hallucinating still, because yes, there it is. There is Mr. Moore's face, smiling from the right breast pocket of the homeless man's new vest.

I want to laugh, or I want to cry, I don't know which. But this is some sort of sign, isn't it? Okay, I don't have a fucking clue what the sign means, but I have no doubt that it is one. I don't know what to do. My hands are shaking. I feel a bit crazy. I know I have to pull over, get my thoughts together. I might be dangerous, driving like this. I make a few turns, too many random turns. I stop on a street in the shadow of the Greek church, with its golden soft-serve-ice-cream top. The Qwik Stop grocery store–gas station is on the corner. I find my cell phone.

"Dad?"

"Is everything all right?" He's beginning to sound like Mom in the way he answers the phone lately.

"I want to spend it," I say. "All of it."

"Indigo, you know, I don't think that's the best idea . . ."

"No. I don't mean just go spend it. . . . I mean, I want to put it places. I was thinking, you know, that maybe what's ugly, maybe it's the imbalances. Like money, *power*, is about imbalances, but all the good things are about balance."

"The good things . . ."

"Love is about balance, and even doing the right thing is about balance, right? And nature . . ."

"Yes."

"And we fuck things up when we let them get out of balance."

"I think that's very true," Dad says.

I sit by the mini-mart and I make a plan. I make a plan with Dad, until my phone battery starts to run out. I write the plan on a pink slip of paper that was in the glove compartment, with a pen from my bag.

"And what about you?" I ask. "What can I give you?"

He doesn't even stop to think about this. "More time with you guys. Another chance," he says.

"Done," I say.

That Emerson—he was pretty funny, too. *What is a weed?* he said. *A plant whose virtues have not yet been discovered.* I think about this as I approach our house. There is our lawn, turning yellow from summer, splotched with the thick scratchy leaves of dandelions, bursts of bright yellow. Sometimes, what is beautiful is ugly, and what is supposed to be ugly is beautiful.

Mom's car is in the driveway, still looking odd and off kilter with its three large tires and one small, round spare. Ron the Buddha smiles serenely at me as I come up the walk. "Peace, Ron," I say. Needlessly—he is always peaceful. I open the front door, causing Freud to leap off the sofa and jet outside. Right away I notice that the television is missing. There are two gaping holes where the bolts had been.

"Severin?" Mom calls from the kitchen. "Are you home? Can you help me? I'm stuck! I got my watch stuck . . ."

"It's me," I call.

"Indigo! Indigo? Is that you? Oh my God."

"It's me."

"Oh my God, come here! You're home!"

Deb Caletti

I go into the kitchen. Mom is leaning over the kitchen sink, her hand thrust down the garbage disposal. "It *is* you! I'm going to cry. Oh, In. You're home!" Mom's face scrunches up, and her eyes fill. "You have no idea . . ."

"I missed you, Mom."

"Oh, In. I was so worried."

"Let me help you," I say. "What happened to you?"

She wipes the tears with her free hand. "I have never been so glad to see someone in my entire life. Oh, my girl. The house key . . . It slid down the garbage disposal, and then when I went to get it, my watchband got stuck around one of these blades, and . . . Who cares!" she cries. "You're home!"

"Just a sec," I say. I wiggle my own hand down with hers, work at the band. "Can you just—"

"Ow, ow, ow," she says.

"Ow, ow, ow," Chico says.

"Okay, wait, now just—"

"There, it's coming loose. It's coming off!" Mom says. The band releases. I retrieve my arm, and then Mom removes hers.

"Man, that was mildly disgusting," I say. I flip on the water to wash my arm, but Mom practically knocks me over.

"Oh, you're home." She flings both arms around me. She starts to cry again.

"I thought you'd be pretty mad," I say.

"Oh I am mad, I am. You have no idea how mad at you I am. But, Indigo, don't you understand? I'm your mother. No matter what you do . . . You children are everything to me," she says.

I hug her hard. "It's the hormones talking," I say.

"Indigo, if you ever do anything like that again, I swear . . . I love you more than life itself."

"I love you, too. I'm so sorry." This time, I mean it.

She holds me away from her, looks at me seriously. "Oh, In. All right. All right. But things can't go on the way they were. You know?"

"I know," I say. "I do. Where is everybody? Where's the TV?"

"Severin's getting a pizza. He's given up on all that protein drink junk. And Bex is playing at An Ling's. After you left, she sold the TV to the Navinskys for fifteen hundred dollars. I told her she could have the money for tsunami relief," Mom says. She wipes her teary face with the back of her hand.

"I only paid a thousand," I say.

"Yeah," Mom says. "Bex knew that." Mom points to the receipt, stuck to the fridge with a magnet shaped like a watermelon. "She told me she had an epiphany. She used that word! I can't believe I was ever worried about her," Mom says.

My world is not large, but it is deep.

I go straight to bed. I am exhausted, and it feels so good to lie my head right here, on my own pillow. In the morning, I make peace with Severin and Bex. The red Porsche in the driveway helps.

"I leased it," I say. "For the summer."

"That's a fine-looking car," Severin says.

"Fast," Bex says. "Real fast, I bet."

"Oh yeah. You're right about that. I forgot to mention," I say to Mom. I reach around in the glove compartment, hold up two pink slips. "My foot got happy."

"Speeding tickets?" Mom says. *"Two?"*

"And the first guy let me go with a warning," I say.

"I'm glad someone stopped you," Mom says.

Deb Caletti

"*Brian* should have stopped her," Bex says. She nudges Mom with her elbow.

"Brian?" The name is familiar. Brian . . . Brian . . . "Officer Brian?" I say.

"He's called Mom three times," Bex says.

"He wants to go out. I didn't really feel like it with you gone," Mom says.

"But now that she's ba-ack," Severin says. He says it like that—ba-ack.

"Enough," Mom says.

"Let's tell him she likes to watch Mr. Rogers reruns," I say. She does, too.

"Just because he's peaceful!" Mom says.

"Briii-aan," Bex sings.

"Well, I was going to turn the car in early to the leasing company, but there'd be some penalty . . . ," I say.

"Yeah," Severin says. He is running his fingertips along the door ledge.

"So I thought maybe you could drive it until then," I say to him.

"You're kidding," he says. His eyes are wide.

"Indigo," Mom says. "What about what we talked about? How things needed to be different? I don't want all this crazy spending—"

"This is just for the summer," I say. "I told you, I've got a plan." I fold up that very plan, written on the back of one of the speeding tickets, and put it in the pocket of my shorts. "This is just one small, temporary indulgence. Trust me, all right?" I say.

"All right," she says.

And then I put the keys into Severin's palm.

Trevor, it's me. Please, I say. *Please pick up. I'm back.* And then, *Trevor! I'm so sorry. Please forgive me. I don't know what happened. I just got stupid.* But he doesn't call back. *Trevor, please, oh please, oh please. Just talk to me.*

I go to Trevor's house, but no one is there, and the van his Mom uses to transport the kids is not in the driveway. I drive to his work. I see Bob Weaver in the parking lot, and my heart thuds with nerves. But Trevor is out on a job, Larry Jakes tells me. They've been especially busy, end-to-end deliveries.

I leave two more messages. I want to see him so bad that I just drive around in my VW, in stupid hope that I might see the delivery truck somewhere. I do this for an aimless, desperate hour, until I get sick of myself, and decide to clean up my other mess. It's much easier to take apart your life than it is to put it together again.

The bells on the door jangle when I walk in, and Jack jumps up, his tail wagging like a grandfather clock on high speed; black Lab *tick-tock tick-tock* happiness.

"Oh, you good old boy. Yes, you are a fine boy," I croon as I scruffle him under the neck and look around for Jane. "Look at that wag, huh? You got the finest wag," I say. It's the lunch shift, and none of the Irregulars are here. Nikki is working, and she tells me Jane is in the back.

"Jane?" I call.

"One of the fucking coffee machines broke," Jane says to me. She is standing in front of one of the two large refrigerators, turns to face me with a carton of cream in her hand. "Is this the return of the prodigal daughter?"

Deb Caletti

"I'm looking for a job," I say. "I'm an excellent waitress with great experience and a newfound sense of humility. And a huge appreciation for my old boss."

"Oh, Indigo. I'm so sorry." She shakes her head at herself, little *why?* and *how?* shakes. She sets the cream on the counter. "I was such a bitch. I've been under such stress with this place. Financially? I didn't want to say it. To everyone. To *anyone*, except my mother, and Nick, who's polite enough to keep his mouth shut. I've been struggling to keep the doors open. And I love this place. More than anything. This place, the people in it. And then you got that money, and it just felt somehow unfair, you know? God, I'm sorry."

I remember Jane and Nick, at the curb long ago. The things she didn't want to tell me. "Jane, *I'm* sorry. I was acting like a brat. You didn't deserve that."

Jane holds her hands together, prayerlike, under her chin. "Can you start tomorrow morning? You haven't been replaced, of course, and everyone is cranky and complaining. Nick only has tea, bobs that damn bag up and down, up and down. Oh! Trina got her car back—"

"No way! That's great!"

"Not so great. The engine died and her cousin wanted her to refund his money. She told him she spent most of it and gave him a few thousand bucks, but it's dead and has a new bash on the front fender. We've missed you, Indigo. *I've* missed you."

"I can't tell you how much I've missed you, too."

Jane holds her arms out, hugs me hard. I hug her back. A lump starts in my throat. I blink away tears. "The weird thing is, this place isn't the same without you," Jane says.

"I'm not the same without it," I say.

Trevor? Please don't hate me. I can't tell you how stupid I was. You were right—I never gave us the chance to handle it. I'm so, so sorry. Another message. *Please—hate me, but don't ignore me. Please just answer.*

My insides are starting to curl with panic, like a newspaper lit with a match. I just want to see him again. I know if I see Trevor and he sees me, I might stop being this person he hates and be just me to him again. I drive past his work, stalker-style, but he hasn't come back for another pickup yet.

I head home, wind back up by the freeway, and then I see something that gives me a surge of happy. It isn't Trevor, no, but it is a large yellow foam rectangle walking along the gravel road, a blotch of orange cheese oozing from the top; he's making slow progress, and he's maybe two miles from Old Country Buffet. Could burritos get lost? Could they meander from their post, become disoriented in a sea of foam with only a slit mesh window to see from? Might they go astray in overcooked confusion, like the poor old people who wander from the nursing home?

I slow. Roll down my window. "Hey! Breakfast burrito! Going my way?"

"Indigo! Is that you? Thank God. This asshole kid who's a pickle spear during the lunch shift swiped my clothes. I've got to walk home like this."

"Can I give you a ride? Do you think you can fit?"

"Hey, it's worth a try. God, I'm hot as hell in this thing."

"Well, if you were cold, I'd have to send you back to the kitchen."

Deb Caletti

"Ha, ha. Hey, it's great to see you. You better get yourself back to Carrera's and fast, because the place is tanking without you. Can you— If you just give some of this egg a shove . . ."

I get out, push and shove all of Leroy into the passenger seat. He has to sit straight, his head way up by the dome light. But we get him in.

"Where are we headed?" I ask.

"I live over by the hatchery. Just a few blocks from Carerra's."

I shift into first, no problem, but punch a fistful of foam going into second and fourth.

"See that house? The little white one? Red trim?"

"It's so cute, Leroy." It's a tiny house sitting by itself, set on a large plot of land at the end of a curved street. Tucked way back in a group of dark, shady trees. There's a crate on his porch, recently delivered.

"Home sweet home," Leroy says.

"Man, what's in the backyard?" The yard is taken up, it seems, with some enormous box of plastic. "It looks like a greenhouse," I say. But, a *greenhouse*?

"Thanks for the ride, Indigo. Man, I sure appreciate it. That little shit at work . . ."

"Leroy, what's that for? What are you growing back there?"

"I hear the accusation in your voice. Get me out of here, I'm wedged in."

I sigh. I cut the engine and come around to his side. I offer my wrists, and he holds them tight as I pull him upright. "I'm not accusing. I'm just trying to understand, is all."

"You think it's pot. Well, it's not exactly hidden, is it?"

"I'm guessing if that was full of pot, you wouldn't need a second job," I say.

"No one knows about this at Carrera's, or anywhere else. Even my mailman's not sure what's in there. I've seen him snooping around."

"Why the big secret?"

"I don't know. I really don't know. I guess I think people might make fun. And it's not a joke to me."

"Tell me."

"Don't laugh, okay? I'll show you, but you gotta promise not to laugh. It's something I care a great deal about. This is where my extra money goes."

"Okay."

"Stay put. Let me change a sec. I'd invite you in, but the place is a mess."

"No problem."

Leroy waddles to his front porch, fishes around a hanging flower basket for a key that must be hidden there.

"Can I help you get that?" The burrito looks tippy as Leroy's arm reaches up.

"No, I got it."

He disappears inside, and is out in a moment, wearing shorts and a Grateful Dead T-shirt, tattoos freed once again. "God, it's good to be out of that thing. Follow me. So, you're maybe the second or third person I've ever shown this to."

"I'm honored," I say, though I don't really know if that's true yet. I have no idea what to expect. I follow Leroy through the greenhouse door. I suck in my breath. I realize it's true—I *am* honored. I can't believe what I'm seeing. "Leroy. Wow."

The greenhouse is full of bonsai. Bonsai—rows and rows of all different and perfectly shaped trees. Little trees, little mossy patches of green lawn and miniature houses and itty-bitty fishermen. Bigger trees, in huge, ancient pots. Groomed and formed into serene shapes, peaceful, quiet forms.

"It's a hospital. They're sick. Some of them are hundreds of years old. I've got a little reputation on the Web, you know, for being able to cure them. So people send them . . ."

"This is amazing." And I mean it. It *is* amazing. There are so many of them. Each and every one is different. I walk down one aisle. They are little worlds unto themselves. A tiny tree growing on a rock, a larger one in a garden of pebbles.

"It costs a fortune. The climate controls, the shipping. See that one there? The bits of yellow leaves? It's a juniper bonsai. Maybe eighty-five years old. I'm guessing it was exposed to a poison in the air, maybe a weed killer. That azalea?" He points to a medium-size tree with tiny oval leaves. "It's recovering from chlorosis, it's a mineral deficiency. I keep any plants infected with vine weevils or other insects isolated. The vine weevil will kill the root system. You have to repot, remove the devils by hand."

"Oh, man."

"The problem comes if I get them too late. Their system gets too fucked up and the damage is beyond repair. Mostly, people mess it up. Too much water. Not enough water. But I can save them, usually. When the plant is a hundred years old, you know, you do what you can."

"Leroy. This is a whole other world here."

"I know." He looks out over the land of tiny trees and smiles. "It's a hell of a lot of work. People think I'm out partying, and I'm here, clipping the mold off leaves."

"Can't you charge the people who send them?"

"Oh, I do. But still, some just leave them. They get forgotten, like some kid in an orphanage. I want to start a business, selling them. I save plants, get them to good homes. Let the cycle take care of itself. But you've got all these fucking start-up costs . . ."

"But Leroy, why are you embarrassed? Why doesn't anyone know this about you?"

"I get so much shit for my tattoos. I don't have an endless capacity for that, you know? People wouldn't get why I take a second job to take care of these guys. I deal enough with people's expectations. It's not what anyone *expects* of me. You don't follow convention, you know the shit you take? And this is my passion, corny as it sounds. My art, like my tattoos are my art. And the trees—what do they care if I have tattoos? Can I treat them right? That's what they care about."

I leave Leroy to his miniature real worlds, peaceful worlds, temporarily out of balance. I call Dad when I get into the car. "Several minor alterations to Plan A," I tell him.

On the fifth ring Trevor picks up.

"Indigo, please stop calling me," he says.

"But Trev—"

And then he is gone.

I go home and fetch Ron the Buddha. I put Ron in the passenger seat, buckle her/him in. I rub his/her tall, bumpy cone hat for good luck.

I drive over to Trevor's house. No one is home, so I sit on the porch with Ron beside me, and I wait.

I wait, and I wait. My phone rings, but it's only Mom. Cars pass, but not Trevor's car. When you are waiting and wanting to be with someone again it is not one disappointment you feel, but thousands of disappointments. I hear a car, but it is only Mrs. Jaynes's son, come over to water her plants for her. It is getting dark, and then it gets seriously dark. I'm getting so hungry, my stomach growls long and low. "You didn't hear that," I say to Ron.

I'm not sure what to do. Maybe he isn't coming home. Maybe his mom has taken one of her occasional trips to see her sister in Vancouver. Maybe he's met someone new and is spending the night.

Oh, man. God, have I messed up. Maybe I've tipped things too far, like Leroy's bonsais. Maybe I've killed something beautiful. I look over at Ron, who just stares serenely ahead. I try to decide what to do, but no great plan comes to mind.

And then, suddenly, there are the two circular headlights of Bob Weaver coming down the street. Two perfect round circles in the now black night.

Trevor doesn't see me. He parks the car in the driveway, slams the door shut. Walks with his head down up the path. I say something like, "Boo," or "Hey!" because Trevor shrieks. "Holy shit!" he says. And then "Christ, you scared me!" He holds his hand to his chest. "Indigo, I told you. I don't want to see you." His eyes shine in the streetlight. God, it's so good to see him.

"Trevor, you can't just throw away—"

"Don't even start with that. Don't even go there. You were happy to throw away . . . What's that?"

"What?"

"Beside you."

I'd forgotten all about Ron. "It's Ron. Our Ron. Our love child."

Trevor sighs.

"He came to plead my case. She came to plead my case. He's still a little gender confused. But he's not confused about the fact that I love you, that I'm asking your forgiveness for being an ass.

For letting money get to my head. I don't care about it. Trevor, I want you to have some, for your business—"

"No, In. No. I'm not going to start my business now. Not right away, anyway. I've been doing some thinking. I've decided I'm going to go to business school first. If I'm going to do it, I need to do it right."

"Trevor, that's great! That's so great!"

"So, you know . . . I don't need it."

"Trevor, Ron . . . He can't stand the idea of being from a broken home. I mean, listen, Trevor, he'd have to have joint custody. He'd have to be on my lawn every week, and then on yours on the weekend and for two weeks of summer, and it's not right, because family belongs together, and anyway, he needs stability to keep his . . . sereneness. Serenity. Whatever."

"Oh, In." Trevor sighs again. He runs his hand through his hair.

"I missed your hair," I say.

He shakes his head.

"I missed your head," I say.

"Goddamnit, In, I missed every part of you."

I start to cry. From relief. From joy. From upset and anger at my own stupidity. "Trev— I'm so sorry."

He puts his arms around me. Like everyone else did. Because that's what people do who love you. They put their arms around you and love you when you're not so lovable. My throat is full and tight with tears. There are probably a hundred types of crying. Fatigue crying and despair crying and loss crying and relieved crying and narrow-escape crying. This is crying that's the sudden knowledge of love and its fullness. And right then I learn something very simple and fundamental about love. That it is there or

Deb Caletti

it is not there. That some of our biggest troubles probably come when we try to convince ourselves it is there when it isn't, or that it isn't there when it is.

I can't speak. "Trev—," I say.

"I know," he says.

"The trees turned yellow," I squeak. "Tonight, before it got dark."

"I know," he says again. "I saw."

I get home very late at night. Mom has left the porch light on for me. I could go inside and sit at the kitchen table, or on my bed in my own room. But I stay here in the car. It is a plan that got made in a car, and will be altered here, in another car. I take the pink slip of paper from my pocket. I read it again, because reading it pleases me so much.

1. *Mom. A house of her own. Don't take no for an answer.*

2. *Severin and Bex. College fund.*

3. *Car, Severin.*

4. *Charity fund in Bex's name. Overseen by Dad.*

5. *Bomba. Tickets to visit us, as often as she can.*

"Or, as often as she can stand," Dad joked. I remember this and smile. I go back to my list.

6. *Invest in Nunderwear.*

I cross this off. Trevor, maybe his ideas weren't so bad after all. I write:

6. *Invest in Trevor. Business school.*

7. *Jane—a vacation.*

I draw a black line through these words, too. I fit in new ones:

7. *Invest in Carrera's.*

8. *Buy Nick a ticket out of Nine Mile Falls.*

The Fortunes of Indigo Skye

9. *Trina—get her car back.*

Strike that.

9. *Trina—restore her car to its former glory.*

10. *Joe: A trip to visit his new grandchild.*

11. *Laptop for Funny.*

12. *Leroy—?*

I click my pen again, smooth the slip of paper out on my leg. I cross off the question mark by Leroy and write *Bonsai Enterprises*. And then, finally, I add number thirteen. Because I know what I love. I've known all along. I don't have to *Be* some big word other people think I should be. I don't want to be a doctor or lawyer. I love being a waitress. I love feeding people. And maybe a person's world can grow bigger in all the right ways, not too wide that it becomes shallow, just large enough to preserve its depth.

13. *Invest in Indigo—College. Restaurant Management.*

I am running out of room; the words are merging into the part of the pink slip that says, *If you wish to contest this ticket . . .* But I write one more thing. I squeeze it in. It's too important to forget.

Insist on yourself.

Deb Caletti

18

"I'd like to call this meeting to order," I say. I like the sound of this. I have brought everyone to the living room; Severin and Bex and Trevor sit on the couch, Mom in her rocker, me sitting with folded legs on the floor. Freud is lying on the "Homes and Lifestyles" section of the Sunday paper.

"I see presents," Mom says. "I thought we agreed on no more stuff."

"They're wrapped in Christmas paper," Bex says.

"It was all I could find," I say.

"Ho, ho, ho," Trevor says. "Me-rry Christmas, boys and girls."

"I hope I got a pony," Severin says.

"And a Betsy Wetsy doll," Trevor says.

"People, please," I say. Maybe I need a gavel. "I'd like to offi-cially welcome you to Plan A." They finally shut up. Bex even folds her hands. "I know I said no more shopping, but these are thoughtful and necessary items. From here on out, it's all about balance."

Trevor holds out his arms and wavers them around like a doomed tightrope walker, but I shoot him a look and he stops.

I read my plan. Everyone is silent. They sit there, quiet. Even Mom. "I expect you to protest," I say to her. "And I'm ready to take you on."

"I'm not going to protest," she says. "I can see you know what you're doing."

"And there's one more thing and I don't want to hear any shit about it," I say. "No jokes, because this is serious. We're all going to drive cars that don't fuck up our planet. The others get traded in. Any questions?"

"The Porsche?" Severin asks.

"*Sayonara.*"

Mom. "The yellow Datsun?"

"Adios, muchacha," Bex says.

Trevor. "Bob Weaver?" He looks stricken.

"Bob Weaver isn't a car, it's a *Mustang.*"

"Thank God," Trevor says.

Now that they've indulged my display of crazed power and dictatorship, it's time for presents. "These are for everyone. I took my time, this time."

I let Mom unwrap. First an iron. Then a vacuum. Then a microwave oven.

"Oh, honey," she says. "We really *need* these things." She's a little choked up. Her voice is high and tight. She blinks back tears. There is one present left.

"I know what it is! I know what it is!" Bex sings. She's so loud that Freud flees under the coffee table, scrunching the newspaper in his panic.

Mom pretends to shake the large, flat box. "Hmmm, an umbrella?" she says. She unwraps. Holds the gift in her lap a moment before she raises it in the air for us all to admire. There is a small round of applause.

It is not gold. It is not padded. But the toilet seat is perfect just the same.

This is not just a simple story of *Money can't buy happiness.* Or maybe that's just what it is. And if it is, why shouldn't it be?

Deb Caletti

Because if this is something we are already supposed to know, then why don't we know it? Why do we chase and scrabble and fight for things to flaunt, why? Why do we reach for power over other people, and through the thin superiority of our possessions, believe we have it? Why do we let money make people bigger, and allow those without it to be made smaller? How did we lose the truth in the frantic, tribal drumbeat of more, more, more?

We're supposed to know this. We should know better.

It took me nearly two months to get all the pieces of my plan in place. We bought the Elberts' house, across the street, when Mr. Elbert got transferred to Philadelphia. It has a bigger, sunnier backyard, a flourishing flower garden in the back, a bedroom for each of us. Freud didn't have to get to know a new neighborhood. We got Bomba a blow-up pool with leaping dolphins on it for her first visit.

Jane accepted my investment, and my offer of any advice I'd learn in school to help her run the business better, and Leroy came out of the greenhouse closet, so to speak, after he, too, accepted my business proposal. Trina was back in boots again, her car at the curb. Roger had returned from Rio and tried to get her back. She told him to go fuck himself, but she was still taking his calls. Joe left for Saint Louis, wearing a suit and tie on the way to the airport, a hat on his head. Funny came in every day with her laptop case strung from her shoulder. But not everything went according to my plan. Nick said he couldn't accept a ticket out of Nine Mile Falls, although his eyes got watery when I gave him his gift. Sometimes he wanted to leave he said, but all the things that made him *him* were here. His memories of his wife were here. And we were here. I understood this.

My guitar playing, too, underwent a change. I played for a little while when I got back, and then I stopped for good. I put my guitar in my closet. It seemed to belong to another time of my life. Some things, I understood, were temporary pieces, passing phases. Other things, the real passions, stayed for good.

When we leave to visit Dad—me, Trevor, Severin, and Bex—Mom stays behind, in spite of her invitation. Dad hoped she'd come too, but Mom said she wasn't sure about that. She is having fun with Officer Brian, even if she isn't the Mariners fan that he is, even if she doesn't like camping. *There's a lot of water under the bridge,* she says. But her eyes look sad, I can see that, when we leave her at the airport.

Dad says he'll ask again, even if it's silly. As we sit on the beach and try to snap on our flippers, I can almost picture her, standing there trying to wipe off all the sand that suddenly clings to her sunscreen. Maybe when her hormones calm down, she'll come for a visit with us.

"Would you guys hurry up!" Severin says from the water. "It's amazing down here. Wait till you see these fish!"

Trevor holds out his arms like a monster, his mask over his eyes, walking stiff-zombie-legged and flipper-footed toward Bex, who screams. "AAAAH," Trevor-zombie says, and zombie-lurches forward.

Bex splashes out away from him, and a moment later, you can see her flowered bikini bottom snorkeling along in the sea.

Dad lies on his towel. He leans back on his elbows, smiles.

"Are you coming?" I ask.

"Nah, I think I'll just watch awhile."

I pick my way carefully to the water's edge. Bex pops her head up.

"Mother Nature is a genius!" she yells.

"The real world," I say, and then I dive in.

298

Deb Caletti

Turn the page for a peek at
another novel by Deb Caletti:

*The Secret Life
of Prince Charming*

When it came to love, my mother's big advice was that there were WARNING SIGNS. About the "bad" guys, that is. The ones who would hurt you or take advantage or crumple you up and toss, same as that poem I would once try to write for Daniel Jarvis. The wrong men—the psychopaths, cheaters, liars, controllers, stalkers, ones too lazy or incompetent to hold a job, to hold their temper, to hold you properly, to hold anything but a joint or a beer bottle—well, there were RED FLAGS, and you had to watch for them. If you were handling love correctly, it should go the way of those Driver's Ed videos, where things were jumping out at you right and left and you had to be on alert—a swerving truck, a child's ball rolling into the street. The important thing was, love was dangerous. Love was that dark alley you were walking down where your purse might be snatched.

Love was also an easy word, used carelessly. Felons and creeps could offer it coated in sugar, and users could dangle it so enticingly that you wouldn't notice it had things attached—heavy things, things like pity and need, that were as weighty as anchors and iron beams and just as impossible to get out from underneath.

"They ought to make people apply for a permit before they can say they love you," Mom said once. I remember this—she was in our big kitchen, holding a mug of coffee in both hands, warming her fingers against an image of Abe Lincoln embossed on ceramic, the oldest mug in the house, from when my father once went to Springfield, Illinois, home of our sixteenth president. Mom was talking to me and Gram and Aunt Annie, who both lived with us, and the sound of cartoons was coming from the living room, where my little sister Sprout was sitting cross-legged on the floor in her pajamas.

"Yeah. Make a man pay fifty bucks and take one of those mental tests," Gram said. She was fishing around in the kitchen drawer as butter melted in a pan for scrambled eggs. "Quinn, help an old lady find the damn whisk," she said to me.

"Cynics," Aunt Annie said, but she did so with a sigh. "You're both cynics." She tightened the sash of her robe around her. She'd just started seeing Quentin Ferrill at the time. We knew him only as the Double Tall Chai Latte No Foam guy, who gave long looks at Aunt Annie when he asked how her day was going across the counter at Java Jive, where Aunt Annie was a barista. Looks that shared secrets, she had told us. "Looks that are trying to get you into bed, is more like it," Gram had replied.

The favorite lecture of some mothers was Don't Talk to Strangers or, maybe, Look Both Ways. My mother's favorite was All Men Are Assholes.

I tended to side with Aunt Annie that they were cynics. I was only seventeen—I wasn't ready to be jaded yet. I was just at the start of the relationship road, where lip-gloss-love ends and you're at that Y where if you go one way, you'll have flat, easy pathways and everlasting happiness, and if you go the other, the rocky and steep slopes of heartbreak—only you have no idea which way is which. I liked to think I was already heading in the right direction, determined to prove my mother wrong by making Good Choices. I was sort of the queen of good choices, ruled by niceness and doing the right thing. Good choices meant asking that weird, solitary Patty Hutchins to your birthday party even when you didn't want to. Good choices meant getting your homework in on time and being on the volleyball team and sharing a locker with someone who played the clarinet instead of someone who drank their parents' Scotch. It meant liking math because it makes sense and liking your family even if they don't make sense and driving carefully and knowing you'd go to college. It meant taking careful steps and being doomed to be someone no one really remembered at the high school reunion.

I think "good choices" also meant *other people's choices* to me, then. I could feel hazy and undefined, even to myself. Was I going to be amazing, the best, the most incredible—win a Nobel Prize in mathematics, achieve great heights, as Dad would constantly tell me? Or was I going to be someone who would only continue to stumble and flounder and search, which is what I really felt would happen, since Dad's words sounded as shiny and hollow as Christmas ornaments to me? Maybe I would be simply *ordinary*. What would happen if that were the case? Just ordinary? And how did you get to a place where you knew where you were headed and what you wanted? I hate to admit this, I do, but the fact was, if most of my friends wanted hamburgers, I wanted hamburgers, and if the whole class kept their hands down during a vote, I would not be the single raised hand. No way. Too risky. When you went along, you could be sure of a positive outcome. A plus B equals C. When you didn't go along, you got A plus X equals a whole host of possibilities, including, maybe, pissing off people and ending up alone. I badly wished I could know my own truths and speak them, but they seemed out of reach, and it seemed better to be sure of yourself in secret.

And in love? Good choices so far meant my boyfriend, Daniel Jarvis, whom I'd been dating for over a year. Dating meaning he'd come over to my house and we'd watch a video and he'd hold my hand until it got too sweaty. Teachers loved Daniel, and he ran track and was polite to my mother and went to church every Sunday morning with his family. Daniel was *nice*. Like me. He made good choices too. He bought that Toyota instead of the classic little MG Midget with the broken convertible top that he'd run his hands over lovingly. Toyota love was only responsible love—remembering to put the gas cap on, refilling the wiper fluid. Convertible love was fingertips drawn slow over the curve of warm metal.

My inner evil twin, the one who would say the things I didn't want to hear but that were the truth, would also say that *oatmeal* is nice. Second-grade teachers are nice. That Christmas present from Aunt So and So was nice, the little pearl stud earrings. My inner evil twin also knows that the kind of nice that appears in the phrase "But he's *nice*," that emphasis, well, it's suspiciously defensive. Sort of like when you buy a shirt you don't really like because it was half off and then say, "But it was a good buy." Justification for giving in to things we don't feel one hundred percent for. Maybe I just wanted to believe in love, even if I didn't all the way believe in me and Daniel Jarvis. Maybe what Daniel Jarvis and I had was half-off love.

With Daniel, there weren't any red flags, but there weren't any blue ones or green ones, either; no beautiful silk flags with gold threads and patterns so breathtaking they could make you dizzy when they blew in the wind. It was enough, maybe, not to have bad things, even if you didn't have great things. For example, my best friend, Liv, went out with this guy, Travis Becker, whom she was totally in love with until she found out he was seeing two other girls at the same time and had recently been arrested for breaking and entering. God. Then again, Liv is beautiful and I am not. Good choices are a little harder, maybe, when you have lots of options.

As for Mom, I'm guessing she began developing her favorite lecture somewhere around the time her own father (Gram's wayward husband, the elusive Rocky Siler) left when she was two, and after her stepfather (Otto Pearlman, Aunt Annie's dad) did the same thing ten years later. She added to the running theme when she and my dad divorced after his affair with Abigail Renfrew, and perfected it some-time after her three-year relationship with Dean. Or, as we call him now, OCD Dean. He and his two horrible children moved in with us for a while after Dad left, before Gram and Aunt Annie moved in. Let me tell you, people of different values don't belong under the same roof. We named Dean's kids Mike and Veruca, after those char-acters in *Charlie and the Chocolate Factory*, Mike Teavee and Veruca Salt ("Da-dee! I want an Oompa Loompa *now!*"). It got so bad with them there that it felt like some kind of home-invasion robbery where the robbers decide to live with you afterward. Mom, Sprout, and me would go somewhere and leave them behind, and when we had to come back, Mom would sometimes drive right past our house. *We can't go in there*, she'd say, as if the building itself were dangerous, filled with toxic fumes, threatened by a collapsing structure. As if the problem was with the house and not the people in it.

My mother, Mary Louise Hoffman, is a graphic designer who used to paint and had shown her work at several galleries. She used to dance, too, which is how she met my father—they actually performed in a show together. It's hard to imagine her as this painter/dancer wearing swirling skirts and swoopy earrings; there's a picture of her from the time just before she met Dad—someone had snapped her in the middle of a cartwheel, only one hand on a deep green grassy lawn somewhere, her feet in the air. It seems odd; it seems like a different her, because her feet were so firmly on the ground after that. She was sort of the super-functioning head woman in our clan. Mom handled things—she could sign a permission slip at the same time she was steaming wrinkles from a blouse and cooking Stroganoff. But if you got her started on the man thing, she'd get a little crazy-extremist, super focused and wild-eyed both, like those anti- or pro-religious people, only without the religion part.

Most particularly, you didn't want to get her started on my dad. "Men" meant him, especially, multiplied by a gajillion. She tended to forget that he was my father, that he was her ex, not mine. And that I wanted to love him, needed for him to love me back because he hadn't been in my life always. Her constant reminders about why I shouldn't didn't help anything. Actually, they hurt her cause. Because every time I heard anything about him, or about "men," I put up a nice new stone in my mental defense wall of him. It's sort of like how you protect the little kid from the bully. You want to say, *Hey, every time you do that, I love Dad more*, but you don't say that. When your parents are divorced, there's a lot you don't say. And another thing you think but don't dare speak: *When you talk bad about each other, you're wasting your breath. I stopped listening years ago.* You stop listening when you figure out that the words aren't actually directed at you, anyway. That you're basically a wire between two telephones.

Anyway. I guess what I mean to say, what I should say right off, is that I knew good choices did not include stealing things from my own father's house. I knew that, and I did it anyway. I had to. Frances Lee, the half sister I never knew but know now, would say this about what we did: sometimes good choices are really only bad ones, wrapped up in so much fear you can't even see straight.

Love. Heartbreak.
Friendship. Trust.

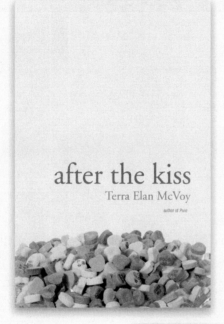

after the kiss

Terra Elan McVoy

author of *Pure*

Pure

Terra Elan McVoy

From Simon Pulse
Published by Simon & Schuster

Need a distraction?

Lauren Strasnick

Serena Robar

Amy Belasen & Jacob Osborn

Charity Tahmaseb & Darcy Vance

Teri Brown

Eileen Cook

Nico Medina & Billy Merrell

From Simon Pulse

Published by Simon & Schuster

Let **yourself go**

with these **books** from

Lisa Schroeder

The companion novel to

Some bonds just can't be broken...

I heart you, You haunt me

a novel by Lisa Schroeder

Also by Lisa Schroeder

From Simon Pulse ✳ Published by Simon & Schuster

"You think he's yours but he's not," I thought.
"You think he's yours but really he's mine."

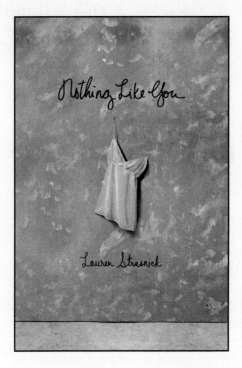

Nothing Like You

Lauren Strasnick

"*Nothing Like You* is candid and quick-paced,
with characters you can't help but want the best for."
–Deb Caletti, National Book Award finalist for *Honey, Baby, Sweetheart*

From Simon Pulse • Published by Simon & Schuster